Caught In The Axe

The Maine Lumberjacks

Book 1

Daphne Elliot

Melody Publishing, LLC

This book is a work of fiction, created without the use of AI technology. The names, characters, places, and events in this book are the product of the author's imagination, and any resemblance to actual events or places or persons, living or dead, is entirely coincidental.

Published by Melody Publishing, LLC

Editing by Beth Lawton at VB Edits

Proofreading by Morgan Leigh

Photography by Lindee Robinson

Models Andrew Lyon & Shelby Poch

 Created with Vellum

Dedication

To all the recovering people pleasers.
Do whatever the fuck you want.
Boundaries are sexy. You are enough.

Chapter 1
Owen

"What do you mean *the police are there?*" I clenched my steering wheel so tightly my knuckles turned white.

"Break-ins, thefts, suspicious activities in the woods. And four ATVs were stolen from the equipment shed up at North Camp last week," Gus grumbled. "We're so behind. March was a wash, and now that things are thawing, everything takes twice as long. Don't even get me started on the truck that almost rolled on Monday or the creditors breathing down our necks."

"And now the fucking police."

Gus grunted. "The chief has it out for us now. After decades of friendship, he didn't take too kindly to the international drug trafficking operation Dad ran right under his nose. Plus all the assault, kidnapping, and murder that went on in the quiet little town of Lovewell made Chief Souza look bad."

My stomach sank like it had been at least once a day for

months. Gus had a point. As the sons of criminal mastermind Mitch Hebert, we should get used to the fuzz crawling all over our business.

Not that any of us deserved it. We hadn't been involved in Dad's nefarious activities. And the next few weeks would be hard enough without the authorities interrupting and causing problems. We had enough of those on our own, hence the reason I was headed home, despite how badly I didn't want to be.

For months, I'd been helping behind the scenes, but I'd adamantly remained in Boston, preferring the comfortable quiet of my condo. I looked over financials and advised Gus and hired lawyers when necessary. But the writing was on the wall. I couldn't do everything that needed to be done from there. We still had too many open questions, and we still had too many disasters to clean up.

So I was Lovewell-bound against my better judgment.

"Just get here," he said. "I can't keep things running on my own. We need investors."

"We need *to sell*," I corrected. For six months, we'd been hemorrhaging money trying to attract investors to our family timber business. At this point, our only hope of getting out of this without losing our shirts was to sell.

Gus didn't respond. He'd been vocal in his opposition to selling, and we'd come to figurative blows over it several times. If I'd been in Lovewell, I had no doubt they would have escalated to the physical kind.

I understood his desire to keep the company our great-grandfather had built. But we were sitting on thousands of acres of timber rights, one-quarter ownership of the Golden Road—the largest logging road on the Eastern Seaboard, connecting Maine to Canada—and various pieces of real estate, trucks, and machinery. It was all worth a lot of money if we found the right buyer. And by ourselves, there was no way we could keep it from sinking.

Even before I'd become an accountant, numbers had always made sense to me. I saw things in dollars and cents. When it came to Hebert Timber, I saw debts and the federal forfeiture of most of my father's assets. I saw an opportunity to make sure my mother and brothers were taken care of after the family business fell apart.

But Gus was the lumberjack. He was emotionally connected to the trees and the land and my great-grandfather's legacy.

A legacy my own father shat all over when he used it as a front to traffic drugs, and even more so when he started murdering people to protect his opioid shipments.

"Two weeks," I warned as I exited the highway and headed toward the mountains. "That's all I've got."

The heavy sigh Gus let out crackled down the line, making my gut twist. It ate at me that so much of our troubles had fallen on his shoulders for so long. But Hebert Timber was his life, his passion. He knew the ins and outs of the industry and how to keep the doors open in the short term. I was the one who had run away and never come back.

He was the oldest brother, the protector, and the problem solver. The solid, strong, dependable Hebert. He'd grown up in the woods, and he'd always wanted nothing more than to run the company with Dad someday. Instead, Dad had blocked him. He'd held him back rather than letting him into his inner circle. With his qualifications and experience, he'd be a valuable asset to any timber company in the United States, but he'd remained loyal.

When Dad went to jail and the entire operation blew up, Gus stepped in and tried to right the ship. He'd been working seven days a week for over a year and was running on fumes. Not that he'd admit that. Nope, he was way too stoic and proud. He'd work himself into an early grave before he asked for help.

And that was why I was finally coming home. To do my part. Even though crossing the border into Maine had me reaching for the Tums I kept in my glove compartment.

I tightened my grip on the wheel and focused on the road as he ran through the outstanding, constantly growing list of crises we were dealing with. Unfulfilled orders, angry customers, employees who were overworked after more than half the team quit, mysterious criminal shit, and the ongoing federal investigation into my father.

I took a deep breath.

Two weeks.

That's all I was giving this shit show.

Two weeks in hell. Two weeks to close things out.

Two weeks until I could make a clean break from my father and all the shit he'd put us through over the years.

I repeated it like a silent mantra. *Two weeks. Two weeks.*

The four-hour drive had felt endless. The straight shot up I-95 should have been easy. One where I could field work calls, talk to my staff at DiLuca Construction, and listen to a few podcasts.

Instead, my racing thoughts had taken over and consumed me for every single mile.

My stomach rolled as I crossed the border into the state

of Maine. I'd been mainlining Tums for the last hour, watching as the exits grew farther and farther apart and the trees and mountains got taller.

In the civilized world, April meant spring. But up here, winter still reigned, as evidenced by the snow piled up on the side of the road and the forty-degree midday temperatures.

"You need to get here," Gus repeated. "Chief is threatening to come back with a search warrant."

Aw, fuck. The feds had already thoroughly trashed the place, and we'd been searching for all kinds of key documents since. The local police playing Sherlock Holmes would only set us back further.

"I left at five," I spat, wishing I'd stopped for a third coffee before I'd left more populated areas. I'd forgotten just how long these country roads felt. "Canceled all my meetings, rescheduled important events, and jumped in the car. I'm doing the best I can."

I made my way through town, down Main Street, headed toward route 106 and the forest. Lovewell, Maine, was just as I remembered. It had been frozen in time.

Same thick forest, same neighborhoods of modest homes, same streets riddled with potholes big enough to sink the Titanic. This place had always maintained the small-town atmosphere, which felt like such a strange contrast against the wild majesty of the mountains and the forest backdrop.

As I put downtown in my rearview, my anxiety worsened. The narrow, winding road was bordered by thick pine forest and led up to the mountains, and with every minute that passed, I was coming closer to the place I'd spent so many years avoiding.

My heart was lodged in my throat, and I'd broken out into a sweat, but I forced myself to continue on.

A looming shape appeared suddenly in the middle of the road, and I all but jumped out of my skin.

"What the fuck?" I slammed on the brakes so violently I was thrown forward, and my chest hit the steering wheel as my car skidded to a halt.

"Owen?" Gus yelled through my car's Bluetooth as I fought to take in air. "Are you okay?"

My hands shook, and all the energy drained from my body. I put the car in park and dropped my head, continuing to focus on breathing without responding to my brother. I didn't think I could form the words even if I tried.

When I finally forced my head up, I startled again. Because standing at the bumper of my Audi, practically staring into my soul, was a moose. A massive moose, literally longer than my damn car.

"Owen," Gus urged, sounding frantic.

"I'm okay," I said, resting my head on the wheel. "I almost hit a moose. It's just standing here in the middle of the road."

"Fuck." He huffed a breath. "A moose will kill you."

I sat up again, and I swore the motherfucker was making direct eye contact with me, sensing all my darkest thoughts.

Breathe. I just had to breathe. It would move eventually, and then I could continue on my way to deal with the endless shit show at Hebert Timber.

"It's not moving," I said with a honk of my horn.

The damn moose was standing sideways in the middle of the road. The forest was dense here, the trees growing right up next to the road, which meant there was no way to drive around the beast.

And the creature didn't even flinch when I honked. That didn't stop me from trying to scare it away, though.

"Don't antagonize the moose!" Gus yelled through the Bluetooth. "Do you want it to charge you?"

"It's blocking the damn road." I honked again, yet it continued to stare. Though its nostrils were flaring. Had they been doing that before? Was it going to attack me? "How do you move a moose?"

"You don't, you moron. It's a fucking moose."

Gus was so absurd. It was just an animal. "Yeah, but I need it to move. So what do I do?"

"You wait until it moves on. You were born here, right? It's not a fucking dog. You can't distract it with a treat."

I unbuckled my seat belt. Okay, so I couldn't tempt it away, but maybe I could run it off.

"Go around it."

"I can't. The woods are too thick and close to the road here."

"And you drive that ridiculous Audi."

"It has all-wheel drive."

My brothers were always riding me about how impractical my car was.

He scoffed. "I'm sure that finely tuned German suspension is great for off-roading through forests and around moose."

"Moose aren't sacred around here or anything, right?" I didn't remember that being the case, but it had been a long time since I'd been back. I'd traveled to India a few years ago and had been baffled by the way the world stopped for the cows that lingered in the middle of the road.

"God, city boy. You're worse off than I thought. No, they're not sacred, you dumbass. It's a fucking moose. Fifteen hundred pounds of unpredictable wildlife. Is it a bull or a cow?"

Its gender was irrelevant. All that mattered was that it was in my way. I'd been in the car for almost four hours and was sleep-deprived and over-caffeinated. In this state, I'd do pretty much anything to get this show on the road.

"Fuck if I know. It's giant. Think it'll take off if I yell at it?"

Gus barked out a deep, full laugh.

Damn. If I'd gotten this much of a rise out of him, then he really thought I was an idiot. Gus was usually pretty deadpan.

"Fuck, I thought you were the smart brother. Just sit and wait."

"But the police are there. And there's so much to do."

The next laugh was even louder, the sound of it sending a shock of irritation down my spine. "Brother. You're in Maine now. Best learn to slow down a bit or you won't survive."

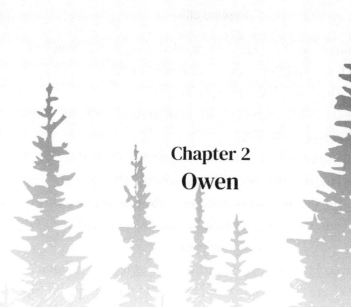

Chapter 2
Owen

For eleven solid minutes, the shithead moose did nothing but stand in the middle of the road and stare at me. While I waited—because I truly did have to wait; there was no easy way to reroute, and Gus had convinced me not to get out of the car—I did a Google search and determined that the antlers on its massive head meant it was a bull.

It also sported a large scar across one of its back legs. Like this asshole had seen some shit and lived to tell about it. So Gus had probably been right about not provoking him.

It figured that my first day in Maine would be filled with moose and police. I could only imagine what other headaches awaited me.

The parking lot was empty, save for a few Hebert timber trucks and three police vehicles. Yes, *three* police cruisers. Probably the entirety of the Lovewell PD force. Like they had nothing better to do in this town.

I heaved open the car door, hauled myself out, stretched, and steeled myself for what I was about to walk into.

And then my phone rang again.

"You're back already?" my mother said without bothering with a polite greeting.

"I just got here. How could you possibly know that?"

She laughed. My mother was always laughing, despite all the shit life had thrown at her. Despite my mood, the sound made me feel a fraction lighter. Fuck, it had been far too long since I'd heard it in person.

"Owen Hebert. It's been years since you've been home. I got texts from two people who saw you at the Pump and Sip in Heartsborough. According to them, you were gassing up a foreign luxury car and buying alcohol at nine a.m."

Jesus. I couldn't buy a six-pack in this town without my mother hearing about it. Or without some kind of comment about my car.

"I'm thirty-eight years old, mother."

"Old enough to buy a six-pack of Allagash, yes, but it's a bit early, don't you think? And on a Tuesday?"

I dropped my head and shook it. Damn, the gossip tip line had even taken note of the brand of beer I'd bought. "I also bought beef jerky, peanut butter M&M's, and dental floss. Did your sources include those details in their report?"

"At least you bought Maine beer. If you'd walked out of there with Sam Adams, I'd never be able to show my face again."

"I love you, Mom."

"And I've missed you, smart-ass."

"Mom." I snapped my head up, taken aback. My mother rarely swore.

"Eh," she said, and I could practically see her wave a dismissive hand at me. "It's fine. I'm living my truth now. Have you read anything by Brene Brown? I can lend you a few titles while you're here. She'll change your life, Owen."

"I don't have time for recreational reading at the moment. While I'm here, I'll be working full time remotely while also managing the sale of the business." Not to mention I had no interest in my mother's brand of self-improvement.

"And dealing with Chief Souza," she quipped.

Stomach sinking, I stopped a few feet from the entrance. "How do you know that?"

She laughed, the sound light and airy, once again lifting my spirits despite the circumstances. "I'm so happy you're here. Your brothers need you. Are you coming for dinner tonight? You've already got a six-pack of beer to bring along."

I sighed. "I've got to get myself settled and figure out how things are going to work here. I'm up to my eyeballs in work for Hebert Timber, as well as my actual job."

Her hum was laced with disappointment. "I'm sure I'll get word when the police leave. Once they do, I'll swing by with something for you."

And this, ladies and gentlemen, is why I don't do small towns. Personal growth in a small town is impossible. A person's childhood indiscretions will haunt them forever, and people make judgments based on the actions of past generations.

In this town, I was Mitch Hebert's second son. That was it.

I wasn't a real person here. I was an archetype. The smart Hebert brother. I wasn't the tallest, or the most athletic, or the one who wanted to take over the business. Each of us boys had been assigned a limited identity at birth.

I'd always pushed back against the confines of this place. Even when I was a kid, it was too small, too rural. I longed for wide streets, more than one option when it came to restaurants and shops, and blissful anonymity.

Once my mom had said her goodbyes, I pocketed my phone and took in my surroundings.

I'd never set foot in this building before. Crossing the threshold felt like a violation of everything that mattered to me, of my value as a person.

When I was a kid, Hebert Timber headquarters were housed in an old brick building on the outskirts of town. There were desks clustered around and my grandpa always had a bowl of candy on his. There was a shop in a pole barn out back and a massive parking lot for trucks and machinery.

It wasn't fancy, but I spent my childhood running around the place with my brothers, causing mischief and climbing on all the trucks. Any fond memories I had of the business were set there.

A decade or so ago, my father built his headquarters. Rather than constructing a new building, he erected an entire campus. Multiple structures and state-of-the-art facilities, including a small hangar and an airstrip.

The office building was a modern mega monstrosity that was completely out of place in rural Maine.

I forced myself through the front door, and as I crossed the grand foyer, I took in the decor. It was ornate and dark and intimidating. I chuckled at the thought of my dad hiring an expensive interior designer out of Portland or Bangor and telling them he wanted something that screamed "swanky law firm in hell."

Bastard.

The money he'd blown on this ridiculous facility would have been better spent on updating the town library or the school or literally anything else. Even the highway sign welcoming drivers to Lovewell was faded and cracked.

But no, my dad's ego needed a campus. If the new buyers wouldn't purchase this building, no one would. In this part of the state, there wasn't a single business that would want or need a facility like this. Not with the way it stuck out against the landscape. And it wasn't like we could convert it into anything useful.

"Thank fuck you're here." Gus was striding toward me. He was a brick wall in human form, dressed in a dark blue plaid shirt, jeans, and boots. It had been his go-to look since high school. His beard was thick and wild, and his hair was on the longish side, curling up from beneath his gray wool beanie.

He pulled me into a hug and clapped me on the back with one of his enormous hands. In that instant, I felt like a scrawny kid again.

And totally freaked out and in over my head.

"So good to see you. Let's get upstairs, play nice with the police, and then get to work, ayuh?"

Once we reached the floor that housed his office, he led me down a long, stark hallway. "The place is a mess," he said. "But I've got faith in you."

I followed him, matching his long strides, past the executive suites. It was hard not to slow when I noticed the framed black and white photos on the walls. This was the one thing they'd done right with this facility. As we continued our trek, I was met with images of Hebert after Hebert. Logging in the woods, dragging logs with chains and horses, riding floats of timber down the river.

The nostalgia that had hit when I noticed the photos was quickly replaced with a surge of anger. All of this history was gone. So many jobs were gone, forcing people to leave town. Because my idiot father had gotten greedy. I'd never had any interest in the family business, but I understood and appreciated what it meant to my family and this town.

We passed several empty offices, some of which looked to have been ransacked. It was unsurprising, I supposed. The feds had tossed this place last year, and that was before the break-ins my brothers had been dealing with.

Gus and Jude had worked with local brokers to sell off the more expensive furniture pieces, the fancy projection screens, and the majority of the electronics.

The massive conference table that sat twenty had been difficult to offload, though they'd eventually found a buyer in Vermont. That sale alone netted enough to keep the electricity on for the next year, so that was a plus.

Now, where that ornate table had once sat, my brother and his staff had pushed together plastic folding tables. Chief Souza stood from one of the metal chairs that surrounded the makeshift conference table when I entered and shook my hand. Two of his officers stood as well, both dipping their chins at me.

"The famous Owen Hebert," Souza said, a toothpick wedged firmly in his teeth. "Came all the way from Boston, did you? Though I was under the impression that you'd be here thirty minutes ago."

I bristled, but I schooled my expression into something I hoped came across as neutral. "I would have been here sooner, but I was stuck behind a moose."

He laughed. "Bastard probably knew you were an out-of-towner. Musta been trying to fuck with you, ayuh?"

Shaking off my annoyance, I gritted my teeth and sat in the chair next to Gus. I pulled a notebook out of my briefcase and found a pen. Then I straightened in my seat and focused on the chief. This was business, and I didn't have time to fuck around with this dumbass.

Chief Souza had been a Lovewell fixture since I was a child. He was known for being good-natured and he was decent at his job, albeit a bit on the lazy side. He had thick gray hair and a Magnum PI mustache that was his pride and joy and could often be found at the local dive bar, drinking beer with some of the people he'd previously arrested.

For several minutes, he pontificated about crime and Hebert Timber and how Lovewell used to be a safe place. His implications were clear. This town had been safe until my father decided to turn to a life of crime.

I kept my mouth shut and let him yammer on. Gus, thank fuck, did the same. It was best we let him say what he wanted to say so he could get the hell out of there.

"We wanna help," the chief said, resting his elbows on the table and affecting a fake-ass look of concern. "Clearly, you're still dealing with the mess your father left. I can assign an officer to drive by periodically."

"That's not necessary," Gus said politely, sitting straighter in the chair beside me. "The place isn't as busy as it used to be, but we've got it covered."

The last thing we needed was the law riding our asses. If

we were going to get this place sold, then the next few weeks would be frenzied. Once I really dug into the financials, I wasn't sure what I'd find, and the last thing I needed was the cops looking over my shoulder as I did.

"Then I'm going to insist you install security cameras."

As if we had the funds for that. I'd bet just about anything that the vandalism and break-ins could be pinned on asshole teens messing around.

"I've got a guy," Chief Souza said with a smile. "He'll do right by ya, and he won't gouge ya if you're a friend of mine."

I opened my mouth, ready to brush off the suggestion. Every word out of his mouth, not to mention his body language and the smarmy looks, made me feel like he was playing with us. Like a cat tossing a mouse around for fun before swallowing it whole.

"Thank you," Gus said sincerely. He stood, silently signaling to the assholes that it was time for them to leave. "I think that's a great idea."

"Because I could get a warrant. If you think that's necessary..." The chief's tone was light, but the threat was clear.

"No need," Gus said, sticking his hands in his pockets. "Help with security would be great. We're eager to stop the break-ins and help you in any way we can. Now that my brother is here to help, I know things are gonna turn around."

I nodded, pretending like I was up for the challenge as opposed to dreading it with every fiber of my being.

"I'll show you boys out," Gus said, leading them away and leaving me alone.

I stood in the empty conference room, taking in the view of the expansive Maine wilderness on the other side of the massive windows. This place was everything I never wanted.

And yet the weight of the situation had settled onto my shoulders. There were six of us brothers, and it was up to me, the one who'd walked away, to fix it all.

Gus's footsteps echoed in the hallway, and then he was stepping back into the conference room. "Thank God they're gone." He heaved out a sigh. "They wandered around the building taking pictures for a damn hour before you got here. I sat them down with coffee and sent Molly out for donuts just to keep them from fucking around too much."

"I don't like him."

He shrugged and sidled up beside me near the windows. "He's the police chief, and he coached the high school baseball team forever. He's not a bad guy, but he's covering his ass. Though I am a little concerned that he's looking to make an example out of us."

His cell rang in his pocket, and he held up a hand. "Hold on." He'd barely gotten a "hello" out when his brows pulled low and his mouth turned down into a frown. "Shit," he said into the receiver. "Give me twenty minutes."

As Gus pocketed his phone again, he turned to me. "I gotta run. There's a truck stuck at the three-mile marker and they need my help. Pick an office and get yourself set up. Supplies are down the hall. Molly left to pick her kids up at school, but she'll be in tomorrow to answer any questions you have."

With that, he strode out of the office and down the hall.

"Hey."

I jogged to catch up to him. How the hell was I supposed to get started? This place was a wreck. My head was spinning as my stomach dropped.

"This is a big job." One I wished like hell I could get out of.

He stopped and clapped me on the shoulder. "I know. That's why Finn and I found an assistant for you."

I frowned. "Sorry, what?"

"She's great." He smiled for what might have been the first time since I'd arrived. "You're gonna love her. She's great at all the nerdy accounting shit just like you." He pulled his phone out and checked the time. "She'll be here in twenty minutes. Meet her down there, would ya? I'll be back in an hour or so to help you get going."

And then he was gone, jogging down the stairs, leaving me staring, open-mouthed.

What the hell had I got myself into?

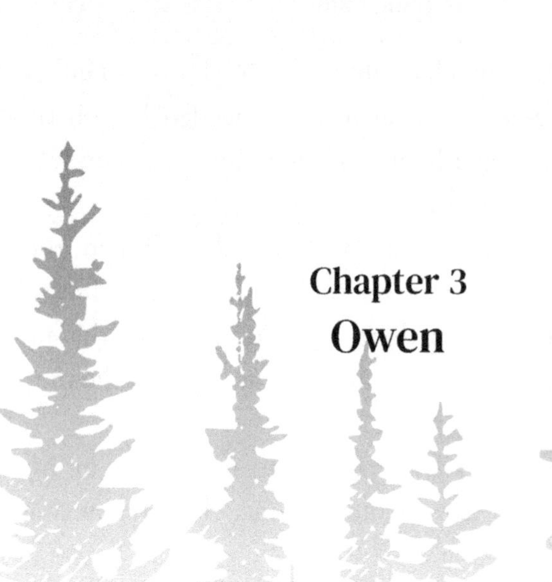

Chapter 3
Owen

I was well and thoroughly fucked.

The feds had returned a few dozen boxes that they'd seized originally. Not one was labeled, and all the documents had been tossed into them haphazardly. So I set myself up in an empty office and decided that my first task would be sorting.

God, I missed Linda. She'd been my right-hand woman for the last eleven years, and if I'd brought her along, she could have this place organized in a matter of hours. I could not do my job without her militaristic organization skills and no-nonsense attitude. In addition to being my assistant, she was a mother to four teenagers, so she had a lot of practice keeping people in line.

As much as I wished she was here to take charge and clean up my father's mess, she was holding down the fort in Boston. DiLuca Construction was now the largest construction company in Massachusetts, and, as CFO, I couldn't take a sabbatical, no matter how badly my family needed my help.

So while I was helping clean things up for Hebert Timber, I'd be working remotely. That meant I needed her on the ground in Boston to coordinate with my staff. Together, we'd keep all the balls in the air.

As I flipped through a stack of papers, they slipped from my hand and scattered to the floor. Cursing my clumsiness, I stood and started gathering them, only then realizing that my new assistant would be here at any minute, so I left the mess and headed downstairs.

While this task really needed a team of four or five MBAs, there wasn't the slightest chance I'd find anyone qualified in Lovewell.

Including this assistant Gus had hired for me. I had no doubt that taking the time to explain the intricacies of what I needed to get done would only put me even further behind schedule. Gus meant well, but he didn't get it.

As I strode down the hall, I assessed the photos of my great-grandfather. With each one I took in, my stomach knotted further. What would he think of this mess?

Once I hit the main floor, I found a woman waiting at the front door. She was tall and willowy, with shoulder-length brown hair. She had on a black puffy coat and jeans—hardly job interview attire—and wore a bright, unassuming smile.

I opened the door, trying to ignore how pretty she was up close.

"Hi, Owen. So great to see you." Her voice was high pitched and musical in a way that made my body want to relax, though I refused to give in to the urge.

Without hesitation, she walked up to me and pulled me into a hug.

God, who was this woman?

She smelled sweet, like vanilla, but with floral undertones. Instantly, my body locked up even tighter than it had been all day. This right here was why I hated small towns. People were entirely too familiar with one another. And far too trusting. This young woman had just waltzed into a half-empty building in the woods without a care. I could be an axe murderer for all she knew.

Jesus.

"It's been so long!" As she unwound her scarf and unzipped her coat, she stepped farther into the building and took it in with wide eyes and a bright smile. "Your mother must be so happy to have you home. And this is such a good time of year to visit!"

Despite my confusion, I nodded and smiled. It was impossible not to. Something about her gray-blue eyes and sincere smile completely disarmed me.

"I came right from the diner. Finn and Gus cornered me this morning and said you could use my help." She walked through the lobby, totally at ease, like she'd been there before.

Did I know this woman? I racked my brain, trying to place the unassuming brunette with the big smile.

I hadn't been home in years, and I hadn't kept in touch with anyone aside from my mother and a couple of my brothers. Given our family's recent infamy, it's likely that she knew *of* me. But I was fairly confident I'd never met her.

She thrust a to-go cup at me. "Do you like coffee? I thought you liked coffee. I don't really know if you like coffee, but there's an amazing new shop at the end of Main Street. They make incredible berry cream cake and homemade scones."

My head spun as I assessed her. This sweet stranger had brought me coffee? Though I was more than a bit confused, I was oddly touched. Until the paranoid part of my brain kicked in and questioned whether the drink could be poisoned. *No.* I pushed that thought away. She was so disarmingly pretty and too goddamn nice to poison a person. Right?

Deciding to take my chances, I took the cup from her hand, and before I could even say thank you. She was chatting away again.

"This is an oat-milk honey latte. *So* good."

"Oh gosh." She tilted her head slightly. "Are you one of those black coffee guys?" she asked, narrowing her eyes. "The kind that pretends to be so tough that milk and sugar are a threat to your manhood?"

"Um, no." I clutched the cup to my chest. Who was this woman?

"Good. If that was the case, I'd stop this interview right now. I bring everyone lattes. It's my little gift. Mostly because I really love the Caffeinated Moose, but also because I like making people smile."

Interview? This was the furthest thing from a job interview I'd ever experienced. Every second of this interaction had been truly bizarre.

I was still filing away her words to play back later when she took a step closer, a smile playing on her lips.

"Try it."

Assessing her earnest expression, I inhaled the delicious nutty scent of really good coffee, then brought the cup to my lips. The latte was piping hot, just the way I liked it. I swallowed, noting the bitterness of the espresso and how the honey and the oat milk complemented and muted the flavor perfectly.

I lived on coffee, so I was a bit snobby about it. When a person consumed as much as I did, it wasn't hard to get really particular about the quality and flavor.

"The honey is local," she said. "Raeanna—she's the barista—was telling me all about how she sources it."

I took another slow sip and held the cup up to survey it. "Where did you get this?" It had been a long time, but as far as I knew, the diner didn't make lattes. If this woman was involved in some kind of espresso operation, then she was hired, regardless of her accounting skills.

"I told you." Her smile was still big, but it was full of exasperation. "The Caffeinated Moose. It's a new coffee bar on Main Street. The people who own it are sweet. They moved here from Vermont. They have bakery items as well as sandwiches and amazing coffee and tea."

"I hardly think Lovewell is the kind of place that can sustain a fancy café."

The second the shitty comment was out, I was hit with a wave of shame. This vibrant, lovely woman lived here. I needed to remember not to insult the locals.

Instead of being offended, she just laughed at me, her eyes crinkling at the corners. "You've been gone a long time, Owen. Things are changing here. And while the older folks in town may complain about paying more than a dollar for coffee, Raeanna is a magician. I guarantee even the cranky old loggers will be lining up for her lavender jasmine tea infusions. But I've decided to become a honey latte ambassador, just in case. I'm getting everyone hooked."

I took another sip. Shit, this was good. It wasn't too

sweet, but it was far more tasty than a cup of black coffee. And damn, was it the afternoon kick in the ass I needed.

With one last smile, she strolled through the lobby, draping her winter coat over one of the remaining chairs as she went. "So talk to me. What's the project?" She spun, producing a small notebook and a pen from her purse, and looked at me expectantly. "Your brothers weren't exactly forthcoming with details."

I felt like I'd been knocked on my ass. This woman's creamy skin and full pink lips were irresistible. The sassy tilt of her head after she asked me a question sent a spark of interest through me. Most of all, I was intrigued by her strange overfamiliarity. I didn't know her. Trust me, if I did, I'd remember this bubbly brunette. And yet she was acting like we were old friends.

Even though I didn't have the first clue who she was, there was something eerily familiar about her.

"Why don't we head upstairs and sit?" I suggested, hitting the call button on the elevator.

While she gathered her coat, I considered discreetly texting my brothers and asking who the hell this was.

But before I could even pull the device from my pocket, she was at my side.

I led her up to the third floor and past the conference room that was littered with evidence of my earlier frustrations. The conference table in my father's office was almost as large, so we could get set up there. The ergonomic leather chairs were long gone, but several hard metal folding chairs had been brought in.

I pulled one out for her and gestured for her to sit. Once she was settled, I sat beside her.

"Listen," I said, rolling my neck, searching for some kind of relief. I'd been here a handful of hours, and it had already felt like days. "I'm not sure what my brothers told you."

"They said you were coming back for a few weeks to handle the sale of the business. And that you needed help with documentation and records while you're here."

Huh. That was impressively accurate. "Yes. But it's a bit more than that," I hedged, going for gentle despite the anxiety and frustration that had taken up permanent residence inside me. "I have a ton to get done in a short amount of time, and I've got to keep up with the workload for my day job back in Boston too. So I need someone with bookkeeping experience who can interpret financial records."

She continued to smile so brightly I had to fight to shield my eyes. "Okay, great."

I blinked at her unhelpful response. "Do you have that experience?"

"Owen," she chided. "Of course I do. Maybe your family never mentioned it, but I finished my BA in business administration last year. It took me a while, given all the moves, but I did it. My work history has been spotty, for obvious reasons." She raised her eyebrows like I was supposed to know what she was referring to. "But I'm a hard worker, and you'd be helping me out."

Despite my better judgment, I found myself leaning forward, totally invested in assisting her with whatever she needed.

Because her presence was turning my brain inside out. I couldn't decide whether I should ask to see her résumé or ask her out on a date. Ha. As if that were a possibility. I'd barely have enough time to sleep and shower while I was here, let alone consider having fun. And even if I did, where would I take a beautiful woman in Lovewell? The diner? After all that my father had done, if I set foot in the place, Bernice would probably spit in my coffee.

I found myself smiling when she spoke, laughing at her jokes and desperate to keep the conversation going. No woman in recent memory had made me feel this way. God, the universe really was fucking with me.

"So tell me about your experience." *Yes, Owen. Get this conversation back on track.*

Since the moment she'd arrived, my brain had been short-circuiting. It was as if I'd never been in the presence of a beautiful woman before.

God, maybe Enzo was right. It had been a while for me.

"I've been back in Lovewell for almost a year. I'm staying with my mom. Before I came home, I was in Florida, doing bookkeeping and advancement work for a nonprofit."

Forcing myself to focus on her words rather than her lips as she spoke, I nodded.

"Before that, it was Providence and Indiana." She shrugged as if I should be familiar with her life story. "I got my associate's degree at a community college and then started working on my bachelor's." Her shoulders rounded a bit then, and her voice went quiet, as if she were embarrassed. "It took me a long time."

"That's impressive," I said, infusing an extra dose of admiration in my voice. It was, and she had no reason to be ashamed of the path she'd taken.

With her bottom lip caught between her teeth, she twisted the silver ring on the fourth finger of her right hand. She was nervous. Was I making her nervous?

She lowered her head and tucked her hair behind her ears. "Anyway, my last job sparked a desire for me to learn more. So I've spent the last year applying to grad programs." Clearing her throat, she dropped her hands to her lap. "I plan to earn a master's in nonprofit leadership. I'm waiting to hear back from a few business programs, but I applied late, so my chances are slim."

I rested an elbow on the table but remained quiet, intrigued by her dedication.

"In the meantime, I'm here, and I like to keep busy. I work at the diner in the mornings, and a few afternoons a week I do math tutoring at the library for a few kids in town. I also teach dance classes at the studio in Heartsborough when I can."

A huff of a laugh escaped me. "And you want *another* job?"

"God, yes. I'm saving up for grad school, so I need all the cash I can get. Plus, this would be helpful business experience, which is hard to come by up here."

There was no way to know if she'd actually be useful, but I admired her hustle. And after a twenty-minute conversation with her, I felt better than I had in weeks. So it was worth a try.

She was determined and cheerful, and let's face it, I needed the help.

"Okay," acquiesced, "but I can only pay thirty dollars an hour."

"Are you shitting me?" She slapped a hand over her mouth, and her cheeks went pink.

I laughed. "I wish I could offer more, but that's all the budget will allow."

"No," she said, grasping my forearm. "You misunderstood. That's so much more than I anticipated."

Ignoring the zing that shot up my arm at her touch, I cleared my throat. "Once we successfully close the sale, you'll receive a bonus, and trust me, it'll be well earned. You'll be expected to work hard, and the hours won't be the traditional eight to five. I have to do my actual job too, so I'll be digging into this stuff mostly on nights and weekends."

Once this was done, I would go back to Boston, but not before I asked her out. She was too beautiful and intriguing to pass up. And damn if she wasn't a bright spot in this shitty town.

She was gorgeous and kind and intelligent, which meant there was no way I'd escape the next couple of weeks without developing a full-blown crush.

It had been years since I'd felt like this, so I'd embrace it. After the stress of the past few years, having a reason to look forward to the long workdays in this hellhole would be a relief.

I was talking her through some of the priorities when the elevator dinged, which meant Gus was back.

"Lila," Gus said, striding into the room. "I'm so happy you're here."

She stood and gave him a big hug. The move sent a wave of confusion through me. And right behind it was a rush of jealousy.

"Owen's been catching me up," she explained, releasing him and taking a step back. "Nothing I can't handle."

He smiled down at her like a proud big brother.

And that's when my brain screeched to a halt. "Lila?"

"Yes. Lila Webster." Gus put his hands on his hips and cocked a brow. "You know Lila."

Recognition dawned on me, bringing with it a hint of the anxiety I'd only just felt relief from for the first time in years. *No.* No fucking way. Of all the shitty office buildings in all the shitty small towns.

"Cole's Lila?" I asked.

Her eyes flashed with anger. "Just Lila. I don't belong to Cole, or any man, for that matter." Her defiant tone was adorable. Despite all the smiles and the lattes, she had a backbone. I liked it.

"Sorry," I mumbled, embarrassed at my gaffe. In my defense, I'd barely spoken to Cole and had been pretty fixated on my criminal father and his crumbling empire for the last year or so.

"Yes, I dated your brother," she said, crossing her arms over her chest. With her bottom lip caught between her teeth, she looked from me to Gus. "Is that going to be a problem?"

"No," my brother grunted.

At the present moment, I couldn't form the words to respond. My brain was too busy spinning.

I squinted. The lovely woman before me bore no resemblance to Cole's on-again, off-again girlfriend. I'd never spent much time with her, I guessed, but the girl I remembered was different in every way. She was all long blond hair, fancy clothes, and pounds of makeup. Always by his side and always dressed to the nines. If I wasn't mistaken, she'd won some beauty pageants or something.

The woman before me was so different. A smiling, barefaced brunette with an eyebrow ring.

I hadn't even realized they'd broken up. That was how distant my relationship with my half brother had become over the years. He and I stayed far away from one another for good reason.

She ran a hand down a lock of her dark hair. "I look different. I should have realized you didn't recognize me." The way her voice faltered was like a punch to the gut. Fuck, I was an asshole. I'd been gawking at her like she was an animal at the zoo. And based on the angry stare Gus was leveling my way, now I was acting like a fool.

"No, it's my fault." I hauled myself up from my seat, banging my knee on the table in the process, all but tripping over myself to make this right. For a moment, I got hung up on her rosy cheeks, her plump pink lips, and the dark eyelashes rimming those gray eyes.

I blinked myself out of my stupor and cleared my throat.

Why hadn't I realized how young she was? She was definitely too young for me, but she had a kind of steely confidence that I respected. And while I had no idea what had happened with Cole, I could guarantee he was to blame.

Her history made sense now. She had been with Cole for years, traveling with him all over the country while he played in the minor leagues, chasing his hockey dreams. I'd never paid her much mind, always assuming she was some kind of hanger-on.

But now? Now I didn't know what to think. Had I offended her?

"I, um. Sorry," I mumbled, unable to string a full sentence together. Determined to apologize correctly, I cleared my throat and opened my mouth, but before I could force another word out, a hot, wet substance hit my chest.

Startled, I jumped back, realizing only then that I had squeezed the paper cup in my hands, popping the top off and spraying my latte all over my dress shirt.

On instinct, I dropped the cup, and it hit the floor.

"Get some paper towels," Gus barked at me, then he turned to Lila and softened his expression. "I've got to get Owen to a meeting. We'll be in touch with the details. Let me walk you out."

Heat crept up my neck and into my cheeks as I scrambled to clean up the mess I'd made. Shame flooded my body. I'd flirted with her and daydreamed about taking her out, all the while failing to recognize her. And then I'd topped it all off by drenching myself in coffee. Disgraceful.

She stepped forward and offered her hand.

I took it, savoring the feel of it in mine, her smooth skin against my calluses and the small connection between us. Lila was something, all right. Something fresh and energetic and a bit terrifying.

"It was nice seeing you, Owen."

As she walked out of the office, I couldn't help but watch the sway of her shapely hips in a pair of jeans that molded to her ass perfectly. Then, with a shake of my head, I cursed myself, wishing I was back in Boston, where I was in total control.

Because there was no denying it. I was now lusting after my little brother's ex-girlfriend.

Chapter 4
Lila

Owen Hebert. Cole's older brother.

Huh.

I flipped the switch on the coffee machine and reached for a small stack of napkins to deliver to table six.

I'd tossed and turned for hours last night, replaying our meeting in my head. The whole thing had been strange and unsettling. Granted, I hadn't seen the guy in years, and throughout the majority of my relationship with Cole, he had alternated between ignoring Owen's existence and talking about what a selfish asshole he was.

In my mind, he was a cruel, money-grubbing city guy. Like Patrick Bateman without the murder, or a younger, hotter Ebenezer Scrooge.

But the man who'd sat with me, asking thoughtful questions and explaining the intricacies of the timber business, wasn't an asshole. Sure, the Italian shoes and blingy watch made it obvious that he had expensive taste, but he was a lot more humble than I expected.

He was calm and collected, despite the defeat and exhaustion that emanated from him. It was easy to see the situation with his family's business weighed on him.

His thick, medium-brown hair only made his dark blue eyes more prominent, and the light peppering of gray at his temples made him look distinguished. He carried himself with quiet confidence, though he wasn't cocky. He wasn't overly chatty, from what I could tell by our interaction, or from what I remembered, but he communicated effectively. I'd taken five pages of notes during our quick conversation, and the to-do list I'd started for myself was growing by the second.

Though I didn't agree with Cole's opinion of his second oldest brother, I could understand why he disliked him. It was obvious that Owen was the antithesis of Cole. He was steady, careful, and strategic, whereas Cole was impulsive and brash. He had a habit of ignoring consequences and plowing headfirst toward whatever he wanted. Once, I'd adored that side of him. The devil-may-care attitude and his insistence that life should be fun had been exciting. But the years had worn on me, and I'd grown tired of being the only adult in our relationship.

Owen was the kind of guy who maxed out his annual 401(k) contributions, flossed daily, and took vitamins. He was the type of person I would have run screaming from ten years ago. Now? I found myself drawn to him and his steady, self-assured energy.

"What did you do to your hair? You used to be such a pretty girl."

I tamped down on my annoyance and forced myself to smile as I topped off Mrs. Dupont's coffee. She'd always been a shitty tipper, but hey, maybe today would be my lucky day and she'd actually throw me more than a few pennies.

With a hum that I hoped conveyed a light, breezy attitude, I touched the ends of my shoulder-length brown hair. "Oh, just felt like making a change."

Karen Souza gave me a pitiful expression while stroking her own artificially blond locks. She was the police chief's wife and the epicenter of the Lovewell gossip scene.

I'd been waiting on her and her bridge club every Friday morning for the last year, and every week, like clockwork, she'd get in some kind of dig at me. Once a judgmental old bat, always a judgmental old bat. And my hair was lovely, thank you very much. I'd gone back to my natural color, and the cut was low maintenance, just the way I liked it.

She could fuck right off with her patriarchal beauty standards. Secretly, I'd love to go off on her and the other small-minded jerks who gave small towns a bad name.

But I wasn't that kind of woman. The instinct to please ran wide and deep. So instead of telling her what I really thought, I complimented Mrs. Dupont's scarf and headed back to the kitchen, mentally cursing the whole table of women from here to Montreal.

And I reminded myself that I was lucky to be here. I got my pick of the best shifts and the best tables, and the job was an easy, enjoyable one. Though Bernice and Louis, technically my great-aunt and uncle, threw me as many shifts as they could, I wasn't rolling in cash. The diner was hardly a big operation, and the tips weren't going far enough these days. But the flexibility of my schedule allowed me a couple of free afternoons a week to tutor the kids of Lovewell at the library.

Sadly, that was not paying the bills either. In Tampa, I'd been able to charge fifty dollars an hour, but up here, even twenty dollars was a stretch for most families.

At this rate, I'd never be able to start grad school.

I shook my head. Nope, I was not going there. Every day was an opportunity to grow, and good things were coming.

Holding tight to that positivity, I headed back to the kitchen to grab the next order.

The sun was shining, and I had a lot to do. I could not spend every waking moment thinking about Owen Hebert and his big hands and kind eyes. Nope. Not doing it.

I was resolved to push all thoughts of the man aside, and I was doing a fine job of it until four giants walked through the door and various heads turned.

Excellent, the Heberts were here.

After I'd dropped off Father Renee's blueberry pancakes, I grabbed menus, gestured toward the only open booth in the back, and grabbed the coffeepot off the counter.

The Hebert family was larger than life, literally and figuratively, in this small town. When I was growing up, they were *that* family. Wealthy, successful, and good at everything.

But since their father had been arrested for all kinds of awful crimes, the tide had turned. Now the gossip mill harped on their notoriety for entirely different reasons. There was nothing a small town loved more than putting people on a pedestal and knocking them off it.

None of this was new to me. My family had always been

a favorite subject of the town gossips. My mother, the teen mom turned three-time divorcée, and I, her ex–beauty queen daughter, were often whispered about in not so subtle ways.

The snide comments wrote themselves, and I'd learned at an early age to ignore them. Sadly, the Heberts were not as experienced with the judgment, and it had clearly been difficult for all of them.

Years ago, I'd learned to laugh it off and even enjoy the twists and turns the rumors took. These days, the rumors had been refreshed. Now I was known as the evil vixen who dumped poor Cole, the town hockey star, destroying him and his career in one fell swoop. It's amazing that in these situations, the default position was always to blame the woman. He got the goodwill and the well wishes, and I got the nasty stares for being a harlot.

Oh how far from the truth that narrative about my on-again, off-again eight-year relationship with the youngest Hebert brother was. But sadly, the folks in Lovewell didn't give a shit about the truth. So here I was, smiling and serving coffee and accepting shitty tips from old biddies who hated me on principle.

I'd learned at a young age that the world always blamed the woman. In the eyes of the citizens of Lovewell, I'd somehow tricked their most beloved hockey star into dating me. Then I'd ruined his life and bled him dry. To them, I was a shameless gold digger. They'd harp on my lack of manners, my morals, or any other value they saw fit to criticize, blaming it on my being raised by a teen mom. Never mind that I was no longer the child they'd looked down at for all those years. I was twenty-eight, and my mother had done a damn good job raising me. But this was the kind of stink that was impossible to wash off in this small town.

"Gentlemen," I said with a smile, holding a fresh pot of coffee high.

Finn, the largest and friendliest of this bunch, gave me a winning smile. "Good morning, Lila," he boomed, sliding his mug toward the end of the table. It looked like a toy in his massive hand.

Gus and Jude, both on the quieter side, gave me more subdued greetings, though they were still friendly. Gus was the oldest brother, a logger who looked like a stereotypical mountain man. His beard was thick and a little unruly, and it was rare to see him in anything other than a knit hat, a flannel shirt, work boots, and at least one item of clothing with a Carhartt logo. Jude, on the other hand, had more of a hipster vibe going, with his thick glasses and ironic T-shirts.

Finn was something else entirely. Long hair and a beard, with the cocky confidence of a prior-service Navy pilot.

And then there was Owen. His blue eyes were bright as they met mine. The hint of a smile he gave me made my stomach clench. He was wearing one of his crisp dress shirts and jeans. Although he was the only clean-shaven one, the family resemblance was overwhelming. Every one of them had blue eyes, square jaws, and massive shoulders.

But the best thing about the Heberts? Despite my history with their younger half brother, they continued to treat me like family. It was a kindness I'd never take for granted.

"How's Adele?" I asked Finn.

His whole face lit up. "Amazing. The third trimester is uncomfortable, but she's managing well. I'm trying to convince her to stop working so much. She can't be crawling under trucks while in labor, you know?"

Gus tossed his head back and laughed. "Good luck stopping her."

Adele was several years older than me, so I didn't know her well, but she was famously tough. I doubted she'd let any man tell her what she could and could not do.

I stuck around for a moment, chatting like I always did when they stopped in. They asked after my mother, showing nothing but respect for her, as usual, and Finn thanked me again for helping his daughter Merry with fractions.

Each time I interacted with them, it felt surreal. For years, I'd believed that one day, I'd be a Hebert too. That when Cole made it to the NHL, we'd get married, have lots of kids, and come back to Lovewell every year for Christmas to see his family, bringing with us tons of gifts and stories about our blessed, exciting life.

Instead, I'd come back home after cobbling together a degree in my twenties so I could save for a shot at grad school and a fresh start in New York. Money was tight, especially since I'd been helping Mom out, and New York rent was no joke.

Willa would tell me to draw a boundary and firmly insist that I was too busy to help the Heberts. But I didn't have the energy to fight my pleasing instincts. Not today. Plus, the promise of thirty dollars an hour was too good to pass up. I didn't need much sleep to function. I could make it work.

The Heberts had been so good to me over the years, so the least I could do was help out while they were struggling. I could file and make Excel spreadsheets with the best of them.

I'd dropped off their usual breakfasts, which consisted of enough to feed a family of ten, then made my rounds, refilling coffee, before Finn called me over.

"Thank you for agreeing to help Owen out," he said, dipping his chin. "We appreciate it."

Gus and Jude murmured in agreement.

With a smirk, I turned to Owen. When our eyes met, a shiver of excitement flowed through my veins, and the world around us went hazy. "Haven't agreed to anything yet."

Those deep blue eyes were the only thing still in focus. They never left mine, almost as if they were challenging me to stay away from him.

"I know he's a pain in the ass," Finn said, pulling me from my stupor, "but I know you can keep him in line."

Jude laughed, and the dimple in his right cheek popped. I'd never say it out loud, but he was my favorite of Cole's brothers. He was gentle, quiet, and kind, but with a dry sense of humor I appreciated. Though I supposed he now had competition for the top spot. Because Owen was sitting back, calmly sipping coffee, saying nothing but communicating so much.

He was silently challenging me. As if he already believed I was capable of all the tasks he needed help with. And as if he looked forward to seeing what I could do.

My heart rate sped up as he continued to assess me, and my knees went a little wobbly.

He was a seasoned negotiator. I'd give him that.

"Pretty sure you're overqualified, but we'd appreciate all the help you could give us," Finn said. "Owen's a bit of a control freak." He laughed. "But if you've got time, he could use help making spreadsheets or organizing files. The rest of us sure as shit don't have the first about doing that kind of stuff."

What did I have to lose? Excitement hummed in my veins at the prospect of a new experience like this. From our short conversation, it was clear that Owen would be a good boss. He hadn't talked down to me, and he'd carefully answered each of my questions. Despite what I considered limited experience, he'd seemed impressed. It was no secret that he was under pressure. Hell, everyone in town knew what the Heberts had been through, and he had every reason to be angry. But he wasn't. A little stern, yes, but still kind.

"I'll do it," I said.

Owen's expression didn't change. He was so serious and controlled.

It shouldn't, but his stoicism sent a frisson of interest through me. What would it take to knock him off his game? He'd been off-kilter for a moment yesterday when he'd squeezed his coffee cup so hard it exploded all over him. Could I rile him up again? Make him lose his cool?

The clang of a fork on a plate startled me. Damn. I'd veered way off course. I forced my attention away from Owen and refilled each of the guys' mugs once more. When Mrs. Souza called out to me, grumbling that her hash browns were cold—of course they were; they'd been sitting in front of her while she gossiped for the last twenty minutes—I excused myself.

The Heberts finished up, and unlike most of our patrons, left a generous tip. As I was busing the table, loading the plates into a plastic bin, a thick business card, embossed and heavy, caught my eye.

I picked it up and studied it. Owen Hebert, CFO,

DiLuca Construction. On the back, he'd scribbled *Call me so we can get to work*. -O

I tucked it into my apron, fighting a grin. It was a certainty I wouldn't be sleeping for weeks. Ostensibly because I'd be working so much. But also because there was no way I wouldn't be spending my time obsessing about Owen Hebert and those damn blue eyes.

Chapter 5
Lila

I accept your generous offer.

Are you sure? I've been staring at a box of files for over an hour, and I'm pretty sure I'd like a hellmouth to open up under this cabin and swallow me whole.

Files don't scare me.

These might.

Never fear, Owen Hebert. I'm gonna make your files my bitch.

As agreed, I'd showed up at the Hebert Timber offices this afternoon. Did I wear a little makeup and my tightest jeans? Why, yes, I did. And No, I did not want to analyze why.

I'd vastly underestimated how much work needed to be done, but seeing Owen cushioned the blow. So did his grateful, enthusiastic acceptance of another honey latte.

We were walking through this week's priorities—and the list was long—when the alarm on my phone sounded.

With a heavy breath out, I stood and gathered my notebook and pen. "I'm so sorry, but I've got to run. Can we pick this up tomorrow?"

He ran his hands through his hair in a way that I'd already pinned as a nervous habit and checked his phone. "I've got some calls scheduled for tomorrow afternoon. Could you stay a few minutes longer? If we could get through the rest of the records, I'd feel a lot better."

I tapped my phone's screen to check the time again, and my heart sank. I really couldn't. Lips pursed, I considered him. "Are you busy now?" I asked. "I've got to do a few deliveries, but if you come with me, we can talk business in the car."

He tipped his head back and frowned up at me. "Deliveries?"

I wound my scarf around my neck and tucked my notebook and laptop into my bag. Then I headed for the door. "Come on. It won't take long."

For a long moment, he didn't move. His expression was serious, as always, as he scrutinized me, like he was trying to make sense of my suggestion. Then he gave the barest of shrugs as if to say *fuck it*—in his own classy way, of course—and stood.

Once he'd pocketed his phone and had thrown his coat on, we headed down in the elevator. All the while, he stole questioning glances at me, but I remained silent. I enjoyed throwing him off balance a little. It was kind of hot actually, cracking the cool, calm exterior of the tall, broody businessman. I had the feeling he wasn't the kind of guy who was frequently caught off guard.

I could have talked accounting with him all night, but it had been a long winter, and Vic was short-staffed, so I'd promised to help out with deliveries tonight.

We left the building just as the last few rays of sunlight disappeared behind the mountains. I couldn't help but scan the horizon, in awe of the beauty surrounding us, as I headed toward my car.

Halfway there, I realized Owen was no longer beside me. I spun, finding him staring, slack-jawed, at my minivan.

I smiled and threw one arm out, gesturing to it like I was a game show hostess and the van was a coveted prize. "This baby is a 2002 Chrysler Town & Country. Don't be intimidated by her grandeur. Priscilla's just a car."

Owen blinked, pressing his lips together in a straight line.

I fought back a laugh at the skepticism written all over his face. I loved my girl. When I found myself back in Maine last year, I needed wheels, and Todd, the owner of the used car dealership in Heartsborough, was a friend of my great-uncle Louis. There weren't a ton of options in my price range, but even if there had been, I would have chosen Priscilla.

She was equipped with all-wheel drive, which was necessary up here, and she was roomy. This was the kind of car I'd wished my mom had driven when I was a kid. The kind of vehicle the normal kids had, with captain's chairs and little baskets of snacks and coloring books for long rides to visit relatives for the holidays.

So what if I didn't have or even *want* kids? The price had been right, and Priscilla and I had understood each other from day one.

And we'd been blissfully happy together ever since.

"She's got new brakes and working heat," I chided. "Get in!"

With a huff, he shuffled toward the passenger door. "What is a single twenty-eight-year-old woman doing driving a minivan?"

"First of all, this beast gets decent gas mileage. Probably a whole lot better than your luxury SUV. Second, she's got tons of space. I've got stow-and-go seats and everything. You don't even know what you're missing." I patted her steering wheel and gave Owen a wink. "Priscilla here is a van-imal."

The man just stared at me like he worried he might have to have me committed.

"Van-imal," I repeated. "Get it?"

He bit his lip and smiled, and my stomach dipped. Damn. I hated how sexy such a subtle movement was. The last thing I needed was to be attracted to my new boss, who also happened to be my ex's older brother. But we were truly past that and now veering into hopeless tween crush territory. If I wasn't careful, I'd dig a Lisa Frank notebook out of my mom's basement when I got home and start doodling his name surrounded in hearts.

"Are you doing home improvement projects?" he asked, peering over his shoulder. "What do you need to transport?"

Shaking my head, I pulled out of the parking lot. "You have so much to learn about Lovewell. Buckle up. You can talk accounting to me while I drive. If we're gonna be working together, you've got to communicate, big guy."

He slid a hand between the passenger seat and the door, then turned to me, wearing a confused frown.

It took me a moment to understand what the look was for. "Ah. It doesn't have fancy controls," I explained. "Just the bar under the seat."

He leaned forward and grabbed the bar between his feet, and suddenly, his seat slammed all the way back.

I couldn't stop the giggle that escaped me. He was so uncomfortable. I bet Mister Thousand-Dollar Shoes had never even come near a minivan.

With a grunt, he adjusted the seat so he had ample leg room but wasn't all the way in the second row and buckled his seat belt.

"Where were we in our discussion about the records?" I asked as I took a turn. "Sorry I couldn't stay any longer. I promised Vic I'd help with deliveries tonight."

He raised one eyebrow, his full lips pressed in a tight line. "You're not running drugs, are you?"

I tilted my head and stuck my tongue out at him. "If I was a drug dealer, I'd probably have a much nicer car." I was not sassy by nature. It went against every polite, pleasing instinct I had. But Owen's stoic demeanor made me want to roll my eyes and make snarky comments just to get a rise out of him.

He crossed his arms and looked out the windshield. "Fair point."

I squeezed the steering wheel and sat up a little straighter. "So about those records."

By the time we reached our destination, we had

discussed GAAP, records retention, and the best way to itemize receipts. Despite the professional, big-city rich guy persona, Owen was a pure math nerd, and I was enjoying myself.

I didn't have anyone in my life to talk about this stuff with. No one who had professional experience to share. Outside of school, I'd been alone, doing my thing and learning as much as I could. Now, though, I had access to a man with decades of experience. Not only that, but a person who could appreciate my hilarious war stories.

"Where are we?" he asked as I parked along the street in front of an old Victorian in town. It had probably been exquisite in its heyday, but these days, the paint was peeling and a couple of the third-floor windows were boarded up.

An old-fashioned cinder block garage sat at the end of the long driveway. Inside the crumbling stone structure were rows of commercial refrigerators.

"It's the food pantry. My friend Vic runs it. Her aunt does, actually, but she's been having health problems and needed a little help."

The sun had fully set, and when I climbed out of the van, I buried my chin in my scarf to stave off the chill. "Vic moved Down East with her husband years ago, but she got divorced recently and is helping out here for a bit."

Owen appeared beside me, shoving his hands into his pockets. "Do you work here too?"

"Nah," I said, heading across the street. "I just volunteer to help with deliveries. Winter is hard. Some people are homebound, and food insecurity is at an all-time high in Maine. Resources are so limited. And the refrigeration garage needs a new roof, so they don't have enough freezers."

With a bump to his shoulder, I steered him to the left of the building. "Here, we go in the back."

He followed me down the ramp into the basement, where dozens of industrial steel shelves were lined with food. It was past closing time, but there were several employees and volunteers scurrying around, cleaning up and organizing all the non-perishable items.

I headed for the front table where patrons checked in and snagged the clipboard sitting on top of a stack of boxes. Each one was labeled with a Post-it detailing the recipient's name and address.

"I guess I'd forgotten this was here." He scanned the space, running his hands through his hair.

"That's convenient," I quipped without looking up from the delivery list.

Beside me, he cleared his throat.

The sound garnered my attention. Clutching the clipboard to my chest, I studied him as he took in the operation, wide-eyed and maybe a little overwhelmed.

"What I meant to say is that it's nice that you don't have to think about this place," I explained. "That you've never experienced food insecurity. That you can so easily forget that there are tens of thousands of hungry people in this state." I shrugged and swallowed back the indignation that always took over in the presence of people who took such basic needs for granted.

He shifted uncomfortably, his jaw rigid and his gaze unreadable.

As he scrutinized me, my stomach sank. What had gotten into me? I wasn't a confrontational person. Had I had these kinds of thoughts before? Absolutely. But I usually kept them to myself, and I never made bitchy comments. And here I was lecturing the guy who'd just hired me at thirty dollars an hour.

"Sorry," I said as hot shame crept up my cheeks. My whole life, I'd prided myself on being polite. I was not the type to rock the boat. Quite the opposite, actually. I'd always worked to make those around me comfortable.

"Don't apologize," he said, catching me with those stormy blue eyes. "I deserved that, and you're right."

He shucked off his coat, draped it over the boxes on the table, and rolled up the cuffs of his dress shirt, revealing tan, muscular forearms that temporarily distracted me from my righteous indignation.

"Put me to work."

"Thanks for coming with me."

"It was worth it for the baby carrots," he quipped with a wry grin.

I squinted at him. "Don't forget about the gluten-free crackers and the string cheese. This is a classy establishment," I said, twirling said string cheese in the air.

Back in the parking lot of the Hebert Timber offices, we sat side by side in my van, listening to *Wait, Wait, Don't... Tell Me* on NPR and eating the lame dinner I'd packed. Owen had been a rockstar with deliveries, and even putting Mrs. Revelle's groceries away since she'd just had her hip replaced.

"I didn't realize I'd have company," I snarked. "Next time I'll pack my finest caviar."

"I'd settle for drive-through fries. Isn't there a Wendy's in Heartsborough now? I'll buy. Anything you want."

"Thanks, but I have celiac," I explained, "so I have to be careful about food."

He bit into another baby carrot with a loud *snap*. "I'm sorry."

"Don't be." I waved him off. "It's not a big deal. I've lived with it for more than a decade. But that's why I always bring my own snacks."

I had a strange relationship with food, because it had the power to thoroughly screw me up for weeks, sometimes months.

"If you don't mind me asking," he said, looking a bit awkward, "does it just make you sick?"

The last thing I wanted to do was talk about the ins and outs of my GI tract with the hot dude who was my new boss. But there was so much misinformation, and he was interested in the details, so I took a deep breath and tried to explain without too many gory details.

"If I eat gluten, I experience acute symptoms. Uncomfortable stomach stuff." I raised one eyebrow, hoping he'd get it so I didn't have to say the word diarrhea out loud.

He nodded once, thank God, so I moved on.

"But that's not the worst. If I consume gluten, even trace amounts, my body mounts an immune response that causes malabsorption. That means I don't absorb many of the vitamins I consume. So if I slip up and eat something I shouldn't, I'll feel awful for weeks afterward because my body can't properly absorb nutrients."

"Shit, I had no idea."

"Yeah, people like to make fun of it, and I know that

going gluten free is considered trendy, but celiac is associated with a significantly increased likelihood of lymphoma and lots of other scary conditions." I'd always been given shit for my eating habits. It seemed everyone and their dog liked to have an opinion on what women ate.

"So that's why, when in doubt, I don't eat something. And sometimes, when there's food I can eat, I eat too much. So it's a whole roller coaster with me."

"I hadn't realized. I'm so sorry."

"No, it's fine. In rural Maine, there aren't a ton of options, but here and there, I've found places that are very careful and accommodating."

"Do you miss gluten? Not to rub it in, but it's fucking delicious."

I laughed. "Not really. Sometimes I crave Froot Loops, but I survive." I thought for a moment. "Ooh. But there is one thing I miss more than anything. Pizza. Really good thin-crust pizza. It's almost impossible to find good gluten-free pizza. Mostly it tastes like a soggy cracker."

"I've seen gluten-free pizza at lots of places in Boston. I'll try some and report back."

"Thanks."

"Least I can do. I can't expect any sane woman to live without pizza. But this explains your impressive assortment of seed crackers. Thanks, by the way. All I've got back at my rental is beef jerky and peanut M&M's."

I hummed and shot him a grin. "Delicious."

"I also have a six-pack and a couple hundred emails waiting for me. I lead a very glamorous life."

"Then you better finish telling me about the cost reports. I wouldn't want to keep you," I teased.

We'd talked as we packed grocery orders and while I drove, and the conversation had continued when we'd made it back to the office. Owen was easy to talk to, and his thoughtfulness and sarcasm only made him that much more attractive, dammit.

He'd spent the evening filling me in on the background of the business, what was left of it, what had already been sold off, and how he had spent most of the last year trying to offload what remained.

He'd gone into all the sordid details about how his father had been working with Canadian drug cartels to move narcotics into the United States via the logging roads their family had owned for generations.

Mitch had finally been arrested last year, and not just on drug charges, but murder, assault, and kidnapping charges as well. I hadn't been living here at the time, but these revelations had rocked the community.

"Were you close with your dad? You know, before all this?"

"Fuck no," he spat. "Sorry." He ducked his head and pulled in a long breath. "I've kept my distance from my dad for a long time. Even before all the crime, he was a piece of shit. If anything, the recent stuff has just confirmed what I've always known."

"I'm so sorry."

"Don't be." He cleared his throat and focused on something across the parking lot. "Some of my brothers are devastated. Gus was close to Dad. And the news hit Jude hard too. Probably because he's the nicest out of all of us. But I detached from my father and his particular brand of bullshit a long time ago."

A silence settled over the car then. I was at a loss for what to say. My heart ached for him and his brothers. My own dad was hardly father of the year, but he loved me and wasn't a criminal.

I studied Owen's profile—his strong nose, square stubble-covered jaw, and his plump lower lip. My stomach dipped every time I let myself really think about him. And every time I had the chance to assess him like this. He was an honest, hardworking, genuine man. Nothing like his father. And I'd help him with whatever he needed.

I handed him the bag of baby carrots again, and his hand brushed mine as he accepted it. That simple touch made my breath catch and my pulse quicken.

And suddenly, Priscilla felt a lot less spacious.

He cleared his throat. "But enough about my shit. Are you sure you have time for this? It's okay if you don't. I don't want you to feel obligated to help."

Humming, I twisted my lips, searching for the best way to respond to him. I did feel obligated. But I was also interested in the work, and, although I'd never admit it, in getting to know him.

With his head lowered again, he scratched at his jawline. "You just seem busy."

A long sigh escaped me. I couldn't tell him the whole truth. It was way too pathetic. I'd wasted most of my twenties chasing the wrong things and now I had to exhaust myself every day to keep from spiraling. About the mess I'd made out of my adult life. About all the stupid mistakes I'd made and all the ways I'd put others before myself.

"I'm sorry I was snappy earlier." I was still feeling guilty.

"I'm really passionate about food insecurity and helping out."

"Don't apologize. I'm an idiot and appreciate the opportunity to learn more."

"It's just..." This was hard to say, especially to someone like him. "When I was little, my mom and I used to sometimes have to go to the food pantry. Vic's aunt, Miss Lou, always made sure we had enough." My voice shook a bit. This wasn't something I talked about. Not that I was ashamed. My mom was a child when she had me and did her absolute best to build a comfortable life for both of us.

His face froze. God, I could see the pity in his eyes.

"I'm sorry..."

I held up a hand to stop him. "Please don't." I didn't want his pity. I wanted him to see me as a capable adult. "But that's why I try to make as much time as I can to pitch in. Small towns run on the energy of their citizens," I said. "I may only be here temporarily, but I gotta help out where I can."

He watched me, gaze intense, for several seconds. I could only stare back while some kind of unspoken understanding passed between us.

"So let me help you," I said softly.

Without a word, he dropped his focus from my face, unbuckled his seat belt, and opened the passenger door.

Then he just stood there, his broad frame blocking out the cold, not looking at me, not speaking, for so long I began to fidget. Finally, he clutched the doorframe and leaned in, studying me.

"You're quite the surprise, Lila."

I turned to him, immediately caught up in the way he watched me, wondering if he could read minds, because I thought the same way about him. Then, as I admired the stubble along his square jaw, I hoped that he couldn't. Thoughts of Owen consumed me so wholly that I couldn't find a way to articulate what I wanted. Which was to work with him. Spend time with him. Help him in any way I could.

This was why I needed to go to grad school. So I could get a good job with decent health insurance. Because I clearly needed a fuck ton of therapy. So I could one day be a functional adult woman who could express herself with words instead of staring slack-jawed at the corporate guy with the distractingly broad shoulders.

"Have a good weekend, okay?" he said. "Don't work yourself to the bone."

"I should tell you the same thing."

He shook his head and gave me the smallest of smiles. "Noted."

He closed the door and tapped the roof of the van. Then he took a step back and stuffed his hands into his pockets, watching me as I drove away.

Why was my stomach clenching? Why was I feeling this strange pull toward Owen and his messy family business?

And what the hell was I getting myself into?

Chapter 6
Owen

I parked my car in front of my temporary log cabin and dug through the glove box for the bottle of Tums I kept handy. Just being here had my stomach churning.

The cabin wasn't the issue. It was far nicer than I had expected and would be the perfect hideout for the next few weeks. It was being back in this town, a place I'd sworn I'd left behind forever, having to grapple with the legacy of my father and the family business.

And then there was Lila. The unexpected upside of this shitty situation. She was smart and curious and fun. I had a blast driving around with her tonight. Her positive attitude was infectious, and shockingly, she seemed to enjoy talking about accounting as much as I did.

Driving around, listening to music and NPR shows, and making deliveries together was more fun than I'd had in months.

She asked question after question about what I did as CFO of DiLuca Construction, eager for every detail. Her excitement reminded me of what it was like when I was trying to figure out my own career, desperate for as much information as I could consume.

I wanted to help her.

She had so much damn potential.

Potential she had no doubt wasted on my idiot brother.

She hadn't said a bad word about him, but I could only imagine what could have gone down. My mind took off with possibilities, each one worse than the one before, making my blood heat and my fists clench.

If he had hurt her in any way...

With a deep breath in, I rolled my shoulders.

Lila was triggering protective instincts I never knew I had. I wasn't usually the kind of guy who got up in arms over drama between other people. Maybe it was because she was so young. I'd never had a little sister, but that was the only reason that made sense. The tightness in my chest was more than just the heartburn I knew was coming.

It seemed impossible that I'd left Boston just yesterday. My normal life seemed so far away. However, one glance at my phone brought reality slamming into me. The one hundred emails or so needing my attention hit like a solid punch to the gut.

I climbed out of my car and slipped my phone into my pocket, determined to avoid thinking about work for just a little longer.

As I carried boxes of files toward the large wrap-around porch, a sharp whistle rent the air. Within seconds, two large dogs were sniffing around my legs. I bobbled the boxes but recovered before they could fall to the ground.

"Rochester. Heathcliff," a booming voice called. "Down!"

I spun at the sound, catching sight of Henri Gagnon, my landlord, and a lanky boy with too-long hair who came up to his shoulder walking down the driveway. It had been years since I'd seen Henri, but he hadn't changed much. His beard was thicker, but he had the same barrel chest and permanent scowl. The dogs abandoned me and took off at a run for him.

Once I'd set the boxes down, I turned and wiped my hands on my jeans. When Henri was close, I offered my hand. Instead of taking it, the flannel-wearing lumberjack pulled me in for a hug.

When he released me, I stumbled, confused. Had a Gagnon—a member of the family my dad had done his best to convince us boys to despise—just hugged me? What was happening here?

"Settled in okay?"

With a nod, I bent to scratch one of the dogs behind the ear.

Henri stepped to one side and tipped his chin at the boy with him. "This is my son, Tucker."

The lanky boy, dressed in a Gagnon Lumber hoodie, had floppy dark hair that he pushed out of his eyes. "Tucker Gagnon." He stuck his skinny arm out, offering me a surprisingly firm handshake.

Henri looked down at him and gave him a smile far softer than I thought was possible for this man.

"You're my Uncle Finn's brother?" he asked.

I shifted, at a loss for how to answer. It seemed simple. Yes, Finn was my brother. But this Gagnon kid had just referred to him as his uncle. Damn, things really had changed around here.

Henri grimaced and stuck his hands in the pockets of his jeans. "He's not your uncle yet," he said.

If I wasn't mistaken, there was a hint of discomfort in his voice. Again, I didn't have a little sister, but it didn't take a genius to figure out that Henri probably wasn't thrilled that Finn had knocked up Adele.

Tucker scowled at his dad. "He's going to marry Auntie Adele, and they're having a baby."

Henri grunted. "Yup. And she's not gonna take it easy on him."

"Does that mean you're also my uncle?" Tucker asked me, his head tilted in curiosity.

"Uh..." That title, uncle, always made me feel a little itchy. Merry was great, but I hadn't spent much time with her, and all this small-town familiarity was making me feel claustrophobic as well.

Thankfully, Henri intervened. "My wife Alice is up at our house making a welcome to town lasagna for you. I'll bring it down later."

"And these are for you," Tucker said, shoving a brown carton of eggs at me.

I frowned at the eggs, then back up at the kid.

Henri huffed a laugh. "My beautiful wife insisted on buying our kids baby chicks. That meant I had to build a predator-proof chicken coop and run. She swore the kids would do all the work. The kids swore they would too. And guess who feeds and waters them every day?"

"You make me clean the coop," the boy protested, crossing his arms over his chest.

He clapped Tucker on the shoulder. "Builds character."

God, this guy was too nice. To say I was shocked would be an understatement. Most people in Lovewell were outwardly hostile these days, if my brothers were to be believed.

Henri had every reason to hate me and my family. My dad had been responsible for the death of his. His business had struggled for years because of my dad's illegal and quasi-legal manipulations.

And here he was, making small talk and dropping off fresh eggs.

Though I suppose this could be pity rather than genuine kindness. That wouldn't surprise me in the least. If anyone understood what we were going through financially, it was the Gagnons. We'd sold some acreage to them last year, which allowed us to pay our employees through the winter. Through the whole process, Henri and his brother Pascal had been professional and helpful. They clearly took no joy in the demise of our family business, thus establishing them as much better human beings than I could ever be.

God, being here was torture. I was a living, breathing reminder of all my father had done. And although I could not atone for his sins, I could at least acknowledge them.

"I'm sorry," I said, holding his gaze. "About your father." It was awkward as fuck, and I felt like an idiot, but I had to say something. There was no protocol for this type of thing. At least I hadn't blurted out nonsense like "sorry my dad murdered yours. Thanks for the eggs!"

He pursed his lips and gave me a nod. "Thanks, man. You gotta know, we don't blame you or your family."

"Yeah," Tucker added with a firm nod. "We like Uncle

Finn. Dad was mad at him for a while, but now he takes me up in his plane."

That sounded like Finn. Kids adored him because, deep down, he was one. It wasn't hard to imagine how perfectly he fit in with this nice, close-knit family. I was happy for him. He'd found what he wanted. Family. Belonging. In the most unexpected of places. Namely, this town.

Sadly, what had become a safe haven for him still felt like a nightmare for me, with unforeseen dangers lurking around every corner.

Henri cleared his throat. "Just thought we'd stop by to welcome you and make sure you're settling in. There's a decent amount of firewood." He gestured to a neat stack on the covered porch. "And there are instructions on the wall about how to light the wood stove."

"I can handle it."

"My wife almost burned the place down a couple of years ago. I wrote them for her, and they've stayed up. Last year, she framed them and hung them on the wall."

Tucker shook his head, executing the perfect teen eye roll. "Mom."

"You should be all set. We've got a whole shed full of firewood up the hill. You can drive up anytime and help yourself."

"Or you could chop some," Tucker said. "My dad and I chop it all ourselves. Sometimes my uncles help too."

I smirked. This kid had zero issue with shaming a grown man he'd just met. I liked it.

It had been many, many years since I'd chopped wood. As common as the chore was up here, it wasn't necessary in a city like Boston. I was probably six or seven the first time

I chopped wood using a small hatchet my dad had given me. Each of us boys had our own. In retrospect, arming us with sharp blades at such a young age was wildly dangerous and inappropriate, but occasions like that, where we got to spend real quality time with him, were few and far between, so we were always eager to go along with whatever manly shit he was trying to shove down our throats.

"I can chop wood," I said, giving the kid a gentle glare. "I may live in Boston, but I grew up here."

"Good." He gave me a chin tip. "Because my dad and uncles compete. I'm gonna too, once I'm sixteen. Sometimes Uncle Paz and Uncle Remy come over and race."

Jesus. The last thing I wanted to do was get into some kind of lumberjack competition with the Gagnons.

"Uncle Finn comes too. Aunt Adele is better than him, but she's pregnant now, so we're helping him train."

Now *that* I'd pay to see. Finn might be an ace pilot, but like me, he wasn't exactly a mountain man.

"Text me the next time Finn comes over," I said. "I'd love to see him make a fool of himself."

That got a smile out of the kid.

Once they'd made their way back to their house, I sat on the porch in an Adirondack chair, taking in the scenery. The moon was almost full and the stars were so bright they lit up the forest. I pulled my knit hat down over my ears, sipped my beer, and tried to make peace with my circumstances.

Yes, I hated this town. But this cabin and this view were pretty great. And then there was Lila.

I squeezed my eyes shut and tried to ignore the pull I felt toward her. She was an employee, temporary or not, and my little brother's ex-girlfriend. Not to mention a decade younger than me.

Yet none of those pesky details mattered when she smiled at me.

And when she did, it was like standing in the sun. Her attention was warm and comforting, and it created an ache inside me, one I'd never felt before and couldn't identify.

But I was here to get the business sold and nothing else. After a good night's sleep and a gallon of coffee, my self-control would certainly return, and I'd stop thinking about her.

But I reached for another beer just in case.

Chapter 7
Lila

I rooted around in the fridge for a hard seltzer, pulling my fluffy cardigan around my shoulders. Magnolia had given it to me a few years ago. Her gifts were always over-the-top.

But it was so soft and so warm. And the house was chilly. Mom and I kept the thermostat at a balmy sixty-six. Oil to heat the house was pricey, and this winter had been tight. So I was bundled up for my Friday night cocktail hour with the girls.

I took the bag of microwave popcorn out and divided it into two plastic bowls. Then I shuffled over to the couch where my mother was absorbed in a Hallmark movie.

She was still dressed in her scrubs, and though her hair and makeup were pristine, there was no hiding the dark circles under her eyes. I wasn't the only one who'd been working hard lately. She'd fought hard to keep this house when she divorced husband number three last summer.

After one failed marriage and one successful night

school program to become a home health care aide, she'd purchased the tiny Cape Cod in town. I was in middle school then, and the night we moved in, we'd brought everything we owned in a few boxes and suitcases. We had no furniture, so we camped on the living room floor in sleeping bags and ate a celebratory blueberry pie Aunt Louise had brought over straight from the tin.

No matter who came into our lives and who left, this house, a tiny Cape painted blue with white trim, was our sanctuary. It was cozy and well-loved and within walking distance of everything we needed, with a rose hedge my mother meticulously maintained.

"Thanks, sweets. Come watch with me." She took the bowl I offered and patted the worn floral couch next to her. "This one is about a florist who is trying to save a beloved community garden from an evil property developer."

"Hm. Lemme guess. He's actually a cinnamon roll in a thousand-dollar suit and will fall madly in love with her and give up his life in the big city to grow flowers in the small town."

With a teasing scowl, Mom threw a piece of popcorn at me. "We can hate watch. Sit down."

"Can't. I've got cocktails with the girls in a few minutes."

She propped her bare feet up on the battered coffee table, her pink toenails sparkling—Mom never neglected her nails, even when times were tough—and reclined further, snuggling into the couch. "Give my love to Willa and Magnolia."

"Enjoy the blandly handsome man who can barely act." I turned and headed for my room, popcorn bowl in hand.

It was small and hadn't changed much since high school.

The twin bed was covered with a purple quilt, and the shelves were stuffed with books and pageant trophies. The desk, a Goodwill find, had been painted purple one sunny weekend afternoon.

While most adults would probably be embarrassed about sleeping in their childhood bedrooms, all I felt was comfort. This house was the only home I'd ever known—a place where I felt safe and secure. And after years of bouncing around with Cole, I didn't take for granted the familiarity and feeling of peace that washed over me when I was inside these four purple walls.

This situation was mutually beneficial too. Mom was getting back onto her feet post-divorce, and I had the ability to help out with the bills while she did. I'd never get her to quit Hallmark movies, but at least she seemed disinclined enough to not jump right into another quickie marriage.

I fluffed my pillows and perched my laptop on the edge of the dresser while I waited for the video call to load.

I'd just settled back when the smiling faces of my two best friends appeared on screen.

Magnolia was waving excitedly, cuddling one of her cats in her lap. She was six feet tall, had the kind of asymmetrical haircut very few people could pull off, and collected tattoos and rescue cats.

"Missed you bitches!" she cheered.

"I've been up for thirty-one hours, so there's a good chance I'll fall asleep mid-convo tonight," Willa warned, rubbing her eyes. "This is your warning."

"Fucking residency," Magnolia quipped. She was wearing a colorful kimono and sipping what looked like a professionally crafted martini. "Aren't you a real doctor yet?"

"Soon," Willa replied. "So freaking soon. I can almost taste the freedom." She pushed her blonde hair behind her ears. "A few more months and then I'll be living the dream, soaking up days off and showers and watching TV. Heck, maybe I'll even date."

"Tell me you're at least getting busy with the hot doctors." Magnolia waggled her brows. "Make sure to sample Baltimore's finest before you come to New York."

Willa scoffed. "I'm not sure you understand what hospitals are actually like."

Magnolia gasped and clutched at a string of imaginary pearls. "Are you saying *Grey's Anatomy* lied to me?"

Willa shook her head gently, her expression one of exaggerated sympathy. "Ladies, this may be difficult to hear, but yes. Shonda lied to us all. The attendings are all married, jerks, or both, and the other residents and interns are my competition. Not to mention that they're more like annoying siblings I can't escape than anything else. Hospitals are *the least* sexy places ever."

"I'm going to need some time to sit with this," Magnolia said solemnly, taking a long sip of her drink. With a loud sigh, she bowed her head. "And process my grief."

"In the meantime," Willa said, a smirk creeping up one side of her mouth, "make sure the liquor cabinet is fully stocked when I move in. I have a lot of lost time to make up for."

Magnolia scoffed. "As if I haven't been preparing for your arrival for months. Your rooms are ready, and we're fully stocked up." She rubbed her hands together. "Finally, our plan is coming together."

A few years ago, Magnolia had inherited a condo in

Tribeca from an aunt. Or maybe a grandparent. She had the kind of multi-generational family money that meant every time she turned around, one of her relatives was inheriting a random house somewhere new.

For now, she and several rescue cats lived there alone, waiting for Willa and me to move in.

We'd been hatching this master plan since we were kids. The three of us together, living it up in the city. It had seemed inevitable after we graduated from high school, but real life got in the way, as it usually does, and it had taken far longer than any of us anticipated.

Magnolia was well established, both with her trust fund and her career as an event planner. Willa had already been accepted into a prestigious internal medicine fellowship. All I had to do was get accepted to grad school.

We'd live our best city lives, finally shedding the last vestiges of the small-town versions of ourselves we'd been outgrowing since high school.

For me, it was a fresh start, a chance to seriously pursue my education, which had felt like an afterthought for so long.

And for Willa, New York was one last taste of freedom. She'd always planned to return to Lovewell, but a three-year fellowship in NYC before her father retired and handed the practice over to her was a gift she would not take for granted.

I closed my eyes and said a silent prayer for a big, fat envelope from NYU to arrive in the mail. I'd visualized the moment many times, but it was beginning to feel real.

Willa launched into a story about the most disgusting thing to come through her clinic that week, and Mags filled us in on a rave she'd thrown for a new sneaker release on Wednesday night.

When it was my turn to share what I'd been up to since the last time we talked, I sat up straight and smiled. "I got a new job."

Willa gave me an unimpressed look. "Another job?"

I shrugged. "It's temporary but good pay and actually relevant."

"The pay is good? In Lovewell?" Magnolia scoffed.

"Yeah." I popped a piece of popcorn into my mouth and chewed. "I'm helping out with the sale of Hebert Timber."

Magnolia rolled her eyes. "Oh no."

Willa huffed. "Nope."

"Girl. We've talked about this. Boundaries." Magnolia pinched the bridge of her nose. "Do you want me to schedule another session with my psychiatric hypnotist?"

I shuddered. Absolutely not. Once was enough. While I took mental health seriously, being hypnotized was not my idea of a good time.

"What happened to getting far away from that family?" Magnolia asked. "It took years to drag you out of the Cole vortex."

"And you've come so far!" Willa said, giving me a genuine look of concern.

"How about you come to New York for a visit?" Magnolia tapped at the screen of her phone. "I'll get you on a flight from Bangor and book spa treatments."

Annoyance and genuine affection battled inside me. Their reactions were over-the-top, but they came from a place of love and concern. I'd ignored my own needs for so long, and I'd been so hurt by Cole, so I couldn't blame them for fighting for me.

As a recovering doormat, sometimes I forgot how much

my inability to stand up for myself affected the people I loved. And it wasn't until I'd sought out therapy that I even understood it was happening.

I shook my head. "Let me explain." My tone was unusually forceful.

Both women went quiet and watched me. This was why I loved them. They didn't agree, but they were willing to listen.

"It's only for a few weeks. I'm working for Owen Hebert. He doesn't even speak to Cole. And it's purely accounting and records stuff. The kind of monotonous, boring work that I actually enjoy."

Willa cocked her head. "Who is Owen?"

"Does it matter?" Magnolia asked, frowning. "That whole family is trouble."

I held my hands up and inhaled deeply, waiting for them to quiet down again.

They were probably right. Most men were trouble, and if our evening spent together was any indication, Owen Hebert was no exception.

"He's going to pay me thirty dollars an hour," I said. "And you know I need that money if I'm ever going to afford to move to New York."

Magnolia wasn't buying it. "You could do plenty of other things for thirty dollars an hour."

"Not in Lovewell, Maine."

"What about stripping?" she asked, grinning. "There's a club in Heartsborough, and you've got great boobs."

"Jesus, Mags." Willa fumed. "Are you seriously suggesting she become a stripper?"

"Sex work is real work," she snapped. "Check your judgment, Dr. Savard."

Oh great, now my best friends were fighting over me. And not even me, really, but over whether I should consider showing my boobs for money.

"I didn't mean it like that," Willa said, narrowing her eyes. "Lila, you are my best friend, and I support you 100 percent regardless of whether you're working for the Heberts or taking your clothes off."

"Those are not equivalent options," I protested with a roll of my eyes. *Why* did my friends have to be so dramatic? "I know I've been a mess for years. I know you both did superhuman things to help me get my life back together, and I appreciate and love you both so much for that." I took a deep breath, closing my eyes and summoning all my courage to be completely honest. My friends meant well, but I was beyond tired of being told what was best for me. Like I couldn't figure it out on my own. "But I want to do this. I need to do this. And I'm going to do this."

I was met with nothing but silence. Cringing, I cracked one eye open and found my friends smiling at me on the screen.

"Boundary drawn!" Magnolia lifted her martini glass in salute.

"I'm proud of you," Willa said. "Even though I don't trust the Heberts, you know what's best for you."

"And anything that gets you to New York faster is a good thing," Mags added.

My heart expanded in my chest, and I couldn't help but smile right back. God, my friends were fierce, and I was lucky to have them.

Chapter 8
Owen

I stepped inside the Caffeinated Moose and froze.

Main Street didn't have much aesthetic charm these days, but the inside of this place was a different story.

The space was filled with mismatched wooden tables and chairs that were clearly handmade.

A massive coffee bar was the focal point. Several townspeople occupied the stools in front of it, chatting and reading the newspaper. Behind the bar, two baristas worked the large copper espresso machines with an impressive efficiency.

The chalkboard menu listed the offerings, which included single-origin beans, every type of espresso drink, and some incredible-looking baked goods. The smell of high-quality beans tickled my nose and drew me in.

Shit, this place was nice.

Near the back of the space sat a massive communal table surrounded by beanbag chairs. Kids' books and toys were neatly stowed on rough-edged wooden shelves on one wall.

It was cozy but clean, and the pastries in the display case were mouthwatering. I couldn't decide what looked better: the homemade quiche, the muffins, or the pre-wrapped sandwiches on artisan bread. No wonder Lila was so enthusiastic about this place.

About half the seats in the dining area were full, and there were another half dozen or so people waiting in line in front of me.

The woman behind the counter had round cheeks and a bright smile. Her red curly hair was tied back with a bandanna, and she wore a denim apron with the shop's logo on it.

I'd always preferred a simple Americano, but for days, I'd been craving another latte like the one Lila had brought me.

"A honey oat-milk latte," I said when it was my turn, handing the barista my card. "And a blueberry scone."

"Are you visiting?" she said, her smile bright, as she swiped my card.

I nodded. "This place is impressive." If the way the hair at the back of my neck prickled was any indication, more than one pair of eyes was watching me, so I ducked my head, intent on ignoring the attention, and focused on friendly small talk.

It wasn't easy. In a city like Boston, I blended in with any crowd, but here, I supposed I stuck out a bit. Was it the cashmere overcoat and Bruno Magli shoes, or was it me? The same thing had happened when I'd gone to the diner, and I wasn't the only one the locals had gawked at. How my brothers put up with this day in and day out was beyond me. The scrutiny was unnerving, and I'd only been here a handful of days. Granted, Gus was pretty antisocial and Finn was blinded by love, but what about Jude? And my mom?

When my latte was ready, I carried it and my scone to the back corner, giving Mrs. Porter, my high school English teacher, a nod as I went. She at least had the grace to say hello. Father Renee, who sat across the table from her, didn't have the same good manners.

I booted up my laptop, thoroughly impressed with the USB chargers built into the tables. This place was very cool. Sadly, it would probably be closed in six months, like many other small businesses that struggled to earn enough to keep the doors open up here.

I'd come here for a change of scenery. Not because I'd hoped to see a certain familiar face. I was reviewing the financials for the GeneSphere campus, the project that had been driving Enzo and me crazy for the past two years. I'd needed the quiet spot so I could focus, and the coffee was a bonus.

That was it.

If asked, I'd deny that I'd spent the last twenty-four hours holed up in my cabin, alternating between stewing over what the hell my father had been doing for the last twenty years—and still trying to understand why—and thinking about Lila: her smile, her laugh, her unabashed love for her minivan.

That thought alone brought a smile to my face every time.

It was a sickness, clearly borne out of the trauma of returning to my hometown. Lila was beautiful and friendly, and she was a genuinely nice person. That was all. And given my shitty association with Lovewell and the not so warm reception I'd received, it was no wonder she stuck out in my mind.

The bell over the door chimed, pulling me from thoughts of Lila I was beginning to worry I'd never escape.

When I looked up, my older brother was watching me, wearing an annoyed frown. He collected his coffee, nodded silently at the barista, and strode my way. Once he'd settled in the seat on the other side of my booth, he sipped his coffee tranquilly. He hadn't said a word. Hadn't greeted anyone he passed on the way.

I, on the other hand, was keenly aware, once again, of all the townspeople who were watching us.

"You get used to it," Gus muttered, coffee cup held aloft.

"Are people always this hostile?"

Young parents with small children and retirees alike were watching us, wearing expressions filled with a mixture of pity and scorn.

"It's not hostility. It's curiosity." Gus lifted one shoulder, seemingly unbothered. "It's gotten so much better. Last year, Adele went on a tirade, threatened the mayor and shamed Father Renee when they were rude to Finn and Merry. I wasn't there, but people still talk about it."

Huh. I had not heard that story. But it would explain how quickly my brother had fallen head-over-heels in love with the woman. "Shit."

He hummed into his coffee. "Part of living here."

I bit my tongue. This was not the place to pick this fight, but it was hard to understand why they stayed. Why here? Did the good really outweigh the bad? Because from where I was sitting, there weren't many items listed in the pro column.

"And since you left, they're gonna be extra critical."

Gus was the practical, serious one. He was hyper-competent and always learning. There was nothing the guy couldn't do. He'd built his own house, for Christ's sake.

He had assigned himself the role of protector a long time ago and had never relinquished that mantle. He shoveled Mom's driveway when it snowed and had driven Nanna to every one of her hair appointments when she was still alive. He was a good, steady guy.

I'd always been the overachiever. If asked, my father would swear that by the time I started preschool, I thought I was too good for everyone.

Where Gus had stayed, embraced his role in this family and the business, I'd run away screaming the minute I graduated from high school.

"I'm the bad guy for leaving, yet no one has a problem with Noah for doing the same thing?" I asked. "What gives?"

Gus cocked one brow, as if he was surprised I needed an explanation. "He's Noah. That kid couldn't stand still with a gun to his head. He's a free spirit."

True. Noah had been in elementary school when he first disappeared into the woods for days. Scared the living shit out of Mom. The only one who could ever track him down was Jude, no doubt because of their creepy twin connection. Noah was larger than life, gregarious, and adventurous. He'd spent his life practically bouncing off walls. The kid hated being inside, hated school. Hell, if it didn't involve running barefoot through the woods, he wasn't interested.

It was a miracle he'd finished high school, and he'd only

done that because of my mom's and Jude's diligence. He'd lived everywhere and tried every type of job and sporadically checked in with us.

But the only one of us who knew where he was at all times was Jude.

Jude, the steady, calm presence that counterbalanced Noah's chaos. He was thoughtful and quiet and preferred comic books and playing his guitar to bungee jumping and all-night raves in the woods. He worked hard for the family business, competed in timber sports with a few buddies, and spent most of his free time hiking with his dog.

He loved rural Maine, the serenity and quiet of it, and the routine of this life.

As grown men, we were all so different. As kids, we were scrappy and close knit. Mom ran a tight ship, and we took care of one another. But over the years, we'd drifted, and our values had changed. Anymore, it felt like any connection we had was long gone.

And truthfully, I'd probably caused more of the distance than anyone else. My desire to get away from my father and his legacy had driven me away from the rest of my family too. And after nearly two decades, it was unlikely I could repair the relationships I'd let wither away.

"You need to go see Mom."

"Yeah. I know."

He pinned me with his older brother glare. "Today, shithead. You've been in town for days and you haven't even bothered to stop by? That's fucked up. That woman went through enough raising us. Don't be a dick."

My gut sank at the reprimand, but I nodded. He was

right. There weren't many people on this earth I loved, but my mother was at the top of the list. Though I wasn't avoiding her, I *was* avoiding her roommate, my half brother Cole. The fewer interactions I had with that dumbass, the better.

"I'll go when I leave here."

Gus gave me a chin tip of approval and then went back to his coffee. After a quiet moment, when I assumed he was done talking at all, he cleared his throat. "I've got the security firm coming today."

The knots in my shoulders tightened. "How much is that going to cost?"

"At this point, who cares? We need it." He took off his hat and ran a hand through his hair. "I've been captaining this sinking ship for a while now. Don't fight me on this."

I nodded and forced out a long breath. He was right. He knew the ins and outs of the business. I was just here to crunch the numbers.

"I've got a meeting next week with the potential buyers," I said, skimming the notes I'd typed out on my phone. "They'll be submitting a written offer in advance. We can head down to Portland together."

He held up a hand. "I can't go. I'm straight out with road repairs. And by next week, I'll be driving log trucks to the mill every day. We're going twenty-four seven right now to fill these orders."

Right. "I guess I can ask Lila. She can take notes," I said, going for nonchalant, even as the thought of spending more time with her sent a thrill through me.

That thrill quickly turned to dread, though, when my brother shot me a glare.

"Don't," he said, his voice low and gruff. "Don't look at her. Don't think about her like that."

"Like what?" I said, playing dumb.

"You are a grown man. I don't need to explain it." He leaned closer. "Lila's a good kid. She's working her ass off so she can move to New York and get a master's degree. *Do not* cause problems for her."

"You're misreading the situation." I lifted my chin, indignant, despite the guilt pooling in my gut. Whatever he had seen, it was a fraction of what I was really thinking about her.

"I'm the oldest of six boys, and I've spent the last twenty-plus years working in the woods with dozens of men. Trust me when I say this. You're not fooling anyone. So let me say it again. Not her."

He was massively overreacting, not that I'd point that out, given his murderous stare.

"She's too young for you," he continued. "And too nice. Not to mention she's Cole's ex."

"You've got it all wrong." I leaned in and ducked my head, lowering my voice. "I didn't recognize her when she came to the office on Friday, okay? The image of Cole's girlfriend I had in my head didn't remotely resemble her. Seeing her just knocked me on my ass a bit. That's all."

Gus buried his face in his hands and growled, clearly not comforted by my half-assed reasoning. "Jesus. This is the last thing we need right now. She's a kid."

"She's twenty-eight. Hardly a kid."

"Said the thirty-eight-year-old man sitting across from me." He fisted his hands on the tabletop. "No way. Off limits. Stop this shit. Please do not complicate things anymore." The glare he fixed on me brought me back to my teenage years, when he'd be pissed when I was too busy to help him with the shit Dad had tasked him with completing out at a logging site. "Weren't you just whining about how you want to get the job done and get out of this town? Get back to that and stay there."

"I've got it under control," I said. That was a lie. Deadlines, expectations, details. I was built to handle the pressure there. Getting things right the first time was a goal I strived for. Putting forth maximum effort to ensure success was my default.

It was the way I existed in this world. Owen Hebert did things the right way, never cutting corners or missing details.

I gave every task 100 percent of my attention, and I didn't believe in distraction.

At least I hadn't before.

Now? This was no ordinary job, and this was no ordinary town. And Lila? She sure as shit wasn't an ordinary employee.

"I want to trust you," Gus said, eyeing a table near the front window. Just about every seat in the place was full now, and the line was out the door. His body was tense, and his jaw had gone rigid.

Huffing and annoyed at how little my brother thought of me if he was this angry, I gritted my teeth and said, "You can trust me."

Only then did I realize the anger coming off him wasn't directed at me. Discreetly, I shifted in my seat and followed his gaze to the coffee bar.

Mayor Lambert, who I'd known since I was a kid, was sipping espresso out of a tiny cup. Chief Souza and Doug

Baker, who owned a few car dealerships in the area, sat on stools beside him. The fourth man with them looked familiar, but I couldn't place him.

He was wearing dress pants and a tie, and his hair was slicked back, which made him stick out even more than I did in a place like this. People in Lovewell were casual, sticking mostly to jeans and flannel.

"Who is that guy?" I asked my brother.

"The tall guy with the hair plugs and the chiclet teeth?" He raised one brow but shifted so he was facing me again. "Charles Huxley. He and Dad used to be friends. He was a state senator for a long time."

Ah. I turned back to survey him again, and recognition dawned. He was tall and thin and blandly good looking for a guy in his sixties. He shifted in his seat mid-conversation, and when he noticed me, his smile faded. Jerk.

"He lives here?"

"Yeah. Ran for lieutenant governor last year and lost. Bought one of those big houses on the lake. He's harmless, but don't let him corner you. That guy never stops talking. Typical politician."

It figured that these former friends of my father would be the ones judging us so harshly now.

Gus returned to his coffee and his phone, shutting me out again. My chest ached as I took him in. For the first time in a long time, I longed for things to be the way they were. At least when it came to our relationship. Back when we joked and busted each other's balls and felt comfortable enough to be completely honest with one another.

He worked long hours, and that was when he was in the office. He often had to leave for days on end to help our crew with cutting. These days, he wore many hats, and each of his responsibilities kept him busy. I wouldn't get much time with him here, but I'd take advantage of what little we had.

"I need your help," I said, finally getting him to look up from his phone. "I need you to teach me more about the business. If we're going to make this sale happen, we've got to work together."

With a wince, he took a long sip of his coffee.

As a kid, Gus had taken the divorce hard. He'd always worshipped our dad, and even after Dad treated Mom so badly, he'd struggled to see the man for who he really was.

But the battle lines had been drawn after the events of last year.

Gus and Jude were on one side, in denial and still believing that the business could be saved.

Finn and I were on the other, wanting to wash our hands of all of it and move on with our lives.

Noah had yet to bother giving us his opinion. If pushed, he would blindly support Jude but wanted nothing to do with the drama.

Cole was too self-absorbed to even participate in these conversations. He was probably sleeping off a bender right now.

"There's only so much I can teach you in a coffee shop."

I let out an annoyed grunt. "I know that. I just want the basics."

"You should know the basics, asshole." He set his cup down a little too hard. "You grew up here just like I did."

I pushed my plate away, no longer interested in the last of my scone. It figured that he wouldn't go easy on me.

"Here's how I see it," I said. "We drive out into the

wilderness and we cut down trees. Then we load those trees onto trucks, drive them back to civilization, and deliver them to a sawmill, where they're cut to fit the specifications of our customers' orders."

With a scowl, he crossed his arms and sat back. "It's a bit more complicated than that."

"If that's the case, then why not teach me more about the intricacies?"

"Why bother? You're more interested in stripping this business for parts and selling them off than understanding it. It's bigger than that. It's more important than that."

Oh, for the love of God. The last thing I needed was another high-handed lecture from Gus. "Spare me the talk about the family legacy today, Gus." I huffed. "I'm here, aren't I? I've put my life on hold—a really fucking awesome life, by the way—to come up here and save your ass."

He snorted into his coffee cup. "Keep telling yourself that, city boy."

My blood heated beneath my skin, just like it did every time we talked about this shit. "Fuck you."

"Listen, little brother. If you could pack up so easily, leaving no one behind to miss you, then maybe your life in Boston isn't so fucking excellent."

His words stung. Shit. Was that what he thought of me? Maybe coming here had been a mistake. If Gus wasn't interested in my help, then there was nothing I could do to fix this clusterfuck.

We hadn't had a knock-down, drag-out fight since we were kids, but I was itching to drag him out to the parking lot and throw a few punches. How had we gotten so far away from one another? How had our family gotten so splintered?

And why were we all so angry at one another? Our dad was the villain. He was the one who'd fucked everything up.

Before I could stand and drag Gus out of the booth by the collar, the door chimed and Lila walked in. The world around me ceased to exist as I watched her greet the barista and several of the patrons with warm smiles, her ponytail bobbing as she waved at each one of them.

Gus growled. "That's exactly what I'm talking about. I see the way you're looking at her."

Ignoring him, I took in every inch of her body. She was wearing yoga pants today, and the view of her ass alone was worth the expensive latte. God, I was already gone for this girl.

"Get your fucking head in the game. We have work to do," Gus said, sliding out of the booth. "And stop mooning over your little brother's ex-girlfriend. It's pathetic."

Chapter 9
Lila

Owen hadn't been lying when he said this was a big job. I spent the first three days cleaning out offices and file cabinets, organizing documents, and then sifting through them to determine what was important and what I could set aside.

It was fairly dull, but I cued up the new season of *Crime Junkie* and listened as I scanned and filed. Folks came in and out of the office on occasion, but the massive building was mostly empty. The employees that remained were all overwhelmed with work and frazzled, but they were friendly and answered my dumb questions with patience.

Gus was here each day, and Jude was usually around, maintaining vehicles or taking inventory of equipment out in the shop. They mostly kept to themselves and kept their distance from Owen.

When Owen and Gus did end up in a room together, their interactions usually devolved into arguments.

When that happened, I'd turn up the volume of my

earbuds and tune them out. Or try to, at least. The tension was so thick that sometimes it was impossible not to get swamped with it.

Owen had now been here for a few days, and other than those occasions when he and his brothers couldn't avoid each other, he hadn't spent any time with his family.

Sure, he could come across as grouchy and unapproachable at times, but only because he was struggling. He cared deeply for his family and their welfare, obviously. Otherwise, he wouldn't have put his own life on hold to help. But he hid that concern well. I could see it, but based on the negative interactions he had with his brothers, I was the only one. If he'd let them see that side of him, I had no doubt their relationships would improve.

In the matter of a few days, I'd developed a new routine. I'd swing by after my shift at the diner with a latte for Owen, then post up in the big conference room and sort. We'd set up folding tables labeled with fiscal years and lined up plastic milk crates for various documents.

Despite the state-of-the-art office building and equipment, Hebert Timber had barely digitized. Most things were still done on paper, and what was available on the hard drives was disorganized.

Owen's lawyers had successfully lobbied for the return of most of the documents and hard drives that had been seized by the FBI, so despite the mess, we were at least working with a semi-complete set of records.

I hummed as I shuffled around the table, depositing invoices and receipts, sipping my latte, and thinking this was probably the easiest thirty bucks an hour I'd ever earned.

Movement in my periphery startled me. With a gasp, I spun and slapped a hand to my chest.

Gus stood in the doorway, cringing.

I pulled my earbuds out and smiled. "Hi, Gus."

"Didn't mean to startle you." He shifted from one foot to another, surveying the room. Gus was thick and strong, and he usually carried himself with ease, but right now, it looked like he wanted to crawl out of his skin. His broad shoulders were hunched and his hands were shoved into the pockets of his jeans. What was it about the Hebert boys and this building?

"Just checking in on you," he said, his voice gruff as always. Gus was the prototypical protective older brother I'd never had. His kindness since the Cole mess would not be forgotten.

"I hope Owen isn't working you too hard."

"Not at all," I said, giving him a reassuring smile. "I make my own hours and listen to murder podcasts while I work. Best job ever."

He rocked back on the heels of his work boots and chuckled. "Good. If he gives you any trouble, call me. Okay?"

I nodded and clutched the stack of documents I was holding to my chest. "Are you headed out to camp today? I saw the schedule you emailed."

"Tomorrow. All this rain has really held us back. The roads are muddy, and as much as I'd like to wait for things to dry up a bit, we've got a lot of orders to settle up before." He kicked at the doorframe. "You know, the sale or whatever. So we're getting creative."

"Let me know if I can help."

According to Owen, operations were continuing, only on a smaller scale with a skeleton crew. After Mr. Hebert was arrested, many of their longtime employees had quit, probably concerned that if they didn't abandon ship, they'd be taken down with it. Most had ended up working for the Gagnons or the LeBlancs, but a dedicated few had remained.

"Do you have a heavy machinery license?"

"Nah."

"Can you use a chainsaw?"

"Wanna teach me?" I gestured to all the files around me. "At this point, I'm pretty much a timber expert. Except for the whole cutting down trees part."

He laughed. "Not today, but I will at some point. It's a life skill, you know?"

I nodded. Now my interest was piqued. I could see myself rocking a chainsaw. "Promise?"

"Just stick to the accounting for now, okay?"

Long after the sun had set, I was still working, but I was beginning to feel the effects of a long day on my feet. I'd been working nonstop since my shift at the diner started at seven this morning, and I was determined to go for a run when I got home. Hopefully, I'd eke out five or six hours of sleep before doing it all over again tomorrow.

Owen came by the conference room, surveyed the carnage, and wandered to the large bay window that looked out at the forest. He ran his hands through his hair, something, by the looks of it, he'd been doing quite a bit today, and tugged on the collar of his shirt.

With one earbud still in place, I tried my best to focus on my podcast, but when he was this close to me, it was hard to focus on anything but him.

Each day, he looked a little more disheveled. First he'd traded his dress pants for jeans. Then his shirts were no longer tucked in. Now his stubble was flirting with beard territory.

He was looking less city boy and more lumberjack by the day.

And it was a problem.

Because he looked *good.*

I had no interest in dating or relationships at the moment, but I wasn't dead. Anyone with eyes could appreciate Owen Hebert's masculine charms. He was handsome, with a hint of ruggedness that was growing by the day. No matter how hard he tried to hide his backwoods lumberjack upbringing with designer suits and fancy cars, the country boy roots remained.

My long-dormant flirting instincts were coming back to life. I found myself smiling at him, playing with my hair mid-conversation, and thinking about him while choosing my outfits. Crushes were supposed to be harmless, but it had been so long since I'd felt even the slightest flutter for a man. I wasn't even sure how to control myself anymore.

"I have a surprise for you."

I paused my podcast. "For me?"

He nodded and lifted his chin, gesturing for me to follow him out the door. Obediently, I trailed behind him to the office he'd been using. It wasn't nearly as grand as his father's, but from what I'd observed over the last few days, he'd purposely steered clear of that one.

There were two large boxes on the table labeled Thrive Market.

"I promised you snacks." He took a multi-tool out of his

back pocket—*hot*—and sliced the top of the box, then slid it toward me.

Inside, neatly stacked, was every type of gluten-free snack I could imagine. I picked up a package of crackers, then a small box of cookies and studied the labels, blinking in amazement.

I unearthed a colorful box and gasped. "Oh my God!"

"You said you missed Froot Loops." He shrugged. "These are the fancy non-GMO organic gluten-free version."

My first instinct was to tear off the top of the box like a rabid raccoon, but I stopped myself. My second instinct was to pack it all back up and return it.

"You didn't need to buy all this for me," I said, guilt swirling in my stomach. He had to have spent hundreds of dollars on this stuff. The gluten-free cookies alone were eight bucks a box.

"I said I'd feed you, didn't I? And," he said, picking up a bag of low-sugar naturally colored gummy worms, "these are at least kind of healthy."

My heart warmed as I took him in, then surveyed all my goodies again. Maybe this was a small gesture for him, and in the grand scheme of things, I supposed it was. But I'd been raised on a steady diet of Hallmark movies and my mother's dramatic relationships, so I'd never been one for big, romantic gestures. Over-the-top proposals and flashy declarations had never done much for me, no matter how much Mom loved them.

For me, what mattered was the little things. The small ways in which it was clear a person noticed me and appreciated me were what made me giddy.

The tiny gestures were what made a big impact. Rob, my mother's second husband, had been like that. Always remembering which days I had piano after school or what my favorite flavor of ice cream was.

While snack food might not mean much to the average person, to someone like me, for whom food could be dangerous, it was huge.

So I rounded the table and pulled him into a big hug. At first, he was stiff, but it only took a moment for him to give in and wrap his arms around me.

I hugged everyone, regardless of the occasion, whether it be joyful or agonizing. It was as natural to me as breathing. But the instant his body heat seeped into me, it was clear that touching him like this had been a huge mistake.

Sometimes, when I went in for a spontaneous hug, the recipient's responding embrace was begrudging. Cole had been that way. His unwillingness to reciprocate my physical affection was one of the things that drove me crazy. I'd wrap my arms around his waist and squeeze him, and he'd give me a halfhearted pat on the back, or worse, wrap one arm around me in return.

Though he'd been rigid at first, once he eased into it, Owen embraced me like he wanted to. Like he had to. The hug was slow and careful, but the affection he gave was as genuine as what he'd gotten from me. And this was a major fucking problem.

Because it felt good. Too good. He smelled like cedar and clean laundry, and the way the scent enveloped me made my knees wobble.

"Thank you," I said into his chest.

Did I have to let go?

I should let go.

But he wasn't loosening his grip.

"You're welcome," he murmured, and then I swore—*I swore*—he pressed his nose to the crown of my head and sniffed. Or maybe not, because suddenly, he was awkwardly stepping back and busying himself with the boxes.

Shit. That was weird. I had made it weird. I should have let go first, and I shouldn't have squeezed him so hard or put my head on his chest. I'd probably made him uncomfortable. He was my boss, for heaven's sake.

And now that I knew what it felt like to have his strong body against mine, I was in even more danger.

"Care to join me for a feast? I've got gluten-free ramen here. Wanna fire up the microwave for a gourmet dinner?" He raised one eyebrow, and a hint of a smile tipped his lips.

My stomach swooped. I liked Owen. He was so much more than the stuck-up city asshole everyone thought he was.

He was thoughtful and sarcastic and he gave excellent hugs.

"I'd love to," I replied. "But only if we can have the Froot Loops for dessert."

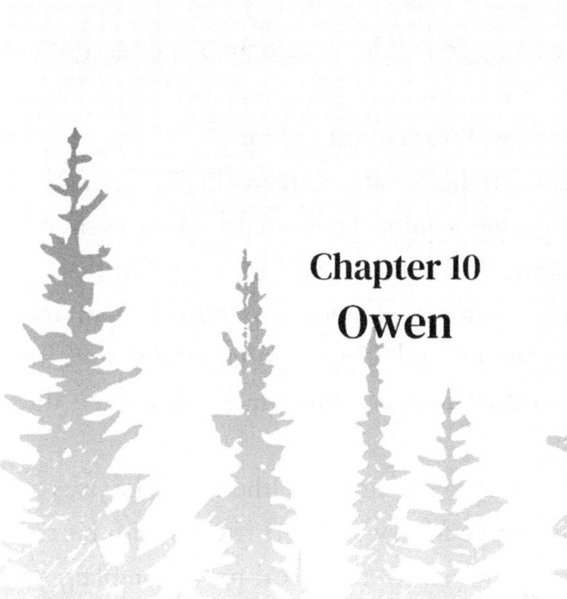

Chapter 10
Owen

I was a coward.

I'd spent the afternoon riding around with Gus, talking through outstanding orders, adding to the list of equipment we planned to sell, and getting a sense of the outstanding maintenance projects we needed to budget for.

It had been a productive day, but I'd done all my work outside the office so I could avoid Lila. Nothing could happen between us, and after I'd gotten swept up in the moment last night, I needed to put some space between us and remind myself of all the reasons I had to stay away.

So when I wrapped up with Gus, I jumped in my car and headed back to the cabin, determined to enjoy what was left of the daylight and avoid any temptation.

But of course, my solitary evening plans were dashed the moment I pulled up to the house.

Finn, who was standing on the small porch of my cabin, gave me a chin tip as I climbed out of my SUV. Gritting my teeth, I tamped down my annoyance and mentally rearranged my evening schedule to accommodate the unexpected visit.

Of all my brothers, I was closest to Finn.

Like me, he'd left home at eighteen. He'd joined the Navy and had become a pilot. I'd visited him on occasion when he was stationed in Virginia, and he'd come to Boston several times. He'd always planned on retiring from the Navy, but when his ex and his daughter moved back to Lovewell, he'd finished up his commitment and done the same.

He'd never intended to return either, but he was a devoted dad to my niece Merry and best friends with his ex. If the move made them happy, then he'd never complain. It wasn't Finn's way. He had the innate ability to roll with the punches rather than tie himself up in knots over things he couldn't control.

And since he'd returned, he'd found happiness in the most unlikely of places. Now he had fallen madly in love, had another kid on the way, and had recently launched a small business.

"You haven't come to visit," he said, his brows pulled low and his arms crossed over his chest. On the surface, Finn was a scary dude. He was taller than me by a couple of inches, covered with tattoos, and typically kept his long dirty-blond hair tied back in a man bun. He was perpetually dressed in jeans and flannel and carried himself with the kind of confidence only earned by serving one's country.

But the asshole was nothing but a golden retriever on the inside.

"Been busy," I said, carrying yet another box of files into my cabin.

In true retriever style, he followed me right in and kept up with the guilt trip.

"I miss you, brother. I was hoping we could spend some time together."

I wanted that too. But right now, my head was a mess, consumed with thoughts of Lila.

We'd hugged, and I had held on too long. She had thrown her arms around me in a friendly embrace, and I'd taken it straight to Creepville, especially when I'd pressed my nose to her head and smelled her hair.

God, I was a disgrace.

I was acting like a fool.

And the worst part was that I couldn't stop thinking about her. Like some kind of lovesick teenage boy rather than a thirty-eight-year-old man, I was desperate to see her again, to hold her in my arms and make her smile.

It had been a few years since I'd seen a therapist, but it seemed as though it was time to schedule an appointment. Clearly my mental health was on the decline.

Over and over, I agonized over how my idiot little brother had ever landed her in the first place. I couldn't wrap my mind around it. She was so wonderful. Even worse than how he'd tricked her into thinking he was anything other than a lazy asshole was that he'd let her go.

"Miss you too, man, but I'm barely keeping my head above water with all this work." It was a mostly legitimate excuse, right?

Finn was not impressed, nor was he accepting my reasoning. "It's Thursday," he said. "We've got to train. Go change. I've got boots for you in my truck."

"Train for what?" I asked, my curiosity piqued.

"Just hurry up and get changed. The last guy to arrive has to clean up."

Giving in to my curiosity and my brother's adamancy, I headed into the small bedroom, unbuttoning my dress shirt as I went. I wanted to be annoyed, but for the first time all day, I found myself pleasantly distracted from my thoughts of Lila.

Whatever Finn was cooking up was probably insane, but if it could get me out of my head, at least for a little while, then I was in.

Once I'd pulled on a pair of jeans and a flannel, I headed outside, where he was waiting at his truck.

He pointed up the hill toward the large timber-style home with a great view of the mountains. Even from down here, it was beautiful. With a nod at the boots on the ground beside him, he said, "Put those on. They were Jude's, so they should fit you."

I eyed the worn Timberlands, then my newer New Balances. "I'm good."

"Nah. Gotta wear a steel toe for this. You're a thirteen, right?"

With a wary look at Finn, I nodded and snagged them off the ground.

"When in Rome, right?" he said with a grunt.

When in Lovewell, I supposed. Letting out a heavy sigh, I sat on the porch steps and changed into my little brother's stinky old boots.

Side by side, we made our way up the path toward the big house. As much as I didn't want to, it was hard not to admire the view. The sun was low in the sky, and the mountains were backlit, showcasing the miles and miles of vast forest. Over the years, I'd forgotten just how wild Maine truly was. I'd grown up here, spent my childhood running wild in these woods, and yet they never failed to amaze me.

"What exactly are we doing?" I asked, jogging to catch up with Finn's monster strides.

"Training," he said, shooting me a grin. "Don't feel bad. The Gagnons are good, but Remy's a professional, so there's no keeping up with him. He's traveling right now, but the rest of the guys still regularly kick my ass. Even the kid."

Was I walking into some kind of backwoods fight club? Did I care? Maybe a good punch to the nose would knock some sense into me. And in what world could anyone kick Finn's ass? The prospect of witnessing that alone was worth showing up for.

As we approached the house, the path veered off toward a large barn surrounded by neat raised beds where a few colorful tulips were popping up.

I followed him around the side of the barn to a large shed. Its doors were wide open, and every inch of its walls was filled with axes, mauls, and chainsaws.

On a raised platform outside the shed, several stumps were arranged in a row.

A few feet from the platform was a large gasoline canister.

And the Gagnon brothers.

"I brought Owen," Finn said, greeting them and turning toward me. "You know, Henri, Pascal, and Tucker?"

I nodded and stepped up close to shake their hands.

"Owen's been working his ass off, so I figured the least I could do was let him train with us so he can blow off some steam." He shrugged off his backpack and gave Tucker a fist bump.

The kid tipped his chin, looking cockier than a scrawny boy his size had any right to. "You gonna show us your skills, old man? My dad's won competitions. He and my uncles are teaching me everything they know."

Pascal ruffled his hair, his eyes lighting with pride. "This kid is pretty good."

"My Uncle Remy set a world record this year for speed climbing." He puffed his chest out and beamed. "But my mom says I can't use a chainsaw until I'm sixteen."

"Chainsaws are overrated anyway," I said. "A real man uses an axe."

The kid's already bright smile turned almost blinding in response to that comment.

"My older brother makes incredible art with chainsaws, but for cutting wood, this is so much better."

Paz gave me a head nod, like maybe I'd said the right thing.

Despite the at-ease front I was putting on, worry plagued me. I was still wrapping my mind around the Gagnons. They had every reason to despise us. Hell, it wouldn't be all that surprising if they each grabbed an axe and attacked. Our families had hated each other for generations. What was worse—so, so much worse—was that my dad, a criminal asshole extraordinaire, was responsible for the death of their dad, a beloved community member and loving father.

Rather than taking a swing with a fist or an axe, Henri waved a hand, motioning for me to follow him to the shed. The structure was impeccably organized, and each tool was clean and in good condition.

He pulled a maul from its pegs and handed it to me. "I assume you know what to do with this?" His tone was gruff, but the corner of his mouth quirked up almost imperceptibly behind his bushy beard.

Pascal elbowed him. "Maybe city boy here should start with the kid-size axe Goldie uses."

"You should talk," Finn said. "Tell us more about your Italian loafers, Paz." He slung an arm around my neck. "My brother was born and raised in these woods just like you dumbasses. He'll do the Hebert name proud."

I took the maul, thankful I'd put on Jude's boots after all.

"Okay. Losers buy the drinks and burgers at the Moose on Friday," Henri said. "Tucker keeps time. Get ready to work, gentlemen."

I wouldn't be able to walk tomorrow. That was a certainty. I was no slouch. Enzo and I boxed almost every morning, and I'd been running for decades. But there was no workout like chopping wood. I'd forgotten just how strenuous it was on the entire body. Holy shit. I felt three hundred years old as we trudged back to my cabin.

Damn, the Gagnons were freakishly good athletes.

Finn clapped me on the shoulder. "Good job out there. You didn't embarrass me."

Biting back a whimper at the contact, I rolled my shoulders. "Tell that to my back. I may not be able to stand tomorrow."

"Nah, you'll recover. And we'll get 'em next week."

I huffed out a laugh at his ever-present positivity. "What's the deal with the Gagnons?"

He tossed his backpack into the back of his truck. "First of all, they're all madly in love. That'll soften a guy up like nothing else can. Second, they're good people. Why we spent all those years suspicious of them is a mystery." He shook his head. "Actually, it's not. We were trained to think that way. Regardless, they embraced me when they had no reason to. They're good to each other. They're protective of Adele, even if she hates it. And they've been nothing but kind and supportive of me. Even gave me a job."

He wasn't wrong. They conducted their business honestly and with integrity. From what my brothers had told me, they'd been thrown into a tailspin when they lost their father, as any family would, but they'd rallied around one another.

"Honestly, being part of their family has really changed the way I feel about this town and how I feel about myself."

I kicked at the gravel beneath my feet. "You have a great support system."

We did not have emotional conversations. Ever. We were Hebert men. We'd been conditioned to repress and then repress some more. But that had never been Finn's style. As a kid, it had been something for our dad to criticize him about, but now he'd become even more open and honest, and he was damn happy with his life.

"I do." He dipped his chin. "Alicia, Merry, Adele, and the whole Gagnon family. I'm working on Jude and Gus, but you know them. I spent so many years hating this place and hating Dad. It took a while after I came back, but eventually,

I let it go. For Merry and for this new baby, but also for myself."

Wiping the sweat still beaded on his brow, he headed for the porch, clearly not ready to leave me to collapse and die a slow, painful death. So I followed, dragging my feet up each step.

Finn sat in one of the Adirondack chairs and put his feet up on the porch rail. "This place is full of so much good if you're willing to open your eyes and embrace it. You can fixate on all the awful shit and let yourself feel suffocated here. Or you can let it go and liberate yourself."

A sardonic laugh escaped me as I dropped into the chair beside him. That was easy for him to say. Finn got along with everyone, no matter where he went. He had the kindest heart of all of us, yet he looked like an action movie star and had the kind of skill set that lent itself to backwoods living.

Some of us *would* suffocate here. And while I used to think he was in that group, it was clear to me now that he belonged in Lovewell, and that he would make this place better.

"Adele and I are carving out our own slice of happy here. I'm not saying you have to do the same. Hell, go find your happy wherever the fuck you want to. But closing yourself off isn't gonna help you find it."

God, why couldn't we just fistfight like we did when we were kids and move on? His words were so much more devastating than a punch to the face would have been. I was here to do a job, and when it was done, I'd hightail it back to Boston. I wasn't interested in having some kind of emotional evolution like he'd experienced in the last few months.

But my brother was sitting on my porch, offering me a

connection. Something we hadn't shared in a very long time. I wanted so badly to reach out and take it. Tell him what I'd been going through, how agonizing this sale process was for me, and how proud I was of the life I'd built for myself in Boston.

I opened my mouth, but the words wouldn't come out. He deserved an older brother who was present in his life, who offered support. All of my brothers deserved that from me. My mom too. So why was it so impossible for me to offer it?

He studied my face for a moment under the porch light, his mouth turned down in a disappointed frown. After a beat, when I didn't speak, he stood. "Better get home to Adele. She may need ice cream, or a foot rub, or a carburetor to take apart."

I didn't move as he jogged down the steps. The words still hadn't come, and I wasn't sure they would, so I stayed put.

Halfway to his truck, he stopped and turned back to me. "I meant what I said. When you're ready, I'll be here for you."

With that, he hopped into the driver's seat and drove off. Leaving me feeling both physically sore and emotionally shitty.

Chapter 11
Lila

I was slathering peanut butter on a rice cake, humming to myself, when my mom wandered into the kitchen and pulled me into a hug.

"What are you doing home?"

I held one arm out to keep from slathering her in peanut butter as well and gave her a good squeeze with the other. "Bernice shooed me out of the diner early, so I came home to go for a run. I'm headed over to the library to tutor next, and then I'll go work with Owen."

"Will you be home for dinner?"

I shook my head. "Probably not. We have to upload a bunch of information for the buyers today." I licked the knife and set it in the sink. "He's got everything ready, but he wants me to double-check it all."

"You're working so much." She pressed a palm to my face and frowned. "You're getting bags under your eyes and forehead wrinkles. Are you taking care of your skin? Hydrating enough?"

"Yes, Mom. This work is temporary. Not to mention the money is good and I like the work."

She tutted. "You never go out anymore. Where are you going to meet people? You're almost thirty."

Oh jeez. This again.

I patted her shoulder and summoned all the patience I could. "I'm not interested in meeting anyone right now. Once I'm in grad school, I'll work on my social life. Right now I want to save money and hang out with you."

She hummed, mollified, at least on the dating front. "Should you be dressing up a bit more for this office job?" She picked up the teakettle from the stove and took it to the sink to fill it. "Wear heels and a skirt, maybe? I could lend you something."

"It's not that kind of office. I'm digging around in dusty boxes and building spreadsheets on a folding table," I said, stepping up beside her as she set the kettle on the stove. "Jeans and sneakers are required."

Boundaries. Boundaries. It really was a mantra. I could love and appreciate my mom and still hold space for me and what I wanted.

When she turned to face me, I took her hand in mine. "Mom, I love you so much. But I feel good about the choices I'm making."

She pressed her lips together in what looked like resignation and nodded. "I just don't want you to miss your chance."

"Miss my chance at what?"

With both palms pressed to my cheeks this time, she gave me a sad smile. "Happiness."

I gritted my teeth. It was better than stomping my feet

and telling her that her version of happiness was bullshit. Happiness doesn't happen by chance. A person has to choose it and work toward it. Which was exactly what I was doing, even if it didn't look the way she'd envisioned.

Tamping down my annoyance, I forced a smile to my face. These conversations went nowhere; it was better to keep moving.

Despite keeping the peace at home, the irritation I'd felt lingered and festered, and by the time I reached the office, I was in a mood. How could I grow and evolve when my mother, along with everyone else in this damn town, wanted to keep me stuck?

They'd be content to stick me in the pretty girl box and never let me do anything. Because finding a rich husband and being a kept woman whose job it was to fuss over her man and please him while denying myself all of my own dreams was, to them, a goal I should be striving for. To me, a life like that was akin to living in a cage.

I'd earned my freedom. There was no going back.

Huffing out my frustration, I moved a couple of boxes, making room to plug my laptop into the external monitors at my makeshift workstation. All the while, I berated myself for not being more honest with my mother *and* for looking around for Owen every few moments.

For all my desire to not be trapped here, he was a man I wouldn't mind getting stuck with, at least for a little while.

I looked forward to these evenings, when it was just the two of us in the office, eating gluten-free snacks and arguing about spreadsheets while I tried to catch subtle whiffs of his intoxicating masculine scent.

I'd even put on mascara today.

It was a far cry from the forty-minute makeup routine that used to be my norm. The one that included blending several shades of eyeshadow, a full contour, and fake eyelashes. But nowadays, it was still more effort than I typically put into my appearance.

I could barely remember why I used to spend so much time on makeup. The woman I used to be was practically a stranger. I'd drifted so far that no matter how hard I reached, there were parts of her that were lost to me forever. Some I was happy to part ways with.

Other parts, the ones I enjoyed, were coming back. And I had Owen Hebert to thank for that.

First up, desire.

It had been so long since I'd felt even a single flutter in my belly or the quickening of my heart rate in proximity to a specific person. That part of me had been offline for so long that I worried it was irrevocably damaged. It was a thrill to know it wasn't. To know that at some point, I'd experience chemistry, connection, and desire again.

Since an early age, I'd been performing. In pageants, on stage, and with boys. I liked what they liked. I dressed the way I thought I was supposed to dress and pretended that life was perfect.

Cole was the first man I slept with, and it had taken me years to orgasm during sex. Not because he wasn't willing to try, but because, after the first couple of times, when it didn't happen, I faked them. It was one more area of my life where I felt the need to be perfect. Perfect hair, perfect body, perfect smiles, perfect orgasms from a little penetration and some halfhearted fumbling. I had no one to blame but myself.

Somehow, my friends had gotten that truth out of me and intervened. Magnolia, in fact, had sent me my first vibrator. Eventually, I explored and learned what I liked and what worked for me. But I'd never experienced the toe-curling chemistry I'd read about in romance novels. The kind that builds and builds until a person feels as though they'll combust.

I'd assumed I was incapable of that kind of passion. I was more Hallmark movie than Harlequin novel. An all smiles and hand-holding, no orgasms kind of gal.

That was until I had to work shoulder to shoulder with Owen Hebert every night.

When he wasn't looking, I'd sneak glances at him, admiring how his ass filled out his jeans or salivating over the corded muscle of his forearms while he typed. He was strong but not bulky. Intense but not domineering. And so careful and controlled.

I couldn't help but fantasize about what kind of lover he was. There was no doubt in my mind he was thorough and focused.

Which was *not* the kind of thought I should be having about my ex-boyfriend's older brother.

I felt my phone buzz in my pocket, interrupting my steady stream of obsessive Owen thoughts. It was Vic.

I stepped out into the hall. "Hey. Everything okay?" I'd been stopping by to help with deliveries as much as I could, but I had even less time than usual. The guilt was gnawing at me. There were so many people in need up here; I needed to find time to do more.

"Yes." Vic sounded out of breath. She was a few years older than me but had also unexpectedly landed back in town last year, so we'd become friends. It didn't hurt that she was hilarious and one of the kindest humans I'd ever met. "Incredible, actually. I'm shaking. We had a delivery today. A new walk-in freezer, along with an electrician who hooked it up and upgraded the circuit breaker in the garage."

"Oh my God!" I gasped. The loss of the freezer, which had been nicknamed Bubba last year, had made it impossible to keep meat and other perishables on hand. Shit, this was a miracle.

"And that's not all. I got a call from a roofing company. Apparently, they'll be here tomorrow to repair the roof. Labor and materials are all donated."

"How? Who?"

"It took some digging, but I was able to determine that the donations are courtesy of the DiLuca Construction Charitable Foundation. Know anything about this?"

The tone of her voice indicated that I should, and I blushed. *Owen.* "I have no idea."

"I'm going to cry again. This is *such* a huge blessing."

We said goodbye, and I headed back to the conference room. What was going on?

"Hey, Owen."

He looked up from where he was leaning over the table, hair a bit disheveled like he'd been running his hands through it and his glasses askew. He looked so delicious I momentarily forgot what I wanted to say.

I shook off the stupor and wiped at my mouth to make sure I hadn't drooled. "I just got a phone call from Vic at the food pantry. She was celebrating a big donation from DiLuca Construction. You know anything about that?"

He looked away and shook his head. "The company has a charitable foundation that makes significant community investments."

I wasn't buying his humble bullshit. "In Northern Maine? Huh." I raised one eyebrow. "And aren't you the CFO of both the company and the foundation?"

"Yup."

"So you sign the checks?"

"No one actually signs checks anymore." He was being intentionally obtuse, and I wanted to slap him. Didn't he realize what a big deal this was? He pretended to be this grumpy businessman, but I could see right through him. He cared. A lot. And if this generosity was any indication, he understood a lot more about this town than he let on.

"I don't know what you did or why you did it. But thank you."

He shrugged. "It's not a big thing."

"Yes, it is. Maybe not to you, but to the food pantry and all the people in this county who depend on it. It's huge." I wiped an errant tear away. The last thing I wanted to do was cry in front of him, but I had firsthand experience with food insecurity, so the thought of other families getting what they needed threatened to overwhelm me.

"I know you hate it here. But you've done so much good." I said softly.

He took his glasses off, always his tell, and gave me a kind smile. "I don't hate Lovewell. I just resent being dragged back here. I have happy memories of this place, I'm glad I grew up here, but..." he paused as if searching for the right words.

"You've outgrown it." I offered.

He nodded.

"I feel the same way. For so long I wanted out, and dreamed of going anywhere else. And when I had to come back it felt like failure. The gossip, the judgment, waking up every day to scrape together tips to try and get unstuck."

"You're not stuck."

I shrugged, "I know that now. It took me a while to realize that being back in Lovewell is an opportunity. To make peace with my past and this town and who I'm becoming."

"That's a very positive perspective."

"It's all about how you frame it, Owen. Think about it. You weren't dragged back. You were given an opportunity to come back here and do something positive for your family. A family you've grown apart from." I gave him an expectant look. Sometimes it frustrated me how obtuse he could be about his family. As an only child with just my mom, I couldn't imagine having all those siblings and not wanting to be close to them.

His lips quirked. "You're something special, you know that?"

I could feel the blush creeping across my cheeks. "I'm not the one who donated a new roof and freezer to the food pantry." He thought he could brush this off, but I wasn't letting him. Beneath that grumpy, corporate exterior was a big squishy heart. And I was determined to make him admit it.

He held my gaze for a moment, those blue eyes shining. "You inspire me." He said softly.

And I could feel my knees wobble and my stomach clench. This man had shown up here and was steamrolling every attempt I made to be practical and logical. I studied my hands as I tried to breathe through the complex tangle of emotions.

He looked away politely as I composed myself, cleaning his glasses and diving back into the spreadsheet he was creating.

I slipped my earbuds back in and tried to focus on work, but this information continued to swirl in my head. *"You inspire me."* God, as if I didn't already have an inappropriate crush on him.

Focus, Lila. You're here to do a job.

But he was right there, looking all kinds of good. Sometimes, when he was puzzling through documents, he took his glasses off and rubbed the back of his neck. When he did, I swore I could feel the tension in his body.

I had just gotten control of my hormones and had started to make real headway when something truly awful happened.

Owen unbuttoned his shirt.

It *was* pretty hot in here. We'd had a couple of warm days, which wasn't uncommon for late April, and the HVAC hadn't caught up. Usually, the building was freezing, but tonight, it was boiling.

And now Owen was stripping.

I shuffled papers in an exaggerated manner, pretending to be absorbed in my work while fixated on him in my periphery. He took his time undoing every button, his large hands working deftly.

Sweet Jesus. He was wearing a white undershirt. I forced myself to focus on the papers in my hands. When I did, I blinked. Then I blinked again. Shit, they were upside down. *Damn, I'm an idiot.*

Despite my best efforts, after I subtly flipped the papers so they were right side up, I snuck another glance.

The shirt was tight, and the thin cotton hugged every muscle in his shoulders. And those were *some* muscles hiding under the designer dress shirts.

My internal temperature rose even more, and a bead of sweat dripped down my spine. Any attempt to work was officially off the table now. Just breathing while remaining standing was hard enough.

"You okay?" With a gentle nudge to my arm to get my attention, he reached for the neat row of folders in front of me where I'd organized all the recent invoices.

"Mm-hmm." My face flamed. God, I was probably crimson by now. Could he read my thoughts? Had I been mumbling to myself? I did have my earbuds in, but I'd been so deep in my Owen fantasy that he'd probably noticed me staring like a sex-starved weirdo.

To be fair, I absolutely was. But he didn't need to know that. I'd much prefer being the mysterious and alluring woman who had her shit together. Ha. Like that was even a remote possibility.

White T-shirt.

Shoulders.

Arms.

That long neck and the stubble-covered jaw. I wanted to lick every inch of him.

My thoughts had veered into full porno territory.

Get a hold of yourself, Lila. I'd slap myself out of my stupor if I thought I could get away with it.

I cleared my throat. "Sorry. I was in my head. What can I help with?"

He lifted one brow and scrutinized me, like he was trying to read my mind.

My skin tingled under his regard, and there went my blood heating again. Goddamn, those blue eyes practically scorched me.

"I need you to check this asset report for me. I've got to get it to the lawyers tonight, since we're headed to Portland on Friday for negotiations with the buyers."

"Right," I said, forcing a smile and patently ignoring the way my core ached. "Of course."

"Are you sure you're okay?" His concerned frown was adorable. "I could grab you a bottle of water. Do you want to sit down?"

Nodding like a bobblehead, I dragged myself over to a chair on the other side of the table. I dropped into it and turned up the volume on my playlist, attempting to lose myself in a sea of numbers.

After fixing a few inconsistencies and sending them off to the legal team, we celebrated with an assortment of gluten-free sugary cereal and tea I heated up in the microwave.

"I've figured out most of the acronyms and the shorthand on the written documents," I said, sorting through our cereal options. "I've got a list on my computer for reference."

He snatched the box of marshmallow cereal out of my hand. "The chocolate bombs are better." When I feigned a scowl, he grinned, looking so boyish. "I said what I said." He was still wearing the T-shirt. His fancy dress shirt was carefully draped over the back of one of the metal folding chairs, daring me to pick it up and sniff it.

I shrugged. "I'm on team fruity sugar cereal. But I will admit the strawberry chocolate turtles were gross."

"Who thought it was a good idea to make kids' cereal out of chickpeas?"

I shuddered. "It's a crime against nature."

The smile he gave me was one of pure contentment. It was impossible not to take a moment to revel in it.

"What?" he said, his cheeks going a little pink.

"I like your smile. You wear this grumpy façade, so most of the time, you're scowling. But once in a while, you smile at me, and when you do, you look like a different person—" The moment the last word left my lips, I stiffened. Dammit, I'd gone too far and been too honest. Yes, we were becoming friends, but he was my boss and my ex's brother as well.

He pressed his lips together and ducked his head. When he looked up again, he searched my face, like he was worried I wouldn't understand his reasoning. "It's hard being here. This town, this building. It makes me feel stuck. Logically, I know that's not the case, but being here puts me on the defensive. I'm sorry if I've been scowling at you."

"Eh." I shrugged, picking out a box of tried-and-true fruity cereal. "I'll take authenticity over artifice any day of the week. Your grumpy scowls and resting boss face don't bother me. Though I do enjoy the rare smile."

He smirked. "Resting boss face?"

"Oh yeah." I slid a finger under the tab of my cereal box, popping it open. "It's like your facial muscles know how to project responsibility and confidence. When I see you, I think *this guy knows what he's doing*."

The laugh that bubbled out of him was deep and loud. The sound caused butterflies to take flight in my belly.

I busied myself with opening the bag inside my cereal box, trying to hide the blush on my face. This kept happening, these tiny moments where I nudged a toe over the line. It was so effortless. Talking turned into flirting so naturally, and I found myself addicted to watching him respond to me.

Desperate to change the subject, I racked my brain for a work-related topic to focus on. "I have a bunch of invoices and receipts for Deimos Industries."

He popped a handful of chocolate bombs into his mouth and chomped on them, narrowing his eyes thoughtfully. "Doesn't sound familiar," he said around the mouthful. "Is it one of the smaller mills? We've shipped to a few in Vermont, as well as some down south."

I shook my head. "I've cross-referenced all our other stuff and the online cost reports. But it's not a client."

He frowned and sat up straighter. "What do you mean?"

"It's not listed in either the client or vendor databases. Which is strange enough. Then there are records of payments coming and going. Random amounts, sometimes a few dollars and other times tens of thousands."

"Flag them," he said. "I'll ask Gus if he knows what that's about. If not, we can always do some digging online."

I pushed my hair behind my ears. "I did, actually. I went to the Secretary of State's website to learn more, and it kind of led me down a rabbit hole." My notepad had been pushed aside while we snacked, but I dragged it in front of me and skimmed the notes I'd taken. "Deimos is an S corp incorporated in Delaware. According to the documents I found, it's an entertainment and merchandising company. Whatever that means."

He sat back and smiled. "I'm impressed."

"Don't be. It's a dead end. There are no corporate filings. The company has no website, and I couldn't find any mentions of it online. It appears to be a subsidiary of Rhiannon Management, which looks like an investment group from the outside, but they haven't filed anything with the SEC. It's some kind of holding corporation that doesn't actually do anything."

"Maybe we can pull corporate records. My friend Amara is general counsel for DiLuca construction. She's great at that."

"There's one problem." A little ball of dread had formed in my stomach when I was digging up information, and it had only grown during this conversation. "It's based offshore in the Cayman Islands."

"That's sketchy as fuck."

"Exactly. If it had been another lumber mill, a construction company, or a materials wholesaler, I probably wouldn't have noticed. But it raised red flags."

He considered me for a moment, his blue eyes piercing and his jaw tight once again. "Thank you for catching this. Let's dig around and find every dealing the company has had with them. Then I can talk to the lawyers and try to pull some strings. Then, hopefully, we can learn more."

He regarded me for a moment before giving a tip of his chin. "Good job."

I shrugged, even as pride filled my chest. "It's my job, boss."

He winced a little at that title. "I suppose you're right. I hired you to be smart and kick my ass when I needed it, and so far, you're succeeding on both counts."

He held out the box of chocolate bombs, so I traded him the fruity rings.

"Do you want to come to Portland with me on Friday?" He tipped the cereal box and poured a few sugary pieces into his hand. "Gus was supposed to come, but he's got to deal with an issue with the roads. You're a better option anyway. I need your sharp mind in there. These types of meetings can get heated, so I need a fighter in my corner."

I kept my expression neutral, but on the inside, I was squealing. He wanted me there. To help him negotiate *a multi-million-dollar deal.* I was already completely distracted by how gorgeous he was in that white T-shirt, and now, after the way he'd just complimented me, I had to focus on my breathing to keep myself from full-out swooning. He needed my mind. No one on earth had ever given me such an ego boost.

I was straight-up giddy at the prospect. "I'll be there. And my spreadsheets will make them weep." I rubbed my hands together and threw my head back, laughing maniacally.

A slow smile spread across his face, and the sight was like a shot to the heart. Teeth, lips and stubble, and that jawline.

"You're really one of a kind, you know that?" He huffed out a laugh and rubbed at his jaw. "How are you so positive all the time? You haven't had an easy road either. This town hasn't been kind to you."

Oh, what he didn't know could fill volume upon volume of books, but I'd spare him the gory details. "As cheesy as this sounds, I'm trying to enjoy the journey rather than fixating on the destination."

"That is cheesy."

"I know. And I'm not ashamed. I spent too many years waiting for my life to begin."

He nodded as if he understood. And despite our vastly different life experiences, I believed him. Like me, he believed that leaving Lovewell was the key to happiness. That real life would begin once we shed the trappings of small-town life.

For me, that meant taking off with Cole as soon as I could. I ended up in Indiana, then Rhode Island, and then Florida, bouncing around from shitty job to shitty job, taking community college classes and piecing together a degree. In the beginning, the plan was marriage and kids and hockey. Then none of it actually happened. Which was a blessing, because somewhere along the way, those dreams had lost their luster.

"I've realized that real life is now. The decisions I make today matter. My attitude and effort and the way I show up for others matters. I don't know what I want long term, and that's okay. I'm evolving, and this town can't stop me."

"Shit." He shook his head, taking off his glasses. For a moment, we were both silent. He lowered his chin and cleaned his lenses on his T-shirt, lifting the hem up just enough to reveal a tiny sliver of abs.

He looked up at me, his focus so intense I could feel it like a brand. I wanted to look away, but I wouldn't. Fuck it. I could be myself when I was with Owen. My heart tripped over itself every time he looked at me, and my core throbbed every time thoughts of him consumed me, which was *a lot*. This attraction was so all-encompassing there was no hiding it. Even if nothing could ever happen, a girl could enjoy a little peek. Right?

I leaned forward and rested my elbows on the folding table. "What do you want, Owen?"

He tipped his head and opened his mouth, but rather than speaking, he snapped it shut again. As he slid his glasses back on, fumbling a little as he did so, he swallowed audibly. "I don't think I can say."

I bit my lip so hard I may have drawn blood. "Why not?"

"Because some things are better kept to myself."

My heart pounded against my sternum, desperate for more. But the look of concentration on his face told me that he wasn't giving up the details. Goddamn, this man had superhuman self-control.

He leaned back in his chair and ran a hand through his hair. "I want to finish this job, do this company justice, and then get the hell out of here. Every minute I spend here reminds me of how awful the world can be. My life in Boston isn't perfect, but I've worked hard for it, and it's my own."

"Wow. Drama much?" I quipped before I could stop myself. Normally, I would just smile and nod, but Owen Hebert's world was not awful, and I wouldn't let him get away with thinking otherwise.

He shrugged. "Life sucks. Over and over, people prove themselves to be pretty terrible. We have to carve out a place for ourselves in this hyper-competitive world. Make our plans, work hard, and hope to find a little happiness along the way."

"Spoken like a true optimist." I narrowed my eyes at him and cocked my head. "You've got a lot to learn, Owen Hebert. Have you ever stopped to think that maybe the world isn't some Hobbesian dystopia where the strong exploit the weak and we kill ourselves struggling for survival?"

"Hobbesian dystopia?" He snorted. "Have you always been this smart?"

With a huff, I rolled my eyes. He wasn't getting away with this doom and gloom bullshit with me. From where I sat, this guy had everything going for him. "Yes. But I used to be pretty, so no one bothered to notice, and I didn't bother trying that hard to convince them."

Instantly, his broody stare was replaced by a gentler expression. His eyes softened and his lips parted just a fraction. Then he was out of his chair, rounding the table, and pulling me to my feet.

With his hands on my shoulders, he looked into my eyes, his face sincere. "Don't say that. You're beautiful. You've always been beautiful. Period. And if people don't notice how smart and empathetic and intuitive you are, then that's their fucking problem."

My breath caught as I studied him up close. His tone was harsh, as always, but his words were like a balm. This grumpy man saw straight through to my heart.

He was still clutching my shoulders as he angled in and brought his lips to my ear. When he spoke, they brushed the shell, sending a shiver through me. "And regardless of how painfully gorgeous you are, your mind, Lila, your mind is magnificent."

My knees wobbled and my body lit up inside at my proximity to his dominant maleness. I'd received plenty of compliments in my life, but that one had just blown every other one out of the water.

He pulled back slightly, his attention fixated on my lips. Time froze as I regarded him, as the weight of his presence settled on me and the heat of his body enveloped mine. I wanted him to kiss me. No, I needed him to kiss me.

He scanned my face, his blue eyes darkening and full of desire as he fought an internal war.

For a brief moment, it was happening. He gripped me harder and leaned in.

I closed my eyes, desperate for the feel of his lips on mine. My heart took off, practically beating out of my chest.

And just like that, it was over.

He released his hold on me and took a step back. Even in the stifling office building, the loss of his heat was excruciating. Taking his glasses off again—another clear nervous tell—he lowered his focus to the table and shuffled long-forgotten paperwork. The self-control had won out.

I deflated. Because, for a moment, a flash of what being with Owen would be like had hit me. And I was desperate to feel it again.

"I've got a couple more things to finish up, then I'm going to head home," he said, keeping his gaze averted. "I've got calls with some environmental consultants tomorrow, so I'll see you Friday morning. I'll pick you up and we can head to the meeting in Portland from there."

"Sure," I said, still rooted to the spot where he'd almost

kissed me. I was being dismissed. My chest ached and my eyes stung, but I swallowed back the hurt. He'd drawn the line. And as much as I wanted to jump over it, I couldn't.

But when I got home later that night, I began looking at the scenario from a different angle. Maybe tonight hadn't turned out the way I wanted it to.

But one thing was clear. He wanted me just as much as I wanted him.

I could work with that.

Chapter 12
Lila

"We should have taken my car. It's much more spacious," I quipped, tilting my head back and enjoying the feel of sunlight on my face.

Without taking his focus off the road, Owen grumbled something unintelligible. He'd picked me up at six thirty sharp, armed with lattes and gluten-free granola bars. The three-hour drive to Portland from Lovewell was one I'd made many times, but sharing a car with Owen Hebert certainly added an element of anxiety to what otherwise would have been a routine trip.

The awkwardness had started when he jumped out of his car and hustled around the hood to open the door for me, all the while blatantly staring at me.

"You look nice," he'd said, finally dropping his gaze to his shoes as I climbed into the car.

"Um. Thanks." I hadn't known whether to be thrilled by the compliment or embarrassed. I was wearing a black skirt suit I figured would be suitable for a contract negotiation. However, a while back, after a decade of obsessing about every little thing I ate, I'd given up my pageant diet. So this skirt, the only one I owned, was on the tight side.

Okay, it had fully crossed over to the far boundary of tight.

My hips were being strangled. There was a chance it was giving businesswoman in a porno rather than a diligent professional woman ready for grad school, but I had no other choice. I'd tossed a pair of jeans into my tote for after, so I just had to make it through the meeting without splitting a seam.

The rest of my outfit—black heels, blazer, and pearls—was the definition of business appropriate. I'd hoped the blazer would hide the too tight skirt, but maybe I was wrong.

Though, on closer inspection, his slack-jawed expression hadn't been one of judgment. Oh no. Those wide eyes and open mouth were all desire. A small fizzle of pride had shot through me. He was looking at me like I'd just slid down a pole wearing nothing but a diamond G-string. The business bitch look worked for him. I'd file that tidbit away for the future.

I wonder if he likes garters.

God, we hadn't even left Lovewell yet, and I was already speculating about his lingerie preferences. Hence the thick fog of awkwardness that had enveloped us the second both doors were closed.

I'd wanted to flirt—still did—to smile and toss my hair and get a rise out of him. But no matter how natural it felt, I wouldn't. Not after he'd made his stance on what was happening between us clear. So I'd taken a deep breath and graciously accepted the coffee. Then I'd made sure my mental filter was firmly in place.

We chatted briefly about strategy, and I pulled out the copies I'd made of our updated spreadsheets. But mostly we sat side by side, listening to classical music while Owen drove south.

After a while, the silence was killing me. I could barely sit still, and words were clawing their way up my throat. Questions, observations, anything to break the uncomfortable silence.

Over and over, I'd found myself checking him out from the corner of my eye. He was gripping the steering wheel tight, his knuckle straining, his hands making the leather creak as he readjusted his hold. For the first time, I really studied those hands. Those very *large* hands.

"How tall are you?" I blurted out. Owen might have been on the small side for a Hebert, but he was still a giant compared to most.

He turned and hit me with a confused frown. "Six-two. Why, how tall are you?"

"Five-seven."

"Okay, now that we've established that, my blood type is A positive. Do you want my social security number too?"

My face heated and a wave of shame washed over me. God, I had the conversational skills of a hamster.

"Sorry," I said, lowering my head to hide the blush I was sure had overtaken my face. "I was just curious. Your whole family is so tall."

"I'm the shortest." He snorted, like being *only* six-two was some kind of shortcoming.

Cole was six-six, and his height made it impossible to

buy clothes at a regular department store. Shoes were an issue too. Hell, even some cars were too small for him to fit into without having to crane his neck or hunch down.

I kept those thoughts to myself, relatively certain that comparing the brothers wouldn't go over well.

Owen was the perfect height. He was broad but lean. Like a swimmer.

Just my type, a weird little voice in my head said. Weird. And wrong. I didn't have a type. I hadn't been attracted to anyone in so long, and when that ability finally resurfaced, it had to be because of this man, a man I couldn't have.

He tapped his fingers on the steering wheel to some kind of pretty music. "You like classical music?" I asked.

He nodded. "Not always, but it relaxes me. You?"

"Yes. Ten years of piano lessons, so I've got a basic appreciation."

He raised a brow and regarded me. "That's impressive."

"Not really. I'm not very good." I clasped my hands in my lap and shrugged. "My mother really wanted that to be my talent. The girls who are musical get a lot of respect from the judges. But I was better at dance, so we stuck with that."

He nodded. "Did you enjoy it? All the pageant stuff?"

I considered his question for a moment before plastering on my best smile and sitting up impeccably straight. "I'm proud to have competed in pageants. I learned valuable leadership skills, developed self-discipline, and discovered my unique abilities and talents."

He turned his head slowly, his brows raised high. "Okay..."

I let the smile fall. It was amazing how out of practice I was. My cheeks hurt already. "The real answer is much more complicated." With a sigh, I slumped back in my seat. Miss Barbara, my coach, would smack me in the head if she saw my shameful posture.

"We've got time," he said, turning the volume down.

How could I explain it to him? For my entire life, I'd been on the outside. My mom and I were looked down on, the image of a family no one would ever dream of having. So she clung to the perfection of pageants. The smiles and sequins and talk of empowerment. As if pretty clothing and fake smiles would make us better. Elevate us beyond the label she'd been given in this small town.

And as a dutiful daughter who adored my mother and wanted a better life for us both, I went along with it. I was desperate to please not just my mom, but the judges, too. I had coaches and teachers and practiced endlessly. Smiling, walking gracefully, faking the kind of *aw, shucks* excitement necessary to convey enough humility to be worthy of the crown.

"I learned a lot about the world and about myself." And that was the honest truth. "I had some valuable life experiences, but I would never, ever put my child in pageants."

He nodded. "They seem pretty silly and exploitive to me. I mean, being Miss Queen whatever is fairly meaningless in the grand scheme."

"Excuse me?" I feigned offense, clutching at the string of pearls at my neck. "How dare you, sir! I was Maple Sugar Princess 2008."

He laughed, the skin at his temples crinkling. "I'm so sorry. I had no idea I was in the presence of royalty."

The prissy scowl I gave him only lasted a second or two before I broke into a fit of giggles.

"Does Your Majesty require a coffee and bathroom break?" he asked in a truly terrible British accent.

"Indeed, I do, good sir."

By the time we passed Augusta, the awkwardness had mostly dissipated, and I was bored enough to push through the lingering remnants. If I didn't find a distraction ASAP, I'd stare at his long eyelashes or strong jaw, and then my thoughts would veer into dangerous territory.

So I chattered.

We were currently debating the merits of various Maine food specialties.

"Needhams are amazing. I will die on that hill," he declared.

"It's potato in chocolate."

"Not much else grows up here. It's amazing. Deal with it."

I shook my head, even as I grinned. "Maine is so fucking weird."

"It is. Tourists think it's all beaches and lobster traps, but most of this state is straight-up bizarre."

I hummed in agreement. "When I was living in Florida, people were so fascinated when they discovered I was from Maine. Meanwhile, I'm like, Stephen King makes it look like a warm and snuggly place."

"Have you ever visited his house in Bangor?" Owen asked.

I shook my head.

"I'll take you. It's super creepy. I've probably been there

a dozen times. When I was in high school, my friends and I went to Bangor every chance we could get. It was like a metropolis compared to Lovewell."

I smiled into my Dunkin cup. The thought of taking a fun trip with Owen made me way happier than it should. "Favorite movie?" I asked, grasping for a way to get us on more neutral ground.

He pressed his lips together and surveyed the road in front of us, considering my question.

"Ooh, no. Wait. Lemme guess." I tapped my chin. "*The Godfather*? That's the ultimate dude favorite."

He shook his head, frowning in concentration. "It's so hard to choose."

"Please don't say *Transformers* or something horrible like that."

"Fuck no." He huffed a laugh. "Don't get me wrong; I do enjoy a good *Fast and Furious* movie from time to time."

"Me too," I conceded, clasping my hands in my lap.

"I just love so many."

"Come on. You have to have a favorite."

"I do? Then what's yours?" He turned and raised an eyebrow at me, one of his sexy quirks I was starting to enjoy.

"Easy," I said. "*Say Anything*."

"Haven't seen it."

I let out an audible gasp and twisted in my seat. "You've got to be shitting me. John Cusack? The boom box? She gives him a pen?"

He shook his head and shifted in his seat like he was searching for a more comfortable position.

"What the hell? Turn around. We've got to fix this right now. It's the most romantic movie of all time."

"Guess I'll have to watch it sometime then. See if I agree."

"You'll watch it today. I decree it," I said in my queen voice. "It subverts the usual hero-heroine dynamic. I could write a paper on the brilliance of the iconic '80s teen rom-com."

"Were you even alive in the '80s?"

"Nope." I tilted my chin up and grinned. "But that doesn't mean I can't appreciate vintage films."

He coughed out a surprised laugh. "Please don't call anything created in the '80s vintage. I may vomit."

I patted his bicep. His strong, hard bicep. "Don't be ashamed. You, Owen Hebert, are one fine vintage piece."

The words were out before I registered the implication, and my tone had been entirely too flirtatious. I froze for a heartbeat, my breath catching, then slapped my hand over my mouth. Goddamn Owen and his ability to make my filter fail. Any sane person would be embarrassed, but if anything, I was emboldened by my inner flirt.

After the moment we shared a couple of nights ago, where he'd come within centimeters of kissing me after declaring that I was beautiful and brilliant, why couldn't I make my attraction known?

Objectively, he was handsome. Especially driving this sexy car through the twisty mountain roads dressed in a crisp button-down and tailored slacks. The grays peppering his temples only made him look more distinguished.

In juxtaposition to all of those details, he still hadn't shaved. The scruff added a hint of ruggedness to his appearance, and I was digging it.

Who could blame me for craving a little flirtation?

Lovewell was a small town, and yes, we had our fair share of handsome lumberjacks, but all the respectable ones were taken.

Owen was a breath of fresh, broody air. Being in his presence had woken my lady parts from what had felt like an eternal slumber.

I'd spent years with Cole, but we'd hardly been hot and heavy, even in the beginning. And the final years had been downright frosty. During that time, Cole's chances with the NHL were slipping further from him, and he was spiraling. While he was concerned with his career and falling into self-destructing habits, I was going through the painful process of realizing that I'd been chasing the wrong dreams for way too long.

And the couple of hookups I'd had after Cole and I broke up barely counted. I had been grasping and flailing. The need had been more about my pride and less about pure desire.

But now, I was feeling desire. A lot of desire. My body was coming alive after being in stasis for way too long.

But still, this situation was beyond complicated, and there was a good chance pushing for what I'd been fantasizing about would make things worse.

So I had two choices. I could sit in awkward silence and pretend I'd never said anything, which was our pattern, or I could keep talking.

I chose option B.

"Your stubble is working its way into beard territory," I observed, not shying away from giving him my full attention for once today.

"Yeah." He lifted a hand from the steering wheel and

scratched at his jaw. "At first, I let it go out of laziness. But I was chopping wood with Finn and the Gagnons the other night, and they were teasing me, saying Tucker could grow a better beard than me."

I laughed, my heart feeling lighter than it had all day. "If any thirteen-year-old could figure out how to grow a beard, it would be Tucker. He's really smart."

"I noticed. And so I figured," he shrugged, "when in Lovewell..."

"Go full lumberjack?" I finished.

"Something like that."

"I like it," I said softly.

Rather than acknowledge my comment, he looked ahead, keeping his eyes on the road. But there was no hiding the smile slowly spreading across his face.

Chapter 13
Owen

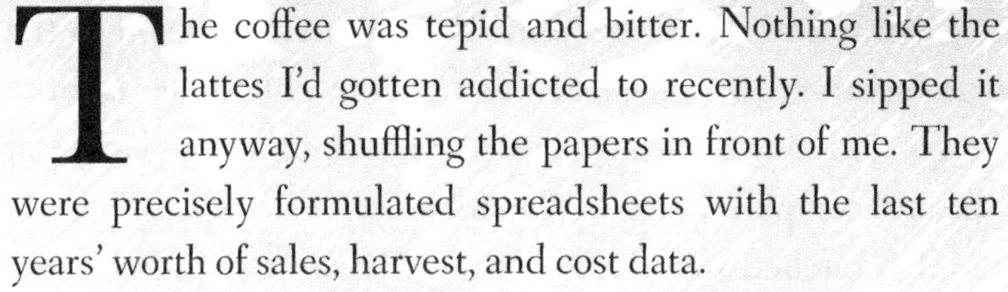

The coffee was tepid and bitter. Nothing like the lattes I'd gotten addicted to recently. I sipped it anyway, shuffling the papers in front of me. They were precisely formulated spreadsheets with the last ten years' worth of sales, harvest, and cost data.

All had been prepared by Lila, and all were perfect in organization and execution. My order-loving perfectionist brain was impressed, but my caveman brain was distracted.

Because I'd almost given in to my baser needs and kissed her in the office. Then, like an idiot, I'd willingly subjected myself to a road trip with her.

We'd spent three hours enclosed in the small space where her scent had wrapped around me and made it hard to focus on anything but what her lips would feel like pressed to mine and how soft her skin might be under my touch. It took some time, but I got myself under control enough to laugh and joke and talk about movies with her. I even indulged when she insisted on getting Munchkins in the

Dunkin drive-through. Then I spent a solid ten minutes getting powdered sugar out of my tie.

Even so, it was fun.

She was fun. Being with her was making it increasingly harder to stay focused and angry.

Focused and angry were my default. It was how I got shit done. I'd built my life and career on focused and angry. And now this smiling woman with the body of a goddess and the mind of a professor was making me question every aspect of my life.

And she was testing my sanity.

She was interested. In me. She liked what she saw.

I was a goner.

Now it was business time, but my brain was still in the car, mooning over Lila, listening to her talk about her favorite songs and '80s teen movies while sneaking flirty glances at me and complimenting my beard.

I scratched my chin. The scruff had been driving me crazy, but now that I knew she liked it? I'd never shave again.

I needed to get my head in the game. Instead of locking in and being present in this dark paneled boardroom at my lawyer's office where it should be, reviewing the offer paperwork and preparing our response, my brain had suddenly drifted even farther. Now I wasn't just reliving every moment of the drive. No, now I was on a beach, rubbing sunblock into Lila's shoulders and sneaking peeks down the front of her bikini top while ordering another round of fruity drinks.

I'd traveled a fair amount, usually with a specific goal in mind. To summit a mountain or visit a world-famous museum. I'd even planned trips around running a specific marathon.

I'd never had the desire to lounge on a beach. But every time Lila smiled, all I could think about was bathing in sunshine and looking out at the ocean with her, watching the waves crash and soaking in the salt air.

Spoiling her rotten by renting a cabana at a secluded resort where her every need would be catered to. She deserved that. She worked so damn hard and deserved to be pampered for once. I wanted to take care of her in every possible way.

"Mr. Hebert?"

I blinked back to the present and came face-to-face with a young associate who was frowning at me in concern. Smoothing out my tie, I gave her a nod, and with that, she led us through the offices toward a large conference room. Inside, a wall of windows faced the harbor, and most of the chairs around a mahogany desk were occupied.

We were introduced to a team of three lawyers and a representative of the buyers. Each one was the generic corporate type with expensive haircuts and the kind of confidence gained from charging a thousand dollars an hour to sit here.

The Carson Group was a group of investors with timber interests across North America. We'd done our due diligence and looked into the organization, though there was very little publicly available information. But if their choice of legal representation was any indicator, they clearly had money to burn.

Our attorney, Tad Pierce, had already arrived. He was a middle-aged golf enthusiast with blinding veneers and obvious hair plugs. The law firm my dad had worked with for years was under investigation, quite rightly, so after the life we'd always known had blown up, I'd had to scramble to find someone else.

This firm had come highly recommended and had offices in both Boston and Portland, which made my life infinitely easier. Our GC, Amara, hadn't liked Tad. According to her, he was "old school." It was her polite way of saying he was a privileged blowhard. Regardless, we had limited options, and he was the best of them.

As we entered, Tad raked his gaze over Lila's body in a way that made my hackles rise. As if she were nothing more than a piece of meat, when, in reality, she was brilliant. There was no way I would have been anywhere near prepared for this meeting without her. He gave her a slick smile, flashing teeth that were at least two times too big for his mouth, and pulled out her chair for her.

She looked beautiful today. Hell, she looked beautiful every day, but she was dressed modestly and professionally in a dark skirt suit and sensible heels. Her hair was pulled back and held with a black clip. All morning, I'd itched to reach over and pull it out, run my fingers through the strands, muss it up a little. Until the moment she stepped out of her house this morning, I'd had no idea that I had a skirt suit fetish. But one look at those hips, and a new kink had been unlocked. Lila had been hiding some serious curves under her casual outfits, and it was impossible not to take notice.

I took my glasses off and pulled a microfiber cloth from my pocket to clean them as the assistant sent in another set of papers to review. This was the worst part of dealmaking—the contractual negotiations. Working line by line through pages and pages until it was done.

When we'd finally made it to the offer stage, I flipped through the portfolio and groaned inwardly. Their offer was far lower than Tad and I had discussed. Where the income related to drugs ended and the actual timber began had been a mystery. The entire Hebert team, including Gus and me, had worked for months to get to a place where we could confidently make projections, and we'd erred on the side of caution and stuck with the low end of those calculations.

I flipped through the pages, annoyed and frustrated, as Tad began to volley with the opposing counsel. William Huxley was a standard-issue New York shark. Ageless, likely because he'd been working one-hundred-hour weeks for a decade and prematurely looked 50ish with a spray on tan. Cocky in an "I went to Harvard and know several senators from my country club" way.

The way he was smiling at Lila made me want to fight him.

And rather than critically examining the proposal, he was speaking as though the deal were already done, as if he had no intention of negotiating. Smug prick.

"Once we get the detailed inventory lists and the first-quarter numbers, we can finalize everything," he said, idly spinning his Mont Blanc pen in his manicured hands. "You can send your girl down with the signatures."

I clenched my jaw, and the nerves I'd battled all morning had officially morphed into anger. "My girl?" I said, keeping my tone measured rather than devolving into feral growls like the caveman inside me urged me to do. "I assume you mean Ms. Webster, my associate?"

He nodded, clearly oblivious to my irritation.

"You can send them by mail," I replied.

He sat back in his chair, lacing his fingers over his abdomen and smirking at the man seated beside him. "Do you even get mail up there?"

"We sure do." Lila sat primly, as if she'd employed her beauty queen demeanor, though she'd tweaked it so her aura was all badass professional. "And we even have running water too," she added, her tone dripping sarcasm.

He assessed her for a moment, then his grin spread further.

The urge to climb over this massive table and choke him with his tie was threatening to win out over logic.

"Could we take a short break?" Lila asked, slipping back into a façade full of sweetness. "I think we need to confer with our counsel."

Tad stood and buttoned his jacket. "Of course. Let's head to a breakout room." He turned to the opposing counsel. "We'll resume in ten."

Without waiting for permission, we shuffled out of the conference room, and Tad led us down the hall to a space designated for our side to engage in discussions.

"I think it's going well," Tad said the moment the door to the small room closed behind us.

I shot him a look, still unsure that I'd leave here today without murdering a man.

Lila was bent over the pages, furiously circling and crossing things out with a pen. "This document is riddled with errors," she said, looking up at me through her thick, dark lashes. "They didn't bother to even look at what we'd prepared."

I sat beside her and scanned the places she'd marked, taking in all the inconsistencies while she pulled out her laptop and tapped furiously, checking details against our recent calculations.

She was absolutely right. The majority of calculations were incorrect. No wonder the offer was so low.

I frowned up at Tad. "You reviewed this?"

He nodded and stuck his hands in his pockets. "Had my best team on it. It all checks out. Don't get all paranoid because the number is on the low side."

"But it doesn't check out," Lila said, her voice as steely as her expression. "If your team really did look at this, then they did a shitty job."

I resisted the urge to pump my fist. Good for her. Lila tended to wear a sweet and polite exterior, but she'd thrown off that façade completely today, and I was here for it. As impressed as I was, her sass was also turning me on, but I'd deal with that later in the privacy of my cabin. For now, I'd breathe through it and focus on how damn magnificent she was. We had asses to kick, and I had every intention of standing beside her and working to do it together.

"What's the strategy?" she asked me, completely ignoring Tad's protests.

"Call them out," I said, angling in closer than necessary. "Let's force them to own their fuckups. Put them on the defensive."

She surveyed me, her bottom lip caught between her teeth, as if uncertainty had sunken in.

I wouldn't have it. She knew what the hell she was doing, and I'd back her up all the way. So I lowered my head, catching her eye, and squeezed her hand. "I couldn't do this without you."

With a nod, she pulled her shoulders back, as if garnering that confidence once again.

"We will not consider this offer," I said, tossing the prospectus on the table as we strode back to the conference table. "It's inaccurate and doesn't come close to reflecting the value of the assets in question."

Every person on the other side of the table blustered. They were all scoffs and nervous tics, like smoothing down ties and shuffling papers. "We employed our best researchers to prepare," Huxley said. "The investors are timber experts."

"We're talking about the largest piece of undeveloped wilderness in Maine." I folded my hands together on the tabletop, sure to keep my shoulders back and my chin high. "Our family owns more acreage, real estate, and machinery than any other timber operation on the east coast."

Huxley leaned forward, his shark eyes narrowing. "It's a good offer."

"Bill," Lila said softly, getting the attention of everyone in the room. "It's a bullshit offer."

All eyes immediately focused on her, and she shrank back almost imperceptibly. She stopped herself quickly, straightened, and eyed me. I gave her an encouraging nod, and that was all she needed to continue.

"The tables on page eleven are based on faulty data." She opened the prospectus and pointed. "These are not the numbers we prepared and supplied to you this week. You've undervalued the real estate, overestimated the tax burden, and neglected to include any of the federal subsidies."

I bit the inside of my cheek to hide a smile as every face

on the other side of the table fell. It was all the confirmation I needed to know that they'd known what they were doing. Huxley's face had gone red, making him look positively constipated.

Watching her school them filled me with a joy I wasn't sure I'd ever experienced. Rather than being dominant or pushy, she calmly flipped through, page by page, and carefully eviscerated them.

They'd been under the impression that they could throw together sloppy numbers and bully us into a deal, and now they were discovering just how wrong they'd been.

"The automation plans and cost-cutting suggestions on page twenty-four are positively delusional. The timber industry is the lifeblood of this region. Most of these jobs cannot be automated. Reducing output is not the answer and will not bring you any closer to profitability."

Tad sat back, thankfully keeping his mouth shut. The man was probably grateful that we were doing his job for him. Though he'd been just as negligent as the rest of the bunch, he was sitting on our side, so though his mouth was fixed in a straight line, his eyes were bright with glee as he watched the opposing counsel angrily argue with us about twenty-first-century technology.

"Have you ever cut down a tree, Bill?" Lila asked, tilting her head sweetly. Damn, she was good at this. Not only had she affected a gentle expression, but she'd tempered her tone, making her sound even more harmless. She was leading him straight into a deadly trap.

"No." He scoffed. "And it's William."

Of course, he hadn't. This guy had probably never seen a

tree up close that hadn't been maintained by full-time gardeners at his country club.

"Hm." She tapped her pen on the desk. "Then you should probably leave the 'innovation' to the professionals. Now, are you ready to talk about the machinery list? Because it's woefully incomplete, and the assumptions are flawed."

With her head cocked slightly, she waved a hand dismissively in their direction. "You should probably take notes."

When she was finished, every one of them was red-faced and sweating.

She looked as fresh as a daisy and positively serene when she flashed her best pageant queen smile and asked. "Any questions?"

Damn, I'd never been so attracted to a woman in my life. Lila could completely destroy me.

And I would gladly let her.

Chapter 14
Lila

I laughed nonstop the whole way up 95, gushing and crowing about how things had gone.

I'd never experienced this kind of high before. One that made me feel like I was flying. Not only had I used my brain to completely shut those guys down, but Owen had encouraged me to. He'd backed me up and urged me to speak up about the errors and omissions I'd found. He'd let me take the lead, and not once had he tried to take over.

When we left Lovewell this morning, I'd assumed I'd sit quietly beside him and take notes. I anticipated being the pleasant scenery I'd been trained to be my entire life.

The last thing I'd expected was to take any sort of lead. But taking charge? Speaking out? Calling out those fancy lawyers for their shoddy work?

I was still giddy.

"You think they'll submit another offer?"

He kept his focus on the road as he hummed, considering my question. While the meeting today had shot lightning through my veins, Owen was calmer than usual. "I honestly don't care either way."

I frowned, and for the first time since we'd left the meeting, my spirits dipped. "But the sale."

"You were right. Their plans are stupid." He glanced over at me, twisting his hands on the steering wheel and making the leather creak. "They clearly don't know what they're doing. If they buy us out, they'll sell everything for parts and screw it up. Not to mention the job loss."

I sat back, watching the wheels in his head turn. The Owen I'd met two weeks ago had been desperate to sign on the dotted line and get out of town as soon as possible. I wasn't sure he'd even thought about the implications of a sale.

"Your words today made me realize that this land means something. This business means something. We have to sell. There's no getting around that. But it's important to wait for the right offer. I'll give them another chance to make a decent offer, but maybe it's worth waiting."

I blinked at him, dumbstruck and unable to formulate a response. I needed a moment to process his change of heart first.

"My brothers are already divided. We're still missing so much information. There's so much we don't know." He blew out a breath. "I'll have to talk to Gus, but maybe we can stay operational for a bit longer while I shop around for the right buyer."

"I don't know," I mused. "I'm spiraling right now."

The moment we'd stepped out of the building, he'd yanked off his tie, and now the collar of his dress shirt was open, exposing the column of his neck and his Adam's apple.

I couldn't say it was an area I'd paid much attention to before, but damn, was it masculine and sexy. I closed my eyes and imagined tracing it with my tongue. Just for a moment.

"Anyway," he said, pulling me from my fantasy and dousing the heat that had already begun to build low in my belly, "I'm just spit-balling. I've got a lot to do before I make any decisions. But," he hedged, side-eyeing me, "you were amazing in there."

His praise made my heart soar even higher.

"I think I like being the bad cop," I admitted, clasping my hands in my lap. "It was fun to let my inner bitch out. For the first time in what feels like forever, I didn't care about being polite or making the right impression. Being heard and being right were more important in that moment."

"You were heard, and you were absolutely right." The smile he directed at me made my heart stutter.

Ignoring the response, I gave him a tip of my imaginary hat and did my best to play it cool. "Why thank you."

"I think you've been forced into playing a specific role your whole life. But the woman I saw in there today, the one I see most days, actually, is the real you. You are fierce. You are smart. And you deserve to be heard."

Shit. Those words turned me on more than any sweet nothing ever could. He knew exactly what kind of praise I craved, and he saw *me*. The me beneath the fake smile and perfect posture and expertly applied eyeliner.

And being seen felt incredible.

"It helped that Huxley was such a douche." I said, steering this conversation back on track. I was feeling a little too exposed at the moment.

"God, they were awful. Bill really has a big stick up his ass, huh?" I unbuttoned my blazer, "not that our guy was much better, Tad was eye fucking you the entire time. I wanted to punch him."

My cheeks heated at that admission. I lowered my head, hoping my hair hid my embarrassment. I hated the way men looked at me sometimes. The feeling that I was just a pleasing object for them to stare at left me sad and empty.

"It wasn't the first time." I sighed. "And it won't be the last. I'm used to it. But I hate the way some men use their expressions and body language to intimidate women, reducing us to objects without saying a word."

Before he could waste his breath apologizing for the misogynistic assholes of the world, I changed the subject. "Hey." I sat up in the seat and turned to face him. "It's only two. What do you think about making a pit stop? There's this place I've wanted to go forever, and it's only a few miles away."

"Depends." He cocked a brow teasingly. "What are we stopping for?"

I tapped my chin. "Something super weird. And not just normal weird; Maine weird."

A huff of a laugh escaped him. "How can I say no to that?"

I rubbed my hands together. "Just remember you consented to this."

From the outside, the Leech Museum was even more bizarre than I'd imagined.

"Where the hell are we?" Owen asked, taking in the large stone mansion surrounded by buildings that looked like bunkers and hundreds of acres of forest. "This place looks like something an ancient alien colony left behind."

I jumped up and down and pressed my palms together in front of my chest and clapped quietly. "It's even stranger than I imagined." Once I'd slipped my sneakers on, I jumped out of the car and proceeded to take dozens of photos to send to Willa and Mags.

"This is the estate of Dr. Samuel Leech," I explained, heading for the entrance. "He was either a brilliant visionary or a total crackpot. The FDA called him a fraud and burned all his books, then locked him up. He eventually died in prison."

At my side, Owen frowned at me, his brows pulled low in confusion.

"It's a national historic landmark." I instinctively reached for his hand and clasped it firmly.

At the contact, he stopped walking, his body stiffening. Shit. I'd made him uncomfortable. I released him and wrung my hands, my stomach instantly churning in embarrassment.

"Sorry," I said, striding ahead to hide the flush in my cheeks. "Let's take a tour."

"Now this room," our tour guide Doris explained, "contained all of Dr. Leech's prototypes." Doris was in her seventies, with waist-length gray hair and bare feet. She fit in perfectly here. "The labs are where the human experiments were conducted. He designed and built his own machinery, you know. The government tried to destroy everything, but these remain."

Owen and I walked carefully around the room, being sure to keep our distance from one another as we noted the various metal contraptions in the glass cases as well as the framed papers and books.

"And when you say human experiments?" he asked, hands clasped behind his back and one brow raised.

"The orgasms," she said matter-of-factly. "Dr. Leech harnessed the life force contained in human orgasms to power his weather buster machines."

Owen's eyes bulged and he almost choked on his tongue. "Sorry. Orgasms?"

She nodded, her face lighting up. "Oh yes. Dr. Leech used orgone, the power generated by orgasms, to control the weather."

I covered my mouth with my hand and turned my back to Doris so she wouldn't catch me trying to control my laughter.

"Genius is always distrusted." She hummed. "True visionaries are never appreciated in their own time. Dr. Leech single-handedly saved the blueberry crop in 1958 from a devastating drought. The Maine economy depended on his science."

Owen nodded solemnly, though his right eye was twitching, as if he was using all his strength to maintain an even countenance.

He gestured to the glass case in front of us. "So these devices," he asked, "were for...?"

"Masturbation," she replied, pointing at a large dildo with rivets on the sides that looked to be made of iron or some other hard metal.

It wasn't something I'd ever let near my lady bits, that was for damn sure.

"Let me show you the lab space. You'll really be impressed by his vision."

We followed her out of the mansion and onto the ample grounds. In the distance, a glistening lake was framed by mountains.

"Dr. Leech believed that Maine was rich in orgone, and that this was the ideal place to harvest it."

That tracked. There was enough weird energy in this state to power several weather machines.

"Many people doubted him. But," Doris turned around and pinned us both with a saucy smile, "orgasms have immense power."

I wanted to be skeptical, but the way Doris deftly hiked the hilly path in bare feet made me think that maybe there was some truth to her orgasm theories. I'd be lucky to be half as spry as her when I was that age.

She showed us the labs, the library, and, of course, the single weather buster that had survived the government raid in the '60s. It looked like a giant ray gun from one of the old sci-fi movies I used to watch with Rob, my ex-stepdad. The entire place was bonkers but in a fun and harmless way.

By the end, Owen had asked a million questions about Dr. Leech's research and had purchased a book of his theories as a souvenir.

"Doris," I said, unlocking my phone, "could you take our photo in front of the weather buster?"

"Of course, dear. I hope you come back to see us soon. Be sure to bring your friends to experience all this."

"Oh yes." The smile that split my face was impossible to stop. "Can't wait to come back."

In front of the weird laser beam statue, Owen and I stood side by side. As Doris fiddled with my phone, he snaked his arm around my shoulders and leaned close.

"Thank you," he said to me as we waited for her to figure the device out. "I needed some weirdness today."

I smiled broadly at him. "Happy to get weird with you anytime."

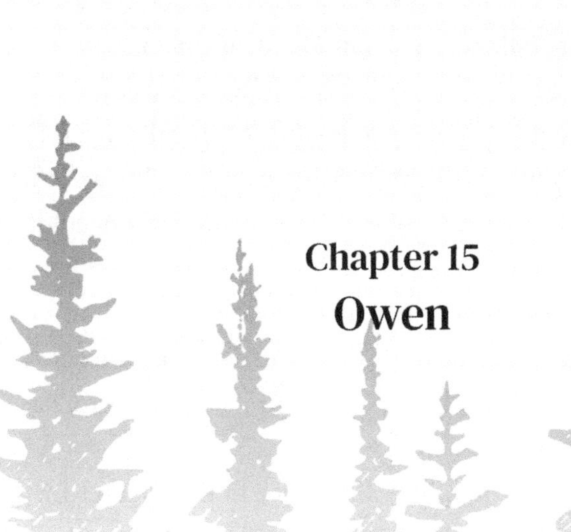

Chapter 15
Owen

The sun had set and the world had gone dark around us as we recapped our visit to the Leech Museum, laughing so hard tears ran down Lila's face. We weren't far from Newport when my stomach growled so loudly that she peered over and smirked at me.

"Hungry? There's a great diner a few exits up," I said. "They have gluten-free options."

"Really?" She perked up. "That's amazing."

With a simple nod, I tapped the steering wheel. In reality, I'd obsessively googled gluten-free restaurants in preparation for our trip. Not that I'd admit that to her. I was surprised by the sheer number I found. Maybe Maine wasn't as backward as I'd thought.

The diner was large and decorated with mid-century kitsch and filled with locals. The booths were vinyl, the jukebox was vintage, and the place smelled incredible.

"I think I want a milkshake," Lila said, studying the

menu. Her eye makeup was smudged and her hair was falling out of its clip, but she looked as incredible as ever.

I'd always been a serial monogamist. I typically went for sophisticated women with impressive careers who were as busy as I was. Women who were, quite often, older than me.

We'd meet for dinner at hot spots, go to the symphony, or sit behind home plate at a Revs game. Nothing too cozy. Nothing too intimate. Companionship, shared interests. That kind of thing.

And it suited me just fine. I was not in the market for a wife, and I'd never been interested in having children. So at thirty-eight, I was content with the routines I'd created.

I'd never found that one great love, and I'd never had my heart broken. I'd spent my life devoted to working and doing the things I enjoyed.

It was good. It was safe and steady and convenient. No risk of failure and no need to make room in my life for the needs of another person.

But sitting here, watching her order strawberry milkshakes for both of us, it hit me. I'd blow it all up for her. It should have terrified me.

Lila wasn't the kind of woman I could compartmentalize. She wasn't a puzzle piece that fit just right into my busy life.

Decades of habits, opinions, and beliefs dissipated as we chatted. We laughed about Dr. Leech and his machines, about the bear meat jerky we'd seen at the mom-and-pop gas station, and about how thoroughly we'd dismantled the lawyers this morning.

"I've had more fun today than I've had in a long time," she said. "Thank you for including me."

"I should be thanking you. I meant what I said. I couldn't have done it without you."

She took a bite of her burger—on a gluten-free bun—and moaned. "Wow. that's really good."

I lowered my gaze to my chicken sandwich, pretending to be absorbed in my own dinner. If I got even the smallest glimpse of the look on her face that accompanied that sound, I was sure I'd throw her over my shoulder and take her back to my cabin, caveman style. It was bad enough that my pants were getting tight again.

I cleared my throat and threw out the first topic I could think of to get my mind off how badly I wanted to strip her out of her clothes and make her moan like that again. "Maine is so weird."

"You have no idea. It's such an oddball state. We have more coastline than California. The home of great thinkers and artists like Longfellow and Winslow Homer. And random stuff has been invented here too, like the snowmobile, the whoopie pie, and my personal favorite, ear muffs."

I shook my head and bit into my sandwich.

"Here." She put her burger down and reached for her phone. "I've got a list in my notes app. I'm so glad we went to the Leech Museum. I've wanted to go there forever."

"Happy to help."

"I made the list so I can soak up all the strange before I leave for New York."

I held out a hand for her phone. "What else did you put on the list?" I scrolled down. "The world's largest crank telephone in Bryant Pond? That's not far. Same with the Moxie bottling plant. Desert of Maine? Isn't that in Freeport?"

She nodded, picking at her burger.

"That's close to the L.L. Bean boot and the fisherman statue. We could group a few of these together in a weekend." The words were out of my mouth before the meaning behind them registered. "I mean you could," I muttered, pushing the phone across the table. To keep myself from saying more, I ducked my head and shoveled several fries into my mouth.

"That sounds awesome," she said, her eyes on her plate too.

I avoided looking at her full-on, but as I glanced up quickly, I caught sight of a faint flush creeping up her neck.

"It would be weird for me to geek out over the world's largest rotating globe alone."

"Right," I said, working through our conversation, searching for deeper meaning. Was Lila interested? She was friendly and a little flirtatious at times, but I'd chalked it up to her sunny personality.

But today alone, she'd called me a fine vintage, then she'd attempted to hold my hand. I'd even caught her staring at me while Doris droned on about masturbation.

But she was so much younger than me. Then there was Cole. And my life in Boston. And her grad school plans.

In moments like these, I really disliked my brother. How could he have found a woman as spectacular as Lila and managed to fuck it up? Not that I was complaining that she was single.

My mind spun, but I did my best to keep my expression neutral, desperate to mask the gut feeling that had swept over me. Despite all the supposed barriers between us, it felt simple. I liked her and she liked me. The pull I felt was natural and completely terrifying at the same time.

I ached to touch her, kiss her, hold her. Was it crazy to think that she could feel the same way?

As I paid for our meal, after I'd declined to let her repay me, reminding her that it was a business expense, I made up my mind. I'd put myself out there tonight. See if this was something worth trying. There were millions of reasons not to get involved with Lila, but when I put my arm around her as we stepped out into the parking lot, none of them mattered.

Being with Lila made me feel brave. I had to at least try.

We were about an hour from home when my phone buzzed on the console. A glance at it told me it was an alert from our security cameras.

I pulled onto the shoulder so I could open the app and monitor the feeds.

Lila shifted to face me. "Everything okay?"

With a nod, I unlocked the screen. "Probably an animal. The damn moose is always creeping around. But as late as it is, it wouldn't hurt to check." We'd thought the thefts would slow down eventually. After my dad was arrested, there were a few disgruntled employees looking to take advantage of the chaos. But break-ins, missing equipment, and vandalism persisted. And, of course, the police hadn't been much help.

My stomach sank this time, though, as I zoomed in. Because the figure on the screen was clearly a person. I was kicking myself for not investing in better lighting when the cameras went up, because like this, the image was too dark and grainy. It was clear enough, though, to make it obvious that they were trying to break into the equipment shop.

Dammit. The last thing we needed was more criminal shit to deal with. Pulse pounding in my ears, I pulled up Gus's contact and got back on the highway.

"Already saw it," he said in way of greeting. "I'm driving there now."

"Don't do anything stupid," I cautioned. "Call the police."

"It could be nothing."

"Given Dad's criminal associations, we can't afford to make that assumption. Just call the police."

I held my breath, certain he'd argue, but he agreed quickly and disconnected the call. Even with his reassurance, as I sped along the highway, I was worried sick that he'd try to be a hero and get himself hurt in the process. There had been way too much violence in Lovewell recently, and although we didn't always see eye to eye, I'd rather die than see anything happen to him.

I broke many laws getting back there as quickly as I could. Lila didn't complain. She sat quietly beside me, watching the camera feed on my phone. The angles were off, so all she could see were headlights and shadows of other people who'd arrived. God, if anything happened to my brother, there was no way I could live with myself.

When the police cars came into view, I let out a sigh of relief.

I pulled in next to Gus's truck, which was parked haphazardly by the front door, and hopped out. With my heart still lodged in my throat, I ran toward the back buildings, where I could see Chief Souza. He was headed my way, along with a couple of deputies. As we got closer to one another, I could make out their faces, as well as the face of the man they were leading out in handcuffs.

Cole.

My stomach dropped. "What's going on?" I demanded, just as Lila caught up to me.

The chief's lip curled as he assessed me. Not only was he suddenly not a fan of the Heberts, he was distrustful of outsiders, and I'd been gone long enough to be considered one, I supposed.

"Your brother here decided to engage in a little vandalism tonight," he said, nodding toward Cole and the deputy holding his arm.

"What the fuck?" I yelled, stepping up close to my little brother.

Cole was thinner than he'd been since high school, and his eyes were sunken. He reeked of weed and booze, and his T-shirt was torn.

His only response was a silent glare.

"Chief," Gus begged. "Is this necessary? An arrest?"

"We caught him damaging heavy equipment, spray painting the building, and slashing truck tires. We've got to take him in and book him."

"What the fuck is wrong with you?" I shouted. Confusion washed through me as pain lanced my chest. Cole was a fuckup, but he wasn't a criminal.

"Why is she here?" he spat, eyes narrowed on Lila.

"Owen and I were on our way home from a meeting," she said calmly, keeping her attention set on him.

He swayed on his feet, clearly blitzed out of his mind.

"Moving in on my girl, Owen? Figures you'd find another way to stab me in the back."

That pain was quickly morphing into fury. I clenched my fists at my sides and bit back a retort.

"You're drunk," Lila said, crossing her arms. "And I'm working with Owen."

"Sure you are," he slurred. "Just remember, he's a pathetic old man who's probably trying to get in your pants."

He turned toward me wearing a cruel smirk. "She'll let you too. Gold-digging bitch."

I lunged at him, intent on punching his smug face. I didn't care that he was my brother and in handcuffs. The way he spoke about Lila sent me over the edge.

Gus grabbed my shoulders and yanked me back before I could make contact. "Do not do this, Owen," he said. "He's spiraling and trying to drag you down with him."

My body shook with rage and confusion. How was this my family? What had happened to us?

Lila walked past me and straight up to Cole.

He towered over her, but she popped up on her tiptoes and slapped him in the face.

The sound carried across the dark parking lot, stunning the rest of us into silence.

"Get your shit together, Cole," she said, her voice strained. "This isn't you."

The slap hadn't fazed him, but he winced in response to her words. His face was etched with pain and his shoulders were slumped.

Despite being livid with him, I couldn't help but pity him too. He was a mess. But he wasn't the only one hurting. All our lives had been upended by our dad and his bullshit, yet Cole was the only one using it as an excuse to behave poorly.

Lila turned toward Chief Souza and affected her best pageant smile. "He should probably sleep this off."

The chief nodded. "A night in a holding cell might help him realize what a fool he's making of himself." When he turned to Gus and me, his expression soured. "You all can come bail him out tomorrow morning and talk to the county prosecutor then."

With that, he waved at his deputies, who led Cole toward the cruisers.

Cole's head was bowed and he dragged his feet. For an instant, I was hit with a flash of him as a little boy, on one of the many occasions he'd been scolded for God knew what. We'd all gotten into our fair share of trouble. I shook off the image and turned back to Gus and Lila.

Gus ran his hands through his chin-length hair. "Fuck." With a frustrated sigh, he kicked a large rock with his boot. "I'll go take photos, see how much damage he did. We can't afford this shit."

I was frozen to the spot, because as I'd turned my focus from Cole to myself and this situation, rage ignited in me and sang through every one of my nerve endings. I was an idiot for thinking I could swoop in, save the day, sell the company, and make my family whole again. Hell, I even thought I could get the girl.

But this family, this life, was too damn broken and fucked up for any of it. This company was a cancer in all of our lives. And it needed to be removed.

Once I'd done that, I'd go. I'd get far away from all the pain and dysfunction and back to my real life.

Chapter 16
Owen

And the hits just kept coming.

I'd woken up to a text from my mother. She'd included Jude and Finn and Gus as well.

Family meeting, the message had said. *9am*.

More than anything, I wanted to lie in bed and obsess about Lila. Or sit on the porch with a cup of coffee, stare out at the mountains, and obsess about Lila.

Instead, I'd get to face Cole after his bullshit performance and deal with the fallout from whatever tantrum he was throwing today. Finn had stepped in and bailed him out. Once that update came through, I stopped paying attention to the family text chain. I was too enraged to do anything but fume each time I thought about last night.

It figured that just as we were ready to close this chapter on our shitty family history, he'd find a way to fuck it up.

Cole had always been an entitled brat. As the result of my father's affair with his twenty-one-year-old secretary, he had always felt like he was on the outside.

My mother had done everything in her power to make sure we all built relationships with him. His own mother had little interest in being a parent, just like our father, so he could often be found hanging around our mom's house. And my mother, the saint that she was, had always treated him like one of her own.

The day our parents sat us down and explained that they were getting divorced was as fresh in my mind now as it was when I was nine years old, so stunned I couldn't wrap my mind around the concept.

At the time, my life was perfect. My parents were awesome. I had four brothers and a forest for a backyard. We lived in a big house with a tire swing and a tree house.

In an instant, everything I thought I knew had been flipped upside down.

Within months, Dad married Tammi. Then Cole was born. Then Mom moved us from our cool house with the big backyard and into a little house in town.

It took years to understand that we'd gotten the better end of the deal. Seeing Dad on weekends and when he felt like it was a hell of a lot better than living with that piece of shit every day. The five of us had turned into semi-functional members of society, thank fuck, and it was all because Mom had been our primary parent.

And now she was standing, arms crossed, glaring at us in front of a needlepoint that read *It's a Good Day to Have a Good Day*.

She looked around the room where we had assembled, her lips pursed. Gus stood against one wall, looking pissed off. Jude was on the couch, perfectly silent and probably writing a song in his head and tuning the rest of us out.

Finn was sitting in an old armchair, one leg bouncing, with his phone in his hand in case Adele needed a pint of ice cream or a foot rub.

And then there was Cole. He was lying face up on the loveseat with a pillow covering his head. I had to fight the urge to stomp over there, yank him to his feet, and shake him until he developed an ounce of common sense.

"You," Mom said sternly, "cannot press charges against your brother."

"Half brother," I mumbled.

"Owen," she snapped.

Shame washed over me as I dropped my head. God, I was such an asshole. But being here in this living room with my brothers, when I could be with Lila, was driving me insane.

"It's not up to us. That's not how it works," Finn explained, his tone as patient as ever. "The district attorney is an old friend of Alicia's. She spoke to him this morning. If Cole agrees to plead guilty, they're willing to drop the charges down to misdemeanor trespass and drunk and disorderly and sentence him to community service only."

If it were up to me, he'd be held accountable, but I kept my mouth shut, grateful that Finn was dealing with this. His ex, Alicia, was a high-powered attorney with all kinds of connections. There was a good chance she could have this taken care of quickly, and if that was the case, then there was a chance it wouldn't set back the sale.

Even so, anger still surged through me. "What the fuck, Cole? Do you have anything to say for yourself?" If I wasn't concerned about upsetting my mom, I'd pick his punk ass up off the couch and punch him in the face.

Or I'd try. He was the biggest of us all. Though if anyone could take him, my money was on Finn. Or Jude, the wildcard. It was always the quiet ones.

He rolled over slowly and narrowed his bloodshot eyes. "I'm a fuckup. Haven't you heard?"

"Cole," Mom chided, her expression a mix of disappointment and compassion.

I tried and failed to suppress an eye roll. My mom had long mistaken Cole for an injured puppy instead of a grown man in need of a lot of therapy and a thorough ass-kicking.

"I am a piece of shit. Please, throw me in jail. At least then I won't be sleeping in Debbie's guest room, watching *Wheel of Fortune* every night."

"Hey, do not bring Wheel into this," Mom warned, planting her hands on her hips.

"I get it. I'm not one of you. I suck. Can you just leave me alone now?"

"Cole." Gus grunted and sat on the sliver of cushion beside Cole's legs. "We want to help you." In true Gus form, he was ready to jump in, protect us all, and fix the situation.

"Fuck off and leave," Cole said into the cushion.

"Yeah, not happening dude," Finn said. "You fucked up badly, and now it's time to face the music. Why did you do it?"

Cole rolled over and pushed his hair out of his face. It was long and shaggy and dirty, and his newly grown beard was bushy and unkempt. He really did look like shit.

A twinge of pity hit me again, but I forced it aside.

"I don't know." He shrugged his massive shoulders. "I was drunk and high, and it seemed like a great idea. A fuck-you to Dad. A way to blow off steam. Who cares?"

And just like that, all my sympathy turned to rage.

"Who cares?" I scoffed, shaking my head. "You don't have the IQ points to understand how your actions affect the rest of us."

I was getting a full head of steam now. One wrong move, and I'd veer right into full-on shouting territory.

"I'm working my ass off, neglecting my actual paying job, to help save your asses. I abandoned my own life to help get this shit fixed so that we can all move forward with our lives.

"And you're up here, fucking things up left and right for the rest of us, sabotaging our chances of moving on without losing everything because you have hurt feelings? Liabilities impact our ability to sell, dumbass."

I was standing now, my fists clenched. "Get your shit together." I hissed, turning to leave. If I stayed, I couldn't be certain I wouldn't clock the asshole, and if I did that, I'd hurt my mom.

He hauled himself off the couch faster than seemed possible and shoved me hard. "Fuck you, Owen. You are the last person to throw stones. You haven't come home in years."

I whipped around and shoved him back, satisfied when he stumbled. "Staying away is not the same thing as petty crime and sabotage, you dumb fuck."

He lunged at me, practically growling, and I pushed him down onto the couch.

"You've had every opportunity laid out for you on a silver platter. The rest of us had to scrape by. We made do without state-of-the-art sports equipment, SAT tutors, or luxury vacations."

My heart was racing now. What I wouldn't give to be

back in Boston. I'd always enjoyed my simple life, and the minute I'd set foot in the state of Maine, everything had gone to shit. And they wondered why I never visited.

"Finn joined the Navy. I bartended to put myself through college," I gritted out, looming over where he was sprawled out. "Every single one of us had hardship, but you don't see any of us throwing tantrums and causing thousands of dollars in damages because our feelings are hurt."

Gus appeared beside me and put a hand on my shoulder, pulling me out of my rampage.

I took a step back and rolled my shoulders. This had already gone too far.

Mom jumped in then. "Boys. What's done is done. I asked you all here so we could figure out what we're going to do about it. Not to make things worse by dissolving into fights."

Chest heaving and blood still boiling, I stomped away from my idiot brother. On the other side of the room, I settled beside the bookshelf where Mom displayed all our high school graduation photos, including Cole's. It took effort not to pick it up and smash it. He didn't deserve my mom.

"We're all hurting. The last few years have not been kind to any of us." She pinned Cole with a glare. "You will make amends, both with the law and with our family."

"Yes, ma'am," he grumbled, hanging his head.

She turned toward me, shaking a finger. "I raised you better than this. We forgive in this family. I'll drag all your lazy asses to church on Sunday if I have to so you can remember your values."

She walked toward me, her expression softening a bit.

I forced my shoulders to lower and blew out a long breath as she stopped beside me.

"Now, how can we repair the damage and work together? Owen has taken on a lot." She shifted and focused on me, even managing to give me a small smile. "How can we help you?"

I shrug. "There really isn't much you can do."

"No." She crossed her arms over her chest. "I don't believe that. This room is full of smart, capable people. If we work toward a common goal, we can do it."

"I have a buyer—they've made one shitty offer. They'll make another, but I don't think it'll be much better. Every decent buyer I've found has been scared off by the incomplete financials and outstanding orders."

Deimos Industries and the mystery invoices were a problem, not to mention the consulting business and the conflicting environmental reports. We'd pull on one thread and find several others all tangled up.

"I've already been here for two weeks," I said. "I need to get back to Boston, but there's still so much to get done."

"I can chip in with whatever you need," Mom said.

Finn tapped out a message on his phone. "I'll ask Alicia to help with legal stuff."

"And if you need to go back to Boston for a bit, do it. We'll hold down the fort here." That from Gus. "We need this sale, but we also need a fair price or we won't even be able to pay off all our debts."

He was right, and until my trip to Portland yesterday, I'd cared more about unloading the company so I could be on my way. But this was a family business, and even though we'd lost the majority of our force, its sale would still affect many in the community. Nothing would be simple or easy.

"You don't have to stay." Jude pushed his glasses up his nose. "Come back and forth if you need to. Gus and I chose this life. You didn't. I don't want you to lose your job or give up your life in Boston for this. It's not worth it."

I considered him for a moment while I worked out how to respond to them all. Jude and I had never been close, but every time I spent time with him, I was impressed by his maturity. Where Gus could be a hothead, Jude was always thoughtful and calm. I tipped my chin, grateful he was on my side.

"We're struggling, as well," Gus said, roughing a hand through his hair. "Jude and I are working with a skeleton crew so we can fulfill the last of our orders. But the roads are shit this time of year, and the soft ground is slowing us down."

"Okay," Mom said with a firm nod. "Cole can help. He needs to spend his time productively."

"Cole?" Finn laughed, stroking his beard. "In the woods?"

"He won't have to operate heavy machinery," Jude said. "There's a ton of grunt work to get done. Checking loads, taking measurements, cleaning equipment, that kind of stuff."

Cole scoffed and slumped back against the cushions.

"We can't default on our outstanding contracts," I reasoned. "The last thing any buyer will want is a company in litigation for a breach of contract."

Mom rubbed her hands together. "Okay, that settles it. Cole will report for work tomorrow. Jude will teach him what he needs to know. We'll all chip in if Gus asks. That includes Finn and Owen."

I spun to face her. "Me?"

"Yes, you. What good is all this work you've been doing if things fall apart at the last minute?"

She had a point there. So with a long sigh, I nodded.

"Now," she said, scanning the room. "You are my boys, and I will say this once. Cut the shit. Work together and support one another. When things are hard, that's when we learn who we really are. And I raised scrappy fighters who aren't afraid of hard work."

She'd perfected the mom look years ago. The one that made us fall in line. And it was just as effective as ever. Every one of us was nodding and acquiescing by the time she put her hands on her hips and said, "Who wants pancakes?"

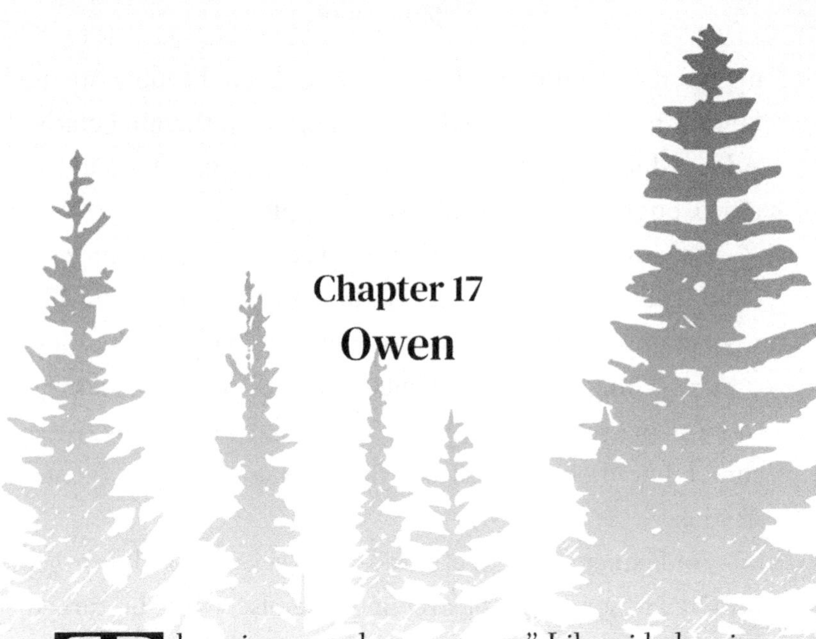

Chapter 17
Owen

"The printer needs more toner," Lila said, drawing me out of a daydream that involved her, a lake, and a sunny summer day. To say my head was not in the game was an understatement.

I'd been a mess since we returned from Portland, questioning my life choices and completely ignoring my responsibilities in favor of obsessing over a woman I couldn't have.

My outlook on life had shifted in a way that I still couldn't articulate.

The flirtation and the sexual tension were only growing by the day, and I had no idea how to manage it. I was an idiot.

Despite being ten years younger than me, Lila was the mature one here. She was starting a life elsewhere and wanted a fresh start. She deserved that. What she didn't deserve was to be followed around by an almost forty-year-old man who begged for scraps of her attention and affection.

I needed to get my shit together. I'd taken the Gagnons

up on their training offers and had been heading up to Henri's to chop wood and share a beer with them regularly. Adele's due date was getting closer, so Finn wasn't around as much, but the Gagnons were good people.

Despite the prejudice that had been drilled into me as a child, I liked them. Tucker continued to bust my balls, but woodchopping was a good workout and made me feel less useless. Things at Hebert Timber were as frustrating as ever, so an hour spent chopping wood relieved some of the pressure I felt there as well as when I was doing my actual day job.

And since I hadn't boxed in weeks, if I didn't get involved in some kind of strenuous exercise, when I returned to Boston, Enzo would absolutely kick my ass.

"Is the toner in the supply closet at the end of the hall?"

"Probably." I stood from my chair and raked a hand through my hair. "I'll help you find it."

As I followed her down the hall, it was impossible not to admire the sway of her ass in those jeans. I chastised myself for being a perv with every step, but I couldn't look away.

We made our way through the executive office space to the supply closet by the stairs. It wasn't large, but it was relatively well-stocked and didn't seem to have been ransacked. Rows of paper, pens, folders, and various other supplies were neatly organized. Probably the work of Miranda, my father's former assistant.

She'd all but disappeared since his arrest. I had the sneaking suspicion she was one of the key witnesses in the case against him. Without her, unfortunately, we were in the dark about so much operational information.

"Looks like the light is out," Lila said, pulling out her phone. She turned on the flashlight and scanned the shelves.

Any day now, we'd have more lights out than working in this building. We hadn't employed maintenance staff for almost a year, and things were falling apart left and right.

I cataloged the items on the shelves as she scanned them, and when the toner cartridges were illuminated, I let go of the door so I could pluck one off the top shelf. The door slammed shut, and the room went dark. If not for Lila's phone's light, it would have been pitch black.

Handing the box to her, I turned, feeling the heat of her body close to mine, and swallowed back the first inkling of fear that rushed through me.

I hated small spaces. I needed to get out of here before I embarrassed myself. My hand was already clammy when I found the doorknob. I gripped it, and as I turned it, I pushed against the door with my shoulder. But it wouldn't budge. I jiggled the knob and tried again. Nothing.

As sweat beaded at my temples, I pushed harder, assuming the bolt was stuck. I twisted the knob hard.

Instead of the click that would signal the latch bolt's release, there was a thud, and the knob fell into my hand, then clattered to the floor.

"Fuck." I dropped to my knees to inspect the door. Yup, dumbass that I was, I'd ripped the handle right off, leaving the lock mechanism stuck in the wall.

Lila laughed behind me, the sound light. "Figures that would happen. Here," she said, nudging my shoulder with her phone. "Use this."

My chest was already feeling tight as I took it and used the light to assess the issue.

Next came a bead of sweat running down my back, and as I worked to figure out how to release the mechanism, my hands began to shake.

Dammit. It wasn't opening. And I didn't have a screwdriver or a multi-tool on me, so I couldn't take the door off its hinges.

Sucking in a harsh breath, I turned and stood, swaying on my feet. I pointed the light at the shelves and scanned them for anything that could help. But all I found were reams of paper and useless office supplies.

Lila stood beside me, still shaking her head at the absurdity of the situation. Her huffs and comments were lighthearted, but I was starting to spiral.

I tried, to no avail, to center myself with the deep breathing exercises I'd learned in therapy. I was beginning to lose feeling in my fingertips, and my lips were getting numb.

"Owen?" Lila said, her voice full of concern but far away.

It was getting increasingly harder to breathe, even as I counted my inhales and exhales. I was such a disgrace. It was a closet, for fuck's sake.

But my nervous system hadn't gotten the memo, no matter how illogical it was.

"Owen, are you okay?" her tone had turned concerned.

Shame washed over me, only making the panic more acute.

By thirty-eight, I should have outgrown this. My childhood fears should be firmly in the past, and I should be well equipped to work through any that might sneak their way in.

But no. I was freaking the fuck out in front of the woman I was obsessed with.

Fucking great.

Lila surely thought I was a basket case by this point. She'd probably run from the building, screaming all the way to her minivan, as soon as we got out of here. And I'd deserve it.

"Owen."

Her hands were on my shoulders now. She still sounded far away, but the scent of her lemony shampoo surrounded me. I focused on it and forced myself to breathe it in, to feel her presence.

"Owen, look at me." She splayed her hands on either side of my face and turned me so I was facing her. "It's okay. Look at me."

I blinked once, then again, and the world around me came into focus a little. Willing myself to be here in this moment, I studied her beautiful eyes. They weren't blue, and they weren't gray or green. They were a color somewhere in between. One that was truly unique. Just like her.

She licked her lips and pressed her hands to my skin a little more firmly. "Are you claustrophobic?"

I nodded, still focused on her eyes. Even in the semi-darkness, the flecks of gold were visible. So was every freckle across the bridge of her nose and a tiny scar at the corner of her top lip.

Seeing Lila had never been the problem. I'd look at her all day if it wouldn't make me a lunatic. But seeing her like this, her eyes filled with concern but without an ounce of pity, made my mind spin out even further.

She pulled me in and squeezed me tight. The feel of her heart beating against mine was like a beacon, guiding me.

"Just breathe," she said, her hold still firm. "I'm going to call Gus and have him come get us out. Okay?"

I nodded, forcing myself to focus on the warmth of her body against mine and the comfort her tight embrace imbued while she spoke into the phone. Then she was quiet again, releasing me but not taking her hands off me. With soothing instructions, she guided me to sit against the shelves.

"Gus will be here in five minutes. Just stay with me." She crawled into my lap and put her arms around my neck, pulling me close.

I clung to her, my anchor, and breathed. I closed my eyes and let the feel of Lila wash over me. The warmth of her body, the weight of her in my arms, made this awful moment a tiny bit easier.

All I had to do was breathe.

Gus had shown up quickly and had taken the entire door apart with relative ease.

I'd barely made it into my makeshift office when the adrenaline wore off and I crashed. With a groan, I collapsed on the old loveseat and closed my eyes. It wasn't comfortable, but it was there.

Lila, her face a mask of concern, appeared a few moments later, armed with snacks, water, and tea.

Gus, who'd witnessed this before, had wanted to take me home, but I promised them I was fine. I still had work to do.

"Can you tell me what happened in there?" She handed me a paper cup filled with tea and sat down next to me on the small loveseat. "Please don't be embarrassed. We all have stuff we're dealing with. And it makes me feel better, actually. All this time, I thought you were some kind of emotionless robot." She turned to face me, wearing a smile.

"Wow. Thanks."

"I mean it. You're so buttoned-up and professional. You never raise your voice, you never get flustered, and you're always in control."

I took a sip of tea and relished the way it warmed me as it slid down my throat.

If only she knew. If only she knew the thoughts that ran through my head. I was not in control. Especially around her.

"I'm claustrophobic." I left it at that while I debated how much to tell her.

Beside me, she watched me with so much concern written on her beautiful face. It made it impossible to hold back. The desire for her to know me, to understand at least a little of my history, was overwhelming.

And so I took another slow sip of tea, settled into the loveseat, and talked.

"I was always a disappointment to my dad." I cleared my throat, searching for the words. I'd never talked about this with anyone but my therapist. "I can't remember a time when he was proud of me. He wanted the Hebert boys to be athletic, dominant, macho. Like a true narcissist, he didn't see us as individuals, but rather as an extension of his fucked-up ego."

Her lips turned down, and she squeezed my knee. "That's so awful."

I shrugged. I'd gotten used to it long ago. "After my parents got divorced, we'd stay with him for weekends once in a while, mostly Gus and me, since we were older. One time, when I was nine, he and Uncle Paul wanted to take us hunting, but I refused. The last thing I wanted to do was kill a deer."

She scooted a little closer, and her arm brushed mine. "I don't blame you."

"Dad was furious. Called me all kinds of awful names because I didn't want to kill an innocent animal." I swallowed past the dread that was welling up inside me. "Then he locked me in the woodshed."

"Are you fucking serious?" she shouted, going ramrod straight. "That's child abuse."

"It was November, and so damn cold. He left me out there all night. The building wasn't all that small, but it felt like a tomb. It was infested with mice, and during the warmer months, it was full of spiders." My body went rigid at the memories. "I remember not being able to breathe and then shivering so hard I couldn't stand up."

Lila put her arm around me, pulling me close. I buried my face in her neck and inhaled. Even thirty years later, I could feel the fear that had overtaken me that night. The smells, the sounds, the cold air against my clammy skin.

"Dad probably got drunk and forgot I was out there. But in the middle of the night, Gus snuck out to rescue me. He'd woken up to use the bathroom and realized I wasn't in my bed. He couldn't find the keys to the shed, so he got a pair of bolt cutters from the garage and cut the lock."

Lila let out a tiny gasp. "Holy shit."

"Dad was furious. He beat Gus up pretty badly for it."

His ribs had been so bruised we'd had to wrap them. Dad knew better than to hit us in the face. Gus had lied to Mom, always loyal to Dad, even when the evidence was on his own skin.

"That's Gus. He takes his job as protector so seriously. I owe him. We may not be close anymore, but he's always looked out for all of us."

Lila wiped a tear from her cheek. "I am so sorry. For both of you."

"That's the biggest part of why I'm even here." I ran a hand down my face. "I didn't come for my dad or the company, but for Gus. No one wanted this place to succeed more than he did. The guy has completed every training course and has earned every machinery certification and qualification in existence."

He was one of the good ones. Always had been. Which was probably why Dad always kept him on the outside rather than bringing him in to run the business side by side. Taking over one day had always been Gus's dream. He never would have gotten involved with trafficking drugs. He was good. To his core. And though he'd struggled to understand why Dad hadn't brought him in, it was really a blessing, because there wasn't a single piece of evidence that could tie him to any wrongdoing.

"So that's why I'm here coordinating the sale and working through decades' worth of records to get the best possible price. If I can get Gus some sort of payout for all the blood, sweat, and tears he poured into this place, then at least he can restart his life and get out from under the shadow of our criminal father."

She put her head on my shoulder, her hair brushing against my chin. That small move soothed my fried nerves. It was perfect. She was perfect. When Lila was touching me, I was okay. I was brave and could talk about things I'd never said out loud. She was magic.

"I'm sorry I freaked out," I said, sitting a little straighter. It was time to regain at least a little of my dignity.

She pulled back and stared at me. "Don't you dare apologize. We all have our shit, Owen."

"True." I lowered my head and sighed. "But mine involves panic attacks in supply closets."

"Stop it. You're not perfect. So what?" She poked my chest. "You're still handsome and successful and you tell hilarious accounting jokes."

I looked up and held her gaze for a moment. Then I seized her hand and held it to my chest, right over my heart.

She twined her fingers with mine and rested her head on my shoulder again.

We were silent for a long time, our bodies pressed together and our fingers tangled, our heartbeats and breaths syncing.

And something shifted inside me. As if parts of me were being torn apart and rebuilt with the scraps.

Chapter 18
Owen

"I need more time." I cringed, bracing for their response.

"Called it," Amara said. Yeah, she did. She'd had my number for years.

I could practically see her pacing around her office with me on speaker. She was probably wearing bright orange or some other ridiculous color.

"Tad not getting it done?"

"He's useless. We need new representation. And things are so much more complicated than I expected." I rubbed at my brow, willing away the dull ache behind my eyes.

"More complicated" was an understatement. I had come to Lovewell two weeks ago with a simple objective. Now I was questioning everything and in over my head.

"Take the time you need, brother," Enzo said. He was my boss, but more than that, he was my best friend. The guy I'd lay down my life for. I had five actual brothers, but no one looked out for me the way Enzo did. "Family stuff is hard.

You're working your ass off. And let's face it, Linda's got it covered."

Couldn't argue with that. Linda kept the team working, and she'd kept me in the loop by forwarding contracts for my review and signature and flagging the important calls I needed to jump on. I truly wouldn't have survived without her.

"But," he hedged. "We've got the GeneSphere status check next week. The entire C suite is flying in, and we need all hands on deck."

I nodded, even though he couldn't see me, and clasped my hands on top of my desk. "I'll be there."

We'd been working on the new GeneSphere Pharmaceuticals headquarters for more than three years. The project was an endless source of stress and angst, but by far one of the biggest things we'd taken on.

"You want a plane?" Enzo asked.

"So that's how it is now? You start rolling with literal billionaires and we've got planes?"

I could give Enzo shit about his roommates all day long and never get tired of it. His girlfriend Delia lived with a couple of billionaires and pro athletes in the most bizarre commune-type situation.

"I'm just saying, if transport is an issue, we can take care of it. We need you here. And the Boston Cares event is that weekend. My mother is on the board, so..." he trailed off.

"Mom will castrate you if you don't show and donate," Amara finished.

Their mother, Elena DiLuca, was a force to be reckoned with. And she had adopted me as one of her own, even though she had four kids and both my parents were alive. She had been working with this organization for decades and would be personally offended if I didn't show up.

"I'll be there," I said. "Can't let Mama D down."

"Good. She'll torture me if you don't show," Amara said. "And we can hang while my siblings are all coupled up."

That had the wheels turning in my head. "Can I bring someone?"

"Who?" Amara asked.

"A friend."

Her responding laugh was so loud the line between us crackled. "She's a lot more than a friend if you're willing to risk exposing her to my crazy mother."

I ignored her, too preoccupied with the plan taking shape in my mind. "Are the Revs at home that weekend?" I wondered out loud. "Enzo, you think you can score tickets from your boy Beckett."

Enzo had recently moved in with his girlfriend and her kids—*and* her friends and their kids and their boyfriends, fiancés, and husbands. It was a whole thing. I didn't give him too much shit, though, because he'd made some very powerful new friends, mainly Beckett Langfield, owner of Boston's baseball team, the Revs. That meant we rarely had trouble scoring tickets to any games we wanted to see.

"Yeah, man," Enzo said. "Let me—"

A shout from down the hall pulled me out of the conversation and had my hackles rising. "Guys, I gotta run," I said, already on my feet and heading to my door.

"*Fuck.*" The words echoed in the cavernous hallway.

I picked up my pace, all but running to the conference room where Lila was working.

When I burst into the room, I found her standing near the windows, staring at her phone.

"Are you okay?" I put my hands on her shoulders, bracing for the worst.

"Oh my God." Her chest was heaving and her eyes were wide with shock as she tipped her head back and looked at me. "It's admission day. I got so busy I totally forgot."

I closed my eyes and said a silent prayer that she'd gotten in. She worked so damn hard, and she deserved this.

"I—" She gripped my arm and blinked, like she was coming back online. "I need my laptop."

Still holding her shoulders, I led her over to the folding table she'd been using as a desk and pulled out the chair. Once she was seated, I leaned in, caging her in with my arms, and waited for her to log into the admission system.

This close, the citrusy scent of her shampoo enveloped me. Her hair was up in a ponytail today, highlighting her graceful neck. I had to fight back the instinct to place a small kiss right there.

With a deep breath in and a silent reprimand, I managed to get myself under control. This was neither the time nor the place, and honestly, I wasn't sure there ever would be a time or a place. Getting involved with her was a bad idea for far too many reasons. The first of which was that she was about to move out of state for graduate school. And then there was Cole.

Nope, I'd muscle through it. No matter how impossible that felt. Because it had been less than two weeks, and I was already deeply infatuated with this woman. With her laugh, her smile, her mind. I had a deep respect and admiration for her and for the way she'd show up, lattes in hand, ready to take whatever life threw at her.

Sometimes, part of me wanted to throw all my concerns out the window. I was greedy. I wanted to stay here, locked in the sea of file boxes, cracking jokes with Lila. I wanted this to last forever.

Then I'd shake myself and remember that I needed to get back to my real life and my actual job instead of sorting through old paperwork in this dusty office building.

These tasks should have been my worst nightmare, but Lila made this entire ordeal fun. When I'd come back to Lovewell, it had felt like a prison sentence. Now, I looked forward to seeing her every day, and the stress of dealing with this mess while keeping up with my day job felt more manageable with her around.

"Crap. I can't even type my password correctly," she said, her voice wavering.

"Shh.," I said, rubbing her shoulders, hoping to imbue her with a sense of calm. "Take a deep breath and try again."

She was so tense she was practically vibrating.

I wasn't fairing a whole lot better. I wanted this for her so badly. I wanted all of her dreams to come true.

Finally, with a long breath out, she typed her password correctly. Then we waited, holding our breath, while the page loaded.

When the NYU logo appeared, she was out of her seat, jumping and screaming. "Holy shit. I got in!" she cheered. "NYU! I can't believe it."

I wrapped my arms around her and spun her around, relishing the way her body felt against mine. "That's incredible."

Quickly, I set her down again and took a step back. The sheer joy on her face when she looked up at me made my stomach flip.

"I can't believe I did it." Her eyes filled with tears.

With my hands on her shoulders again, I gave her a gentle squeeze and dipped down so she was forced to look at me. "You deserve this, Lila. You are going to do amazing things. I'm so proud of you."

I'd never been a touchy-feely person, but I found it hard to keep my hands to myself around her. I constantly itched to stroke her hair, squeeze her hand, or put my arm around her shoulders.

Thankfully, I had the presence of mind to knock that shit off. This moment was supercharged, and I could easily let things get out of hand, but I wouldn't do that to her. Not when she was flying high like this. So I took a step back and shoved my hands into my pocket, determined to let her have her moment.

"God," she sighed. "I feel so lucky."

"Lucky?" I scoffed. I couldn't stop myself. How on earth could this woman think luck had anything to do with this? "You are smart and determined. You worked hard for this. Take the credit."

She tipped her head and studied my face, her cheeks flushed.

"Say it," I commanded.

"I did this," she whispered.

I crossed my arms. "You can do better than that. Own it."

She bit her lip, and it took every ounce of self-control I possessed not to grab her and kiss her until she realized how spectacular she was. Instead, I arched a brow, waiting for her response.

"I did it," she said, lifting her chin, her voice clear and confident.

"Congratulations, Lila."

"Thank you." She beamed. "I worked hard."

"And you deserve it. You deserve the world. Never, ever doubt that. Understood?"

She didn't respond. She didn't even nod. She just regarded me, her eyes wide and her smile broad. And before I could process what was happening, she jumped up and threw her arms around my neck, and then her lips were on mine.

Sweet and firm and insistent.

And for a moment, everything was right in the world.

I grasped her hips and slid my hands up her ribs, around to her back, finally exploring her the way I'd wanted to since that first day.

This kiss was messy, joyful, and enthusiastic. Just like Lila.

I slid my hands lower and cupped her ass, and in response, she wrapped her legs around my waist and raked her hands through the hair at the back of my neck. She moaned into my mouth, the sounds vibrating through me, as I pushed her back against the wall. And just like that, I lost hold of the last shreds of my self-control.

Wild, messy, and desperate, we kissed and touched and explored, as I lost my mind completely.

And then she was pushing me away. I eased her to her feet and took a step back, out of breath and desperate with need.

"Shit. Shit." She hung her head, refusing to look at me. "I'm so sorry."

Those three words were like a punch to the solar plexus. All the air escaped me as I searched her expression. My heart was racing and my cock was hard as steel, causing a lack of blood flow to my brain. I heaved in one breath after another, unable to interpret her words or her expression.

"Don't apologize," I said, working my way closer to coherent thought.

An apology meant she regretted it. And how could anyone regret what we had just shared?

My heart pounded out an erratic rhythm as I took one step closer and used two fingers to tip her face up to meet mine. "Lila, look at me."

When she focused on me, her eyes were filled with a fierce, raw vulnerability that made me want to hug her until she never doubted herself again.

"You have nothing to be sorry for."

She put her face in her hands. "I mauled you, Owen." Her groan was muffled. "I pounced on you like a jungle cat."

I huffed a breath. Did she think I wasn't into that? If that was the case, then it was time to correct that misconception. "First of all, what you just did was hot. Don't think for one second I didn't enjoy the hell out of it. Second, you're welcome to do that whenever you want."

She slumped and hit me with an exasperated scowl. It was the cutest expression I'd ever seen.

I tucked a loose strand of hair behind her ear and cupped her jaw. "Good-girl Lila always plays by the rules. She never takes what she wants and worries too much about what people think. But this version of you—the ass-kicking grad student who goes after what she wants—is irresistible and powerful and incredible."

She inhaled sharply and took a step back, and my heart sank to my feet, taking my stomach right along with it.

"I can't do this right now," she said, ducking her head and sidestepping me. "I need to go tell my mom the good news. And call Willa and Mags. Is it okay if I head out early?"

I swallowed past the boulder that had lodged itself in my throat, mentally kicking myself for coming on too strong and scaring her off. "Of course."

She gathered her stuff and headed out without looking back, leaving me breathless and confused.

My head was spinning and my heart was bruised. Lila had kissed me. And it had completely rocked my world. And then she'd walked away.

Maybe I should be thankful she had. She was headed to New York, and I was headed back to Boston.

Her life was just starting and I was settled. And then there was Cole. As much as I resented his part in all of this, he was the elephant in the room. They'd been together for eight years, and he was still wreaking havoc, if only indirectly.

I had no loyalty to him, especially after what he'd done a few days ago. But if it made Lila uncomfortable, then I'd have to step back and keep things the way they had been.

Logically, I had plenty of legitimate reasons to stay away.

But then I touched my lips. That kiss had rearranged my brain cells, and despite my better judgment, all I could think about was doing it again.

I'd had plenty of first kisses in my life. Some were

awkward, others passionate. But this one had been filled with pure joy. And it was Lila. Sunshine in human form, a woman who was free to do what she wanted, when she wanted it.

And just knowing that she had wanted me, if only for a moment, made my heart crack wide open. Maybe there were other possibilities for me too.

Chapter 19
Lila

"I'm so proud of you!"

"You're amazing!"

News of my acceptances called for an impromptu Zoom happy hour, so we'd all gathered provisions and logged on.

"Every school you applied to." Willa shook her head, grinning. "We knew you could do it." She was toasting with a Diet Coke from an on-call room at the hospital.

Magnolia was wearing a leopard-print silk robe and petting one of her cats. The villain in a James Bond movie look was typical for her.

"Are you planning to visit any of the campuses?"

I shook my head. "Not yet. I'm waiting for the financial aid packages. If any of them offer something really amazing, I'll consider it. But nothing short of a full ride and being crowned queen of the universe would keep me from New York."

Despite my acceptance into several excellent schools, I was sticking to my plan.

"We are going to live it up, ladies," Willa declared, stifling a yawn.

"Why are you so sleepy?" Magnolia teased. "Long night with your boy toy?"

Willa pretended to dry heave. "No. Just the chief riding me. The charting is never-ending, and she wants me to be harder on the first years during rounds. So now I've got to prepare extra hard and get comfortable being a little meaner."

"At least you're kind of getting laid," Magnolia complained. Her shoulders slumped, but an instant later, she perked up again, startling her cat, who jumped off her lap. "Lila," she sang, "are you banging your hot boss yet?"

My face flamed before I could look away from the camera. Even so, I went with it, pretending to be occupied by the stack of random papers on my nightstand. There was no way I was getting into this right now. I was still in recovery from kissing Owen.

That moment was all I could think about. The crush of his lips, the strength of his hands, the way he'd pushed me back against the wall. The thoughts were plentiful and all-consuming, each one dirtier and raunchier and more fun than the last.

I wasn't inexperienced, but I wasn't particularly experienced either.

I'd lost my virginity to Cole when I was nineteen after I'd deliberately waited, and only after taking every precaution. Being the daughter of a teen mom meant I'd spent my life being reminded of the need for birth control. Double birth control at that.

So I waited. Because I was a good girl and I'd internalized the misogynistic views that drowned out all the rest. The ones that said I should save myself and not experiment. The ones that assured me that being inexperienced and not understanding sex was an attractive quality to men.

"You know we can read you like a book. May as well come clean."

My stomach lurched. Dammit. I scrunched up my face, trying to keep the secret, but there was no use. I told my best friends everything, so it would come out eventually. "Owen and I kissed," I sighed, keeping my head down and picking at a piece of lint on my comforter. "It was really hot, and now I'm confused and horny and did I mention confused?"

When silence ensued, I forced myself to look up. Both of my friends were gaping at me, slack-jawed.

"Well done." Magnolia put her glass down and clapped so loud, the sound coming through the speakers made me cringe. "I didn't know you had it in you."

"I'm in over my head, guys. I'm feeling things and thinking things, and he's this successful older guy. He's probably been with dozens of women, and I'm just a lame small-town girl who mauled him with her mouth."

Willa shook her head. "You are none of those things and, given the shade of your cheeks, he kissed you back and kissed you back good."

I nodded, my cheeks flaming hotter. "I feel like such an inexperienced kid around him."

"You know," Magnolia mused, "I think all that virginity purity shit is just an excuse for men to be bad at sex."

"What do you mean?" Willa had waited even longer than I had. She was a textbook good girl, but in recent years had loosened up a bit.

"Think about it. If you save yourself for your husband, then you won't know he's lousy in bed and he never has to work to get any better."

Willa's eyes went wide and her mouth formed an O. "It's the patriarchy's way of denying us pleasure!"

"Preach, sister," Magnolia shouted, sloshing liquid over the rim of her martini glass.

All my life, I'd assumed that I wasn't a sexual person. And I was mostly okay with it. I had many other interests and attributes. Especially given my friends' experiences, it had never really been important to me.

After Cole and I ended, I'd taken advantage of my single status and hooked up with a few guys.

The sex had been fine and relatively uneventful, but it had felt like a necessary step. To help move away from the compliant, complacent Lila and closer to a woman who did what, and whom, she wanted.

The experience had broadened my horizons and opened my eyes to the reality that sex was more than I'd ever understood. Still, I hadn't felt the urge in a while. Despite my toy collection, courtesy of Magnolia, I didn't have much of a sex drive. It was probably a result of living with my mom and working constantly.

"If you like each other and are interested in taking the next step, none of that matters, sweetie," Willa said gently. "From what you've said, he's been a perfect gentleman."

"Yes," I hedged. Though I wished he would be a bit *less* of a gentleman sometimes.

"And you've got time," Magnolia added, bringing her drink to her lips. As she sipped, she watched us over the rim of her glass, keeping us in suspense in a way only she could pull off. "You aren't even in your prime yet. I've heard mid-to-late thirties is when shit gets good."

"I don't know about you girls, but I want it to be good now." Willa harrumphed.

"You've got... uh... Anderson," I said. I was pretty sure that was the name of her current hookup.

"Eh." She waved a hand. "I'm not into it anymore."

"Why?"

"It's purely a convenience thing." She blew out a breath, sending the fine hairs around her face floating. "He's a dorky attending. I'm a dorky attending. We can't screw our residents, and we don't ever leave the hospital, so it just made sense to screw each other."

"Damn, that sounds so unsexy. *Grey's Anatomy* taught me that all doctors are super hot and everyone is banging in on-call rooms all the time."

Willa rolled her eyes. "He's decent in bed. Not world-rocking, but he gets the job done. He's a doctor, so he knows where everything is and, while he tends to be a premature ejaculator, he does always get me off first."

"Wow." Mags snorted. "You're talking about sex like you're preparing a tax return."

"Hey, we'd all love fireworks and passion every day, but some of us don't have time for more than a decent, complication-free lay once in a while." Willa shrugged. "It was good while it lasted."

"Lila, cover your ears. Don't listen to Dr. Gloom and

Doom over here. The passion and fire are out there. You just have to chase them."

That was exactly my problem. They *were* out there. I was feeling a lot of passion. And it was inconvenient and confusing.

Sex had always felt transactional. Cole, as imperfect as he was, had always been a gentleman. But I'd always felt like I had to perform. Like sex was for him and not for me.

It was part of my role as a trophy girlfriend. I didn't realize it at the time, but that outlook was unfair to him. It meant that I never gave him true intimacy. I never spoke up about what I wanted or how I wanted it. Instead, I let him take the lead and played clueless virgin.

And in some ways, I was clueless, but as I got older and more comfortable with my body, I'd suspected I was capable of more. But I was stuck in the mindset that I couldn't ask him to help me explore what that might entail.

"You know what you need?" Willa asked. "Audiobooks. I've got great recs. Get yourself out of your own head and let the sexy vibes flow."

"You're a genius." Magnolia picked up her phone and scrolled. "I'm looking at my Audible library now. Let's get Sebastian York or Jacob Morgan in your ears. Do that, and you're guaranteed to find your inner sex goddess."

"Guys." I threw myself back against my headboard. "I don't need motivation."

I suspected sex with Owen would be a hell of a lot more than fine without additional motivation. If his approach to work was any indication, he was meticulous and thorough. His hands were large and strong, and if I closed my eyes, I could almost feel the pads of his fingers brushing against my clit.

Shit. I forced my eyes open and sat up straight again. The timing could not be worse.

"There's also a complication," I admitted, worrying my bottom lip. "He asked me to come to Boston with him this weekend."

Magnolia leaped out of her seat and danced around her chair. "Fuck yeah! Our little Lila is getting some."

"It's for work," I explained. "Gus was supposed to go with him, but there was some road issue, and Finn can't go because Adele is due any day now."

I'd had to physically restrain myself from pumping my fist when he asked me, and I was still giddy. He'd gone on about how he'd like me to come with him to meet with the new lawyers and how good I was at catching errors and fact-checking. They were minor compliments, but each one made my heart sore. Because he wasn't blowing smoke. He was impressed with my abilities. This wildly successful, highly intelligent man was impressed by me.

I plucked at my comforter again, lowering my head. "I really like working with him. The respect he shows me is something I don't think I've ever experienced. He asks thoughtful questions, and he always carefully considers my work and opinions."

He'd trusted me to run with the Deimos Industries research and had let me loose on those bozos in Portland. Every step along the way, we worked as a team. This brilliant, accomplished guy and me, the girl who'd bootstrapped a degree out of community college credits and online courses.

And part of me was afraid of ruining what we had. Because as good as kissing Owen felt, working with him felt better.

Willa waggled her brows. "Damn, girl. He's attracted to your mind, not just your ass. This work trip would be the perfect opportunity to jump him."

I blushed again. Dammit. I should be used to their teasing by now. "We're meeting with new lawyers and a land use consultant, and then there's some big event he's got to be back for. I'll have some time to spend in the city while he's busy with that."

"Ooh," Magnolia said. "You should visit U Boston. The campus is gorgeous. This will give you a chance to at least take a tour before you turn them down."

"No," Willa protested with a huff. "She's going to NYU, and we're all going to live together in New York."

Magnolia waggled her eyebrows. "What if she wants to be in Boston? With a certain hot, older guy who loves her sexy brain."

"I don't." I rushed to object to keep Willa from blowing a gasket. Our New York plans had helped her through her grueling residency. I could never disappoint her like that. "I may walk around and take a look. But I'm not moving to Boston, especially for a guy. I've been down that road, remember? I know better now."

That reined Mags in. She and Willa both murmured in agreement and sipped on their drinks. They wholeheartedly agreed with my logic on this front. I'd never, ever derail my plans for a man again.

Even as I repeated that promise to myself, my brain, my stupid, weak, terminally horny brain, started to wander.

Maybe I *could* go to school in Boston. And if I did, maybe I could date Owen...

No. Bad. I needed to stay focused.

"You should seduce him on this trip." Willa was cracking her second Diet Coke. "Get it out of your system. Bang him and then move to New York and live your life. That way, you don't have to wonder any longer."

"Are you staying at a hotel? Fancy hotels are so sexy."

"No. He has a guest room. He offered to put me up at a hotel, but I'm fine staying at his condo. I looked it up on Zillow. It's like two thousand square feet."

Magnolia's drink had disappeared, and she was rubbing her hands together, once again looking like a movie villain. "I'm with the good Doc. Jump his bones. First, you'll get all hot and bothered talking about accounting..."

"Yes." Willa laughed. "Maybe create some pivot tables in Excel. That's when your panties will incinerate."

"Then he'll eat you out while you talk about cost analyses."

"Stop," I said, putting my hands up. "I give up. You two are lunatics."

Willa's answering smile was big and genuine. "We just want what's best for you, sweets."

"And what's best is multiple orgasms," Magnolia said, her expression nowhere near as innocent as Willa's.

I pinched the bridge of my nose. God, my friends were nuts.

Or were they?

Boston was nothing like Lovewell. We'd be away from the gossip and the drama and all our baggage for a few days.

And that kiss, it had been something. The start of something.

Would it be so bad to do a tiny bit of follow-up?

I shut the thought down before I went too far down that road. Owen was a colleague and a friend. Sexy make-out session notwithstanding, it was important to keep things between us professional.

I'd have to find some way to deal with this crush that didn't involve mauling him like a horny feral tiger.

Chapter 20
Lila

Owen's big GeneSphere meeting on Thursday meant I had some time to explore Boston on my own. I didn't know much about the project, but based on how tense he'd been on the flight last night, it was important. Once we'd landed, we'd taken a car to his condo, where he'd given me a quick tour before disappearing into his room to work.

The sun was out in full force and the spring air was crisp and refreshing as I made my way to Back Bay, where I toured the Boston Public Library, then strolled down Newbury Street toward the Public Garden.

I took a selfie with the Make Way for Ducklings statue and sent it to my mom. It had been my favorite book as a kid, and the copy in my room was almost falling apart from so many readings.

I'd scheduled a tour of the University of Boston ahead of time, and when I arrived, the dean of the management school even welcomed me and chatted with me about their program and the massive nonprofit network in the city.

The campus was gorgeous. Just for a moment, I let myself imagine living here, walking down the Charles River path to get to my classes in ancient brick buildings that proudly lined the streets and studying at a battered oak table in the massive library.

New York was my destiny. My dream. But Boston was gorgeous and intriguing.

I sat in the park, sipping a coffee and taking in the sights and the sounds of the city. This was what I'd been waiting so long for. A new place filled with infinite possibilities. Where I could carve my own path, far away from the person I used to be.

Once in a while, I spiraled, stressing about all the wasted years. It wasn't just hindsight. It was muscle memory, imprints of the constant ache of disappointment.

Despite the perfect day and how alive I felt, I was hit with the regrets and what-ifs right there on the park bench. I closed my eyes and breathed through the tidal wave of shame that came.

I've evolved, I reminded myself. *I freed myself from limiting beliefs*. Falling into old patterns was too easy. Just another reason that my fresh start in New York was so necessary.

Most days, my natural positivity made it relatively easy to avoid these feelings. I'd muscle through with a smile and the belief that everything would be okay.

It was more than a belief. It was the truth and an eventuality. I'd grown through the tough years. I'd learned so much about myself and what I wanted. The lessons I learned during the hardest times, and the person I'd grown into because of them and in spite of them, were far more valuable than any degree, job, or money could ever be.

It had taken a long time to come to terms with the path I'd taken and to embrace the journey I was on. But now, just a few months away from graduate school, a real career, and making a real difference in the world? I was so ready.

Only a few years ago, I was destined to be someone else entirely. A pretty trophy on someone's arm. A kept woman who spent her life bending over backward to please others. I shrank, took up less space to make room for the wants and needs of others, until I didn't recognize myself. Now I took up the space I needed. The space I'd earned. I woke up every day and presented my true self to the world, brown hair, flat shoes, and all. It took a long time to get to where I was, and I had a way to go yet, but I was doing things my way. I'd earned that degree, and when I did, I'd do so much with it.

I had a bank account filled with shitty diner tips and tutoring money, and I was ready for the next step.

I smiled at a group of senior citizens power walking, then tilted my face to the sky and soaked in the warmth of the sun.

Good. Positive. This was who I was. A woman with grit and determination. There was nothing I couldn't accomplish with a little elbow grease and a smile.

Right? I popped in my earbuds and cued up my "good vibes" playlist.

Life was great. The day was perfect. This moment was bliss.

And then my thoughts veered into dangerous territory. *What if I came here instead?* The University of Boston was gorgeous and prestigious. I'd even applied for several scholarships. At least I thought I had. I'd applied for damn near every stipend, scholarship, and grant I could find, so it was hard to remember the details.

It was closer to home, and the cost of living in Boston was cheaper than in New York. And Owen was here.

I huffed out a breath and tipped my head back. I'd made it all the way back to square one again. I cursed my stupid, optimistic, romantic brain. It had gotten me into trouble so many times before.

God, I was such a silly girl, considering the idea of making plans around a guy I'd kissed once.

I knew better. I had plans and goals, and every day, I was striving to be the kind of woman who wouldn't rearrange her life for a man.

Especially when said man may have zero interest in me following him back to his city and his life like a lovesick schoolgirl.

I was *not* lovesick. It was only a teeny-tiny crush. Nothing more. And who could blame me? He was better looking than any Hallmark hero my mom had drooled over in my lifetime, and he said the kindest, most insightful things to me.

And then there was the kiss.

Owen kissed like a man who understood that a kiss shouldn't be rushed. It was not an appetizer, but a full, satisfying meal.

His lips, his hands, the feel of him pushing me against the wall. I clenched my thighs together, willing the warmth in my belly to dissipate and scolding myself. Here I was, sitting on a bench in public, having a sexual flashback.

In my defense, it was hard not to fantasize about him, especially while I was sleeping in his home, surrounded by his things, engulfed in his scent. He'd been a perfect gentleman, and I had no doubt that would continue for the whole weekend. We were here for work, and tonight, we'd be working through the new offer from the buyers and prepping the new lawyers.

But I couldn't help but wish he'd be a little less of a gentleman.

DiLuca Construction, housed in a massive building in Boston's Seaport District, was a ten-minute walk from Owen's very impressive but minimally furnished apartment.

We were set to meet with the new lawyers on Friday morning. When I arrived, I was directed to set up in a large conference room with windows that overlooked Boston Harbor. I should have been reviewing numbers and working through the Deimos issues as our meeting drew near, but instead, I couldn't help but marvel at the facility.

It was huge, with people bustling about everywhere. Some were dressed formally, while others looked as though they'd just come from a job site. Every aspect of the office was state-of-the-art, and every person here knew Owen and seemed in awe of him.

During my exploration of the city, I saw DiLuca Constructions signs everywhere, and Owen was confident and knowledgeable and fair. Witnessing him in his element was thrilling, and the energy of the place already had me buzzing. No wonder they were so successful. Everyone here was working hard and excited about it.

The door to the conference room opened, and a broad-shouldered man in jeans walked in. He wore a wide smile as he held his hand out. "Enzo DiLuca. You must be the famous Lila."

As I slid my palm against his, I marveled at this guy. He was handsome, with thick dark hair and a neatly trimmed beard. He wore a dress shirt, jeans, and work boots rather than the stuffy suit one would expect from the CEO.

What was even more unexpected was the way he turned the chair around and straddled it, then put his elbows on the table.

"I've heard so much about you. Sorry the office is crazy today. Our biggest client was in yesterday, and the adrenaline hasn't quite worn off."

I straightened a stack of papers beside my laptop and nodded. "This place is beautiful."

"Thanks. As usual, your boy Owen came to the rescue. I don't think he slept last night, but he has all the new calculations ready to go." He scratched at his beard. "A lot of professionals warn against working with your friends, but there's no one I trust more. I wouldn't last a week here without him."

I'd known this man for two whole minutes, and already, it was clear that he was whip-smart but down-to-earth. No wonder he and Owen were so close.

"He's brilliant." The moment the words were out of my mouth, my cheeks went hot.

Enzo nodded in agreement, but he narrowed his eyes, as if evaluating me. Rather than feeling anxious about the scrutiny, I felt proud. Let him judge me. I had nothing to be ashamed of.

"I've heard a lot about you. Owen said you plan to study nonprofit management. Is that right?"

"Yes. I've been accepted to some great programs. It's my dream to develop my leadership skills and business acumen in a mission-driven setting so I can use my skills to have the greatest impact."

A broad smile spread across his face. Like I had passed some kind of test.

"That settles it. You've got to join us at the Boston Cares event tonight. The foundation is connected to every major philanthropic effort in the city. It would be a great networking opportunity for you, and I've got two empty seats at my table."

"Um," I stumbled, my stomach twisting at the prospect.

I wasn't the charity gala type of girl. I was a waitress in a small-town Maine diner, not the kind of accomplished city socialite who belonged on Owen's arm.

"I'm not sure," I hedged, racking my brain for a way to politely decline without insulting him.

I was saved from having to stutter my way through a lame excuse when Owen walked into the conference room.

"Lawyers will be here in twenty minutes." He handed me a cup of coffee, then jerked a thumb at Enzo. "This guy bothering you?"

With a roll of his eyes, Enzo stood and gently punched Owen's shoulder. "I was telling Lila that she must come to the party tonight."

Owen winced. "Don't force her." He pulled out a chair

and sat down across from me, carefully opening his laptop. "We're here to work."

"She's a future nonprofit star. Have you considered how many people we can introduce her to at this single event? You're already here, and there will be free food and alcohol, so why not?" He picked up his coffee and held it out in my direction. "You dragged this poor girl all the way from Maine. Might as well show her a good time."

Owen looked at me, brows furrowed and his mouth pressed into a straight line, as if considering.

As I took him in, I couldn't help but feel a little curious. What would it be like to attend a glitzy event on Owen Hebert's arm?

It only took a moment for reality to sink in, and when it did, I had to keep from slumping in my chair.

"It's so kind of you to include me," I said, "but I didn't pack any gala-appropriate clothing."

I did not *own* any gala-appropriate clothing, so that was a nonstarter. Not that I'd admit that out loud.

Enzo waved a hand. "That's no problem. I live with four women and a couple of billionaires."

I frowned at Owen. *What was he talking about?*

Owen only shrugged and took a long sip of his coffee.

Enzo dug his phone out of his pocket, set his own coffee down again, and tapped at the screen furiously.

Still at a loss, I sat back and watched both men. "I'm confused."

Enzo held up a finger and stared at his phone, as if waiting for a response. Then he nodded so vigorously I worried he'd give himself a headache. "We've got a guy," he said, still texting. "At Saks. Gabriel." He looked up, his brows raised high. "What's your number?"

I rattled it off, worried about what I might be agreeing to by doing so.

"All set. Liv is going to contact you shortly. She'll make sure everything is taken care of."

"Sorry," I said, unease officially settling in my stomach. "I don't follow."

He shook his head and laughed at his phone. Shit, he was even better looking when he laughed.

I could only imagine how women would line up just to watch these two men if they discovered them in the wild.

A pang of jealousy joined the unease brewing inside me.

Owen wasn't mine. He wouldn't ever be.

I swallowed thickly at the thought. "I can't."

He pocketed his phone and leaned down, bracing his strong arms on the table across from me. "Delia really wants to meet you," he said. "Trust me, you're doing me a favor. Because generally, I do everything I can to give her whatever she wants."

Owen laughed and sat back. "How is Medusa these days?"

Enzo's eyes twinkled. "So fucking good, man."

Owen's brows rose, but his only response was a half smile and a nod.

"Career-wise," Enzo said, homing in on me again, "it's great for you. Plus, you'd be helping me out. My mother insisted we buy two tables. One would have been sufficient, but she wouldn't listen to reason. Now she's freaking out about filling them. She doesn't want to be embarrassed in front of Monroe Langfield." He waved a hand, as if I should know who he was talking about and understand. "It's a whole thing. And the last thing I need is my mom teaming up with my girlfriend to kick my ass."

"Owen?" I peered over at him, hoping he'd inject some reality into this conversation.

But he was busy typing away. "It's fine," he said without looking up. "I've got to attend anyway. Just gotta run home and change into my tux."

I turned to him and let out a huff of disbelief. "I'm sorry. You *own* a tuxedo?"

He shrugged, glancing at me, then went back to typing. "This job comes with some obligations."

Enzo laughed and stood up straight. "That's putting it lightly. You really should come along, Lila." He rapped his knuckles on the table. "The food is usually mediocre, but the booze will be top shelf, and it'll give you a chance to rub elbows with the most influential people in Boston. If what Owen's told me about you is true, then I have no doubt that once they meet you, they'll be lining up to offer you jobs."

He was so kind and confident that I should be there. It was hard to argue with him. My stomach twisted into knots at the idea, but I couldn't deny that I was curious. I'd probably never get another opportunity like this, so it would be silly to waste it, right?

Plus, I was dying to see Owen in his tuxedo. I'd need that image to get me through long, lonely nights.

So I pulled my shoulders back and nodded. "Thank you for the invitation," I said in my best pageant queen voice. "I'd love to attend."

Enzo's face lit up. "We'll have a great time. The girls are gonna love you." Snatching up his coffee again, he headed to the door. "I'll let you guys get ready for your meeting. This is so great. Oh, and Lila," he said from the doorway. "Do you prefer baseball or hockey?"

"Not sure," I said, tilting my head in confusion. "Why?"

"So I know who to introduce you to. I'd be shocked if all the pro athletes in attendance weren't lining up to ask you out tonight."

With that, he shot me a grin and closed the door.

Mind spinning, I looked at Owen, who was violently typing away on his computer, his face red with anger.

Huh. This trip was about to get a lot more interesting.

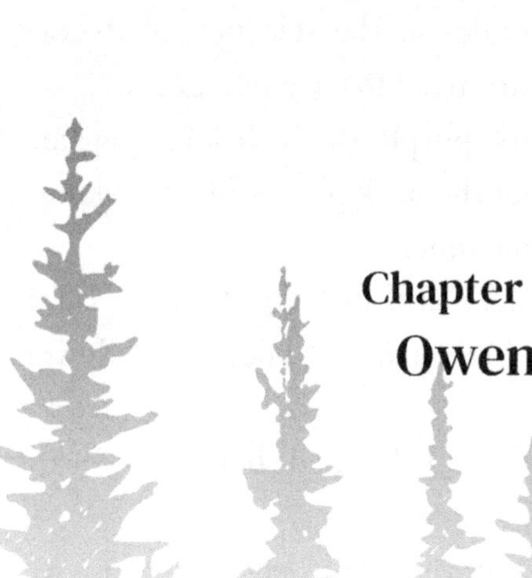

Chapter 21
Owen

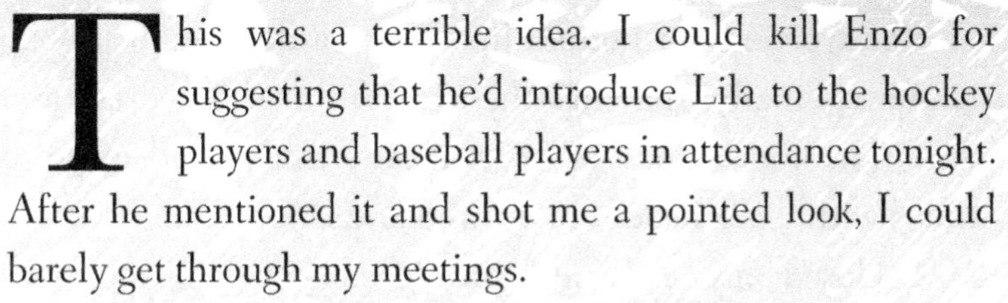

This was a terrible idea. I could kill Enzo for suggesting that he'd introduce Lila to the hockey players and baseball players in attendance tonight. After he mentioned it and shot me a pointed look, I could barely get through my meetings.

And then I had to sit on my couch while Lila tried on a bunch of dresses, each more gorgeous and sexy than the last. Each time she'd disappear into the guest room to change, my heart would take off in anticipation. And each time she'd come out to ask my opinion, I'd have to hold my breath and silently tell my dick to stand down.

I swore Enzo was straight-up fucking with me.

I'd punch him, but Delia would be at the event, and I knew better than to piss her off.

And I'd be too distracted by Lila's presence to remember anyway. After our meeting, we headed back to my building, where my doorman informed us that several garments and shopping bags had been delivered.

Lila had lit up in wonder at the selection of dresses, shoes, and purses Liv had arranged to have sent over.

She'd settled on a dark purple dress. It was long and simple, with cap sleeves, but the back plunged low, making it demure and sexy at the same time.

While Lila fixed her hair and makeup, I texted Linda with instructions to send Liv a massive bouquet of flowers tomorrow to thank her.

"You okay?" I asked as I handed her coat to the attendant.

"Yes." She nodded, but the smile she gave me was uncertain.

I cocked a brow and waited for her to elaborate.

She worried her bottom lip and regarded me for a long moment. Finally, she smoothed the front of her dress and said, "I'm not a fancy event girl. Any time I had to go to things with Cole, he left me behind and ignored me."

I closed my eyes and promised not to fly into a murderous rage even as fury coursed through me. Every single time she mentioned that dipshit, I disliked him more. Which was a feat because, after his mini crime spree, he was at the top of my shit list already.

"I won't leave your side," I said, patting her arm. "And we don't have to stay long. We can leave before they serve dinner if you want. We could be out of here and back in my condo in sweats in fifteen minutes."

She turned and straightened my bow tie, giving me the sweetest smile. Damn, she was gorgeous. She was always beautiful, but her shimmery eyes and glossy lips mesmerized me every time I looked at her tonight.

"Have I told you how handsome you look?" she said, brushing at my lapels.

"Only fifteen times." I shot her a grin.

Lila had been complimenting my tux since I pulled it out of my closet. With her on my arm, I felt like James Bond striding into this party.

"And you are drop-dead gorgeous," I said, tilting my head so I could get closer to her. "You look like a princess, but not one of those lame, helpless ones. You're like a badass princess."

"I did pack my hip daggers," she joked, eyes dancing.

"I'd expect nothing less from the Maple Sugar Queen."

I offered my arm, and she took it, and then we strode into the ballroom.

"Princess," she corrected as we maneuvered around people. "Miss Maple Princess."

"Nope." I shook my head. "You've been promoted to queen."

I was practically floating tonight, full of pride, as I introduced Lila to my life and showed her my home and my business. The things I'd accomplished.

In Lovewell, it was hard not to feel like a stumbling failure, but in Boston, I was someone. Not a big deal like Enzo or his rich friends, but a man who had made a place for himself in this world.

Lila wasn't the kind of woman to be seduced by glitz and glamour, but even so, she was wide-eyed and excited.

As I steered her toward the bar, heads turned, and I'd definitely noticed a couple of photographers point their cameras in our direction. Before Amara could swoop in and steal her away, and before Enzo's brownstone roommates found us and circled like vultures, I wanted a few minutes alone with her.

I ordered two glasses of champagne, and we toasted.

"To grad school success," I said, clinking her glass.

"Can we talk about your success for a second?"

She licked a drop of champagne off her bottom lip, and the room spun around me. I'd probably give her my social security number and bank PIN if she asked while licking champagne off her glossy lips. Who knew I was a lip guy?

"I heard that name, GeneSphere, thrown around all day, but I don't actually know what you've been doing."

"We call it a skyline project. A building so significant that it will alter the skyline of the city." I rubbed at the back of my neck, suddenly a little uncomfortable. I didn't want her to think I was bragging, but I was damn proud of this project. "Long after we're gone, this building will be part of Boston, the fabric and the visual of our city and what it represents."

Her eyes were wide and full of honest excitement. "Wow."

"We've been working on it for almost three years. When we first bid, we were underdogs. Enzo had just taken over the company, and it was a big swing. A brand-new multi-building research facility and campus for one of the world's largest biotech companies. It was a dream come true."

She grasped my forearm. "It's incredible. And you guys did it."

I laughed. "Sort of. We're mid-build right now, which is when the shit usually hits the fan. We've encountered so many setbacks, permit issues, weather, a couple of strikes. You name it, and we've faced it. But we're close to the finish line. And then these buildings will be there for generations to come, and all our hard work will have been worth it."

"You know, deep down, I think you're a romantic, Owen Hebert."

A surprised huff escaped me. "Me?"

"Yup. Maybe not in the cheesy, stereotypical way, but no one could do what you do and not be. Putting in years of hard work and sacrifice for the skyline of the city you love?" She splayed a hand over her heart. "It's beautiful."

Her words ricocheted through me, lighting me up. Lila found the beauty and the good in everyone and everything. Even me, a grumpy thirty-eight-year-old accountant.

I surveyed her, memorizing the lines of her gorgeous face, racking my brain for a response. But words escaped me. All I could think was that I was so happy to be standing here with her. This tiny moment in the grand scheme of my life somehow felt significant.

"There you are."

Amara's words jolted me out of my stupor. I sucked in a breath and blinked, only then realizing she was standing beside us.

"Lila." She threw her arms around her and gushed. "I have been waiting to meet you."

God, she had the worst timing. This woman lived to mess with me. I didn't have an annoying little sister, but with her around, I didn't need one.

"Lila, this is Amara DiLuca, our general counsel and Enzo's sister."

She elbowed me. "And one of Owen's closest friends. You're so pretty. Let me introduce you to everyone." She looped her arm through Lila's. "My mother is dying to meet you."

My stomach bottomed out. Mama DiLuca was a force to be reckoned with. She'd probably have Lila and me married by dessert.

Without giving either of us a chance to object, Amara dragged Lila away. As I watched them go, that dread morphed into something like hope or anticipation. Because it wouldn't be the worst thing in the world if I got to keep her.

Only Lila did not want to be kept. My brother had learned that lesson the hard way, but I was determined to protect myself. It was one more reason to resent Cole. He'd had so many years with her, years he wasted and didn't appreciate, while I would likely only get tonight.

Lila working the room at a Boston charity fundraiser like a professional socialite was a sight to behold. She charmed every person I introduced her to, asked thoughtful questions, and left an incredible impression each time.

My chest was so filled with pride I thought I might burst.

She didn't have the first clue how spectacular she was. How smart and capable she was. Hopefully being here, even if only for a couple of days, could remind her of that.

My heart sank. A couple of days. That was all we had here. Soon, she'd be headed to New York, where she'd no doubt kick ass and have a line of young, successful guys desperate for a chance with her.

I clenched my fists at my sides and choked back the jealousy clawing its way up my insides. I couldn't logic myself out of this, no matter how hard I tried.

Lila wasn't mine. And I had no right to even consider the possibility.

I should be grateful to have this night with her. To be the one standing by her side as she blossomed.

This woman was going to take over the world, and I'd hold on to the knowledge that I played the smallest role in her journey. She'd do anything she strived for. Hell, I wouldn't be surprised if she was running the Boston Cares Foundation someday.

It was a relief to be the one smiling and supporting tonight. All I had to do was stand by her side and let her shine. Funny enough, I'd be very happy doing that for the rest of my damn life.

Enzo and Delia had been placed at our table, along with two of Enzo's sisters and their husbands. She bonded with Delia over their mutual love of old houses and charmed Amara with her encyclopedic knowledge of some television show I'd never heard of about teenagers in Southern California. She even suffered through thirty minutes of Enzo showing her photos of a robot he was building with Delia's twins. At one point, she had the DiLuca sisters taking silly selfies and texting them to their kids.

We danced, we laughed, and we suffered through the speeches together. As Delia entertained us with a story about her brilliant twin daughters, Lila reached under the table and squeezed my hand.

This was it. The thing I'd been looking for. The feeling of contentment that came from being in her proximity.

Usually, I was bored to tears at events like this. I felt like an idiot in a tux, and I had to make nice with a bunch of powerful people I wasn't overly fond of. But tonight, I was having a blast.

With Lila, I danced and chatted and enjoyed every minute.

After she'd squeezed my hand, all I could focus on was her smooth skin and her curves in that dress, even as the rest of the table fell into a fit of laughter as Delia talked about her twins and how their lifelong goal was to control the robots of the world. So, in an effort to control myself, I headed to the bar to get my girl a refill.

"You should come to the game tomorrow."

I turned at the sound of the voice and found Beckett Langfield standing next to me, slowly swirling his whiskey glass. It wasn't a question. It was a command. Which wasn't surprising, coming from him.

"Damiano is pitching. You haven't been to the box in a while." Langfield owned the MLB team here in Boston, and I'd been invited to watch a few games in the owner's box before.

"I'm not sure," I hedged.

"Bring your girl. It's a casual thing. The kids will be running wild, as usual. And the weather is supposed to be perfect."

I surveyed the table where Lila was deep in conversation. She sat straight, looking far more comfortable than anyone had the right to be in formalwear. Her legs were crossed, showing one creamy thigh through the slit of that purple dress.

When she threw her head back with laughter, it was as if

we were tethered. The movement and the pure joy in her expression made my blood sing in my veins. Just seeing her across the room took away all the tension that had been weighing on me.

She turned and caught my eye, as if she could feel the way I soaked her in, even in a large ballroom filled with hundreds of people.

I didn't turn away. I couldn't take my eyes off her even if I wanted to. Was I a creep? Yes. But I was also desperate to soak up every moment with her I could get.

Beckett tilted his head and assessed me. Then he shook it and held up his whiskey between us. "You're so fucked."

I didn't bother turning away from Lila. Yeah. I absolutely was.

He patted my shoulder. "Your VIP passes will be at will call. Don't be late. First pitch is at one."

Once Beckett had wandered back to his table, I composed myself and returned to my own, only to be dragged onto the dance floor. Holding Lila felt like heaven, and dancing with her in my arms easily topped it. The smell of her up close, the feel of her in my arms, was a high I'd never experienced.

I'd only just gotten my head in check at the bar, and, already, it was in the damn clouds again. So when the song ended, and before the band had moved on to the next, I excused myself. I needed a bit of distance before I did something stupid like kiss her, or worse, get down on one knee and propose on the spot. Because I was fully smitten. The excitement of the evening and the thrill of finally being back where I belonged were making me reckless and stupid.

"Are we going to talk about this?" Enzo asked, holding out a glass of whiskey as he sidled up beside me.

On the dance floor, Lila was dancing with a group of women to an acoustic version of a Rhianna song.

"You're in love with her," he said when I didn't respond.

I did my best to remain stoic, even as pain lanced my chest. But this was my best friend.

It was no use even trying.

"No. I'm infatuated with her."

He chuckled darkly into his glass. "Same thing."

"Not even close."

He wiped his mouth with the back of his hand and cocked a brow at me. "You want to be in denial, that's your business. But a few months ago, you and I were standing at a similar event, wearing the same tuxes and probably drinking this damn Hanson whiskey. Remember that? You called me out on my bullshit that night when you caught me drooling over Delia and finding every excuse imaginable to spend more time with her."

God, he had been so ridiculous. "You were out of your mind, dude. You couldn't keep your tongue in your mouth when you were in the same room as her."

He laughed. "Still can't, my friend. She puts my tongue to good use now, though." He raised his glass toward where his girlfriend was now dancing barefoot. "I'll say this once. Go after what you want. Even if it's terrifying."

My stomach was already twisted into knots, but just the thought had them tightening. "I can't."

"Bullshit. Remember when we were debating about whether we should bid on GeneSphere? We didn't think we could do it. We didn't think we could manage a project of this size. But then we said *fuck it. It's a chance to make a lasting impact on this city*. We knew we had to get out of our own way." He nudged me. "That girl over there, she's a risk. But I see the way you're looking at her. You've talked of no one else for weeks. Don't think for a second I haven't noticed. Hell, I'd bet part of the reason you haven't come home yet is because you want to spend time with her."

I held up a hand and shook my head. "There have been issues with the sale."

"Which you could handle from Boston." He gave me a challenging look. "Admit it. You're gone for her. I'd be a terrible best friend if I didn't tell you to take your shot." He handed me his empty glass and straightened his cuffs. "Now, if you'll excuse me, I've got to take my woman home."

With that, he waded into the throng of women, threw his arm around Delia's shoulders, and kissed her. As if that was a signal they'd agreed upon before the event, she instantly turned to her friends and waved goodbye.

I swirled the whiskey in my glass and considered his words. Would it be so bad to take a shot? I didn't have a lot of time left, and being here, surrounded by my friends, in my home city, bolstered my courage.

Moments later, Lila was hugging some of her new friends and heading toward me, her shoes dangling from her fingers.

"Tired?" I asked.

She threaded her arm through mine. "Yes." She sighed. "Also, I was under the impression that people were expected to keep their shoes on at fancy parties."

I shook my head. "Not when Dylan is here. She's begun a barefoot dancing revolution. For the last year or so, at every black-tie event she's been to, she's gotten everyone to take their shoes off. It's her thing."

She smiled as she took in the glowing redhead who was wearing her infant daughter in some kind of complicated fabric wrap and was slow dancing with her fiancé.

Dylan and Cortney, who was a retired MLB catcher and was now the GM for the Boston Revs, were two more of Enzo's roomies. Their infant daughter and teenage son lived with them as well.

"Owen."

I bowed my head and took her in. She was all pink cheeks and misty eyes and her usually bright smile. Fuck, she was gorgeous. "Yes, Lila."

"It may be the champagne talking, but I like your fancy friends."

With her arm still tucked in mine, I led her to the coat check.

While we waited for the attendant to retrieve them, she beckoned with her finger, and I bent down to get closer.

"And," she whispered, her lips just millimeters from my ear, "I think I like you too."

I blew out a long breath and stayed where I was so she couldn't see the effect her words had on me.

Once I was certain I had control over my expression, I pulled back. "How are your feet?"

"Killing me. The thought of putting these shoes back on makes me want to chop them right off."

"We're only two blocks from my condo. Want a piggyback?"

When Enzo had roped Lila into coming, I would never have guessed my night would end with me, still decked out in a tuxedo, giving her a piggyback ride through the Seaport District.

But I couldn't think of a more perfect way to end our night.

"Are you sure I'm not hurting you?" Her lips were dangerously close to my ear again.

Clearing my throat, I leaned forward and pushed the elevator call button. "Not at all."

That wasn't entirely accurate, but I'd happily gallivant around the city with Lila clinging to me until my bones turned to dust.

The feel of her body against mine, the way her arms wrapped around me, was intoxicating. I'd never felt stronger or more masculine. That, combined with the whiskey, was sending my caveman urges into overdrive.

Once we were inside my condo, I crouched and supported her as she slid to her feet. The instant our connection was broken, the Neanderthal buzz wore off. What was I thinking? That she'd tear off that sexy dress and beg me to make her mine?

She was glowing, she'd had fun, and she'd been drinking. So I'd do the right thing. No matter how much it would kill me.

I shoved my hands into my pockets, suddenly feeling the weight of all my expectations come crashing down on me. "Can I get you anything? Water? Tea?"

She blinked up at me for a beat before her face fell.

Shit. I'd done the wrong thing.

She shook her head. “I just need to get out of this dress and take off my makeup.”

“Okay,” I choked out, feeling awkward as fuck and unable to formulate any sort of plan. I wanted to know what she was thinking. Or, more importantly, what she was feeling.

Because I was feeling all the things.

Chapter 22
Lila

My face burned with humiliation. After the night we'd had, I was sure he would make a move. I'd flirted with him and danced with him, throwing out all the signals. Did I need to wear a flashing sign that said *tear my clothes off, please*?

Grumbling to myself, I unzipped the dress and laid it on the bed. I had no idea how I'd pay for it. The dresses had just appeared, and the doorman had taken the ones I didn't want before we left. But there was no returning this one now. It hadn't been marked with a price tag, but I wasn't dumb, and I wasn't interested in charity.

But that was tomorrow's problem.

Tonight, I was frustrated.

Sexually frustrated.

Anger coursed through me as I undressed and threw on an old T-shirt, then stomped to the en-suite bathroom.

Why was this so hard?

I cared about him so much, and I wanted more. But I couldn't get out of my own damn way.

I was tired of playing it safe all the time. Being a good girl.

Worrying about what other people wanted and thought.

Ignoring my gut.

My gut that was, at the moment, telling me to take the leap.

And I swore Willa and Magnolia were perched on my shoulders, like an angel and a devil—only neither was being very angelic—urging me to take what I wanted.

So I washed my face, brushed my teeth, and formulated a plan.

Once I was fresh-faced, I marched out the door and across the living room to Owen's bedroom. I didn't stop, afraid that if I did, I'd talk myself out of it. So I pushed the door open without knocking. The moment my feet sank into the plush carpet of his room, I came to an abrupt halt.

He was standing near his bed wearing a pair of boxer briefs and nothing else.

"Lila?" he said, his eyes wide. "You all right?"

I didn't respond. I was too busy processing the sight of him almost naked in front of me. The broad, strong chest. The thick thighs. The heat that ignited in his eyes as they roved over me.

Overwhelmed, I strode straight for him, and once we were toe to toe, I threw my arms around his shoulders, popped up on my toes, and kissed him.

For a split second, his body went rigid, and I was sure he'd step back. Instead, he clung to me and pulled me flush against his body.

"What are you doing?" he asked into my mouth, his voice low and husky.

I pulled back a fraction. "I can't lie in the guest room all night thinking about how I want to be in here with you." I inhaled a steadying breath. "I'm tired of playing it safe. I'm taking what I want."

He put his hands on my shoulders and pushed me back a bit. "This isn't a good idea."

I popped up on my tiptoes again and kissed his jaw while trailing my fingertips down his chest until they landed on the waistband of his boxers. He was hard against my stomach and swelling with every second we were pressed together. Knowing I had such a visceral effect on him sent a surge of power through me. He wanted this too. It was time to stop letting all the bullshit life threw at us stand in our way.

"I don't care. We're not in Lovewell, Owen. Tonight, I got to be the best version of myself, and that's all thanks to you. You inspire me and push me. I'm tired of pretending I'm not wildly attracted to you."

With a single step back, I pulled my T-shirt over my head and tossed it to the floor. Chin tipped high, I stood before him in nothing but a pair of panties.

"Fuck." He hissed. "Are you seducing me, Lila?"

Pressing my teeth into my lower lip, I nodded. "Are you going to let me? Or should I beg?"

He threw his head back and groaned. "How are you so perfect?"

I stepped in close, pressing my breasts against his warm, naked chest, and kissed him, long and deep.

"How am I supposed to control myself with you?" he

asked against my mouth, skimming his hands up my hips and ribs and settling on my breasts. "How can I hold back?"

"Don't," I said, shimmying out of my panties. "Just don't do it. Control is overrated."

Blue eyes lit with desire, he brought his fist to his mouth and took me in.

"Don't hold anything back. What if we're completely real with one another? No pretense, no artifice, just authenticity."

With a grunt, he picked me up and carried me to the bed. "I've never felt this way with anyone." He gently guided me to the mattress and hovered over me. "I'm more myself when I'm with you."

"Same," I whispered as he lowered himself on top of me, kissing my neck and exploring my naked body. "And if I don't take this chance, I know I'll regret it. The connection I feel with you is special, and, just for one night, I'd like to be yours."

"So that's what you want? For me to make you mine?"

"Yes, please." I arched off the bed, moaning. "Make me yours, Owen."

His hands roamed hungrily over my body as we kissed. His weight pinned me to the bed, his skin pressed to mine driving me wild with lust. This feeling, the need, the want. It was exhilarating.

His stubble scraped deliciously along my neck as he kissed his way down, teasing, torturing.

I wiggled beneath him, angry that he was having all the fun.

My fight was interrupted, though, when he grasped my

wrists and pinned them above my head. "If you're not going to behave," he growled. "I'll have to punish you."

Heat flooded my core. My brain didn't have the first clue what that might entail, but my throbbing clit did.

"I just want to touch you," I whispered, wiggling beneath him.

Keeping my arms immobilized with one hand, he used the other to grab my chin so I was looking straight at him.

"Since the moment you first walked into that office building, I've been thinking of your naked body under mine. I've waited so long for this moment. You're going to be a good girl and let me play."

Holy bossy Batman. My body lit up at the demanding tone. There was nothing tentative about his touch. He knew what he was doing and did it well. Unlike the reserved man I'd come to know, bedroom Owen was all confidence, especially as he kissed, licked, and nipped his way down my body.

When he took one nipple into his mouth, biting down, I arched off the bed.

"Oh yes. God, these are perfect. You have no idea how crazy you make me. How badly I've craved your body." He trailed his hand down my stomach, idly stroking my inner thighs.

My eyes rolled back at the sensation. "Please." I gasped as he scraped his beard over my sensitive nipples. "Touch me."

"I've waited so long for you to say that."

He pushed my legs open with his knee and teased me with his fingers, making me writhe with anticipation. His fingers were gentle but firm, giving me just enough to drive me wild but not provide any satisfaction.

"Patience," he growled, nipping at my earlobe. "You're so damn wet."

He slid a finger inside me. It wasn't nearly enough, but I moaned at the friction, relishing the tingles that worked their way through me. But then he pulled away quickly, leaving me bereft.

He brought that finger to his lips and licked it. "Fucking delicious," he declared with a smirk. "You gonna let me eat your pussy, Lila?"

"Later." I'd never been into oral. I always felt guilty, like the guy was doing me a favor. I'd rather just get to the main event, especially since I was more than ready. "I want to feel you inside me."

His eyes widened. "I want you warmed up first." His hand returned, fingers teasing my clit. "If you won't let me taste you, at least ride my hand a little."

Before I could object, he slipped two fingers inside me, and I temporarily lost the ability to speak. Goddamn, he was good with his hands. He used his fingers and the heel of his palm against my clit, making it impossible to argue with him.

"That's it," he said, curling his fingers and ratcheting up the tension building inside me. "Oh, I can feel you clenching my fingers. Right there, keep going. Come for me."

As if my body was desperate to follow his every command, I hurtled toward the edge. I closed my eyes and cried out, pleasure mounting as I gripped the sheets and arched my back.

My mind went blank as the pleasure washed over me.

"Fuck," he growled, still stroking my clit as I shivered beneath him. "Even more gorgeous than I imagined."

Panting, shaking, totally wrecked, I opened my eyes and tried to find my bearings.

Owen was sitting back on his knees, stroking his hard cock. The sight alone almost sent me over the edge again.

"God, this view," he said, his blue eyes ablaze. "You. Lying on my bed, naked and spent. Dream come true."

I pushed up onto my elbows, the heat pooling inside me going molten, and palmed his cock. When he groaned in response, my heart flipped over itself.

With a hum, I slid my hand down his thick length, loving the feel of him. "What else did you dream about?" I asked, watching his chest rise and fall as he fought to keep control.

"You riding me." He panted. "Lying back and watching you come on my cock."

I pushed up to sitting, then pressed a hand against his chest, gently forcing him to lie back, then leaned down to kiss him.

"Condoms?"

He nodded toward the bedside table.

Once I'd pulled one from the box, I straddled him, tore the foil, and carefully rolled the condom down his length.

I positioned myself over him, keeping my focus locked on his face and reveling in the power of this position. His eyes were hooded and his chest was heaving as he watched me just as intently. He wanted this just as badly as I did.

With one hand flat against his chest, I slowly lowered myself onto him. Beneath me, he tensed, gripping my hips and guiding me until I had taken every single inch of him.

Once I was fully seated, I let out a long breath, adjusting

to his size. Then I started to rock gently, letting myself warm up.

He groaned, pulling me down for a kiss as I circled my hips, increasing my speed.

My eyes were scrunched shut as I worked his length, pausing to find the perfect angle and fighting not to lose myself in the feeling of being so full.

"Eyes on me," he growled, snaking his hand up my chest to grip my chin hard.

I obeyed, taking in the hard lines of his face and the desire in his eyes.

"Look at me, Lila. I need to see you when you take my cock."

His words sent a shock straight to my clit, urging me to arch my back and grind against him. My God, this felt incredible.

Not one to sit back, Owen slid a hand down to my breast, teasing one nipple, then the other.

I worked myself over his length, throwing my head back and letting my body take over.

His hands went to my ass, gripping me hard as I found a rhythm. "That's it," he encouraged. "Take what you need."

The muscles in his neck and shoulders went taut as he tilted his head back. He was close, but he was holding back.

I knew what he wanted, and I wasn't sure I could get there. Not twice. Even so, this felt so good, and I was beginning to think it may be possible.

"Don't overthink. Just feel." He trailed his fingers around my hip and put pressure on my clit.

Instantly, a jolt shot through my body.

"Let go. Just let it all go."

I rolled my head back as I let the sensations caused by his cock, fingers, and words wash over me.

I increased the pace, feeling all my nerve endings light up as I got closer.

And then I let go.

Of my self-consciousness.

My doubts.

My anxiety about what this all meant.

And I soared, crying out as the wave broke over me, freeing me from all the baggage I'd been carrying.

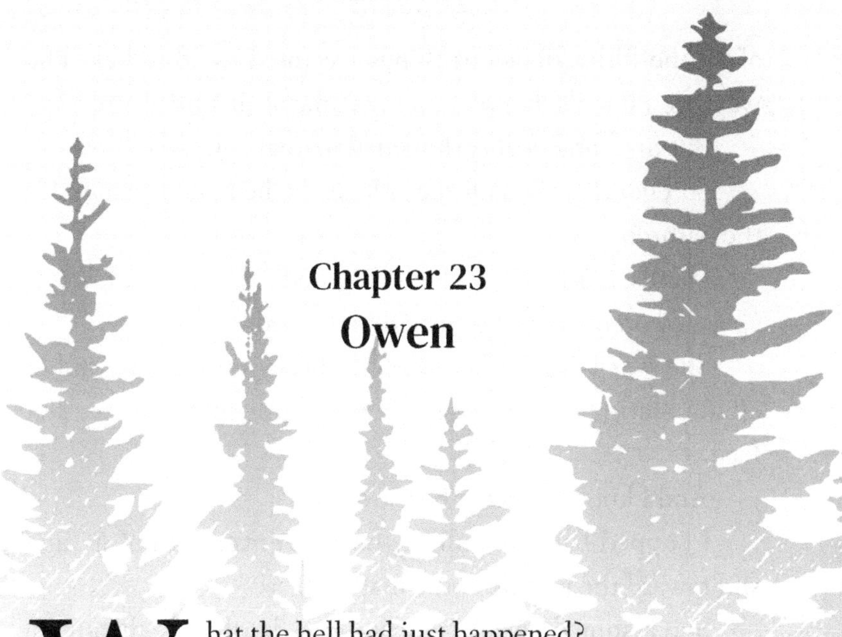

Chapter 23
Owen

What the hell had just happened?

I squeezed my eyes shut, certain this had been a really good, exquisitely detailed dream. Except the woman snuggled into my chest proved that it was real fucking life.

I didn't want to move or speak for fear of ruining the moment. Lila had walked into my goddamn bedroom and stripped off her clothes.

Begged me to fuck her.

And then it finally happened.

My life had been changed. The moment I got up from this bed—and I really needed to deal with this condom—I would be changed.

I'd been lusting after her for weeks, thinking my need unbearable. But the joke was on me, because now that I'd had a taste of Lila, my desire had been fully unleashed.

The post-orgasmic haze was dampened by my racing thoughts. Thoughts of how badly I wanted her again. Visions of all the filthy, delicious things I wanted to do to her. The way I could make her scream my name again and again.

But first, practicality. I needed to deal with this.

So I gently rolled off the side of the bed and sprinted for the bathroom.

Hands washed, condom disposed of, and cold water splashed on my face, I returned to the bed.

She was lying on her side, her head propped up on her elbow, staring at me. Slowly, a wide grin spread across her face.

And I knew I'd never be the same.

I hopped back in, pulling the duvet over both of us, and slid toward the middle of the mattress.

She assumed her place next to me, her hands already on my chest. God, I could get used to this.

I shifted, pulling her on top of me so I could get a handful of that amazing ass.

"Owen—"

I grasped the back of her neck and gently guided her mouth to mine, shutting her up with a kiss. Her mouth was so soft and perfect.

"Owen." She pushed back and shook her head. "It's late."

If this woman thought I'd be taking my hands off her, she was sorely mistaken. I'd gotten a taste, and I wasn't sure I'd ever be satisfied. The feel of her, the sound of her voice, the way she took charge, and got exactly what she needed. Every facet of her was so fucking hot.

"I'm not tired," I said, arching up to take one of her rosy nipples into my mouth. "And I'm not finished with you yet."

"But—"

The words died on her lips as I bit down gently. Her fingers were in my hair, tugging, driving me wild.

I grinned up at her. "Butt stuff?" I gave her a cocky wink. "Hell yeah. If that's what you're into, I'm down."

Her eyes grew wide with shock. "No," she sputtered. "I mean yes. Shit." She covered her face with her hands, looking so goddamn adorable.

She took a deep breath. "What I meant to say is that you've done enough."

I barked out a laugh and grabbed her hips. Then I flipped her onto her back and hovered over her. "There will never be enough when it comes to you."

She grasped the hair at the back of my head in response, her eyes hooded and her chest rising and falling rapidly.

Game. Fucking. On.

I slid down her body and pushed her legs apart. Then I dipped down and gazed at her perfect pussy.

"What are you doing?" Her voice was breathy.

"I'm a growing boy," I teased, slowly lowering my face. "And I need to eat."

She made an unintelligible sound, but it died on her lips the moment my tongue touched her clit. Just as I suspected, she was sweet, delicious, and responsive to my touch.

I didn't waste any time. I was done teasing. I dove in, spreading her with one hand and licking and sucking like a man obsessed.

Her moans and shaking legs urged me to keep going, and her hands were in my hair again, driving me fucking wild.

"That's it," I urged, suckling at her clit. "Ride my face, Lila. Show me how much you love my tongue."

She moaned in response, tossing her head back and

arching up. Fuck, I felt like a goddamn king. I added one finger, then another, loving the clench of her muscles as I worked my mouth over her.

This was actual heaven. There was no doubt in my mind I'd never find anything like this again. Every gasp, every moan, urged me to keep going, to give her everything I had so she could understand just how badly I needed her.

"Ah, shit. Owen," she cried as her body began to convulse. There was no better feeling in the world. I kept going, focusing on feeling every single tremor as she came all over my face, bucking and writhing. I held her down, continuing to use my tongue and fingers until she was fully spent.

When she'd gone boneless, I sat back, admiring my work. Lila, arms thrown out, eyes closed and panting. Her legs were spread wide and her pussy was glistening. I had worn her out, and I'd never felt so proud of myself.

I lay down next to her, giving her some space to recover but unable to hide the satisfied grin on my face.

Once her breathing had evened out, she turned to face me. "That," she said, her eyes sparkling, "was incredible." She grabbed my face and kissed me. "I usually don't like oral."

I froze and my stomach bottomed out. How was that possible?

"But you're some kind of expert."

Now that was the best compliment I'd probably ever received. Fuck my diplomas. I wanted that matted, framed, and hung on my office wall.

But I diverted my thoughts back to her comment about not liking oral. Who had she been with? Idiots who couldn't properly worship her gorgeous pussy? I inhaled, ready to rail against them, but stopped when I realized that one of those idiots was my brother.

"You are now my favorite meal. Get used to it, because I'm going to be eating you every day."

She laughed and cupped my cheek. "I wish. But we should talk."

Fuck. My heart sank.

"I think that—well, maybe." She studied me for a moment, worrying her lip. "We don't need to confine this to one night. Maybe we can keep having fun."

My heart soared. Fuck yes. My cock also got the memo, hardening against her stomach with the need to be inside her again.

"Until we go back to Maine."

The damn floating organ plummeted back to earth. Oh shit.

"Enjoy each other for the weekend?"

She was so sweet and hopeful. It was impossible to say no, even if I wanted a hell of a lot more than a weekend.

She walked her fingers down my abdomen, then wrapped that warm hand around my length, making it a lot harder to focus.

I did the math. It was early Saturday morning. We were due to fly home on Sunday at ten. Which gave me approximately thirty-two hours to show Lila how much more I could give her. Prove to her that a weekend would never be enough.

And I was up for that challenge.

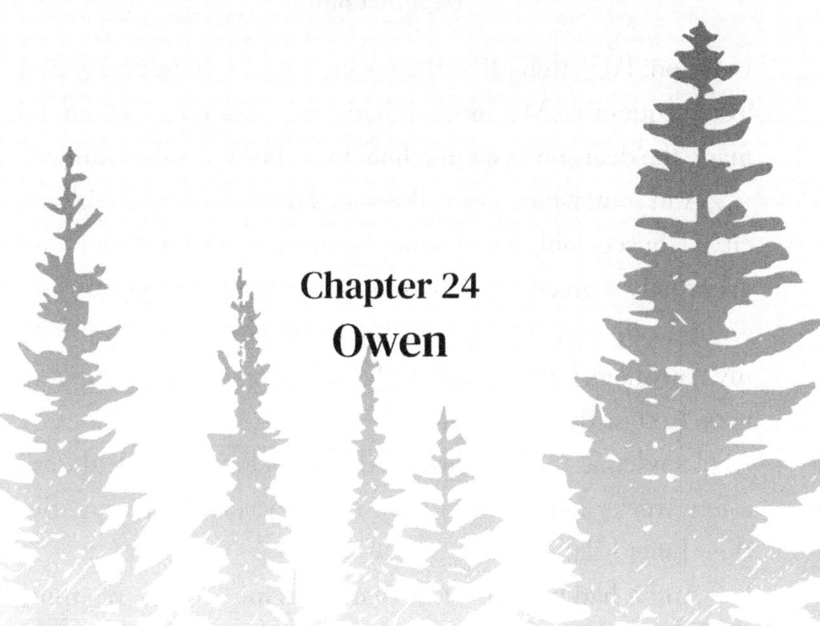

Chapter 24
Owen

I'd missed this place. The city, my office, my apartment, my friends. But we needed to get back to Lovewell today. I had yet to sleep, but as the sky was turning from the darkest shade of blue and the sun was just peeking over the horizon, I poured coffee from the fresh pot into a mug and wandered out to the balcony to watch the sun rise over the harbor.

DiLuca had built this high-rise about seven years ago. Enzo owned the penthouse, but my unit was two floors below. It was too big for just me, but it faced due east, giving me a view of the harbor, the Tobin Bridge, and the most spectacular sunrises. It was clean and modern, and though it was a bit sparse, I was proud of it. It had been my first real adult home. Enzo and I boxed in an old gym a few blocks down the street, and the restaurant on the street level always saved me a seat at the bar when I needed dinner.

When I'd arrived in this city at eighteen, I'd had no clue what I was in for. I'd spent most days feeling overwhelmed.

Early on, I'd gotten off at the wrong subway stops and gotten lost frequently. My mother had been hysterical when I'd made the decision to go to school here, but I was determined.

And somewhere along the way, I'd fallen in love with the city. I bused tables at a fancy restaurant in Back Bay and eventually worked my way up to bartending. I'd get off work around one and then go out for late-night pizza slices with my coworkers before crashing for a few hours and getting up to go to class the next day.

I smiled at the memories. I'd come a long way. And until a few weeks ago, I would have said I was really happy. But then I met Lila.

And it had become clear that I was missing one big thing in my life. Her.

I'd never longed for a girlfriend or a wife—some nameless, faceless idea of a person to fill a void. When I met a woman I liked and had things in common with, I dated, and I was single when it suited me.

I didn't want a girlfriend.

I didn't want a wife.

I wanted Lila.

Only her.

And if my past was any indication, I'd never want anyone else.

This weekend had changed things. It wasn't just the sex, although that part had been incredible. It was how I felt when we were together. How even though we'd spent just about every waking moment in one another's company, I still couldn't get enough. How easy it was to be with her, having fun, working hard, enjoying one another. We'd shared meals and cracked jokes and sifted through endless spreadsheets. We'd danced, and I'd finally been able to hold her close.

It was so damn perfect I had to pinch myself in order to make sure it had really happened.

Once we'd given in to our mutual attraction, it was almost impossible to stop. For a few hours, we managed to get dressed and act appropriately at the baseball game Beckett had summoned us to. But the moment the game ended, we ran back here and tore each other's clothes off.

Last night, we'd sat on this balcony, eating gluten-free pizza at one a.m. and swapping stories about growing up in Lovewell. Intimacy—something I'd always struggled with—was so easy with her. We were honest and vulnerable. We laughed and fooled around and watched movies. She teased me and wore my shirts, and already my condo felt less empty.

But now we had to go back to Lovewell. And reality.

"Owen?"

My heart stuttered at the sound of her voice. I shifted in my chair and found her standing in the doorway, wearing one of my DiLuca Construction hoodies and nothing else. Her hair was messy and there were sleep lines on her face. God, I was so fucking lucky.

I tilted my head, inviting her to join me on the balcony.

She sat and pulled her legs up under the hoodie. "Wow. This is beautiful," she said softly as a large cargo plane flew overhead on its way to Logan Airport.

"You're beautiful," I countered, unembarrassed by my cheesiness. "Come here." I patted my thigh.

Instead of getting up to snuggle with me, she sighed and gave me a pained look.

Oh shit. That simple look was enough to make dread curdle in my stomach.

I sat up straight and set my coffee on the small table between our chairs. "You okay?" I'd been so distracted by my thoughts and a night spent with Lila that I'd missed something.

She sighed. "I just think we should talk."

I held my breath and waited for the axe to drop. Whatever was wrong, I doubted my proposed solution of staying here, in my condo, forever, would be well received.

She brought her knees up closer, my sweatshirt creating a cocoon around her body.

My heart sank. Her defensive posture told me everything I needed to know.

"I've had so much fun."

"But?" I whispered as an ache formed behind my ribs.

"But I think we need to make sure we're on the same page before we head back to Maine."

"And which page would that be?" The words were harsher than I meant them, but I couldn't help myself. I was sleep-deprived, and my brain was still flooded with oxytocin after spending a dream weekend with my dream girl.

She pinned me with a chiding look, and damn if my cock didn't thicken at the reprimand. I considered picking her up, carrying her back to bed, and eating her delicious pussy until she saw sense. Instead, I laced my fingers over my abdomen and waited.

"I care about you so much," she said, resting her chin on her knees so her hair fell around her face like a curtain. She sniffled and wiped at what might have been a tear with the sleeve of my sweatshirt. "This weekend was amazing. More than amazing. Being here with you, seeing the city and being part of your life for a couple of days, has meant everything to me."

I swallowed as a lead ball sank in my gut. God, I'd been given the most incredible chance with the most incredible woman, and I'd managed to fuck it up. "Tell me what you want, Lila."

"It's not about what I want," she said, giving me a sad smile. "It's about what I need. I need to preserve the amazing memory of this weekend. I need to hold on to the connection we've shared."

Hold on to our connection? That was exactly what I wanted, yet her resignation said that she and I had different definitions of that phrase. "But it can't continue?"

She shook her head. "The last thing I need is to face the firing squad in town when it gets out that I've hooked up with my ex's older brother."

Hooked up? The words hit me like a punch to the gut. Here I was, mooning over her, feeling like I'd found *the one*, and, to her, I was nothing more than a casual hookup.

"My brother got you for eight years," I spat, the anger inside me bubbling up. "And I only get a weekend?"

The moment the words came out of my mouth, I wished I could breathe them back in. God, I hated myself right now. I sounded exactly like Cole; selfish and petty.

Her face fell. "Is that what I am to you? A trophy? A revenge fuck? A toy you want to steal from your little brother?"

"No. Of course not." I shook my head. "Lila, I'm sorry."

She held up a hand. "That was shitty, Owen. The

circumstances then and now are vastly different. You should be able to understand that."

I put my head in my hands and cursed. God, I was making this worse. "I'm so sorry. I'm spiraling. I've got feelings for you. Real, complicated feelings. And I guess I saw this weekend as the start of something."

She lowered her gaze. "We can't start anything. I'm moving to New York in August. And you're coming back here in a couple of weeks."

"I don't care," I said. "I don't care what people say or what they think. And I don't care if we live hours apart. You're amazing, and I want to spend as much time with you as I can."

"We're both so busy, and I can't risk any more drama. We've had so much fun together." That brought a sparkle to her eye that, even through her tears, told me she'd like to have a lot more fun.

I'd happily oblige.

I opened my mouth but snapped it shut again quickly. Nothing I could say right now would change her mind. The sadness etched into every line on her face made me want to hold her close and never let go.

She averted her gaze and clasped her hands in front of her. "We can still be friends."

"I'm a shitty friend."

"No, you're not. All weekend, I met person after person who adores and respects you. You have no idea how lucky you are. You've built an incredible life for yourself. I'm proud of you, and I hope you can leave all the Lovewell bullshit behind soon and get back here."

"The bullshit is so much more bearable when I'm with you."

"I'm not going anywhere. We're weeks away from closing this deal. Then you can go back to your life, and I'll go start mine."

I leaned back in my chair, pinching the bridge of my nose. There was nothing I could say that would change her mind. If I knew one thing, it was this woman was determined. And what did I have to offer her anyway?

"We should get packed up," I said, standing so quickly my cold coffee sloshed over the rim of my mug and onto my sweats. "Car service is picking us up at nine."

Chapter 25
Lila

I needed to run. Every muscle fiber in my body twitched with tension. It took all my self-control not to grab Owen by his handsome face and stick my tongue down his throat.

God, that man.

He was so controlled, so careful. He did everything with precision and care and never raised his voice.

He didn't have to. He emanated power and brilliance.

But he had one weakness. Me.

And it thrilled me.

I was drunk on the power. Knowing that his superhuman self-control wavered when he got too close.

If I were a different type of woman, I could abuse that power and use it for my own orgasmic gain.

But I had a plan. And as much as I ached for him, I had to stick to it.

I had promised myself that I wouldn't get sidelined by

dick. Even good dick. And Owen was *the best* dick. Not that I'd tell him that. His ego didn't need the stroking.

So far, after our incredible weekend, I'd kept my distance. But the memories just refused to fade. Hell, I still had beard burn on my inner thighs.

But we kept growing closer, and it was getting increasingly harder to stand my ground. With each minute I spent with him, I cared about him more and more.

After so many years of letting life steamroll me, I'd set a boundary. Not just with him, but with myself. NYU was only a few months away, so I didn't have to fight this too much longer.

Saturdays at Hebert Timber were quiet. Typically, Owen and I were the only ones in the building. He'd be in eventually, but I'd come early to get a run in first, hoping it would help me get my head on straight.

After our weekend in Boston, I needed to run farther and faster than usual to shake off the need to be near him. So I headed out, set on physically exhausting myself before facing him.

The Hebert Timber campus was a great spot to run. The paved roads were fairly empty, and the trails heading up through the woods were beautifully maintained. I could go down the airstrip, through the wooded paths, and come out by the lake.

I could get a little fresh air and work up a sweat, and in turn, keep my pants on around Owen.

Running used to be a punishment. I'd push myself to go farther and faster, logging every mile on my calorie app. I'd run a few half marathons, which I despised, and had used early training runs as an excuse to skip out on fun more times than I could count.

But it wasn't until recently that I realized that moving my body could do more than burn calories. And that I could pick the pace that worked best for my mood and goals for the day. In Lovewell, surrounded by breathtaking scenery and serene quiet, running was a great way to get out of my own head.

These days, I rarely ran more than a few miles. I only ran when I wanted to, and I stuck to a pace that my pageant self would have considered a warm-up.

When I came to the end of the paved path, I turned and headed down toward the lake. The trees on either side of the path were just starting to bud. In no time, they'd be in full bloom. My running playlist kept me going, even as I got distracted by my surroundings. My heart lurched and I almost tripped over my feet when movement ahead of me caught my eye.

I pulled up short and froze as I took in the massive moose standing in the middle of the path about ten yards away, blocking my access to the lake.

I stumbled backward, panic rising up inside me. A lone bull moose in the woods was fucking dangerous, and this one was as big as a truck. Sure, moose weren't uncommon, but I'd never been this close to one, and certainly never alone in the damn woods.

I gasped for breath even as I willed my heart to calm and my legs to function so I could head back up the path, hopefully without the beast noticing me.

I'd taken a single step back when he bellowed. A loud, moaning roar.

He turned enough to make the thick scar cutting across his back and hindquarters visible. Shit, it was Clive. The notorious bull who liked to wander around town wreaking havoc on its citizens.

Most moose were afraid of people and didn't come too close to town, but not Clive. He didn't give a shit. I'd heard stories that included him disrupting fireworks shows, crashing weddings, and stealing belongings. They were all so ridiculous it was hard to tell which were truths and which had been made up.

What I did know was that wild animals that were too comfortable around people were more dangerous.

Fuck. This moose could straight-up murder me just for crossing his path.

Okay, new plan.

Slowly back away, cut through the woods if necessary, and avoid detection.

I took a step back, then another, up the hill, sticking close to the tree line in hopes that he wouldn't spot me.

I'd only gone a handful of feet when he grunted and swished his tail. When he turned his enormous head and pinned me with one big moosey eye, my body locked up.

Aw, fuck.

Should I run?

No. I knew better than that. I may have been gone for years, but I was a born-and-bred Mainer. Moose may look slow and lazy, but they could run thirty miles per hour and take out a truck.

This close, I couldn't scramble up a tree fast enough to avoid him if he decided to charge, even if my upper body strength wasn't shit. And out here, there weren't any places to hide.

He made a loud, scary noise, causing me to jump and slap a hand to my chest. Fuck me. I'd rather run up a mountain in hell than tangle with Clive. He had no fear and could gore my ass with minimal effort. The grunt he let out sent snot flying from his massive nostrils, but he didn't come closer.

He moaned again, his focus still fixed on me, as if he was telling me to get the fuck out of his yard.

I was more than happy to oblige, so I backed away slowly again, breathing a sigh of relief when he didn't come closer.

When I made it to the bend in the path, I turned and ran like hell toward the parking lot.

I headed up toward the parking lot, avoiding the airstrip and looping around the machine shop and where the fellers, cranes, and loaders were all parked neatly in rows. I'd become familiar with each of them and their uses over the last few weeks. It was a shame. This place had once been bustling, with employees everywhere.

My heart ached like it always did when I thought about how much the Heberts had lost.

I banked around the building, avoiding the row of dumpsters. Once I was safely behind it, I stopped to catch my breath and tighten my ponytail. Running like hell from a wild beast took a lot out of a girl.

With my hands planted on my knees, I heaved in one deep breath after another. Finally, as my heart rate was returning to normal, I straightened. As I readied to head inside to splash water on my face and chug a bottle of water,

I caught sight of a single boot tipped on its side in the middle of the parking lot.

Frowning, I headed for it. It was clear, as I got closer, that it was a man's hiking boot. And its mate was nowhere to be seen. Weird. I stopped in front of it and scanned the parking lot, a chill going down my spine. There were a few cars parked near mine, which was typical for a Thursday afternoon, but something was off.

Hackles rising, I looked over my shoulder, then slowly toward the main building. I hadn't made it far before my curiosity got the better of me. So with another deep breath, because my heart had taken off at a gallop again, I jogged back around to the shop.

And there, lying next to the row of black dumpsters I'd just hustled past, was—I stopped short. Holy fuck. There, on the ground, was a man. His face was bloody, and he wasn't moving.

Fuck. *Fuck.*

I fumbled to get my phone from my waist pack, my fingers shaking as I unlocked it.

Walking closer, I assessed him. It was impossible to tell if he was dead or alive. I could barely make out his facial features beneath all the blood, and his body was crumpled.

Right in plain sight.

"Nine-one-one. What's your emergency?"

"I'm at the Hebert Timber headquarters," I said, gasping for breath. "There's a man on the ground. He's bleeding."

My brain went offline. Dammit. What was the address of this place? "527 Cumberland Road," I rushed out when it finally came to me. "Down the road past the main building, next to the machine shop."

"Okay, ma'am. Help is on the way. Can you tell whether he's breathing?"

I crept closer and squinted, looking for the rise and fall of his chest. I wished Willa was here. She'd know what to do.

His head was bleeding. That was for sure. As I got closer, I scanned his body, looking for weapons. When I didn't see signs of anything near him, I knelt beside him. I trembled as I put the phone on speaker, set it on the concrete, and stripped off my hoodie. I used the shirt to apply pressure to his head wound, then snaked my fingers to the side of his neck to check for a pulse.

I wasn't entirely sure what I was feeling for, but after a moment, I detected a slight rise and fall of his chest.

He was alive.

Fuck. Now I just had to keep him that way until the ambulance got here.

Ignoring the blood on my hands, I tried again to locate his pulse. The flutter in his neck was faint, but it was there.

My stomach revolted as the coppery scent of blood hit me. I choked back the bile that rose up my esophagus. I would not get sick, and I would not let this random person die on my watch.

I shifted closer, shaking more urgently now, and wiped the blood out of his eyes as best as I could.

He looked like he was a few years older than me, and he was only wearing one boot. Clearly, the other was the one I'd seen in the parking lot.

What the hell had happened? Could he have been hit by a car?

"Please live," I whispered as my eyes welled with tears.

"I don't know you, and you don't know me. But help is on the way. Just hang in there."

By the time I heard sirens, tears were pouring down my face.

Response times weren't spectacular, as was typical in rural towns, but Lovewell had an excellent fire department. Sure enough, the ambulance crested the hill first, followed by a fire truck.

Unsurprisingly, the police were the last to arrive.

The paramedics were out and rounding their vehicle in seconds. I was still on my knees beside the man as they found his pulse, put an oxygen mask on his face, and checked for spinal injuries.

As they worked, they reported to the police officer that there was no phone, wallet, or identification.

Terror washed over me as I took in the scene. How could something like this happen?

I startled when a gentle hand landed on my shoulder. Blinking, I tipped my head back. Rob hovered above me, holding out a hand. Shaking, I slid mine into it and let him help me to my feet and lead me away from the paramedics.

When we were out of the chaos, he stopped and put his hands on my arms. "Are you okay?"

"I—" I shook my head and held my bloody hands out in front of me. "I don't know."

"Okay, let's sit down and get you a coat. Then we can talk."

We were halfway to the entrance when Owen came storming out. He stuttered to a stop when he saw me, and his eyes went wide. Then he broke into a run.

"Can I help you, officer?" His tone was sharp.

"Just taking Lila inside to get warm. Then we'll chat."

"Is that necessary? We have cameras. Gus will be here any minute to assist you."

"She found the body," Rob said firmly.

The two men glowered at one another, neither willing to bend and allow the other to take the lead.

"Owen," I rasped. "Officer Fielder is my ex-stepdad. It's fine." Rob was by far the best of my mom's ex-husbands. They married when I was in junior high, and even after they divorced a few years later, he'd looked out for me.

"Fine." He gave me a sharp nod. "But I'm coming with you."

Chapter 26
Owen

I paced uselessly in front of Lila, offering her gluten-free cookies and water. The police had finally left after several hours, yet she was still wrapped in my jacket and staring at the wall.

Gus had pulled surveillance footage. Whoever had done this had clearly known where the gaps in our cameras were, because all that was visible were the tires of one vehicle and the boot in the middle of the parking lot.

The place was swarming with police, firefighters, and paramedics. On TV, when law enforcement converged, it looked so efficient and coordinated, but in reality, it took forever. After the mystery guy was taken by ambulance to the hospital, the police spent hours taking photos, asking questions, and thoroughly searching every inch of the property.

A police presence was not a new thing for us, unfortunately, but it was still disruptive as hell. The business may be half dead, but we were still trying to operate.

Thankfully, Gus walked the whole area with them, unlocking every garage bay and storage shed we had. He'd spoken calmly to the police and looked at the photos, but was unable to identify the man. I was so far removed from this life that I was no help with identification or details.

The man's face was so beaten it was impossible to say for sure who he was, but we didn't believe he was a Hebert employee or anyone we knew from town.

Which only made this situation scarier.

Lila had been pale and shaking since Officer Fielder had brought her inside and cleaned her up.

She was in shock, and every protective instinct inside me had been activated. The police wouldn't let me take her home, but at least Officer Fielder was kind and patient. Chief Souza, the prick, had been a judgmental ass since I was a kid. He'd love to find an excuse to arrest any of us. Every time we crossed paths, he practically salivated at the possibility.

Hell, he'd looked positively gleeful booking Cole last week.

For years, he'd been tight with my dad, always kissing his ass. But the minute Dad was arrested, he'd turned hard on the rest of us. Probably mortified that he'd been so blind to all of Dad's crimes.

Or maybe the opposite. Maybe he was putting distance between himself and our family because he hadn't missed the signs of Dad's nefarious activities. That, in my opinion, was far more likely. I kept that theory to myself, but a small-town cop turning a blind eye to a lucrative drug trafficking operation was hardly a leap.

My mom knew what brand of beer I'd bought before I made it to the parking lot of the store the day I'd arrived. It wasn't a stretch to assume at least some of these guys had been in on it.

But I bit my tongue and gritted my teeth while they asked Lila dumb question after question. And finally, they gave me permission to take her home.

I wrapped my arm around her as I led her to my car.

"You don't have to do this." She peered up at me, her face still wan.

"Of course I do. It's just a ride, Lila." That was a lie. It was so much more to me. The woman I cared for deeply was hurt and scared. I'd do anything to make sure she was safe and cared for. So I'd gladly take her home and keep an eye on her. Even if that meant camping out in her driveway for the night.

"Thank you," she said softly as we stepped into her house. "I should probably take a shower." Her eyes were wide as she focused on me. "Can you stay? I don't want to be alone."

With a relieved sigh, I nodded and pulled her in for a hug.

She removed my jacket, letting it fall to the floor, then disappeared into the bathroom.

I scooped it up and hung it by the door, then wandered to the kitchen and put the kettle on for tea.

The home was quaint and only a few blocks from where I'd grown up, on a side street lined with cookie-cutter houses. The walls were all painted bright, cheery colors, and photos of Lila were hung on just about every wall.

As I took them in, one at a time, I found myself pulled into her life story. Lila as a tiny baby with chubby cheeks on the hip of a teenager with massive bangs, then a skinny kid with a big smile wearing several glittery pageant outfits, and everywhere in between.

She was adorable and always smiling.

I made two mugs of tea and found the honey Lila liked on the countertop. In my pocket, my phone was buzzing almost nonstop. No doubt my brothers were panicking about today's incident and expecting me to fix it. I ignored it. I was here for Lila.

I was so lost in my thoughts I didn't hear the door open.

"Oh my God, is she okay? Where is she?"

I spun and came face-to-face with Lila's mom. Sandra looked like an older, fancier version of her daughter. Even in her medical scrubs, she was dressed up. Hair done, lots of jewelry, and perfect red lipstick.

I nodded down the hall. "Shower," I said, offering her my hand. "I'm Owen."

Taking it, she gave me an appraising once-over. "Finally I get to meet the famous Owen Hebert. Thank you for taking care of my baby."

"Today was a lot." I sighed, rubbing at the back of my neck. "The police, the questioning—"

She held up a hand. "Not just today. You've been good to her. You've done so much for that girl's confidence. I'll miss her, but I know she'll be ready to take on the world when she leaves."

I cleared my throat, surprised at the direction of this conversation. "She's incredible," I said, only realizing how potentially creepy that sounded once the words were out. "At accounting. Work, you know," I stuttered like a bumbling idiot. "She's very smart."

Sandra pursed her lips and crossed her arms. For a long moment, she scrutinized me, then dropped her arms and stepped over to the stove. "Let's sit down." She handed one mug of tea I'd prepared to me and pulled another mug from the cabinet.

"I don't want to intrude."

She pinned me with a look that reminded me so much of Lila I did a double take. "Don't you dare leave." Once she'd added honey to her tea, she nodded toward the living room. "Go sit your ass down so we can have a chat."

I followed her into the cheery space and sat on the sofa.

"I apologize for the chill," she said, blowing on her mug. "I'd light the fire, but we're out of wood, and I can't bring myself to order more. It's May, for Christ's sake. I've lived here my entire life and still get angry every year when spring never arrives."

I nodded politely, but I kept my mouth shut, terrified that if I spoke, I'd say something stupid. Rather than a successful businessman, I felt like a teenager waiting to take Lila to prom.

"This place," she mused, "is not for everyone. I've grown a thick skin over the decades, but Lila deserves a hell of a lot more."

I sipped my tea to give myself something to do while I deciphered her words. Was this a test? It had been a long time since I'd had to deal with the parents of a love interest.

Of course Lila deserved more. She deserved the world.

But I didn't want to show my hand to her mom, especially with the skeptical way she was looking at me.

"You know," she said, "if I were the type of person to listen to the rumors, I'd kick you out of my house right now. According to the gossips, you're one of those greedy city types. Got too big for your britches and forgot where you came from."

I opened my mouth, but nothing came out. My stomach had sunken to my feet and my throat had gone dry.

Sandra didn't seem to mind that she'd stunned me speechless. "And the fact that you're a Hebert? Trust me, one of the reasons I want her to get out of this place is to get as far away from the Heberts as possible."

I cleared my throat, finally finding my voice, and sat a little straighter. "I am not my father."

She gave me a pitying smile over the rim of her mug. "Of course not. He's a one-of-a-kind piece of shit."

I laughed. Despite the sweet, feminine exterior, and the bubbly energy, Sandra had claws. It made me happy that Lila had someone like this in her corner.

"And your brother."

I raised an eyebrow.

"I've heard all the rumors about you Hebert boys."

I sucked in a breath, irritated that I'd once again been lumped in with Cole. He'd made a name for himself, and it wasn't a good one. And the rest of us were guilty by association.

"It's a good thing I don't put much stock in rumors. This town has been talking shit about me since I was a kid. Trailer trash, teen mom. I'm sure they've called me worse behind my back."

The ache in my chest throbbed at that admission. "I'm so sorry."

She waved her hand. "Don't be. I've got a good life, and I take great pride in pissing off the sanctimonious jerks. But my girl." She shook her head. "She puts on a good front, but it's not as easy for her to tune it out. She's dealt with her fair share of shit too, and come out stronger for it."

I likely didn't know half of it, but I respected what she was saying. Lila had a quiet strength, and she bore her scars privately, but she had plenty. The way she'd reacted after our weekend in Boston revealed that she wasn't as free-spirited as she pretended to be.

The bathroom door opened, and soft footsteps sounded down the hall, followed by the soft snick of a door closing farther away.

She leaned forward and lowered her voice. "I know something happened between you two."

I stiffened but pressed my lips together. I had no interest in giving away anything Lila hadn't shared with her mother.

"But I'm not a meddling mom. My girl knows what she wants." She squeezed my hand. "Promise me something?"

I gave her an encouraging nod.

Her expression hardened. Not in an angry way, but in a way that made it clear she was dead serious and concerned for her daughter's well-being. "Do not trap her. Do not clip her wings. Let my girl fly. Because I believe she can soar."

The lump in my throat made it hard to speak. "I'm not —" I coughed. "We're not—"

She shook her head. "I'm not saying stay away. I'm not saying give up. In fact, I'm impressed with your efforts so far.

She's gonna make you work for it, but if I had to guess, you're the kind of man who likes a challenge."

I roughed a hand down my face, then busied myself with my tea. Wasn't that the truth. She'd been hot and cold and everything in between for weeks. Flirtatious and seductive and then closed off and cold.

Then there were the most glorious moments of vulnerability sprinkled in. When she confided in me about her fears about graduate school, or when she was so kind and patient when we'd gotten locked in the supply closet.

Sandra put her other hand on top of mine. "She's not going to be someone's obedient housewife. She won't be content to take the back seat and always be the runner-up. If you can't deal with that, then please walk away now."

Her words hung in the air between us, threatening to swallow up all the oxygen.

But then Lila appeared. She was wearing a Boston Bolts sweatshirt, her wet hair hanging around her shoulders, and I jumped to my feet.

"Can I get you anything?"

She shook her head and headed straight for her mom, who stood and wrapped her arms around her, pressing a kiss to her forehead.

"Have you heard anything?" she asked, her face buried in her mom's scrub shirt.

"Yes." I pulled my phone out and double checked the information I'd been given. "The police were able to identify him. His name is Hugo Barrett. He's an employee of the Department of Fish and Wildlife."

She cleared her throat and tilted her face lower. "Is—is he alive?"

I nodded. "Officer Fielder texted me and asked me to assure you he was okay. He's at the hospital now."

Sandra blushed at the mention of Officer Fielder.

Huh. Interesting.

Lila straightened and wrapped her arms around herself. "How does something like this even happen?"

I shrugged and tucked my phone back into my pocket. "He met with Gus a while back, I guess. Gus didn't recognize him until the police showed him a copy of his driver's license. I think he works in the area." I didn't mention that Chief Souza now wanted to question us about our company's relationship with him or how that would only add to the dozen issues I was already dealing with.

Sandra smoothed Lila's hair and kissed her once more. "I'll call Bernice. Tell her you need tomorrow off. It'll be good for you to take a day to rest."

"I should go." I could use some time to myself to process how the woman I loved had stumbled upon a man beaten unconscious on my family's property, only yards from where I sat working. And I wasn't sure I could even get into the complete shit show that was going down at the office right now.

"You should stay," Lila said.

I shook my head. "Your mom's got it covered. Can I bring you ladies anything?"

Sandra shook her head. "This one should probably get a good night's sleep. Tomorrow, we'll take it easy and have a Hallmark marathon." She smiled at Lila. "Do it right. Full cozy girls' day. Popcorn and snacks and PJs?"

"I'm fine, Mom." She waved her off. "You don't have to fuss."

"Text me if you need anything." The offer was lame, but what I really wanted to say was that I'd take care of her forever if she let me, and I was pretty certain that wouldn't go over well.

Lila walked me to the door, and once I had my jacket slung over one arm, she looped her arms around my waist. I held on for a moment too long, soaking her in, just fucking thankful she was safe. Being chased by a moose and finding a man clinging to life all in one day was a lot, even for someone as tough as her.

She popped up on her tiptoes and kissed me on the cheek. "Thank you, Owen."

With one final goodbye, I walked back to my car, trying to make sense of my life.

In the last couple of weeks alone, she'd witnessed my panic attack in the closet and we'd had life changing, mind-blowing sex. And now all this.

This wasn't the linear progression I was used to when it came to relationships. We'd never even had an official date, but our lives were intertwined in so many ways. I'd shown her parts of me that no one else had ever seen.

On paper, we made no sense. But when I was in her proximity, I felt more alive than I ever had. In the light moments, while we laughed about orgone and the Leech Museum, and the dark ones too.

The pain I still felt from the trauma and the anger and confusion over what my father had done to this town, the Gagnons, and our family, lessened when she was near.

The only thing that grew was the sense that the life I'd built away from my family and this town was a hollow one.

This was too much for me. I thrived on being in control, on having a plan and setting parameters and boundaries.

I entered and stayed in relationships on my terms and never pushed myself too far.

But this time, I'd gone too far, and there was no going back. I was in love with Lila Webster.

Chapter 27
Lila

Despite it being May third, I was snuggled up in a cardigan and old sweats and drinking hot tea. Outside, it was still cold and cloudy, and the mountains in the distance were still capped with snow.

It had been a while since Mom and I had time to just be together. We'd both been working so much that I'd barely seen her in months.

As much as I couldn't wait to start my life somewhere else, the knowledge that my time with her was running out made my heart heavy. I'd moved back here to help her, to spend time with her, and I'd failed at it miserably.

Because the weather was getting us both down, all the movies we'd lined up for our Hallmark movie marathon were set at the beach or in other sunny locations. We'd pulled out all our favorite snacks and planned to do nothing but snuggle and zone out all afternoon. Despite my mother's protests, I'd gone to work this morning, and my feet were aching from a busy shift at the diner and my mind was spinning with thoughts of Owen.

In the week since we'd returned from Boston, I'd been unsuccessful in putting emotional distance between us. If anything, the incident yesterday had brought us even closer.

My mom was making popcorn when tires crunched on the gravel out front. I hauled myself off the couch and peered through the curtains. Instantly, I had to do a double take. Owen had parked his Audi next to my van in our tiny driveway. Just the sight of him had my heart pounding out a joyful rhythm in my chest.

I was bare faced and wearing old sweats. They weren't the cute kind of sweats that made my ass look great. No, these were an oversized pair that were extra soft and terribly faded from hundreds of washes.

Could I hide in my room? Pretend I wasn't home? Even as my heart leaped at his presence, my stomach knotted.

God, I was regressing. This man had appeared, and suddenly, I'd been reduced to an insecure teenager.

"Who's out front, sweetie?" Mom called from the kitchen.

Without responding, I grabbed a fleece from the hook beside the front door, stuffed my feet into a pair of wellies, and headed outside. Obviously, my desire to see him had won out over my vanity.

When I opened the door, he smiled and held up his hands in surrender. "I'm not trying to intrude. I know it's girls' day. I just wanted to check on you."

My stomach dipped at his thoughtfulness. And did he have to be so damn attractive?

"And I wanted to drop these off." He leaned into the car

and stretched over to the passenger seat. When he straightened, he was holding a small pink box tied haphazardly with string.

I wandered out to meet him and took it. Immediately, I was hit with the most heavenly smell.

"They're gluten-free scones. Cranberry orange." He ducked his head and kicked at the dirt with a well-worn work boot I'd never seen him wear. "I figured they would go well with your tea."

I cocked my head and frowned, processing his words. "Did you—" I clamped my mouth shut and swallowed, hoping when I spoke again, my voice wouldn't sound so crazed. "Did you make these?"

He shrugged and stuffed his hands into his pockets. "Got a good recipe on the internet. Not a big deal."

I blinked, as if that would somehow make this make sense. "You baked for me?" My inner lovesick teen girl was squealing with delight.

"I thought you could use a cozy fire too." He rounded his car and opened the hatch. "So I brought firewood."

He loaded his arms with logs and carried them toward the backyard.

I took a moment to center myself before I said or did something stupid. This man had shown up to my house bearing homemade gluten-free baked goods and firewood?

Was I asleep? Was this some kind of Hallmark-induced fever dream?

I followed him, finding him neatly lining up the logs. I was frozen to the spot, unsure I could trust my legs not to give out on me, when he passed me and headed back to his car.

"Go inside," he said when he returned with an axe. "It's cold out."

"It's forty-five degrees. That's bikini weather in Maine."

He froze his efforts to set up a log and looked up at me, a full smile spreading across his face. "Do you want to put on a bikini, then? I won't object." With a wink, he went back to the task at hand.

I stepped forward, wobbling as my boot caught on the loose paver.

A wink.

Owen Hebert, Mr. Super Serious Corporate Bossman, just winked at me.

And it caused my legs to stop working properly.

I knew what he was capable of. I'd gotten a taste in Boston. But I was beginning to think that was only the beginning. That he had more sexy layers for me to peel back.

"Where did you get those?" I asked with a nod at the small pile of logs, desperate to change the subject and recover my dignity.

"My family owns a timber company."

I pinched the bridge of my nose and bit back a huff. "Okay. Wrong question. Why did you bring them here?"

"Your mom mentioned that you'd run out of firewood." He shrugged, still focused on the task at hand. "I wanted you to have a nice day."

Jesus. There was no recovering from this man. Distance and professionalism were not getting the job done. If I wasn't certain that my mother was spying on us through the kitchen window right now, I'd be dry humping his leg already.

"Go inside," he demanded, holding out the axe in my direction like he was pointing at me.

I shivered. Not because of the cold. Nope. But because that deep, bossy register unlocked some deep, primal muscle memory. I was fairly certain the responding fluttering in my belly was my ovaries spontaneously ovulating.

As I shuffled up the back stairs and into the warm kitchen, I found my mother standing by the sink and smiling maniacally at me.

"Don't say a word."

She laughed. "I'm just here for the show."

I set the scones on the counter, ready to protest, but then, outside the window, movement caught my eye. Owen began unbuttoning his dress shirt, and I lost the ability to speak. He carefully shrugged out of it and draped it over the deck railing, then he stepped away, wearing just a white undershirt, jeans, and those broken-in boots.

"Daaayuuum," Mom hissed under her breath.

"Is this actually happening?" I asked, my heart pounding in my ears. Because I thought maybe I'd died in my sleep and now resided in lumberjack heaven.

"Does it matter?" She elbowed me. "Shut up and enjoy it."

This was unfair. Truly unfair. How was I supposed to resist him when he was stripped down to a white T-shirt and chopping wood in my mom's backyard?

He lined up the log and swung the axe, then brought it down. The movement was hypnotic.

The strength and precision were intoxicating.

Beside me, my mother fanned herself. "Talk about arm port. Those dress shirts do not do him justice."

She wasn't wrong. They hid just how muscular and lean he was. As each muscle bunched and clenched beneath the thin cotton, it hit me just how hard it was going to be to keep my damn pants on around him. "Remember to practice safe sex, sweetie."

A scoff ripped its way out of me. "Mom. Stop."

"The man is chopping wood for you. Just give it up already."

I ignored her. I was too busy watching him to bother continuing the argument.

He kept going, swinging and chopping, each cut precise.

As if this buttoned-up corporate executive had been born with an axe in his hands.

After a solid fifteen minutes of chopping, then stacking the cut wood next to the back door, he'd prepped enough to last an entire winter. But I couldn't help but think it might not be enough. Because I wasn't ready for the show to end. I'd personally take down every tree in town just to keep watching the Owen Hebert Lumberjack Spectacular. Screw raffles. The town should use him to fundraise for the new library. If we streamed this on YouTube, this town would never want for anything again.

And then he was at the door, all sweaty and masculine and lickable.

"Ms. Webster, sorry for the intrusion." He dipped his chin politely at my mother.

Her response was nothing more than a dazed smile.

He toed his boots off and carried a small stack of wood to the fireplace. Once he had it placed the way he wanted it, he opened the flue and got the fire lit quickly.

The two of us stood side by side, possibly with our mouths open and our tongues lolling, surely looking completely idiotic. But there was no helping it. My mind and body could not process what was happening.

He rubbed his hands together and stepped back to admire the blaze. "Here you are, ladies. Enjoy your Hallmark movies."

I was still staring, slack-jawed, when my mother poked my side, startling me.

"Th-thank you," I said, concerned the words may have been incoherent. My brain was far too preoccupied to focus on syllables and pronunciation.

"You should stay for dinner," my mother said.

At least one of us was semi-functional.

He shook his head. "Oh no, I don't want to interrupt girl time." He gave me a soft smile and headed for the back door.

I followed him onto the porch, where he sat on the top step and laced up his boots. "You didn't need to do that." I cringed. The words sounded ungrateful, which was the last thing I wanted, but I was confused and mad and really turned on.

"I wanted to," he said firmly, standing to his full height.

My heart stuttered in his chest. Dammit, that bossy tone did things to me. "Why?"

He closed the distance between us and tipped my chin up with his knuckles so I was forced to meet his deep blue eyes.

I held my breath and locked my knees to steady myself.

"Because I don't want you to be cold. Or hungry or tired. I care about you. And if I can make your life easier, even in the smallest of ways, then I'll do it. Every time."

"So this wasn't just about putting on a show by chopping wood?" I teased, finally coming back to myself.

He smirked. "I have no idea what you're talking about. I had a job to do."

I crossed my arms and cocked a brow. "Bullshit. You knew what you were doing."

He shook his head. "Nope. Totally innocent. Just trying to help my friend." The way he emphasized that word hit me like an arrow to the heart. "But I don't mind it when you ogle me." He waggled his brows.

I made a throaty sound of dismissal at the notion that I was ogling him, even though I really, really was. "They sell firewood at the gas station. You didn't need to bring your own and chop it here."

He put his hand to his chest and lowered his brows, feigning insult. "I'm surrounded by wood all day. My wood is the best wood."

I bit the inside of my cheeks to keep from laughing. "Now you're just being cocky."

He leaned in close, the warmth of his body overwhelming me, and brought his mouth to my ear. His lips ghosted over the lobe as he whispered, "We both know I've got the goods to back it up."

And then he turned, snagged his shirt from the railing, and rounded the house, wearing a shit-eating grin.

"Bye, Lila. Have an amazing day."

Chapter 28
Lila

Work. That's what I needed to focus on.

Mr. Spellman at table four needed a coffee refill, and Mrs. Souza in the corner had demanded crispier bacon.

I plastered a smile on my face and tried to focus on tables, busing, orders, and making change.

But that bastard Owen Hebert had fully infiltrated my mind. It was bad enough that my body remembered just how good he felt on top of me, but now my mind was spinning, because I so badly wanted to talk to him and make him smile.

It was a challenge, to earn one of those smiles. I swore his facial muscles only had the capacity to contract a couple of times each week. And I wanted all of them, damnit.

"Lila dear." Mrs. Dupont beckoned me in the most obnoxious way. "I specifically said I wanted cheddar in my omelet. This is American."

I blinked. Seriously? They were basically the same thing. And her palate was not particularly refined. How she could taste anything after smoking a pack a day since I was in grade school was a mystery.

"Of course. I'll get this fixed right away."

As I scooped up her plate, she rolled her eyes at her tablemates. In turn, they all looked at me with scorn. There was nothing better than spending a Monday morning surrounded by judgy old bats.

I sleepwalked through the rest of my shift, only making a few more mistakes as I went. I'd been waiting tables here for the better part of a year, but it was starting to feel unbearable. For a long time, it was easy to ignore the little slights. I'd dealt with them all my life, really, so it was almost second nature. But lately, every comment needled at me.

Maybe it was because I'd been accepted to several great grad schools, yet they treated me like I was below them. Or was it because my freedom was so close? Maybe I was just embracing my inner bitch?

Whatever the reason, not drowning Mayor Lambert in his oatmeal when he spent a full minute staring at my rack was a true victory.

I was wiping down tables when I caught pieces of conversation from the knitting group set up in their usual spot. "Very serious... Dr. Savard... so young?"

"What was that?" I asked, standing up straight.

Loraine Gagnon gave me a genuine smile. "Oh dear, apparently Dr. Savard had a stroke this morning."

My heart plummeted to my feet. Willa's dad? With a gasp, I fumbled for my phone in my apron.

When I'd finally freed it, I was met with a whole slew of missed calls from Willa. Shit.

I tapped on her contact and turned, waving a shaky hand at Bernice, signaling that I was going outside.

"What happened?" I asked as soon as she picked up.

"Lila," she said, her voice trembling. "Dad. Had a stroke."

Heart aching for her, I slumped against the brick wall in the alley and slid to the ground.

Dr. Savard had been like a father to me since the second grade.

He had been the one to encourage me to apply to college, even editing my essays for me. He'd been the one to take the training wheels off my bike and chase me down the street for hours until I mastered the ability to ride on two wheels.

I was the only kid in third grade who still needed training wheels. But I'd only gotten a bike the year before. I'd begged my mom for months, and she'd finally found one second hand. But she was too busy working to teach me to ride it.

Even though Willa had long since mastered two wheels, Dr. Savard had stayed out with me, patiently helping me every time I wobbled or fell.

My heart cracked at the memory. He was one of the absolute best.

"Where is he? I'm getting in my car."

"He's been airlifted to Portland. I'm waiting at the airport now. My flight leaves in thirty minutes." A cry escaped her, followed by a sniffle. "I'm just so scared. It was bad."

I swallowed back my own emotion, desperate to be strong for her. "What can I do? What do you need? I can be there in a few hours."

"No, stay. Don't drive down yet. We've got to figure out what's going on. Mom says he's stable."

I took a deep breath and closed my eyes, searching for the right thing to say to my terrified best friend. "He's so young and healthy," I said lamely.

Her hiccup on the other end pulled at my heart. God, what I wouldn't give to ease her pain and worry.

"He's going to be okay, Willa. Between you and your mom, he will get the best care and the best chance at recovery. I'll be by your side for every minute. You're not alone."

I sat on the ground, my back pressed to the brick wall, with the phone pressed to my ear, as she cried. Sometimes the only thing a person could do was be present, as shitty as it felt.

"I'm so sorry I didn't see your calls," I said. "I put my phone on silent when I'm at the diner."

"S'okay." She hiccuped. "You're here now."

"Of course I am. You should be boarding soon, right?"

"Hopefully," she rasped. "I'm still on standby. Can you distract me?"

"Done." I cleared my throat and racked my brain. "Ooh. My mom and I did a Hallmark marathon yesterday. The last movie we watched was batshit crazy." I grinned, because it truly was. "So these two families rent the same cabin for a week of vacation in the mountains. Hot single mom and hot single dad and the cabin is creepy A.F. and in the middle of nowhere."

"Did they get murdered?"

"Worse, the power goes out and they make a fire and fall in love. They go to forage for stuff in the woods and I wasn't sure if it was one of those survival shows."

I could hear her giggling in the background.

Willa snorted on the other end. "They are trying to forage for food and the kids are just hanging around in a cabin. Never mind they have cars they can get into and drive away in. But the need to survive bonds them."

"Dumbasses. Maybe they were just horny so they pretended to be stuck there?"

"And these people? They were ridiculously irresponsible." I waved a hand as I went on. "Like they are full-on neglecting their children."

I described their attempts to make fire and the bear cub that had been thrown in for comic relief and before long, we were both howling with laughter.

"You know," she said, her voice lighter, even as it was clear her tears hadn't stopped, "I'm beginning to think Hallmark has been lying to us all this time. These hot, emotionally stable men with full heads of hair don't really exist."

My mind flashed to Owen. That wasn't quite accurate. They existed, all right. They just weren't forever. Which was almost a crueler reality.

"But since Hallmark men are nonsexual, maybe they have tiny penises," Willa said, snorting into the phone.

"Aren't you in public?"

"I'm too upset to care. Plus, the terminal is pretty empty right now."

"My theory is that they're like Ken dolls." I giggled through my tears. "That's the secret flaw. The corporate titan turned small-town florist? Or the carpenter who drives a Mercedes and lives in a gorgeous house? They've got nothing downstairs."

Willa gasped for breath on the other end of the phone.

"Yes. I'll never swoon over a Hallmark man again. Those poor women. Lured in by the small-town charm, broad shoulders, and deep voices. Only to find out it's all smooth down there."

Even as my heart ached for my bestie, I roared with laughter. This conversation was beyond absurd, and it made me miss her so much.

She sniffed. "I love you."

"I love you so fucking much. And I'm here for you. Always."

The walls were closing in on me. I'd gone for a run around my mom's neighborhood to give myself something to do. Then I headed to the Savards' house, where I fed Madam Flo, a.k.a. Florence Nightingale, Willa's ancient cat. I'd taken care of her when Dr. and Mrs. Savard went to Florida in January and still had a key to the house. I texted Mrs. Savard to let her know I'd check on her for as long as they needed. Then I cleaned her litter box, took out their trash, and got the mail.

Willa had texted to tell me he was stable and that the doctors were optimistic. I'd passed the information on to my mom and Magnolia.

Mom didn't question me when I cleaned and alphabetized her spice cabinet, but every time she checked on me, her brow was knit with concern. I was about to start on the medicine cabinet when she strongly suggested I snuggle up with a good book and try to get some sleep.

My fingers itched to text him, but I held strong.

What good could come of it if I did? Soon, we'd be in different states, likely to never see one another again. We'd had our fling in Boston, the one meant to allow us to get the attraction, the passion, out of our systems.

Only, the opposite had happened.

These feelings weren't going away. In fact, they were becoming more overwhelming by the day.

And life was so precious. I needed no greater reminder today.

For years, I'd been with the wrong person.

And although Owen couldn't be a forever option, he felt so right for today. And why deny myself happiness and connection and affection today, when tomorrow wasn't guaranteed?

So after a full hour of pacing, then throwing myself onto my bed and rereading the same page of my current read over and over, I made sure my mom was asleep, then snuck out. Because the pull was too strong. And I was tired of resisting.

For once, I'd take what I wanted and let the consequences be damned.

Because I needed to feel his arms around me, his lips on my skin, more than I needed to breathe right now. I needed to be in the presence of the one person who could comfort and thrill me at the same time.

A smarter woman might stop and reflect on this. Maybe pump the brakes and think through the potential consequences.

But I silenced my logical brain and instead went with my gut.

I didn't know how much time we'd have together, but it

didn't matter. I'd take as much as I could get, and I'd ensure that time started right now.

He answered the door wearing an old Boston Revs T-shirt and a pair of sweatpants. As if I needed another reason to do this.

"Lila? Are you okay?" Frowning in concern, he pushed his glasses up his nose.

I pushed past him, slammed the door behind me, and threw my coat on the couch. "I just needed to see you."

Without hesitation, he opened his arms.

I walked right into them, letting his strength and warmth envelop me in a kind of comfort I'd never known. "I don't want to fight it any longer," I admitted. "This. Us. I want it. I want you." I was tearing up. Instead of a smooth seductress, I was a blubbering idiot.

But there was no stopping the emotions bubbling up within me. Memories of the moments we'd shared, the way we'd each let ourselves be vulnerable, his gentle kindness and care, blended together, creating a tsunami of emotion, gratitude, and desire.

Owen pulled back but didn't step away. He peered down at me and wiped away my tears with the pads of his thumbs. "You can have whatever you want. I'm all yours. For tonight, this year, or forever. I'm here if you want me." Hitting me with a look as sincere as it was sexy, he leaned down and captured my mouth in a gentle kiss.

I clung to him, my hands twisting his shirt. "I can't stay away. I can't pretend anymore."

He gently kissed my neck, pulling a gasp from my lungs, and pressed his body flush to mine.

His sweatpants hid nothing. The feel of his hard length against my belly ignited a flame inside me.

Desperate to feel his bare skin on mine, I pulled him toward the bedroom.

He followed willingly, though his lips never left my skin.

"I know we can never—"

He pinned me against the door, cutting me off. "Stop." That demanding tone only fanned the desire heating my blood. "Be here with me. In this moment. We'll worry about everything else later."

I nodded mutely, captivated by the way he commanded the situation and the set of his jaw.

Despite his insistence, his control was unraveling, and that was even sexier.

"I want you."

A shiver worked its way through me as his pupils blew out and a groan worked its way up his throat. Trembling, I snaked a hand down to the waistband of his sweats.

"Undone. No control. No perfectionism," I begged. "Give me the real, raw Owen."

He tilted my chin up and stared into my eyes, his fingers caressing the column of my throat. "I'll give you everything."

Chapter 29
Owen

This was my moment. She was here.

Every day since we'd left Boston had been torture. Keeping my hands to myself made me twitchy and angry.

What I felt for Lila was complicated and messy, sure, but the intensity couldn't be denied.

I adored her. And I'd do anything to make her happy.

Correction. I'd do everything. Starting right now. These opportunities didn't come around too often, so I'd do all I could to convince her that we could do this for real.

I leaned down and took her mouth gently, letting the feel of her kiss course through my veins.

This.

This was what I had been missing.

And now I had a chance to help her understand. To make her mine.

I threaded my fingers through her hair, cradling her head, and dove in again, more aggressively this time. My body lit up as she matched my intensity. The air around us crackled with electricity, and the connection strengthened and grew. How did we ever think we could deny this?

She was just as energized as I was, grabbing at my shirt and pulling me closer.

There wasn't enough time. There never was. And there were so many reasons to stop.

But I couldn't.

Not when she'd shown up here, looking so vulnerable and needy.

I'd give Lila anything she wanted.

And by the way she was pawing at my belt, it was clear what she wanted. "Owen." She gasped. "Bedroom."

I threw her over my shoulder and jogged to the bedroom, ignoring the shoes that slipped from her feet as we went.

I laid her down on the bed, then stripped my shirt off quickly.

"Fuck. That was so hot," she said, sitting up on her elbows. "You can throw me around anytime you want."

I winked. If she liked my inner caveman so much, I'd have to let him out a little more often.

Angling over her, I tugged at the waistband of her leggings, and she lifted her hips and allowed me to ease them down.

"Shit." I exhaled as I tossed them over my shoulder. "No panties?"

She shrugged. "They get in the way."

"Spread for me," I commanded, a bit louder than I had anticipated. I could barely contain myself, so modulating my tone of voice was probably not in the cards.

But her eyes flared in excitement in response, and without looking away, she obeyed.

I stood back, studying every inch of her body, spread out for me to consume.

Creamy skin, gorgeous curves, and rosy pink nipples.

And that pussy. So sweet and warm and wet. And mine.

"Please, Owen," she begged. "I need to feel you inside me."

God, was there anything sexier? My cock strained against my zipper as I considered exactly what I wanted to do to her.

But then my heart stuttered and all coherent thought left me. Because she'd slid her hand down her torso, and now she was gliding those fingers over her clit.

"Can't wait for me?" I growled, barely able to stop myself from mauling her.

She shook her head. "I'm already so wet. Please."

I stood, slack-jawed and vision blurring, as she fingered herself in front of me.

All my careful plans went to hell the minute she sank her fingers inside her wetness. Yup, talk about caveman brain. All I could think about was getting inside her.

Practically vibrating, I pulled out the box of condoms I'd optimistically bought after returning home from our Boston trip and shucked my jeans.

Once I'd sheathed myself, I kissed my way up her body. Then I captured her mouth and lined myself up.

"*Yes*," she cried as I sank inside her, slowly savoring her heat. This was so much better than I remembered, and I'd spent a lot of time remembering those nights together.

Every thrust was better than the last.

With her head tossed back, she spread wider, taking me deeper, and I swore I was losing my mind.

"You feel incredible," I gasped. Damn, I wasn't sure I'd last. "You're so perfect. Like you were made for me."

"What if I was?" She gasped. "Made for you?"

Fuck. Those words just about did me in. I gritted my teeth, holding tight to the last vestiges of my control.

Withdrawing, I shifted back and kneeled, then lifted her legs onto my shoulders.

When she focused those hooded eyes on me, lightning surged through my veins.

"Just like that." I pushed inside her, reveling in the tight fit and the way she cried out. "Fuck, you're so tight."

Using her legs as leverage, I focused on deep, hard strokes, keeping an even pace to make this incredible feeling last.

"Tell me you thought about it," I said, bottoming out and loving the total control I had over her body. "Tell me you thought about how good it was when I fucked you."

She writhed underneath me, clinging to my forearms. "Yes. I thought about it all the time. No one has ever made me feel this good."

Fuck, my ego might never recover.

"Good. Because no one ever will. You're mine now." I grunted. "This pussy, it's mine."

I was going hard now, pounding into her so violently those glorious tits shook with every thrust.

"Say it," I demanded.

"I'm yours," she cried, digging her fingers into my arms. "Please, I'm close."

"You wanted to make me watch before." I hissed. "So rub your clit while I fuck you. I wanna watch you come."

With her teeth pressed into her lip so hard I worried she'd draw blood, she nodded and slid one hand down to where we were joined and rubbed slow circles around her clit. Instantly, she tightened up around me, making me see goddamn stars.

"That's it," I encouraged through gritted teeth. "Give me a good show."

She was laid out in front of me, totally powerless and chasing her pleasure. I wasn't sure I'd ever recover from this.

"Good girl. You're so tight. I've been dreaming of feeling you come all over my cock again."

As her muscles began to clench, I unleashed, thrusting hard and fast.

"Yes," she cried, trembling and arching her back. One hand still rubbed her clit while the other pinched her nipple.

I couldn't take my eyes off her as she rode out her orgasm. She was so beautiful and so damn sexy and 100 percent made for me. There was no other explanation for the intensity of these feelings.

I'd spent decades living a careful, controlled life. Being strategic and always planning ahead. But this woman had taken all of my careful constraint, my strategy, and patience, and she'd ripped it all to shreds.

With her, I was reduced to nothing but a beating heart.

And I wouldn't want it any other way.

Chapter 30
Lila

I woke nestled in Owen's arms, the gentle rise and fall of his chest against my back nearly pulling me under again.

Last night had been intense. Emotionally and physically. If I could, I'd bottle up this feeling of contentment and save it for the lonely days ahead. Eventually, we'd have to say goodbye. There was no way around it. And I wasn't sure how I'd survive it.

So much had changed for me since Owen had come to town. For years, I'd been pushing myself to grow and evolve, to move beyond the girl I used to be. Owen may not have known it, but he'd helped me realize that the woman I wanted to become had always been a part of me.

The first time I'd ever been complimented on my intelligence, I was twenty-two years old. I'd dropped out of school to follow Cole to Indiana, where he was playing for an ECHL team.

We'd been broken up for a bit, but he begged me to take

him back. Said he needed me. Swore he'd never make it in the pros without me. So, like a stupid, silly girl, I caved. College had not been going well for me anyway. Even with the pageant scholarship money, I'd struggled to pay my tuition, and I hated the merchandising courses I was taking. So rather than buckling down and working hard, I was more focused on partying with a group of sorority girls I'd befriended.

Leaving with Cole seemed like an adult decision. The two of us, in a new city, following our dreams. In reality, we were chasing *his* dream, but he made me feel like I was an important part of it, even if I was nothing more than his support. There to cook for him and have protein smoothies waiting when he got home from practice and always present to cheer him on from the stands.

I got bored quickly, so I enrolled at a local community college, hoping to find something that interested me.

I was a solid B student in high school, which my mom had celebrated. Her expectations for my grades were low, just as her parents' had been for her. Plus, finding time to study was challenging when I spent all my free time dancing, cheerleading, and traveling on the pageant circuit.

"You're beautiful," she'd always say. "You don't need to be smart. Your future is so far away from here. The first step is just getting out."

And I'd believed her. No one on earth loved me as much as my mother. It had taken a long time to realize just how misguided she had been.

At the community college in Indiana, I was required to take a math assessment to enroll. I aced the first test, and then they gave me a harder one. Eventually, one professor,

Ms. Lipman, asked me to meet with her. She went on and on about how I had the makings of an excellent math student. She encouraged me to enroll in calculus and accounting and consider pursuing a business degree.

No one had ever told me I was smart before that day. Not because I wasn't, but because the world saw me as nothing more than a pretty face. But on that day, in that dingy office, I felt like I was capable of doing something worthwhile.

When we moved to Florida, I transferred my credits and got serious about earning my degree. Cole didn't understand why I bothered with school or why I picked up a waitressing job to pay for it. The job meant I couldn't attend all of his games, but for the first time in my life, I was pursuing something for myself rather than living to please others.

The idea of working for nonprofits inspired and motivated me. So I researched and I studied the best way to go about making a difference in the world.

Then I made myself a promise. I was creating a life for myself. I'd use my brain and my work ethic rather than clinging to a man or getting by on my looks.

So where did that leave Owen?

A shiver worked its way through me as he nuzzled into me and dropped a soft kiss on my naked shoulder. It would be so easy to fall in love with him. He was older and successful and already established. I'd ridden on Cole's coattails for years, but I had too much respect for myself to do that again.

"Morning, gorgeous," he said, rolling onto his back and pulling me with him so I was sprawled out on his chest.

God, he was so warm and strong, and being here with him made all my baggage seem insignificant.

"I want to talk about last night," he said, tucking a strand of hair behind my ear.

My stomach sank. Owen was a mature, adult man. Of course he wanted to openly discuss things. In most circumstances, I would find that scorching hot. Accountability and honesty were major turn-ons. But for now, I wanted to run and hide from my feelings. I wanted to live in this little bubble, here in his cabin, and ignore real life.

So I did what any girl in my position would do. I created a diversion.

I kissed his neck, then worked my way to his earlobe and nipped at it. "Can you give a girl some coffee first?"

While he put the coffee on, I dressed in yesterday's clothes, like I was putting on armor to fortify myself against what he'd say. We stood in the kitchen, sipping coffee silently while my mind raced and I dug deep for courage.

I'd come over here. I'd made the big gesture. That meant I should be the one to step up and make this right.

"I know you want an explanation." I shifted on my feet, pushing back the trepidation rolling through me as I searched for the right words. Avoidance and a smile, my go-to coping mechanism, wouldn't cut it here.

He set his mug on the countertop and sighed. "I do. You were very clear in Boston, and I'm struggling with the mixed signals."

Yup. I deserved this.

I choked back the nerves clawing their way up my throat. "I meant what I said. I needed to see you—I was desperate to see you. You see me. And being with you makes me happy, protected. I've tried so hard to fight the pull between us. I've tried so hard to be friends and colleagues and nothing more."

I tucked my chin and searched my coffee for the courage to continue rather than give up and fall into his arms and stay there forever.

"But then you showed up and chopped wood at my house. You took care of me. You got to know my mom. And you show me every day what a kind and compassionate person you are."

A slow smirk spread across his face. "So you're telling me this is my fault?"

I crossed my free arm over my chest and huffed, patently ignoring the incredible view of his naked chest. How dare he stand there in his sweatpants and nothing else and smirk at me like that?

"Can you put a shirt on?"

He cocked a brow, and that grin grew. "Why?"

"Because I'm trying to have an adult conversation, and you're not making it easy."

He crossed his arms, making his biceps bulge. *Fuck me.* As if I needed that visual.

"You're doing great so far. Say what you need to say."

I paced from the kitchen into the living space, taking a moment to marvel at the view of the mountains while I collected my thoughts. I could do this. I needed to do this.

Honesty. Vulnerability.

But the desire to tell Owen what he wanted to hear was

strong. The desire to turn this around and make it about him. To hide my messy thoughts and feelings.

Fuck, growth was painful.

"I want to be with you," I said softly. "I don't want to fight it anymore. But it can't last. I know it will hurt when it's over, but it would hurt more to lose this time with you."

He ate up the space between us in three long strides and rested his hands on my shoulders. Dipping his chin, he searched my face, his blue eyes burning with intensity. "You keep saying it has to end, yet it hasn't even begun. Can't we just see what happens?"

I shook my head, tears welling in my eyes. "Can we just take the time we have and make the most of it? Before you sell the business and go back to Boston and before I start school in New York. Whatever it is, however long we have, let's take it and cherish it."

He angled in and kissed my head in response.

It would be so easy to fall into his arms and let him tell me that we could be together forever. But I was no longer the kind of woman who stood on the sidelines, who gave up my dreams so another could pursue their own.

He pulled me in and pressed his lips to the crown of my head. We stayed like that, his arms around my shoulders, our bodies close, for a few moments. Even the silence was comforting when he held me.

"Okay," he whispered into my hair. "I'll give you all the time we have left. I respect your wishes. I want you to go to New York. When the time comes, I'll step aside and cheer for you from the sidelines."

My gut clenched. He was saying the right words, but they felt wrong.

I looked up at him. "Are you sure?"

"Yes. But before I can dive into this completely, I need to know what happened between you and Cole."

I sucked in a breath, and my stomach twisted. I'd known this was coming. The history between his brother and me was long, so of course he'd need some clarity. But I barely had the words to explain it to myself. And I was protective of him, as well as the version of myself who'd fought like hell to make it work.

Part of me would always love Cole. We'd grown up together. We'd become adults together. Even though those adults were incompatible and had made each other miserable, we'd gone through some of life's biggest achievements and disappointments together.

I sat on the worn leather couch and pulled my knees up to protect myself from the emotional fallout of his conversation. Owen padded over and draped a blanket around my shoulders before sitting next to me.

"He never cheated on me, if that's what you're thinking."

His eyes widened. "Yeah. I guess I was." He rubbed at the back of his neck. "He's so much like my dad, self-centered and egotistical."

"No, Owen." I frowned. "You are dead wrong."

He huffed. "Why are you defending him?"

"Because someone has to. Don't think for one moment he had it easy. Your lives have been vastly different, sure, but you and I both know that you got the better deal." I hugged my knees tighter. "You have a loving mother and four brothers. Cole was the leftover no one wanted."

"Bullshit. My mother wanted him. We all accepted him." He fisted his hands on his thighs. "And it's not my job to heal his childhood wounds, anyway. He's a grown man. He can get therapy like the rest of us."

"You're right." I pressed my lips together and nodded. "That's on him. And I hope that one day he'll get there. I'm not asking you to forgive him, but I am asking you to show him some empathy."

He grunted down at the floor in front of us, which I took as a signal to keep going.

"There was no cheating, there was no big fight, he didn't hurt me. We just were not a good fit. We didn't have the same values, and I never felt good enough." I licked my lips and sighed. "He didn't support my desire to finish my degree, and he was embarrassed that I worked as a waitress to pay my tuition."

"There is nothing wrong with honest work, not that my entitled prick brother would know that."

I glared at him. "Stop." I waited for him to look at me before I continued. "You wanted the truth; I'm giving it to you. Stop bad-mouthing him. In the end, we wanted different things out of life. I should have seen it sooner, but for so long, I felt stuck and unable to leave."

"Why?"

I picked at a piece of lint on the throw blanket and gave him a small smile. "Because I cared about him. And he needed me."

"But your needs are just as important."

"It's easy to say that, but far harder to live it when you've spent your entire life doing what everyone else wants and believing your needs don't matter."

Owen bowed his head in silent understanding.

"We clung to one another. For eight difficult years. We

were young, and we'd been tossed out into the world, doing our best to swim while also keeping one another from going under. He was pursuing his dream of playing pro hockey, and I was pursuing my dream of getting the hell out of this small town and making something of my life. So, for many years, we hunkered down and weathered the storm."

I worried my bottom lip for a moment, wondering how vulnerable I should be. In the end, I chose to put it all out there. If I wanted to be with this man, then I needed him to see all of me.

"I blamed myself for our unhappiness. I thought if I made more of an effort, dressed up, made sure my makeup was perfect, hid behind the sweet façade I'd created long ago, and bent over backward, it would be enough. That he would love me the way I wanted to be loved and that our life would be perfect. It wasn't, of course, and that's not his fault. That's my fault."

I wasn't honest about what I needed. What I wanted. For a long time, I blamed him for not being able to read my mind.

When, in reality, I had a lot of growing up to do. I needed to learn how to set boundaries and take the time to figure out what the hell I wanted out of life.

It had been my own fucked-up belief system that led me to feeling unseen and unloved.

So I worked like hell to deprogram all the toxic thought patterns.

"It's taken a lot of work and reflection, but I learned to believe in myself and in my own abilities. I have to be my own hero, stand on my own two feet."

He'd turned to face me now, his full focus intent on my face.

"I spent eight long years in a crappy relationship before I finally realized that Prince Charming wouldn't show up and save me."

He took my hand in his and brought it to his lips. "Lila," he said, kissing my knuckles. "As the guy sitting here, watching you shine, it's more than clear to me that this princess is going to save herself."

Chapter 31
Owen

This was not the kind of relationship I'd hoped for with Lila, but I'd take whatever she was willing to give. For now.

Even if that meant keeping things quiet. No one despised the small-town rumor mill more than I did, but when it came to her, I couldn't care less. Lila, on the other hand, was terrified of being discovered. She put up with a lot of shit as a kid and had watched her mom suffer from their judgment, so the last thing she wanted was to give the people of Lovewell a reason to criticize her.

But I was developing a complex. We had so little time together, and we were wasting it by hiding how we felt from the world.

She couldn't be swayed, though, and I was too busy juggling my time with her with my day job and the sale of the company to argue.

We'd gotten another offer. It was better, but still low. I'd had to run back to Boston once to go over some of the preliminary documents and was running on a few hours of sleep a night just to keep all the balls in the air.

But when I woke up to my dream girl curled up next to me with a serene smile on her face, all of my complaints and hesitation vanished. The secrecy was frustrating, but I knew better than to push her too hard.

We'd fallen into a pattern. She'd go to the diner while I crossed off as many tasks as I could as the CFO of DiLuca construction and delegated the rest. Then she'd meet me at the office, and we'd get through as much as we could before we dragged ourselves back to my cabin.

There were still enough people working in the office to keep us from pushing past flirty glances and occasional kisses in my office. It was juvenile, but fun. Sitting side by side, reviewing spreadsheets was magical. Listening to music through a Bluetooth speaker while eating gluten-free cereal was better than any fancy date I'd ever been on.

Some days, we took off, hitting more spots on her weird Maine bucket list.

The world's largest chocolate moose in Scarborough.

The desert of Maine in Freeport.

The world's largest rotating globe in Yarmouth.

We drove around the state, talking about our favorite movies and books and the places we wanted to visit someday.

We had so much work to do, but if we slept less, we could accomplish it all. Right? Because I couldn't fight the desire to spend time with Lila. To savor every laugh and smile and contented sigh while I could.

"Why aren't you married?"

We were midway through our hike to Moxie Falls, one of

Maine's tallest waterfalls named after Maine's signature drink, when she dropped that bomb.

My lungs seized as the words registered. "Sorry?"

"You're handsome, successful, and great in bed. How has some smart woman not locked you down yet?"

I scanned the trail, searching for the next trail marker, stalling. This was not the conversation I expected to have today. It wasn't a conversation I ever expected to have with her.

"Answer my question." She didn't stop, but she zeroed in on me. "I know you're stalling."

I turned and stuck my tongue out at her. For someone who claimed to be a people pleaser, Lila really enjoyed calling me out on my shit.

And I loved it. I loved that she was comfortable enough with me to put away the pageant smile and be herself.

"I don't know. The easy answer is that I work a lot. But you're not going to let me get away with leaving it at that, are you?"

"Nope."

"It's so cliché to say, but I've never met the right person. I don't care all that much about marriage, but I have always wanted to find my person. A partner, someone to share all the good, bad, and weird parts of life with."

I kept my focus fixed on the path in front of us. The last thing I needed was to look at her gorgeous face. Because what I wasn't saying was that she was the person I'd been looking for. She was the person I wanted to share it all with.

But that wasn't our deal. And I refused to push her into something she didn't want.

So I gritted my teeth and kept my pace steady, determined to enjoy every moment I could.

"In thirty-eight years, you never found her?"

"I've dated, and I've been in a couple of relationships, but nothing all that serious. Maybe I wasn't ready, maybe it was timing, or maybe I'm too selfish and work-obsessed, who knows?"

"You keep claiming to be a workaholic, but you're out here with me, in the glorious Maine wilderness, on a Wednesday afternoon."

I stopped in the middle of the trail and finally turned to her. The beauty of the vast valley below was nothing in comparison to her, but the sunlight made her skin glow. She was impossibly gorgeous, and I was impossibly in love with her.

"You're the reason I'm out here, Lila. You make me want to skip work and have fun. Or take a road trip to see a giant chocolate moose."

Her face lit up. "His name is Lenny."

I closed the distance between us, my heart racing. "You make me want to stand still and savor every second. I want to take road trips with you, watch old movies and hike to hidden waterfalls." I blew out a breath and gripped the back of my neck, bolstering my courage. "You asked why I've never been married."

Her eyes widened as she surveyed me. Her chest rose and fell rapidly, and the air escaped her in harsh breaths. Good. She was feeling it too. The magnetic pull, the strength of this connection.

"This is why. Because no one has ever made me look at

the world differently until now. No one I've ever met has altered my perception the way you have."

I ran my knuckles along her jaw and tipped her chin up. Then I lowered my head and pressed my lips to hers.

I could stay here forever with her. Fuck work, fuck the business. Fuck the world's expectations.

This feeling, right here, was all I wanted.

Chapter 32
Owen

"What am I going to do with you?" I nuzzled her neck and gently nipped at her soft skin.

She arched up into me, pushing her breasts into my chest. She'd come in to show me a pattern of deposits from Deimos Industries, but her words were lost on me. Because she was wearing a tank top.

"Focus," she snapped. "I think I've worked something out."

I nipped her earlobe and tried to force my brain to function.

She handed me a spreadsheet. "I isolated all the transactions. For Deimos and some of the other unknown vendors. And they follow a weird pattern."

She pointed to the lines highlighted in yellow. "Those deposits occurred every twenty-nine or thirty days. And these withdrawals followed a similar pattern, occurring fourteen or fifteen days after the deposit."

"Okay..." I wasn't totally following, but in my defense: tank top.

"And there were twelve of these cycles each year, except for every two and a half years, when there were thirteen."

I looked at her, still not clear.

"The lunar cycle," she said, a self-satisfied grin on her face. "Each of these massive payments occurred on a full moon, dating back for at least seven years. I don't have access to the records before then, but I'd bet on it."

"And when did they stop?"

"There was a full moon six days after your dad was arrested. No payment."

Shit. Something was related, but what?

"And I did some more digging. I can't believe I didn't think of it before. Deimos is one of the moons of Mars. These couldn't have been legitimate business expenses, because they followed no discernible business need or pattern. Instead, they paid out on the full moon. Even those on weekends, when no other payments were made."

"Someone thinks they're clever."

"Yup. And while we don't yet know what these transactions were for, it's starting to look a lot like money laundering."

I pushed my hands into my hair. "Fuck."

"We have no hard evidence. It's not like I can go to the feds and talk about the damn full moons. They'd laugh me out of their offices. But at least we know these weren't legit, that the books weren't accurate. Now we can at least account for it and make accurate projections."

She was right. Any information that helped to discern

legal versus illegal conduct could only help us in a sale, but fuck if I wanted to get mixed up in this.

"I'll talk to Gus," I said, pulling her close. "You're fucking brilliant."

She arched back against me, and I thanked the wonky HVAC system as I grasped her waist, deposited her on my desk, and kissed the hell out of her. God, I would never tire of this. Her lips were intoxicating. Even though we'd snuggled for so long after the alarm had gone off this morning, she was almost late for her shift at the diner, I needed more.

She threw her arms around my neck and slid her knees farther apart.

Taking the move as an invitation, I stepped between her legs, all the blood immediately flowing south. This woman made me hungry and reckless.

"Owen."

The sound of my name in a low tone barely registered.

"*What the fuck?*"

Lila tensed in my arms, and her eyes went wide. Her back was to the door, but she recognized the voice, I was sure.

I shot Gus a glare. "You don't believe in knocking?"

He stood in the doorway with his hands fisted at his sides and a murderous expression on his face. "I did. About twenty times. What the hell is going on?"

Lila pushed me aside and hopped off the desk. She subtly wiped at her mouth, then scurried to the door. "Hi, Gus," she squeaked, keeping her head down.

Without a word, he moved aside, and she rushed out. That hurt. We were supposed to be in this together, and she ran away the moment my brother walked in?

I sank into my desk chair and stared up at the ceiling, studying the beams and clenching my jaw, waiting for the lecture.

The door slammed so hard against its frame the whole room shook.

"What the fuck, Owen?" my brother hissed, stomping toward my desk. "I told you to stay away from her."

I laced my hands over my abdomen and glowered in response. "Didn't you realize you were her older brother too."

"I'm everyone's older fucking brother these days. God." He ran his hands through his shaggy hair. "This is the last thing we need. She's a good kid."

"She's a grown woman, and this is none of your business."

Gus's overprotective instincts ran deep. Since we were kids, he'd felt as though he was responsible for not only all of us boys, but for his friends too.

"This is why I can't talk to you. You jump to baseless conclusions, you blow up over nothing, and you don't trust me."

With a shake of his head, he sighed. "I trust you with a lot of things, but everything is shit right now, and Lila does not deserve to be dragged into it."

Roughing a hand over my face, I leaned back in my chair. He wasn't exactly wrong.

"Wait a second." He braced his hands on the desk and leaned forward, his eyes narrowing. "Is this why the deal is taking so long? Because you're fucking her?"

I shot up out of my chair, and my vision went red. "Do

not talk about her like that. You have no clue what you just saw and instead of clarifying, you go right into fight mode."

Gus stared at me for a moment, his hands still splayed on the top of my desk. Then he stood and nodded. He pulled up a chair and sat, his forearms braced on his thighs. "I'm exhausted. I don't want to fight. I'm so done. So if you want to explain, here's your chance. That girl's had a rough time here." He laced his fingers and dropped his head. "People say awful things about her and her mother, and she's spent her whole life fighting for the respect she deserves. The last thing she needs is to be dragged down by another Hebert."

He was right. Of course he was. And the thought that I could drag her down just about killed me. "We've been together for a few weeks now," I said slowly. "She's incredible. I—" I cleared my throat. "I'm falling for her."

He groaned and slumped back. "Jesus."

"I know. Trust me, this was not the plan. But we click. We have fun no matter what we're doing. She's smart and hilarious and we like the same weird stuff. And strangely enough, she's into me. So I realize that this is inconvenient for you, but fuck off."

"So you're not using her?" The question was ridiculous, but his concern was clearly genuine.

My blood pressure spiked, but I breathed through it and kept my cool. "I should punch you for suggesting that. Don't lump me in with Cole."

"If you've been together for weeks, why did I just find out?"

I shrugged. "If I had my way, I'd walk into the diner every morning and kiss her in front of Father Renee and the knitting club. But this is what she wants, and I'd give her anything."

"What happens when she goes to school?"

"I will let her go." Just saying the words out loud made my stomach churn. "It may kill me, but I'll do it. She deserves it."

He nodded, his lips pressed together in a way that signaled his approval. Then the expression dropped, and he pinched the bridge of his nose. "Don't hurt her."

"I would never. Just please keep what you saw to yourself."

He frowned at me. Gus was pretty much a vault and probably spent more time chatting with his chainsaws than actual human beings.

I shifted in my chair, ready for a change of topic. "So why did you barge into my office?"

"Two things. First, the Barrett kid. I handed over everything I had about my interactions with both him and his predecessor at the Department of Fish and Wildlife."

"Okay." I leaned forward and rested my forearms on the desk. "Do we need a lawyer? Are we in trouble?"

"Nah. They seemed satisfied. He's only been on the job for about six months. Gary retired, and this guy came out here a few weeks ago to talk about the bats."

Ah. The bats. The fucking bats. Specifically the northern long-eared bat. The little fucker was an endangered species and nested in our forests. That little fact meant lots of regulatory work to ensure their safety and constant visits from our friends at Fish and Wildlife. Just another fun fact about the timber industry I wish I didn't know.

"Who would want to hurt the bat guy?"

Gus shrugged. "Beats the shit out of me."

"Is he gonna be okay?"

"Still in a coma. Officer Fielder told me they moved him to Portland. He's got family there. Poor kid. I feel so badly that it happened here."

"We're doing what we can to catch the people responsible. Just keep me posted if the police come poking around again, okay? I don't trust Souza. It feels like he's looking for an excuse to fuck us over."

Gus grunted. "No shit. He's so worried about his reputation since he was friends with Dad. Jude's convinced he wants us shut down and run out of town."

I agreed with Jude, but I wasn't interested in diving into the motives of small-town law enforcement with Gus. I had a shit ton of work waiting for me already.

"Lila found something too," I said, giving him a brief rundown of the questionable transactions.

He took his hat off and leaned back in his chair. "Fucking great. Gotta love Dad's web of lies and crime."

I laughed. At this point, there was nothing else I could do.

"I did the basics after Dad and Uncle Paul were arrested," Gus explained. "And I never saw any of this. If there was an invoice. I paid it. Miranda helped me, but we got the bills out, so everyone got paid."

"None of this was in the official databases," I explained. "You wouldn't have known unless you dug deep into the paper like we did. But this money exchange has been turned off for more than a year, and have you noticed anything shady with any accounts?"

Gus shook his head. "Not at all. But I was just trying to keep my head above water. If I missed something—"

"No," I interrupted. "You didn't. It's just more evidence that this shit went further than Dad. There were more people involved, so the sooner we get ourselves away from this mess, the better."

"Is this gonna ruin our sale?" Gus looked stricken. It was amazing how he'd come around to selling recently. We'd spent a lot of time going through the business together, him teaching me about logging and me teaching him about accounting, and we'd reached a mutual understanding of how badly we needed to be rid of this mess.

I shook my head. "Don't think so. There's no concrete evidence, and I'm certainly not looking to poke around in a drug conspiracy. The buyers are well aware of the company's criminal past, and this just helps me give them a better financial picture."

"Okay, good." He looked relieved. "Actually. That's why I came in here. To talk to you about the sale." He took a deep breath like he was steeling himself for battle and locked eyes with me. "I need help."

If I hadn't been sitting, I might have stumbled at that admission. Gus did not ask for help. Ever. He was a one-man show. He could do everything and anything better than a team of ten. He was always learning, always training, and could pick up any skill.

"We're behind. The cutting is done, but all the rain fucked us. We're behind on almost a dozen orders, and we're going to start incurring financial penalties if we don't deliver soon."

I had suspected as much, but Gus wasn't exactly an open

book, and my job was to sell the company, not run it, so I'd kept my nose out of his business.

"What can I do?"

He swallowed audibly. "I need to dip into the cash reserves."

My stomach sank. "There's nothing left."

"Dammit." He shook his head, but he looked unsurprised. "Even so, I need to hire a weekend crew. Maybe some of the guys I know who work for the Gagnons and the LeBlancs. We've got a couple million dollars' worth of trees in two separate log dumps up in the mountains. We need to get them down the roads and to the mill in the next couple of weeks."

I nodded. He was right. The contractual penalties for late deliveries were steep. And we couldn't fuck over the few loyal clients who'd stayed with us through all the rough years.

"Everything has to be wrapped up before the closing on July first."

He grunted. "Exactly. Which is why we've got to get on this now. And I'll need you too."

Dammit. I'd promised to help, but I wasn't much use outside the office. "I can't operate a crane or drive a commercial truck."

"Doesn't matter." He slid to the edge of his seat. "We need people to do inventory, make counts, track gas mileage, and direct traffic. Make sure things run smoothly."

I wasn't sure how much help I could be, but I nodded. "I'll do whatever you need."

"I'm gonna need Finn and Cole too."

"I'll rally the troops."

"Thank you." He shifted in his seat and grimaced. "I mean that. You've given up a lot for us. We'd be fucked without you. I hope you know how much we appreciate it. I'm sure Dad does too."

"Fuck, Dad." Anger flared hot in my veins. "I did this for you, and Finn, Jude, and Noah. Even Cole. We're brothers, Gus. No matter how far apart we've drifted, I love you guys. And I'm not going to screw you over. I hate this deal. I'd love to spend a year searching for a better one, but we can't make it that long. All I can do is get things wrapped up as quickly as possible so you can take your share and live your life."

He hung his head for a minute, and when he looked up at me again, his expression was pained. "About that."

I raised an eyebrow.

"After the sale closes, I'll stay for a couple of weeks to make the transition if you need me."

I wasn't surprised by the offer, but I nodded graciously. "That's generous of you."

"But then I'm leaving."

That had my breath stuttering in my lungs. Gus was Lovewell and Lovewell was Gus. This forest and this land were part of his DNA.

"I'm heading out west," he said. "I got an offer. In Oregon. To run operations for a big corporate outfit."

I blinked, at an absolute loss for words. He was going to move across the country? This man who'd spent his life taking care of the people he loved was going to leave them all?

"I've spent forty years in this town. There's nothing left for me. She's never coming back." The sigh he let out was full of resignation. "I need to push myself a little, get out into the world."

I was speechless. On the one hand, I was proud of him for putting himself first, on the other, I was still flabbergasted at the idea of him leaving behind the only place he'd ever called home. Also, who was the "she" he referred to?

"It's a great job," he said. "I'll run several crews, and I'll be closer to Noah. It's time I experience something different."

"Different?" I couldn't help but chuckle. "You know Oregon is Maine, but with a different ocean, right?"

He shot me a glare. "Thanks for your support, asshole."

I held my hands up. "I support you. If anyone deserves to leave all this drama behind, it's you."

He did. Gus had borne all the responsibility for the company since Dad's arrest. He'd dealt with the police and the lawyers, and he'd fought like hell to save as many jobs for his employees as possible. Years of working seven days a week and trying to salvage the family legacy had taken a toll.

I cracked a grin. "Is it weird to say I'll miss you?"

"Yes. Especially since you haven't visited in years."

"Hey, I-95 goes both north and south, dick. You could have come to me."

"You know I hate cities. And you've got your fancy life down there. I never wanted to intrude."

"You're my big brother. I'd be thrilled to have you. But make me a promise, okay?"

He nodded once in his gruff way.

"Before you go, come down to Boston. We'll go to a Revs game, drink a few beers, and eat good food. Let me show you my town before you head out."

He stood and held out his hand.

I heaved myself out of my chair too and took it.

"Done," he said, squeezing tightly. He already looked more at peace.

A fresh wave of guilt washed over me. I'd gotten to leave, experience life elsewhere, and I'd built something for myself. Gus had spent his life waiting for his turn to run the family business, and now we were selling it off, leaving him with very little to show for a lifetime of hard work and devotion.

After he left, I sank back in my chair, feeling the weight of that conversation. We'd need to push extra hard. We only had six weeks until closing. I was due back in Boston before then, so I'd have to delay again. Enzo had been understanding, but that was because I'd still been putting in the hours and dialing into every call and meeting I could. If I had to start working out in the woods, there was no way I'd keep up the way I had been.

But I'd deal with the details later. Right now, I needed to put my head down and get back to work. My family was counting on me.

Chapter 33
Lila

"Where are we going?" I asked, gripping his arm for dear life.

Owen had insisted I meet him in the parking lot of Hebert Timber, and when I arrived, he tied a scarf around my eyes as a blindfold.

"Shh. Just a bit farther." He led me down what felt like a dirt path. "Okay." He stood behind me and turned me toward the light that filtered through the scarf. Then he gently slid the fabric over my head and whispered, "Surprise."

I shook my head to get my bearings and took in my surroundings. We were in the small paved area behind the machine shop. Twinkle lights hung from the building and nearby shipping containers. A flatbed truck had been moved close, the bed set up with a big couch and ottoman and piled high with hand-knit blankets.

"What is this?" I asked as I turned slowly.

I'd just caught sight of a massive projection screen

mounted to the side of a shipping container when he pressed a kiss on the sensitive spot behind my ear.

"This is a movie date, gorgeous."

He stepped up beside me and offered me his elbow. Once I'd looped my arm through his, he guided me to where several folding tables were covered in a variety of gluten-free snacks and a bottle of prosecco chilled in an ice bucket.

"You did this?" I turned to him, my heart skipping.

He nodded, clutching my hands. "I wanted to have a special movie night with my girl."

"Owen," I pleaded. "You don't have to go to all this trouble for me."

He laughed and tilted my chin up, then gave me a chaste kiss. "I know I don't *have* to. And this is nothing. But since I've never seen *Say Anything*, I wanted to make this showing of it special."

"*Say Anything*!" I squealed, throwing my arms around his neck. "Thank you."

"Now get comfy. I'll bring snacks and drinks over."

He gave me a hand climbing up into the truck bed, and once I was settled, he loaded up on treats, then draped a blanket over us both and snuggled close.

"How did you set this all up?"

It was incredible. Who knew a couple of pole barns and old shipping containers could look like this?

"Gus helped with the lights. He's an electrician."

I shifted to face him. "I thought he ran the cutting operations."

"He does. But he went to technical school to become an electrician. My dad thought it would be an asset to the company."

At the mention of Gus, I immediately felt guilty. He'd caught us together and I'd run away like a child.

"I need to apologize, actually. When he walked in the other day, I panicked. I feel like such an idiot, leaving you to talk to him."

"It's fine. He's my family, and we had a good talk." His voice trailed off like there was something else he wanted to say. There was definitely a but coming.

"But I don't love how this feels. I don't want to hide you or my feelings for you. You're worth so much more than that."

And the realization of just how selfish I was being hit me square in the gut. Owen was patient, mature, and selfless. He was trying to build something with me. And I was acting like a child.

"I'm sorry," I said, wringing my hands. "I want to be ready to tell people. But first, I need to talk to Cole."

He froze. We'd danced around the Cole issue a few times, but we'd yet to dive in. Mainly because it was painful and awkward, and I wanted the small amount of time I had with Owen to be fun. But again, this was on me and my constant desire to avoid conflict.

"I'm almost ready," I promised. "I just need to do this at my own pace."

He put his arm around me and kissed the top of my head. It was a far kinder reaction than I deserved.

"Gus came around quickly. He's just overprotective. But he helped me do all this."

I relaxed into him, enjoying the change of subject. "A man of many talents."

"You have no idea. He's also a really accomplished

chainsaw artist, can cook like a Michelin star chef, and built his own house."

"Overachiever," I coughed into my hand.

Owen shrugged. "Oldest child syndrome. He's one of those people who's always learning something new, always pushing himself." His tone implied some mockery, but in a lighthearted way.

I gave him a gentle shove. "Like you should talk, Mr. Ambitious Perfection."

He put his hand on his chest and scoffed. "Me?"

I leaned forward, pulling him in for a kiss. "Yes, you. You set up an outdoor movie theater for me. You don't need to try so hard." I kissed him again.

He pulled me so close I was almost on top of him. He was always like this, urging me closer, his hands always on my body. It thrilled me.

"You were getting laid anyway," I said, biting my lip.

He reared back a little, his brow furrowed, and gave me the stern daddy look that made my knees weak. "Lila, this has nothing to do with getting laid. I'm trying to show you how damn special you are."

My heart practically floated right out of my chest at his sincerity. God, how did I have a chance in hell with this man?

I pulled him close and put my head on his chest. I knew I couldn't keep him. That this couldn't last forever. But was it wrong that I wanted it so badly?

"If you were home in Boston right now," I asked, "what would you be doing?"

He blew out a breath. "On a Friday night? I'd be in my office," he mused. "Enzo would stop by for a beer, and

Amara would stop by to drop off contracts and get some sassy comments in. And then I'd work."

I snuggled closer. "And after?"

"In our younger days, Enzo and I would work late and then hit a bar or club, have a few drinks, and unwind."

"And meet ladies?" I hated how clingy I sounded.

"Sometimes." He smoothed a hand down my hair. "But I was never great at that."

"Bullshit." I grinned up at him. "We both know the ladies of Boston were throwing themselves at you."

A deep laugh rumbled out of him. "Not even close."

I gave him an eye roll. "Okay, keep talking."

"In the last several years, instead of going out to bars, we'd usually grab dinner and talk about work and sports. Then I'd go home and crash. Enzo started dating Delia a few months ago, so that's changed too. Now he spends every free minute with her. Not that I can blame him. She's way better looking than me."

"That must have been hard to adjust to."

He shrugged. "Enzo is my brother in every way but blood. He deserves his happiness. Delia is a handful, and so are her twin girls, but he is so damn happy. And he's finally working less. It's good to see him so content, even if I don't get to see him as much. But this is what he wants. He's a big family guy."

Maybe it was the wine or the mild weather or the adorable romantic gesture he'd gone to all this trouble to set up, but suddenly, I wanted to share. Hell, I needed to share.

"That's actually one of the reasons Cole and I didn't work out," I said tentatively.

I felt his body stiffen next to me. "What do you mean?"

"He wanted a very specific kind of life. Marriage, lots of kids, house up here in Maine."

"And you don't want that."

I shook my head. "I don't. I guess I thought that once he got a pro contract, we'd settle in the city and I'd build my career and we'd travel in the off-season. But then it started to look like hockey wasn't going to work out, and he started to talk about having kids soon and buying a house up here.

"My mom had me when she was in high school. You know that." I sat up so I could face him completely. "For every single minute of my life, I've been aware of just how much of a burden I was."

"You are not," he protested, grasping my hand.

"Logically, I know that. My mom has never made me feel as though she didn't want me, and she has devoted her life to caring for me. But I've seen the toll it's taken on her. She put her own life on hold for me."

He stared at me, his lips parted as if he was surprised by this revelation.

"My whole life, the world has just assumed I'd get married and have kids. Be some guy's wife and some kid's mom. It took me a long time to realize that I get to call the shots and decide what's right for me. The real me, not some idealized version. And I'm good with just me."

I could remember the sheer panic I felt when Cole brought it up. The immediate desire to run away and hide. Our relationship was hanging on by a thread at that point, so even if I'd wanted kids, I wouldn't have wanted to bring them into that dysfunction. And I'd spent so much time supporting his dreams, and he hadn't even bothered to ask me what mine were. It was so typical of Cole. He just assumed I'd go along with whatever he wanted.

"I realize that's probably a deal-breaker for you," I said, feeling nauseous. We hadn't defined the future yet. We were still tiptoeing around the fact that he was leaving soon.

He took a sip of his prosecco and looked out into the dark for a long moment before peering down at me. "Can I be honest?"

"Always."

He looked away again. "I don't want kids either."

I bolted upright. If I'd been drinking my prosecco, I no doubt would have done a spit-take. Owen Hebert? He had *responsible family* man written all over him.

"I want a partner," he clarified. "I want to be one-half of that kind of family. I want nights where we cook meals together and vacations, just the two of us. I want someone to come home to, someone to share my life with. Maybe a pet or two." He took another sip. "But kids? Nah, probably not for me."

I was well and truly shocked. Owen Hebert would make the best kind of dad. He was authoritative and could be strict, but he was patient, kind, and successful.

"Really?" I asked.

His nod was slow. "My family is huge. Our house was pure chaos. I guess I've never felt the urge to create a life like that. It's not to say that I don't like kids. I love Merry. And I can't wait for the new baby to arrive.

"And being here these past few weeks has made me realize how much I want to be closer to my brothers and my mom. I want to work on strengthening those relationships.

But I have just never had any interest in children of my own."

Huh. This conversation had taken a very deep and very strange turn. But I wanted to know everything about Owen. I wanted to dig down deep and get to know all the parts of him, even the not-so-great ones. I'd never experienced this kind of honesty and intimacy before, and I was hooked.

I shifted, nestling myself in closer again.

"Ooh," I said. "I forgot to mention a cat. I really want a cat. I'm getting one as soon as I've got a home and a job. Maybe two cats. We'll see."

He was silent, like I'd stunned him speechless, so I gave him a shove.

"What?"

"Nothing." He shook his head. "I just didn't figure you for a cat lady."

I elbowed him. "Big time cat lady. When I die, I'm going to leave them everything. I'll make sure they have a butler to wait on them and everything when I'm gone."

We were both laughing now, but the air had grown heavy, and a weight had dropped into my stomach.

Likely sensing it too, he pulled his phone from his pocket, pressed a few buttons, and pulled me close.

I closed my eyes for a moment, taking a mental snapshot of this perfect night. Something I could look back on to give me hope when things were difficult. To remind myself of how two struggling people came together and built one another up while having a lot of fun in the process.

"You've set me up with high expectations. I hope this '80s teen rom-com can deliver."

"Oh, it can and it will. Just shut up and enjoy your vintage Cusack."

"You know, he's old enough to be your dad."

"How dare you? His charm is timeless. Pay attention, Hebert. You could learn a thing or two from Lloyd Dobler."

Chapter 34
Lila

I was bone tired. Working multiple jobs, sneaking around with Owen, and filling out financial aid forms had me running myself ragged these days. But Magnolia had flown in to check on Willa, so I had to rally for girls' night.

Poor Willa had been in Portland with her parents for the last few days, making arrangements and talking to doctors. Her father would return home after he completed a stint in a rehab hospital down south, and she was taking it all so hard.

Willa was short and curvy, with honey-blond hair and dark brown eyes. She was one of the most motivated people I'd ever met. Since we were little kids, she'd worked harder and longer than everyone, always striving to be the best, but she'd done it all with a smile on her face.

Seeing her so pale, with shadows under her eyes, was killing me.

I put my arm around her and pulled her close. Magnolia had arrived early and convinced Jim to give us the huge booth in the back so we could have a little privacy, away from the prying eyes and listening ears of Lovewell.

As much as I'd love to be at home curled up in my sweats with a Hallmark movie, Willa needed us.

Magnolia raised her wineglass. "First order of business. A congratulatory toast to our girl Lila. Accepted to every grad school she applied to."

Warmth spread through me as I clinked my glass with theirs. It had been unexpected, to say the least. But the notifications had kept coming in. Five acceptances. I was still waiting on financial aid decisions, but there wasn't much that could keep me from New York and our plan.

Willa teared up. "I'm so happy for you." Sniffling, she accepted the cocktail napkin I held out to her. "You'll have to have fun in New York without me."

"Don't say that," Mags said, pulling her shoulders back resolutely. "We're not doing this without you."

She shook her head. "I can't. I have to take over the clinic here while Dad recovers. This county desperately needs doctors, and I'm board certified now."

"You don't know what the future holds." I set my drink down and clutched her hand. "You could be in New York doing your fellowship in six months."

"Doubtful." Her shoulders slumped. "Dad is looking at probably a year of concentrated rehab to get his quality of life back, and even then, he may never be able to practice medicine again." She swallowed thickly, then gave us a sad smile. "This is where I belong. It's the family legacy. The Gagnons and the Heberts have their timber, and the Savards take care of people."

She had always been so proud of this history, but that

didn't mean she wasn't struggling with the responsibility. Willa was a great doctor. She could do this, but my heart broke for her. Like me, she'd been dreaming about the freedom and excitement of New York for so long.

Her great-grandmother had been a midwife, and she'd delivered every baby in this town for more than thirty years. Her grandfather and her father had served our community as doctors. Her mother was a psychologist who operated a sliding-scale practice to support mental health access for low-income families.

"They all devoted their lives to Lovewell. It's my destiny too. I know that. But I thought I'd have a little time for myself first. I'd get my three years in New York so I'd know what it was like to just live for a while before all the responsibility kicked in."

As she drained her wineglass, Magnolia gestured to Jim to bring the bottle.

"These were supposed to be my years. I'd do my fellowship in New York, work normal hours, and have a life. I'd date. I was going to get in shape. I was even going to find a few hobbies."

Magnolia arched an eyebrow at her. "Really? Dr. Willa Savard is going to develop hobbies?"

She frowned, affronted. "Maybe table tennis. Or knitting." She tilted her head. "Or falconry."

"Falconry. Now you're just fucking with us."

"Falcons are very majestic birds," she said, covering her mouth to hide her giggles. Willa had no poker face.

God, even when things were rough, I could always laugh with my girls. I was so lucky they'd stuck with me through all the Cole drama. Each had warned me about giving up on myself and my future several times. They'd even staged an intervention before we moved to Florida, but I wouldn't hear their concerns. I was sure that if I could just be a better girlfriend, if I could wear the right clothes and do my makeup perfectly, be friendlier, more supportive, then things would get better, and eventually, I'd get the happily ever after I'd been searching for since I was a kid.

I closed my eyes and thanked the universe for bringing these insane, beautiful people into my life.

"This is why I love you," Magnolia said. "You are going to be just fine, Dr. Willa Savard. We won't let you miss out on anything."

"I shouldn't even be saying this stuff out loud." She deflated. "I'm such a terrible daughter. I could have lost my dad. Really, I'm so grateful he's okay."

I covered her hand with mine and gave it a squeeze. "You can say anything to us. It's not selfish to have complex feelings about something this major. Your plans and priorities are shifting, and that's hard. We're always here and willing to listen without judgment."

And the tears were back. She blotted at her eyes with the cocktail napkin again. "He's always been my hero."

My heart clenched. Willa had the kind of loving nuclear family I had longed for as a kid.

"It breaks my heart that he's hurting. There's no question that I will pick up the slack. I'll get things worked out at the clinic. I have to finish my residency program in June, but I owe it to him to do my best. It just feels like so much."

"It is a lot," Magnolia said, scooting closer and putting her head on Willa's shoulder. "But you can do hard things. And you won't be alone. I can come up every couple of weeks and help however I can. We can come here for drinks. Ooh, I have an idea." She perked up and flagged Jim, the curmudgeonly owner of the Moose, down. "Jim, would you be opposed to going to mixology school? I'll pay. That way we can elevate the cocktail game in this place."

Jim threw a bar towel over his shoulder and scowled before stomping to the other end of the bar.

"Okay, we'll work on him. I'll get you New York caliber cocktails, babe, just wait. There's not much I can do about the waffle fries, though."

"You can't change the waffle fries," I said. They were unarguably the superior fry in Penobscot County, but sadly, until Jim invested in a dedicated fryer, I couldn't eat them. So instead, I got a side of celery that usually accompanied the buffalo wings. Not exactly the best bar snack.

Magnolia popped one into her mouth and chewed. "True. They're not sushi at Nobu, but they taste pretty damn good."

Willa broke out in a watery smile. "I love you both so much. But let's not kid ourselves. I'm going to be working nonstop, keeping up with patients and billing and insurance and making house calls. Any hope of having a life has vanished. But it's okay. It's a privilege to serve the people of Lovewell and keep them healthy. I'll probably have to move in with my parents, but I'll make it."

"Wow, that's the spirit," Magnolia deadpanned. "How about this? Take my house. Live there. Do whatever you want."

"I couldn't. What if you need it?"

"Given that it's a seven-bedroom lakefront mansion, I'm pretty sure there's room for me to visit." She picked up another waffle fry and dipped it in ketchup. "It rarely gets used. After all the money I spent on the damn roof last year, someone should live there and benefit from it."

Willa worried her lip and studied her wineglass. "I'm not sure."

"You were going to live in my house in New York. Why not live in my house in Lovewell instead? I'll make sure Mr. and Mrs. Lewis take good care of you."

"They're still alive?" The Lewises had been caretakers of the house back when we were kids.

"Yup." She sipped her wine. "I built a retirement cottage for them on the property. They don't do much anymore except call me when something needs to be fixed. But I love them. They have been far kinder to me than any of my actual relatives."

This was textbook Magnolia, so generous and so loving.

I nudged Willa. "Do it. You could wake up every morning with a view of the lake. I've been living here for more than a year now. Trust me, there are a lot of plus sides."

Willa practically gaped at me. I'd been complaining about this place my whole life, but it was the truth.

I held up one finger. "Natural scenic beauty." I added a second. "A slower pace." Then a third. "Real, genuine people—"

She grasped my hand, interrupting me. "I get it. Thank you for trying to cheer me up."

"This place is leveling up," Magnolia argued. "Have you been to the new coffee shop yet? It's not the only new business in town either. I've heard rumors that they're bringing back the River Festival. And the Smiths are selling the inn."

Magnolia tapped her metallic gold nails against her wineglass. "I'm thinking I might buy it."

I choked on my wine. Eyes watering, I slapped a hand to my chest and gasped. "You're going to buy the inn? *How rich are you?*"

She shook her head. "Don't ask. It's just so charming. The town needs it if we want any of the other local businesses to survive long term. And you know I love a renovation project."

Willa shook her blond hair. "I'm confused. You, Magnolia Stephens-Thomas, are going to give up planning events in the Big Apple to become a backwoods innkeeper?"

Magnolia threw a balled-up napkin at her. "Gross, no. You make it sound so sad. I won't be the one running it. I'll buy it and fix it up, then I'll find someone to run it for me. It would be a strategic investment in the economic future of Lovewell."

"You're insane," Willa scoffed.

Magnolia flicked her hair. "Oh, I know it. Here's the thing. We can't control the future, but we can control how we show up for one another. So just because you'll be here and Lila and I will be elsewhere doesn't mean we won't have your back every single day."

Willa lowered her head, fighting back another round of tears. "Thank you."

"We will find a way to live our dreams. We're scrappy, gorgeous, and smart." Magnolia held her glass aloft. "The world better get the fuck out of our way."

The girls ordered a second basket of fries and we were feeling much better by the time the band set up for the night. I hadn't really participated in the Lovewell nightlife scene since I'd been home, but even I knew about Jasper Hawkins and his band. A few of them were local timber guys, and a couple others worked down at the hydroelectric plant in Woodville. They mostly played covers and performed at town events and weddings.

Magnolia was trying to convince us to come back to her house for a sleepover when the air in the bar shifted. The Heberts had arrived. En masse.

Including Owen.

And damn, he looked good. Was he wearing a flannel shirt or had I had too much wine?

Despite my better judgment, I craned my neck to get a better look.

"Ooh." Magnolia bounced in her seat and rubbed her hands together. "The lumberjack brigade has arrived. We've got Scruffy Lumberjack, Corporate Lumberjack, Man Bun Lumberjack, and, ooh, my personal favorite, Sensitive Musician Lumberjack. It's a goddamn buffet, ladies."

I slid her wineglass away. It was probably time to cut her off.

With one brow lifted, she smirked at me. "You calling dibs on Corporate?"

I only spared a second to glare at her before my attention diverted back to Owen. He was like a homing beacon, and I couldn't look away. His hair was a little longer than when he'd returned to town, almost shaggy, and his perpetual stubble had officially transformed into a full-blown beard. He was wearing jeans and a pair of broken-in work boots. And yes, he really, really was wearing a flannel shirt.

Damn him. I swore I ovulated on the spot. That was the magic of Lovewell. It could turn even the most impeccably groomed Tom Ford–wearing city guy into a feral lumberjack in a matter of weeks.

The moment he came into view, my pulse had taken off, and my core had tightened. That was the effect this man had on me. He'd been out in the woods helping Gus for a couple of days, so I'd been starving for him already. Now that he was in my proximity, I was ravenous.

But what was he doing here? Owen avoided town events and crowds if at all possible.

When Jude climbed up on stage, it made more sense. They'd come to watch him play. So adorable.

Jude slung his guitar strap over his head and ducked down, tuning the instrument. He sometimes played with the band, but he was so reserved that he usually faded into the background.

"Are we going to talk about this?" Willa asked, slapping my hand gently. "Or do you expect us to pretend you're not eye fucking your hot boss right now?"

"Pretty sure she's done a lot more than eye fucking, Willa," Magnolia leaned forward, a Cheshire cat grin spreading across her face. "Now be a good girl and spill. He's incredible in bed, right?"

"Stooop," I whisper-yelled, my face flaming.

Owen stopped at a table and greeted Henri Gagnon and his wife Alice, then wandered to the bar and spoke to Jim for a moment, probably ordering drinks. He looked so comfortable here, almost like he was enjoying himself.

"I get it, I really do." Willa sighed. "Those Hebert boys are fine specimens. I dig what he's got going on. Polished enough to look like he's super in control, but then you've got the beard and the rolled-up sleeves, which make it clear he's all business about making you come, too."

All the air whooshed from my lungs. "Willa!"

She shrugged and brought her wine to her lips. "I'm just calling it like I see it," she said over the rim.

"I bet business daddy is great with his tongue," Magnolia said, nudging Willa. "Now start talking, Lila." She pinned me with a look. "Or else I'll go ask him myself."

Sadly, she was not bluffing.

Whimpering, I dropped my head into my hands. Then, with a sigh, I spilled. "We went to Boston for work. And things heated up. We said it was a one-time thing."

"Only one time?"

"One-weekend thing," I corrected. "And I tried so hard, you guys. I tried to stay away. But he kept being really sweet and sexy and vulnerable."

"And?" They were both staring at me, eyes wide and mouths agape.

"And so we've been sneaking around. He may have built me an outdoor movie theater where we watched *Say Anything*."

"So Cusack is involved?" Mags asked. "This is serious."

I hung my head. "I'm fucked. Someone is going to find out, and it's all a mess, and I really like him."

"Hey." Willa rubbed soothing circles on my back. "Slow down."

Reluctantly, I looked up, fully spiraling now.

"You don't have to justify anything to us," Magnolia

assured me. "We're your best friends. And given that we both have functional eyes, we can see what you've been up against."

"And that's so great that you like him!" Ugh, Willa was such a romantic sometimes.

"No it's not." I dropped my head back and groaned. "We crossed the line in Boston, and it was supposed to stop there. Like a hall pass. But I can't stay away from him. And it's not just a sex thing. I adore him. He's sweet and protective and incredibly supportive of my dreams."

I was being torn in two. Part of me was angry that I couldn't draw and maintain a boundary when it came to him. But when was the last time I'd been impulsive? When had I last done exactly what I wanted to do when I wanted to do it? I'd lived my life pleasing others. For once, I'd gone after what I wanted, and it was incredible.

Willa frowned and swirled her wine. "So why is this a problem?"

"Because she's still hung up on Cole," Magnolia said, shooting me a look of pity.

"No," I practically shouted, almost knocking over my wineglass in my haste to object. "Not at all. Just because I won't publicly date his brother doesn't mean I'm still in love with him. I just want to get out of Lovewell unscathed. Build my life in New York. Can you imagine what people would say if they found out about Owen and me?"

"They're going to talk regardless." Magnolia shrugged, as if it was no big deal. "At least give them something juicy."

"That's not helpful." This from Willa. Thank God one of them had a little sense. She'd been through the wringer with this town too. "Sure, people here might think you're some devil woman who dumped the sweet, handsome hockey star when he got seriously injured."

Oh God, it sounded even worse when she said it out loud.

"But we know he spent years driving you away with his narcissistic behavior and non-stop partying. We know that he was distant and unresponsive and treated you like a maid most of the time."

I pinched the bridge of my nose. God, why did I stay so long with someone who was so wrong for me? My friends thought I was this strong, independent woman, but that was such a lie.

"Stop that," Magnolia snapped. "Self-doubt gives you wrinkles. You've done nothing wrong here. Enjoy your fling with the hot, kind man."

"I'm going to NYU."

"Exactly." She nodded once. "Make the most out of your time here. Plus, sneaking around is hot."

"I'm obviously terrible at it if you guys could tell we were fucking the second he walked in."

"We can tell because we know you so well. I've never seen you look at a guy like that. No one will catch on, and he's leaving soon, right?"

I nodded. "But he's my ex's brother."

"The brother said ex has practically no relationship with. You haven't crossed any ethical lines here." She splayed her hands on the table and inspected her nails. "And sure, Cole is great if you're into gigantic hockey players who are six-six and built like a Mack Truck. But Owen, he's mature and capable, and even from here, I can tell he's the kind of man who's focused in the bedroom. He pays attention. Wants to get things right."

She raised one eyebrow, and my responding blush confirmed her suspicions.

With my lip caught between my teeth, I scanned the bar again. It was impossible not to seek him out. He and Gus were shooting pool with a couple of guys who were dressed like they'd probably spent the day in the woods too. The sleeves of Owen's flannel were rolled up, the muscles in his forearms tensing as he set up his shot. As he pulled back, he turned my way and caught me watching him. He slid the pool cue through his fingers and completely missed the ball.

A laugh bubbled out of me. That was pure Owen, trying to do something slick and not quite nailing it.

"Go talk to him." Magnolia nudged my arm.

"No." I forced my attention back to my friends. "It's girls' night, and he's with his brothers."

Cole wasn't here, though that wasn't surprising, especially after the arrest for vandalism. He'd always believed he was the black sheep, but he made things harder for himself. I'd spent years trying to talk sense into him, to no avail.

"Okay, then just keep staring." Willa said, though I didn't register her words. I was too busy watching Owen again.

God, he looked good. And while I'd seen him two nights ago, my body was already aching for him. I wanted to throw my arms around his neck and melt into him while we slow danced. I wanted to claim him as mine in front of all these people.

Which was dumb. So fucking dumb. The dumbest idea ever.

So instead, I'd sit here and watch him.

I was reentering the conversation with my friends when a tiny redhead wandered toward the pool table and greeted the assembled crowd like an old friend.

Who was this girl? She wore sky-high heels and had wild, curly hair.

Another woman I didn't recognize, with long legs and thick bangs, trailed her and joined the conversation too.

"That's Liv," Willa said beside me.

I hummed, going for uninterested, but then she got closer to Owen and shook his hand a little too enthusiastically, and my ability to play it cool evaporated.

I twisted my napkin as he smiled down at her.

"She's a famous author," Willa explained. "She visits from time to time. I think she's friends with the Gagnons. My mom's book club has read all her books."

"And the tall one with her?"

"No idea." She shrugged, her arm brushing mine. "Maybe someone from Portland."

I gritted my teeth, wishing I was the one over there with Owen, laughing and touching his arm. Playing with my hair and tossing him saucy looks as we played pool together.

My heart panged. This was so unfair.

"You could sit here pouting or you could go talk to the man," Willa deadpanned.

"Just don't stick your tongue down this throat," Magnolia added. "No one will know. If you lose control and get too handsy, I'll create a diversion."

Feeling a fraction lighter, I laughed. "Thanks for having my back, girls."

I should stay put with my friends and enjoy the live music and the rare night out.

But my body was impossible to reason with, and Owen was too far away. I needed him close, even if I couldn't touch him the way I wanted to.

"Maybe I'll just go say hi," I said, sliding out of the booth.

"Keep your hands to yourself and your tongue in your mouth."

Whirling around, I blew a raspberry at them, then I strode for the pool tables.

I wasn't sure what I'd say or do, but I'd die if I didn't get closer to him. The rest I'd figure out later.

Chapter 35
Owen

I registered Lila's presence the moment I walked into the bar. Keeping my eyes off her while she laughed and joked with her friends was pure torture.

For two days, I'd been out in the woods with Gus and Jude, driving between camps, taking inventory of what we had, and making plans to close out our last orders. My dad had been arrested more than a year and a half ago, and despite the fallout, Gus had kept our customers happy and the trucks on the road. I knew this was bittersweet for him.

Our new lawyers were burying us in document requests and scheduled virtual meetings almost daily to discuss projections, and Lila had handled everything with ease. God, she was going to kick ass in graduate school.

She had the makings of an incredible leader. I'd be shocked if she wasn't running a major foundation in five years.

And she looked so pretty in the booth. Her hair was down and her eyes were sparkling as she laughed on the other side of the crowded bar. I wanted to throw her over my shoulder and take her back to my cabin so I could ravage her.

But I was here for Jude tonight.

Generally, I avoided the Moose, since it was busy and loud and filled with people who didn't like me. Plus, I should be working. But it had been years since I'd seen Jude play.

He'd always loved music. Mom had bought him his first guitar from a second-hand shop in Bangor when he was seven, and he'd quickly taught himself just about all he needed to know.

If things had been different, if there had been money or opportunity, and if he'd been interested, he could have studied music, and maybe he could have made a go of things professionally. He'd never publicly considered it, but he wasn't the kind to ruffle feathers or push too hard against either of our parents' wishes. Like Gus, he'd earned all his licenses and certifications quickly and had come back to work for Dad.

He never stopped playing guitar, though. Noah used to talk about the songs he wrote, but he was the only one who'd ever heard them.

A few years ago, Jude had started playing with a local band, fronted by Jasper Hawkins, a full-time lumberjack and part-time small-town rock star. My mom had pushed Jude to officially join the band, but he insisted on only filling in on occasion.

But he was slowly coming out of his shell, and tonight, he was playing lead guitar for the first time. According to Gus, Jude still wasn't sharing any songs he'd written, but it was a start.

After years of never showing up for my brothers, I hoped

I could make up for lost time. At least while I was here. So I was nursing a beer and doing my best to ignore scrutinizing looks from folks I hadn't seen in decades. Thankfully, I was decent at pool, which was a good distraction. And it was the one activity where Gus wouldn't mop the floor with me.

Eventually, every person in the place had gotten into the music, which was a mix of indie and country covers with a few originals mixed in. These guys were really good. And shit, my brother was talented. He barely even looked out at the crowd, instead putting every ounce of focus into what he was doing, playing with his entire body as the music flowed through him.

I was bursting with pride. I was caught up in it when Gus elbowed me and handed me another beer.

"Good, ayuh?" He lifted his chin, gesturing to our little brother.

I nodded. "How did he get this good?"

He shrugged. "Beats me. The kid works hard and spends most of his time wandering around the woods with his dog, but this is his true love. I can feel it."

On the other side of the dance floor, a tall, willowy woman with thick bangs and a hipster vibe had her hands clasped in front of her and was focused intently on Jude.

"He's got fans," I said to Gus.

"Don't know her." He took a long pull of his beer and nodded at the redhead who'd come up to talk to my brothers. "Think she's friends with Liv. There are a lot of them. Every time he plays here, the women line up. It's the quiet ones, you know?"

I turned, needing another hit of Lila, but her seat was empty. A sadness far too acute for the situation hit me. More than anything, I wished she'd walk over here and kiss me in front of the whole bar. Claim me the way I wanted to claim her. This sneaking around shit was getting old.

Frustration had just pushed aside the sadness when there was a tap on my shoulder.

One glance back, and all those negative emotions dissipated. She was standing behind me wearing an innocent smile.

I wanted to reach out and pull her in close and press my lips to hers, but I gripped my beer bottle instead, squeezing so hard I worried it would explode in my hand.

"L-Lila," I choked out over the music.

She wedged herself in front of me, boxing out the redheaded woman friend of the Gagnons.

My heart flipped over in my chest at her proximity. We were in public, yet she was standing so close I could feel her warmth. Huh.

"The band is great," she said, already swaying to the music. "I love Zach Bryan."

We stood facing each other awkwardly for a few moments before she stood up on her tiptoes and whispered in my ear. "A flannel shirt? Are you trying to kill me?"

I snorted, and when she dropped back to the balls of her feet, I gave her a wink. "I've been spending a lot of time with the boys out in the woods. I'm embracing my inner lumberjack."

I'd ordered a dozen online last week after she'd made an offhand comment about how I'd look hot in one, but she didn't need to know that.

Her eyes were dancing, even as she rolled them at me. "Not fair."

I chuckled to myself. Hell no, I wasn't playing fair. She should know that by now. I knew what I wanted, and I'd do what I could to get it. I wanted her to be mine. Now and always. Officially and publicly. So if I had to grow out my beard and embrace the flannel, then so be it.

When the band took a break, she gave me a pointed look, then sauntered toward the back door. Halfway there, she peeked over her shoulder and winked.

I pulled my phone from my pocket and checked the screen, like I'd gotten a call I needed to answer, then made my way through the crowd, heading out the front. Once I hit the sidewalk, I rounded the large building. The parking lot was down the hill and well lit, but this side of the bar backed up against the forest.

"This isn't sketchy at all," I said, striding right up to her. "You miss me?"

In response to my question, she splayed her hands on either side of my face and pulled my face down to kiss the hell out of me.

I braced one hand against the side of the building and let her go wild. God, I'd missed her. We'd texted and spoken on the phone, but the relief of being able to touch her was palpable. She gripped my hair as she slid her tongue into my mouth, and I temporarily forgot that we were making out like teenagers behind a dive bar off Highway 16.

I pulled back. "Good to see you too."

"You're an asshole. Coming in here, looking like that," she teased, pulling her lip between her teeth. "How am I supposed to keep my panties on?"

Desire stirred inside me as I zeroed in on her mouth.

Damn, I loved her sass, and I loved that she was comfortable enough to be her true self when she was with me.

"I still have beard burn everywhere," she said.

I squeezed her ass hard. "Good. Evidence that I did my job." I bit down on her earlobe.

She arched her back and my mind was flooded with the need to taste her. Right here and now.

"Were you trying to make me jealous?" She moaned.

My laugh bounced off the wall behind her. "Jealous? Because I came to a bar and drank a beer while my brother played music?"

"You were flirting with those women." Her tone was light, but she couldn't hide the worry in her eyes.

I shook my head. "I exchanged pleasantries with a few members of the opposite sex. Hardly flirting. But," I bent down and kissed her neck, "jealousy looks good on you. I think I like you like this."

She pushed me back. "Really? Angry and horny?"

"Oh yes. I love it." And I had the hard dick to prove it.

I picked her up and pushed her against the wall, relishing the way she wrapped her legs around my waist. God, I could get lost in her all night.

She let out a needy whimper that shot straight to my cock. Shit, I needed to get myself under control.

I put her down gently and smoothed my hands down her arms. "I'm not fucking you next to a dumpster outside the Moose."

She glared up at me. "Then take me home and fuck me."

Jesus. That sounded good. No, perfect. I would trade a kidney if it meant she'd say that to me every single night.

But... "I'm here to support Jude," I said. "And my brothers. I don't get to spend a lot of time with them."

I dug my keys out of my pocket and slid the one to the cabin off the ring.

"I'm going to stay for the next set. Go to my cabin. Take a bubble bath, have a glass of wine, and wait for me."

She nodded and took the key. "Okay. Stay as long as you want. It's important."

The smile she gave me was genuine, but disappointment flashed in her eyes.

"When the band wraps up, I'm out of here. And then you're all mine for the entire night." I gave her ass a hard squeeze. "Rest up now. If you're a good girl and listen, I'll make you come at least ten times."

Chapter 36
Lila

Hanging around Owen's cabin was more fun than I'd expected. Willa and Magnolia had left the bar early with plans to go to Magnolia's to watch movies and do face masks, so I didn't feel guilty heading here and waiting for him.

When I entered the cabin, I noticed something strange on the kitchen island. It was a large rectangular appliance. On closer inspection, it was some kind of oven. I plugged the brand name, Breville, into Google and searched for the model.

Oh shit. It was a countertop pizza oven. And it cost almost a thousand dollars. Damn. I didn't realize Owen liked pizza that much.

But then I turned around and saw the dozen bags of flour lining the small area between the sink and the range. I picked up a glossy bag of designer flour. The entire label was in Italian. But two words stuck out: senza glutine. Gluten free. Huh.

The other bags all read gluten free.

I picked up a stack of flour-crusted printouts. Each one was a recipe for gluten-free pizza dough. His messy handwriting was on each page. There were notes, highlights, and alternative measurements. Was he running some kind of test kitchen in here?

As I sealed each bag and wiped down the counters, my mind wandered. Was he doing this for me? He'd baked scones before. And those incredible blueberry muffins after he got one at the Caffeinated Moose and I said I was jealous. Was he really trying to crack the pizza code? For me?

My heart clenched. Some girls were about the flowers and jewelry. But this right here was my love language.

I took a photo of the pizza oven and the flour and texted it to the girls.

MAGNOLIA

He's not cooking meth, is he? Potential deal-breaker.

WILLA

Potential? Absolute deal-breaker. But that's not meth. It's bread flour.

LILA

Imported Italian pizza flour, actually. I think he's trying to make good gluten-free pizza for me...

WILLA

SWOON

MAGNOLIA

Wow, he really knows you. You complain endlessly about pizza.

WILLA

He spends his nonexistent free time elbow-deep in flour so you don't feel left out on pizza night? That's husband material right there.

I gasped and almost dropped my phone. Husband material? Willa wasn't wrong. Not that I was looking for a husband. Fuck no.

But I couldn't help but daydream a little. Owen would be an incredible husband. God, I was insane. A few bags of flour, and I was practically writing vows. And we still hadn't talked about what was going to happen when he had to leave Lovewell. Would he want to do long distance? Would I?

This was real, no matter how much I might like to deny it. And letting him go was unconscionable. So we'd have to figure it out. God, I was such a mess. I'd come over here to seduce him, and now I was spiraling into what-ifs.

Positive thinking, Lila. I'd come here to get laid, and clearly, I needed to take my mind off everything.

So, at his suggestion, I did take a bath. I couldn't resist the claw-foot tub situated in front of a massive window that looked out at the moonlit mountains. I enjoyed a glass of wine and a spicy book in that bath, which only served to make me ravenous for him to get home.

Neediness was one of my worst traits. I'd promised myself I'd work on it, but it was virtually impossible where Owen was concerned. Something about him made me ache. I never felt the need to keep up some cool girl facade with him. No need to feign indifference. Nope, I was a full-on crazy woman, getting jealous and mounting him behind a dive bar.

He'd come so far, and I loved that he was making an effort to spend time with his brothers. I wanted him to cultivate those relationships. But I also wanted him here with me, preferably naked. God, I was so ridiculous.

So I entertained myself, first with a rom-com and a second glass of wine, and later by looking at the collection of brand-new, ultra-soft flannel shirts neatly hanging in the closet. Huh. Between these, the cedarwood beard oil I found in the bathroom, and his new affinity for chopping wood with the boys after work, he had clearly taken to the mountain man lifestyle easily.

Which was good for me. It was hot as fuck.

But standing there, staring at those neatly hung shirts, I had an idea.

When I heard his car pull up, I rushed into position, giddy over the thought of surprising him.

I perched on the freshly cleaned countertop, shaking with excitement.

"Lila," he said, toeing off his boots at the door.

"Holy shit," he exclaimed when he saw me. "Are you wearing my shirt?"

With a feral growl, he stalked over to me and picked me up.

"And nothing else?" He ran a hand over my bare hip as I wrapped my arms around his neck.

He set me on my feet and took a step back. "Let me look at you."

I put my hands on my hips, and the lapels of the shirt slid farther open, exposing my breasts.

Groaning, he bit his fist. "You are a masterpiece. God, you in that shirt."

"Did you buy a pizza oven and attempt to make gluten-free pizza for me?" I asked.

His gaze never moved from my body. "Yes. I'm awful at it. Almost burned the place down one night. But I'm getting better."

"You don't have to do that."

"Course I do. My woman wants pizza, I will provide her with the best damn pizza on planet earth. Even if I have to study hydration ratios and yeast fermentation rates to do it."

"I love it when you talk dirty. I've been waiting ages for you. Take me to bed, Owen."

He tapped his chin, still admiring the sight of me naked in his shirt. Owen looked at me like I mattered more than anything in his world. Whether I was naked or dressed up or in sweats, his eyes always lit up when they found me. And right now, they were on fire.

And so was I.

"Are you gonna look?" I asked, shrugging the collar of the shirt off my shoulders so it caught at my elbows, "or are you gonna touch?"

Grasping my upper arms, he pulled me in for a kiss.

I wound my arms around his neck, my fingers threading through his hair while our lips and tongues tangled. I was wild and frantic, desperate for him, but he was as controlled as ever.

"I wanted to do this at the bar," he said, kissing along my jawline and hitting the spot that drove me wild. "Kiss you, hold you, and claim you in front of everyone."

I threw my head back, savoring the feel of his lips on my skin.

"Instead, I had to keep my hands to myself. Do you have any idea how hard that is? With you sitting there, eye fucking me in your little skirt? Tempting me and driving me insane in public?"

I splayed my hands over his chest and pushed. "It was torture for me too. Watching you talk to other women. Witnessing the way they look at you."

A slow smile spread across his face. "You jealous, baby?"

Yes. I was jealous. Also frustrated and angry at myself, but it was easier to blame jealousy at this moment than dive into the complicated feelings I was harboring about Owen and our current arrangement.

I nodded.

He ran his hands through his hair and shook his head. "I guess I've got to teach you a lesson, then."

Before I knew it, he was leading me to the bedroom.

"On the bed," he said gruffly, starting to unbutton his shirt. "On your knees."

I hesitated, and that earned me a challenging look. Ooh, this was going to be fun.

Slowly, I kneeled on the mattress, facing away from him.

Then he was behind me—close enough that I could feel his heat—caressing my hips and running his fingertips over my bare skin.

A *crack* rent the air, the sound accompanied by a sharp sting as he spanked me.

I gasped.

He immediately leaned down and kissed my red skin. The tender move made me a little dizzy.

"This okay?" he asked softly, his fingers roaming all over my skin.

"Yes," I said enthusiastically. "More than okay." I'd never been spanked before, but already, I fucking loved it.

Crack. This time he spanked the other side.

"There is nothing to be jealous of."

I threw my head back. God, this was so hot. The slaps were light enough to not be painful, but sharp enough to make my clit throb even harder.

Here he was, fully clothed, while I was bent over and naked, at his mercy.

"Other women don't exist for me." Another slap.

I squeezed my thighs together, trying to alleviate some of the tension.

"I don't want anyone but you. Do you understand?"

Another slap. Oh fuck, I thought I might pass out.

"Yes." I moaned. "Yes. I understand."

"Good." He angled over me and peppered kisses all over my tender skin. "It's okay if you don't feel the same way, but I need you to hear me. You're it for me. Got that?"

I nodded, desperate to know what he'd do next and so turned on by the possibilities.

"Now I'm gonna kiss it and make it all better."

Then his hot breath was on my skin, and he was lowering his mouth and licking straight up my seam, making my legs shake with anticipation.

A low groan rumbled out of him, and then he dove in, all pretense of going slow lost. He was licking and sucking my clit with abandon while his hands traveled everywhere, sending wild sensations through me.

The angle was dizzying and the pressure exquisite. I had

no control, and I loved it. Owen knew how to touch me. The combination of his hands, fingers, and mouth was sending me higher and higher.

"It's so good." I cried out, gripping the sheets to keep from floating away.

Just as I felt about to break, he surprised me again, pushing his thumb against my back channel.

The moan that escaped me was throaty and loud as I dropped my head to the mattress and pushed back against him.

And then I detonated, fully and completely, as wave after wave crashed over me. As I shook and moaned, he continued working me over, prolonging every single second of delicious pleasure.

He lit up my nerve endings, and elation coursed through my veins. Owen was more than just a part of me now. He was mine and I was his and there wasn't any way to fight it anymore.

I collapsed on the bed, panting and spent. With my face in the sheets, I attempted to catch my breath and regain coherent thought. But I was lost in the incredible sensations. My legs were jelly and my stomach was flipping with glee. Because this man had just delivered the world's most intense orgasm on a goddamn silver platter.

And then the heat of his body was there again and his lips were on my skin. He kissed my neck and shoulders.

"You're so fucking beautiful when you come." He sighed into my skin. "But I'm not done with you yet."

I picked my head up and smiled at him, my eyes still unfocused. "I'm not sure I can walk after that."

I heard the tear of the foil, then he was lifting my hips.

He carefully placed each of my hands on the headboard, then ran his fingers down my spine. I arched up for him. I couldn't help myself, because as spent and boneless as I was, I could always take a bit more.

"That's a good girl." He groaned, palming my ass cheeks as he lined himself up. "Always ready for me."

He pushed inside me, the pressure making my eyes roll into the back of my head. I was still tingling and sensitive from whatever magic he had performed earlier, and as he filled me, it felt like I was already on the verge of coming again.

He didn't move right away, instead running his hands all over my body, as if committing every inch of me to memory.

"Please," I groaned, needing friction.

And then he pulled back and thrust into me slowly. Once. Then again. Deep and rhythmic, but with enough power that I had to clutch the headboard to keep steady.

It wasn't long before he picked up his pace, that perfect control wavering as he slid one hand into my hair, gripping it and tugging with enough force to make me moan.

Fuck, I loved it when he got all possessive and feral over me.

"I can feel you," he gasped, "squeezing and ready to explode. Keep going."

Back fully arched, I relished the way he kept a firm hold on my hair and played with my nipples with his free hand.

My body trembled, and that was all it took for him to snap. Then he was fucking me with abandon and sending me hurtling over the edge. He cried out my name as he rode out my orgasm with me. I was still soaring when his groans filled the air and he succumbed to his own.

He collapsed on top of me, rolling to the side and pulling me close.

"You are incredible," he said into my hair as I tucked myself into his chest. For such a dominant boss man in the sheets, Owen was quite the cuddler.

Eyes closed, I was just beginning to drift when he placed a kiss on my head. "I don't know how I'm ever gonna let you go."

My heart clenched painfully.

Because eventually, I'd have to let him go. And when I did, it would crush me.

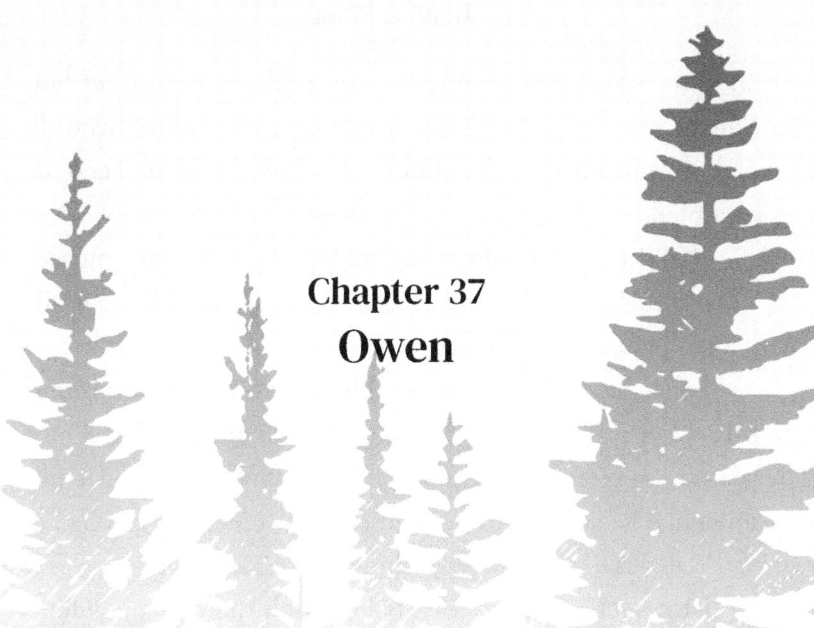

Chapter 37
Owen

"Dinner?" I asked, leaning over the console to kiss her. I'd been kissing her all damn day and I didn't want to stop.

"I'm famished," she said, pulling at my shirt to bring me close again. It was still early, but dread was already creeping back in. We had to head back to Lovewell tonight, and keeping a lid on my feelings for her was beginning to feel impossible.

We'd spent the day in Bangor, checking off weird spots on our list. The Paul Bunyan statue, the art museum, and, of course, Stephen King's greatest hits.

We'd blown off work for the day to have fun and forget about reality after Lila had learned that she hadn't received a scholarship to NYU. She could still take out loans and apply for grants, but she'd gotten her hopes up that this next part of her journey wouldn't be quite so expensive.

The sadness that had plagued her had made my chest ache, so I'd done the only thing I could think of. I'd taken her on a mini road trip to random, weird places to distract her. Bangor was the perfect spot. It wasn't too far from Lovewell, and it was filled with plenty of strange shit to keep us occupied.

"I didn't know you were such a big fan," she mused. "The water tower that inspired *It*? Most people just go to his house. That's more of a deep cut."

I shrugged. There was no hiding my nerdiness around Lila. "I'm a big reader. Maybe I live in Boston, but I'm a Mainer, so of course I'm a fan. Never done any of this stuff, though. The cemetery was definitely the creepiest."

"Oh yes. *Pet Sematary* is the scariest book ever."

I bit back a laugh. "Really? Church the cat is nowhere near as scary as Pennywise. Ugh. Clowns." I shivered.

My brothers had fucked with me endlessly when they'd discovered my fear of clowns.

She laughed and rubbed her hands together maniacally. "Okay, terrified of clowns; noted. I kind of want to have a Stephen King movie marathon now."

"I'll bring the popcorn. As long as you promise that we can watch *Stand By Me*. That was a childhood staple for me and my brothers."

Humming, she looked out at the restaurant on the other side of the parking lot. "Never seen it."

"Excellent. I'll put the wood stove on in the cabin and we can snuggle up and watch."

She turned back to me and raised her brows. "You gonna feed me first?"

"Don't move." I got out and jogged around to get her door. Yes, it was cheesy, but I liked this. The small gestures that went along with being with someone. Caring about someone.

She was so tense and on guard in Lovewell, so I had to seize these opportunities when I could.

I held out a hand and guided her out of the car, then toward the entrance. The Timber Kitchen was fancy by Northern Maine standards only, and its website promised many gluten-free options, so it was the best I was going to do. Finn had mentioned it once, and I'd filed the name away for future use. I'd love to pull out all the stops, and I would, if I thought it would impress her. At this point, I was so desperate to take her on an actual date that even the Wendy's in Heartsborough was looking pretty good right now, and in comparison, this was a three-star Michelin restaurant.

She took my arm and buried her face in my shoulder. "This has been an amazing day."

Inside, the hostess seated us and placed menus in front of us. The restaurant had an industrial vibe and balanced the exposed ductwork with details that were specific to Maine. There was wood everywhere, mason jar water glasses, and of course, a moose head mounted over the fieldstone fireplace. Poor bastard.

Across from me, lit by candlelight, Lila glowed. She looked so at peace. I hated sneaking around, but moments like this made the secrecy worth it.

I slid my hand over the table and squeezed hers.

"I have a new appreciation for this state. You've forced me to admit how great parts of it are," I admitted.

She laughed. "I think you mean how weird parts of it are. And we're just getting started."

We kept our conversation light, avoiding any talk of what would happen when the sale closed in a couple of weeks. I was still in denial. I'd already spent way more time here than I could afford to. Enzo needed me back weeks ago, and I was barely sleeping keeping up with the workload.

But this right here. These moments with Lila made all my worries seem unimportant.

Once we'd placed our orders, she headed to the restroom. While I had a minute to myself, I sat back, sipping my beer and taking the place in. It was nice. As long as the food was decent, I'd definitely bring her back.

The front doors were oversized, with large wrought-iron handles. They'd clearly been salvaged from an old barn. One swung open easily, and a group of people entered. I was pulled from my perusal when I was met with a familiar face.

It was a face I knew almost as well as my own.

My mother's.

In Bangor?

I sat up and gaped as Karen Souza stepped up beside her, along with her husband, the goddamn chief of police.

What were they doing here?

Finally, a tall, well-groomed man joined the group.

I was pretty sure Gus had pointed him out to me once or twice. He was some local bigshot who probably used to rub elbows with my father.

And then he put his hand on the small of my mother's back.

Anger rippled through me. Who the fuck did he think he was?

I stood, clenching my fists and itching to fight. It only took a couple of heartbeats to realize how stupid I must look.

In a rush, I dropped back into my chair and ducked my head. But it was too late. Mom had spotted me and was headed over.

"Owen." She greeted me with a big smile and a hug.

She was wearing a dress and lipstick and smelled nice. Suspicious.

"Mom, what are you doing here?"

"Just out to dinner with some friends. Come say hello."

The last thing I wanted to do was speak to Chief Souza, but I had no interest in upsetting my mom. "Sure."

As she led me toward where the hostess had seated them. I typed out a quick text to Lila.

Code red. My mom is here. With other Lovewell people.

My phone vibrated in my hand almost immediately.

Fuck. I'll hide in here. Let me know if I have to climb out the window.

My mother tugged on my arm before I could reply and presented me to the table.

"Obviously you know Chief and Mrs. Souza."

I shook the chief's hand and tried to hide my grimace. He had done nothing but crawl all over us since the incident with that poor kid. According to Gus, he was still in a coma. Lila had probably saved his life by finding him that day.

I trusted the chief even less now that the security cameras that his "friend" had installed had failed to catch any evidence of the crime.

I bent down and kissed his wife on the cheek. "Good to see you, Mrs. Souza."

She swatted at me and smiled. "Please call me Karen. You're all grown up now. We're so happy you've come back to town."

My mother, who still had hold of my arm, pulled me closer. "And this is Charles Huxley."

The tall guy stood and shook my hand. "Such a pleasure to meet you. Debbie has told me so much about you."

A shudder worked its way through me. One I hoped I'd hidden from him and my mother. It took everything in me not to run to the bathroom and scrub my hands. The guy gave off a sleazy charm that made my stomach churn. His teeth were blindingly white, and no one in Maine had a tan this time of year.

"I've been trying to fix your mom up for years," Karen said, beaming. "And now she's finally double-dating with us."

My vision blurred a bit at that word. *Dating? This fucker?*

The prick was wearing an Hermes tie. That alone made me vow to myself that I'd burn all mine when I went back to Boston. I wasn't sure I could wear them without vomiting.

"Mom," I said. My tone was tense, but there was no helping it. "You're dating?"

She patted my arm. "Oh, Owen, it's just an evening out with friends." The smile she gave me turned a little feline then. "And you never told me what you're doing here."

The look on her face was pure challenge. She was silently warning me to keep my mouth shut on the topic of her dating.

For now, I'd do just that. I'd save all my questions for

another day, after I punched my heavy bag for a few hours and talked to my brothers.

I wasn't involved with the operations side of the business, but I knew Gus could easily disappear this fucker out in the woods.

"I met a friend for dinner," I stammered as my phone vibrated three times in my pocket. Dammit. I needed to give Lila a heads-up.

She glanced back at my empty table. "Where did she go?"

I held back a sigh. Of course she'd assume it was a she.

"Just stepped out for a moment. Work thing." I shrugged casually. "I better get back."

Stuffing my hands into my pockets, I turned and headed back to our table. I waited until I was halfway across the dining room to pull my phone out.

LILA

Motherfucker.

Okay, it's getting weird in here. I'll climb out a window and meet you at the car.

Or... should I go through the kitchen? Can you text me some photos of the layout so I can plan my escape route?

Hit with a wave of weariness, I sighed. Not only was my mom dating, but she was dating someone who made the hair on the back of my neck stand up. And she was hanging out with the Souzas? I couldn't prove it, but there was no way the chief didn't have some inkling about what my dad was up to, yet he had turned a blind eye.

And now Lila was willing to climb out a window to avoid being seen with me in public. Fucking great.

Or you could come out, and we could bite the bullet and come clean. Be honest that we're together.

With your mom? She'll hate me forever.

Are we talking about the same woman? Debbie Hebert? Medium height? Sensible bob haircut? Loves to knit and bake pies?

I can't face her. Who else is there?

Chief Souza and his wife and Charles Huxley. Don't know him, but I don't trust him.

Now Charles was holding court at their table, telling some funny story. Probably about golf. Fuckers like that always thought golf stories were interesting. My mom's tinkling laughter floated across the restaurant, and it made me see red.

Wait. Is your mom on a date?

I can't answer that right now. I'm having some kind of rage-induced panic attack.

This is too weird. We have to leave.

My damn heart was bruised and in my throat. I desperately wanted to leave. But I also wanted to stay and salvage my romantic dinner with Lila. This day had felt so perfect, and now everything had gone to shit.

What do you want me to tell them?

Say you were meeting a date and she ghosted you.

Wow, thanks. Also your wineglass is half full and has your lipstick on it.

Come up with something.

Should I create a diversion? Set a small fire?

No fires, please.

Fake a medical emergency.

No that's insane. Take a breath. Let's just approach this like adults.

Have fun with that. I'll hitchhike back to town.

Stop. If you want to leave, I'll make an excuse and meet you in the car.

Damn, I really wanted that scallop risotto.

How about I get our meals to go?

You are my favorite person, Owen Hebert.

I flagged down the server and asked her to box up our meals, paid, and said my goodbyes to my mother and her companions. After hearing that my "friend" had a "work emergency," they invited me to join them. I declined politely. I'd rather lie on a bed of nails than sit at that table.

Lila and I ate dinner in my car in the parking lot. It was a far cry from the lovely meal I'd envisioned.

Frustration and confusion had overtaken me, so I was terrible company, I was sure. Yes, we'd agreed to keep things quiet. I could understand her concern about what people would say, and I respected her desire to finish her last couple of months in town without stirring up drama.

But this felt an awful lot like rejection. For as much as I honored her wishes and feelings, mine had been tramped and tossed out. Did barriers exist that made our relationship less than ideal? Absolutely. But after all this time together, it was hard not to hope that she'd let go of her paranoia about people finding out.

Because I was totally and fully in love with her. I hadn't told her that. If I did, she'd think I was insane. But since the night we'd danced at the gala in Boston, I'd known she was it for me. And it was bad enough that our time together was ticking away without having to worry about hiding in bathrooms to avoid being discovered.

I was itching to fight. To let out some of the aggression boiling inside me. Instead, I called Gus and made him conference with Jude and Finn while we drove back to town.

"This better be good. We're on baby watch over here," Finn complained.

"Mom is on a date," I said.

"What the fuck?"

"Are you sure?"

I squeezed the steering wheel until my knuckles were white. "Yes. She's on a double date with Chief and Mrs. Souza and that guy, Charles Huxley, at the Timber Kitchen in Bangor right now."

"Fuck," Finn moaned. "That restaurant is ruined for me now."

"I don't like that guy."

"Neither do I."

"And what does she need to date for?" Jude said. "Plenty of us don't date, and we're just fine."

"Debatable," Gus quipped.

"Like you should talk."

"Focus," Finn said. "We need a plan of action here." His voice got muffled for a moment, and another voice, this one more feminine, responded. "Hold on, Adele is making me put this on speaker so she can contribute."

We all fell silent.

"Boys. I'm a hundred weeks pregnant and do not have time for bullshit. Why are you all shouting at each other on the phone at nine p.m.?"

With a sigh, I explained briefly.

"And why are you all having temper tantrums? Your mom is a grown woman. She can go on a date."

"She-Ra," Finn said in a soothing tone, "you don't understand. Mom doesn't date. After what Dad did and all she went through."

"After all that, she can do whatever the fuck she wants," Adele protested. "She raised you assholes on her own. The least you can do is stay out of her business. The woman is in her sixties. Let her live."

"But Charles Huxley?"

"It's just a dinner. People go out to dinner as friends all the time. You're all overreacting, and coming from me, that's serious. Now stop being shitheads and leave your mom in peace. If she wants your input, she'll ask. Go do something productive and stop acting like Neanderthals. You were raised better than this."

I growled. God, how had this perfect day gone to shit so quickly? "My phone's about to die anyway. I'll text you guys later."

The moment the call was disconnected, Lila burst into a fit of giggles. "Adele." She wiped at her eyes. "I love her. I feel like she could teach me so much."

With a roll of my eyes, I took the exit toward Lovewell and once again got lost in stewing and ruminating on my ruined night.

Chapter 38
Lila

The ride home was tense, and that was my fault. The farther we got from the restaurant, the sillier I felt about the way I'd behaved.

The panic had felt so real at the time. I hadn't thought about Owen's feelings at all; only my own embarrassment.

And what did I have to be embarrassed about really? Being in a consensual relationship with a man I cared deeply for? That was hardly a criminal offense, even in small-minded Lovewell.

"Do you want me to drop you off at your mom's house?" he asked, his focus still fixed on the road ahead of us.

My stomach sank. The plan had been for me to stay at his cabin tonight. I had an overnight bag in the back of the car and everything.

I'd told my mom about the sleepovers, knowing there would be no judgment there. She did dive into a lecture about safe sex, but that was to be expected. I'd been getting the same one pretty regularly since the day I turned thirteen.

"I thought I'd spend the night," I said softly, fixing my attention on my hands in my lap.

Clearly distracted, he let out a hum and continued on.

I didn't want to be that needy girl, but he'd gone so distant, and I could have really used a little reassurance. Not that he owed it to me. I'd created this problem. God, I was such an idiot. Would it have been so bad to smile and keep my chin held high while the town gossiped about how I was dating my ex's brother? My tips at the diner were already shitty, and everyone thought my mom and I were trash. Would this really make things any worse?

Back at the cabin, Owen lit the wood stove and I went to the kitchen and put on the kettle for tea. I would make a cup, steel myself, and talk to him. He was too important to me. I needed to put on my big girl panties and have the adult conversation.

My heart ached in my chest. I wasn't sure I could let him go. I wasn't sure I could walk away from what we had. But I also wasn't sure I had a choice in the matter.

I wandered back to where he was fiddling with the wood stove. It was better to just tell him. Flat out. I was falling in love with him and panicking and acting like an immature fool. I'd own my shit and be honest.

Yup. Solid plan.

He straightened and wiped his hands. "Why are you giving me your pageant smile?"

I deflated. Dammit. I hadn't realized I was doing it. The moment things got tense, it was like I reverted back to my factory settings.

Be pleasant. Be quiet. Don't say anything.

"I'm sorry I'm in a mood. But you don't have to do that."

Frowning, he gestured at my face. "That's the smile you give nasty customers at the diner." He stepped in closer and tipped my chin up. "I only want your real smiles, Lila. If you're mad at me, tell me. Yell at me. I'll do better. But don't pretend everything is fine. Trust your feelings."

God, I loved this man. And I needed to say it out loud.

With tears pricking at the backs of my eyes and my heart threatening to crack in two, I put my arms around him and buried my face in his chest.

"I'm just..." I trailed off and pulled back so I could look into his deep blue eyes. Shit, this was hard. Why was it so impossible to just say what I wanted out loud? "I'm ashamed of how I acted tonight. I can't believe I hid in the bathroom."

"It's fine." His tone disagreed.

"No, it's not. Don't do that, Owen. You can hold me accountable. I was being selfish and immature, and I'm sorry. I just wasn't ready to face those people, and I should have handled it better."

"You're young, Lila."

I could hear the record scratch in my head. Why was he brushing me off? I was trying to be an adult and take responsibility for my actions. My age had nothing to do with it.

"And I know you're disappointed about the NYU scholarship."

As upset as I was about the scholarship, I was more angry about my behavior at the restaurant and the situation I'd backed us into.

He kissed the top of my head and held me tighter. "I'm so sorry. But I can give you the money for tuition."

I jerked back. "Excuse me?" Hold up. This was not how I'd seen this conversation going.

He tilted his head, his face a mask of pity.

Oh, hell no.

"Or lend it to you. I just don't want you to have to worry about money."

I blinked, thinking that might pull me out of what had to be a hallucination.

He rubbed my shoulders, completely oblivious. Then he stiffened. "Shit. My phone."

He jogged around the kitchen island and plugged in his dead phone as I stewed. I didn't want his pity or his charity. I wanted a teammate, someone who pushed me to be better and called me out on my shit.

"I don't need your money, Owen."

He wasn't getting this. I opened my mouth, willing something logical and reasonable to come out. But I snapped it shut again when his phone erupted with one notification after another.

"Shit," he said, unlocking the device. "I have a bunch of messages from Sara."

Sara was the lawyer we'd met with in Boston. She'd intimidated the shit out of me, but she was great at what she did, and Owen had a lot of faith in her.

His eyes widened, and he rubbed at his beard. "Okay, a lot of messages."

"Call her," I said, my anger dissipating.

God, I prayed there was nothing wrong with the sale. After all the work we'd done, Owen and his brothers needed a win. They deserved it.

"It can wait," he hedged, setting his phone down.

I put my hands on my hips and looked up at him. "Don't make me call her myself. Just do it already."

He swallowed audibly and searched my face, his brow furrowed, before he finally picked it up and dialed, careful to keep it plugged in.

She picked up on the first ring. "It's about fucking time."

"Sorry, Sara. My phone died. I've got you on speaker with Lila."

"Thank God. I was debating whether I should drive up to Maine and track you down myself."

I smiled. She would do that. I got the sense that no one ignored Sara's calls and lived to tell about it. But she was a way better lawyer than Tad the asshole.

"I got a call from Williams & Freund today. They represent an investment group called Strategic Timber."

"Okay," Owen said, tapping his nails on the countertop nervously.

"They're making an offer."

Owen visibly startled. "Sorry?"

How was that possible? We were already in negotiation with another buyer.

"Yes," she said. "Canadians. Big money backing. Some former Wall Street types. Anyway, they want to acquire Hebert Timber. All of it."

"We already have a buyer." He wiped at his face, frowning.

"But nothing is final. And this is not an offer you want to ignore. It's big."

Owen looked at me, as if needing reassurance, so I gave him a thumbs-up. I knew nothing of the legalities, but a big offer could change things for the Heberts.

"How big?" he asked.

As she gave him the number, the phone fell from his hand and clattered to the floor.

Holy shit. As silently as I could, I jumped up and down, clasping my hands at my chest. That was more than double the first offer.

With shaky hands, Owen recovered the phone, plugged it in again, and sucked in a deep breath, his chest rising, then falling again.

"Owen? What's happening?"

"Sorry, Sara. I dropped my phone. Did you say what I think you said?"

"Yes, I did. This is real money. More than you're worth, frankly, but we'll take it. And it gets better. They intend to continue to operate the company locally and will keep on any existing employees."

I let out a sigh of relief. If Hebert Timber could continue to operate in some capacity, it would save many jobs in Lovewell, and all the land and generations of work wouldn't go to waste.

"There are conditions," Sara warned.

"I don't care what they are." Owen had composed himself and was using his bossy professional voice. The one I loved far more than I should. "We'll make it work. This is better than we could have hoped for."

"Good. I'll have the full written offer sent over as soon as I receive it."

He hung up, took three giant steps toward me, and hauled me off my feet. My anger was forgotten as he spun me around and kissed me, his smile so big I thought it might crack his face.

"You did it," I said softly.

"No, Lila, we did it." He set me on my feet and held on to my arms to steady me. "I owe you so much." His shoulders relaxed as the news set in.

Everything we'd worked for was finally coming together. He held me close, and I clung to him in return, savoring the moment. We needed to talk. About a lot of things, apparently, but I couldn't bring myself to spoil the mood.

"Shit, there's so much work to do." He pulled back. "I gotta review everything, talk it over with Gus, check in on the trucks." He was reaching for his phone again, but it was already after nine.

I put my finger to his lips. "Tomorrow," I said. "Just enjoy this moment."

He sagged against me and kissed me again. "There's no one I'd rather enjoy it with."

I should speak up. Continue our conversation and establish some boundaries. But his kisses felt so good that I let it slide.

"Then take me to bed so we can really enjoy ourselves."

Chapter 39
Owen

I'd barely slept. My mind was buzzing, and I needed to get to work. So I left Lila asleep in my bed at the cabin and headed out early.

It was about an hour and a half drive up through the woods, but this was news I needed to deliver face-to-face. The sat phone wasn't going to cut it.

Since venturing out into the woods to help out, I'd become more familiar with the roads and the scenery and found myself enjoying the drive to the main logging camp, where we were staging and stacking wood that needed to be transported to the mill.

I wasn't particularly useful. I was usually the guy with the clipboard, counting and keeping notes, recording weights, and radioing instructions, but it felt good to contribute.

And it gave me a new appreciation for what Gus did.

"Gus, I have news," I yelled up to him as soon as I put the truck in park.

"What are you doing here?" He was wearing his usual jeans and flannel and worn work boots, along with an orange safety vest. He removed his headset, swung himself out of the nest, and climbed down, then signaled to the guys on the ground to turn off the equipment.

"I have news," I repeated, unable to hold still. I was bursting to share it with him, and the long drive had done nothing to calm the excitement that had kept me up all night.

He lowered his brows and frowned. "You couldn't call?"

"And wait hours for you to call me back?"

"I'm a little busy at the moment." He held out an arm, gesturing to all the work being done around us. "But please, interrupt my morning and tell me what you need."

I nodded toward the small building, then took off for it, not waiting to see if he'd follow. Once we stepped inside, I whirled around, unable to keep a grin from spreading across my face. "We got a new offer."

He scratched his beard and huffed. "We already have an offer. You said it's shitty but that we gotta take it."

I shook my head. "This is a new offer. A company called Strategic Timber out of Canada. Sustainable forestry investment. They've offered double what The Carson Group did, and they want to remain operational."

He collapsed into the chair behind his desk. "Fuck me."

"Yup." Damn, my heart was pounding out of my chest. "I can't wrap my mind around the number, but it's enough to set you all up, pay everything off, and give bonuses to the loyal employees who stayed with us until the end."

"What about Carson's offer?"

"Sara will contact them today and give them a chance to counter, but given how they've been fucking around for the last few months and that they no doubt plan to just sell off the assets, I doubt they'll be interested."

Gus flipped on the coffee maker perched on the wooden slab counter. His movements were so slow and deliberate.

I wanted to jump out of my chair. "Seriously? This is your reaction?"

He regarded me for a long moment, his face an unreadable mask. "I'm just letting this sink in."

He turned back to the coffee maker and carefully prepared two cups, taking his time. When they were just the way he wanted them, he handed one to me, then sat and sipped his slowly.

"We need to take it," he said after a solid five minutes of silence.

Fucking finally. "Yes. I agree. But..."

He raised one bushy eyebrow, bringing his mug to his lips.

"There are a few conditions," I explained. "First, we have to close out all open orders."

A simple nod. "We're doing that right now."

I cringed and braced myself for his reaction. "By June tenth."

"Are you fucking kidding?" He jackknifed up in his seat. "That's in three weeks." Setting his coffee on the desk, he stood and paced. "I could call in Mike, maybe shift some guys around." When he spun and headed back toward me, he ran a hand through his hair and tugged. "If Finn can fly some of the guys up north, it would save time."

This was one of the things I admired most about my brother—his ability to manage the logistics of the people, equipment, and trees.

"I gotta make a few calls."

I cleared my throat. "There's more."

He came to a stop and crossed his arms, silently waiting for me to go on.

"The offer specifically requires that you, August Gabriel Hebert, stay on as operations manager for at least one year."

Disappointment flashed in his eyes, but it was gone as quickly as it had come, replaced by his usual stoic glare. "Fine," he grunted.

"Stop and think about this before you make a decision. I don't want to fuck you over."

"Nothing to think about." He shook his head. "Our family needs this. Our town needs this. Those guys out there?" Nodding toward the door, he lifted a brow. "They've stuck with me through all the bullshit. I'm not going to risk their jobs and their families. Jude, Noah, Cole. Hell, Finn is about to have a baby. I'm not going to take money out of their pockets."

Typical Gus. When given the choice to take care of himself or others, it was always the latter.

"But you've got another job lined up—"

"Doesn't matter." His expression was hard, unyielding.

"And are you sure you can work for someone else? Now that we've lost it all?"

"I'll deal." His shoulders tensed, and the tendons in his neck went taut. "And we didn't lose anything. Dad did. He fucked us over. This is on him."

My chest went tight at that comment. Gus took personal responsibility for every aspect of this business and had been hesitant to blame my father, but finally, he was catching up with the rest of us.

"There is no discussion. Talk to the lawyers. Do your financial shit. I'll make it happen."

"Okay..." I blew out a long breath.

"Seriously. Get your ass back to the office. I've gotta make a plan for how to get all this shit done in half the time I'd planned. I'll come to town tonight and talk through what I figure out."

With that, he strode out of the building.

Admiration flooded me. For so many years, I'd assumed we were too different to ever get along again. But that was my own baggage. Gus would do anything for me and the rest of our family.

And finally, I could do something for him in return. This sale would give him a nest egg to use for whatever he wanted. To help him start over when he was ready. For decades, I'd been a shitty brother, but at least I could give my family some financial security.

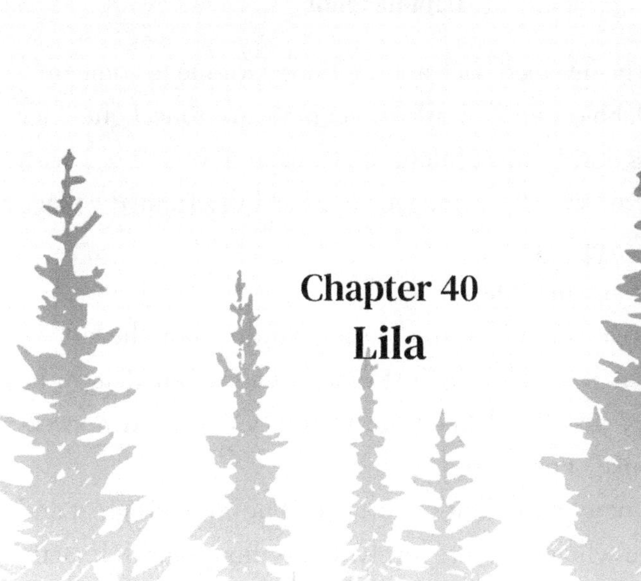

Chapter 40
Lila

I rolled my shoulders, giving myself a pep talk in the car. This was necessary.

Growth.

Maturity.

Fuck, I didn't want to do this.

But there was no going back now.

I'd texted him this morning after Owen left to go to work, and he'd agreed to meet.

Stomach in knots, I knocked on the door and gripped the latte from the Caffeinated Moose, a peace offering, a little tighter.

It took several minutes, but finally, he opened the door.

Cole looked like a stranger standing in the doorway of the small home in his sweats, his medium-brown hair grown out and hanging over his forehead.

He'd lost so much weight that his T-shirt hung on his frame. Just the sight had my caretaking instincts kicking in, but I pushed them away.

Silently, he stood back and motioned for me to come in.

"Is Debbie here?" I asked, keeping my tone light. Her home was lovely, meticulously clean, and very cozy, with photos of all six boys arranged in an artfully framed collage above the fireplace.

"She's at work. Have a seat."

"Brought you something," I said, handing him the latte.

He took it, and for the first time, smiled. Immediately, he took a sip, just like I knew he would. Cole loved a sweet coffee drink. "That's good."

"The new place. You've gotta go. The coffee is great and the people who own it are lovely. Everything's local. Exactly the kind of spot we need up here."

He made a noncommittal noise and took another sip. I rarely saw him around town. He'd been going to physical therapy for his hip injury, but outside of that, did he just spend all his time here?

I surveyed him from head to toe. He'd changed so much. I couldn't put my finger on it. Low energy, maybe? Or was he just defeated?

Cole had always had a big personality. Not loud, but commanding. He was so tall and broad, with a cocky self-confidence that hockey players always possessed in abundance. It made it hard to not be transfixed by him.

But the guy sitting across from me on the paisley couch with the dark circles under his eyes bore no resemblance to the ambitious, impulsive boy I'd fallen for almost a decade ago.

"Why are you here, Lila?"

I shifted as nerves prickled along my skin. It was time. I needed to be honest and up-front.

"I wanted to talk to you about a few things."

"You gonna blame me for ruining our relationship? Tell me all the things I did wrong?"

The way his eyes narrowed reminded me of how cruel he could be sometimes. I had no intention of provoking him today. I had come here to tell him about Owen. Calmly and compassionately. Not because I required his approval, but because I wanted him to hear it from me rather than through the rumor mill. After eight years together, he deserved to process this information on his own time.

"No. I don't blame you for anything. I wanted to share my good news. I got into graduate school." I sat a little straighter and pressed my hands to my knees. "Several actually."

"Good for you."

He didn't sound particularly happy, but I wouldn't let him get to me.

"Thank you. I've worked hard for this," I said. "I'm moving on. I got help to sort through my shit. I had to let go of my old dreams and embrace who I've grown into."

"No shit." He planted his elbows on his knees. "You gave up on our dreams a long time ago."

I gritted my teeth. This was supposed to be a friendly visit. But his combativeness had anger welling up inside me and was bringing back so much of the hurt I'd left behind. At the way he'd ignored me and minimized my feelings. In the time since we'd broken up, I'd believed that one day we could be friends, but that fantasy was fading away quickly.

"Don't go there, Cole. We didn't have dreams together. You had dreams, and I was just there, hoping someday you'd wake up and support me the way I'd been supporting you."

He launched to his feet and paced the living room. "You know how much pressure I was under!"

I stayed seated. I'd seen this reaction too many times to count.

"Every minute of my life was about one thing. Going pro. Getting the big contract. I'm sorry you felt *neglected*," he said the word as if it was preposterous, "but I couldn't lose focus."

I shook my head. It was all the same old bullshit. "Oh, right," I said sarcastically. "I forgot. Drinking and partying all night at strip clubs helped your focus."

"Fuck off." He tugged at his hair. "I was blowing off steam, and I never cheated on you."

"None of this matters anymore," I said as years of pent-up frustration simmered in my bloodstream. "We're done. We've been done for a year and a half."

"Don't lie to yourself, Lila. You were done with me way before that."

Maybe he was right. Who the hell knew anymore? And as much as it pained me not to jump in and defend myself, I wasn't here to play the blame game. I'd moved on, and I'd worked hard to distance myself from the toxicity of the relationship we once had.

"I came here to make peace. To tell you I've moved on and am working on myself."

"Moved on?" He scoffed, crossing his arms. "With who?"

I squeezed my eyes shut, reining in my annoyance. I could get up, leave this house, and never look back. But growth was uncomfortable and sometimes painful. If I had any hope of settling into a real, adult relationship with Owen, then I had to push past this discomfort.

"I'm dating Owen," I said, keeping my head held high.

"The fuck you are." Cole whipped around, his face a mask of fury. "Owen is a pretentious asshole. And you work at the diner, for fuck's sake."

I balled my fists. I wasn't sure which part of that statement made me want to punch him more. The part where he called Owen an asshole or the part where he looked down on me because I worked as a waitress.

It took me a moment and a few deep breaths to realize that his goal here was to provoke a response.

"I don't owe you any explanation. We're dating. It's new, and so far, we've kept it to ourselves. I wanted to tell you first, out of respect for the years we shared." With that, I stood and smoothed out my shirt, ready to get the hell out of here.

"He's using you," he said, putting his hands behind his head and reclining on the couch like he didn't have a care in the world. "You're just a piece of ass to him."

It would be so easy to punch him in his smug face right now.

Instead, I took the high road. "Stop feeling sorry for yourself and get your shit together."

His eyes widened and his mouth dropped open in response.

I'd never spoken to him like that. But he needed to hear this. "I'm going to say this once," I continued. "You are not okay. There are a lot of people, me included, who care about you and are willing to help you get better."

"I don't need your help."

"Maybe you don't, but I'm offering it anyway. And I'm not the only one. You have so many gifts to share with the world."

He regarded me with a frown before he sank lower into the couch. "You're wrong," he said softly. "I'm nothing. I was good at one thing, hockey, but I fucked that up. Now I'm almost thirty and have no degree, no skills, and I'm sleeping in Debbie's guest room because my actual mother wants nothing to do with me.

"I've been working with my brothers a little, but the company's being sold, so it's not like I could even be a part of the family business someday. What the hell am I going to do?" He slid his hand down his face. "And how the hell can I even figure that out when I've got probation and hundreds of hours of community service to deal with?"

My first instinct was to rail at him and remind him that he'd dug this hole for himself. Instead, I remained silent. I'd been in a similar position before, feeling scared and reactive and worried that there was nothing more out there for me.

He didn't continue, so I headed toward the door, aware that this conversation was going nowhere. "Sorry I bothered you," I said. "I'll be here to help when you're ready. But until then, stop lashing out and acting like an entitled asshole."

He grunted. "Easy for you to say."

"Yes." I turned and raised a brow. "Shockingly, it is easy for me to refrain from getting drunk and high and committing petty crimes, then verbally abusing the people who care about me." I was both shocked and a little proud of myself for my retort. Usually, I placated him and kept my true thoughts to myself. But he needed to hear the truth as much as I needed to speak it.

"Spare me the sarcasm." He waved a dismissive hand. "I have to go. Gus summoned me to the woods. Maybe I'll get hit by a falling log and be put out of my misery."

Ignoring him, I walked to the front door. With my hand on the knob, I gave him one last look, taking in his slumped posture and the defeat in his expression. Then I opened the door.

"Goodbye, Cole."

I headed straight to the office to start tackling the pre-closing to-do list Sara had emailed in the middle of the night. That woman was hardcore.

I was stewing and frustrated and all bent out of shape when I arrived. For a few minutes, I sat in my van, breathing deeply to calm my nerves. I had no interest in encountering anyone here while I was this fired up.

Just as I pushed my door open, a Hebert Timber truck parked beside me.

"Lila." Owen jumped out of the cab and jogged to me. "I'm so happy to see you."

I blinked, still out of sorts. "You're already back?"

"Yeah. We've got a lot to get done here. Gus is getting everything organized, and then we'll head out for a couple of days to get things moving." He pulled me in for a hug and kissed the top of my head. "I hated leaving you all peaceful and asleep this morning."

I closed my eyes and took a moment to absorb his warmth and affection. Owen gave the best hugs. He used his whole body and didn't hesitate to squeeze when necessary. The simple act alone was the reset my nervous system needed.

"It's okay," I said. "Things are busy."

He pulled back and rested his hands on my shoulders, studying my face. "Are you okay? You seem off."

Bowing my head, I gave it a small shake. "I went to see Cole this morning."

He squeezed my arms gently, soothing me.

The sweet act of comfort immediately brought tears to my eyes. "I needed some closure. I wanted to tell him about school. And he was such an asshole."

He scoffed. "Shocking."

"And I yelled at him."

"Which he deserved." There was a hint of pride in his voice.

"And—"

"Shh," he said, smoothing my hair. "It was kind of you to try and talk to him. But he's not going to hear you right now."

Annoyance coursed through me. I was trying to explain to him that I'd told Cole about us. That I was ready to go public because I was in love with him and damn the consequences.

But he was fixated on comforting me, which I didn't need. I needed him to hear me and to talk to me.

I cleared my throat. "Can I ask you about something?"

He tilted his head and kissed me gently. "Anything," he said against my lips. "Let's head inside, though. I've got to get some things together before I leave."

Silently, I followed him through the lobby. There were a few people here, and they gave us big smiles as we passed. Apparently, the news of the sale had spread already.

When we reached his office, he unplugged his laptop charger and wound it up, then started sorting through files.

"Last night, when we got home from dinner, you said you would pay for my graduate school."

He looked up and smiled. Damn, it was that soft smile that made him impossible to resist. "Of course, babe. Whatever you need."

Despite his sweet expression, that phrase made my anger well up again. "I don't want that."

He was still shuffling papers, not giving me his full attention. "It's no problem. I'd be happy to."

The urge to slink away and internalize all this was overwhelming. I didn't want to bother him when he had so much going on, but this had been eating away at me, and I'd lost my nerve last night.

"Owen, please look at me."

He did just that, his eyes wide and his lips parted in surprise.

Okay, maybe my tone was a little more yelly than I had intended.

Regardless, I had to say this. "I know you're busy, and I'll be quick, but this is important to me."

He walked around and sat on the front of his desk, crossing his ankles. "I'll always make time for you."

God, he was so perfect. Instantly, my anger deflated. Even so, this was important, and I wouldn't let myself push it aside.

"Your generosity is wonderful. And I know it comes from a good place. But when you offered, it didn't feel good for me."

He frowned. "I just wanted to help."

"I know." I licked my lips and took a single step closer. "And that's why I want to explain myself to you." I took a deep breath. "I want more with you. Something real. But I don't want to be a kept woman. I've lived that life. And I swore I'd never do it again. I'm gonna get out of Lovewell on my own two feet." My hands were shaking, and my voice was entirely too loud. But I had so much pent-up emotion inside me I couldn't control myself.

He crossed his arms and hit me with a smile so warm I almost stumbled back. Here I was, lecturing him, almost yelling, and he was so calm and collected.

"Lila, there's no one I believe in more than you. I've never seen such determination, and I've spent time with some incredibly successful people. I just want to invest in your potential in any way that I can. I'm so sorry if I insulted you or made you feel uncomfortable."

My eyes stung and my throat went thick. God, he was such a grown-up. An actual man. He listened, he validated my feelings, and he apologized so willingly. What a fucking turn-on.

He opened his arms, and I walked right into them, kissing his handsome, bearded face.

"You are obnoxiously mature," I complained.

He shrugged. "I want something real with you too. Don't think I forgot about that part. But you have to realize that one of the keys to success is knowing when to accept help."

"How about I promise to work on that?" I lifted a brow and nipped at his bottom lip.

He dropped his head back and groaned. "I hate that I need to leave. We have so much to talk about."

"It's fine. We can talk when you're back."

Pulling me close again, he hummed. "It's only two days."

I soaked in the feel of him, knowing it wouldn't tide me over. "I'll be here."

He rested his chin on the top of my head. "I don't want to leave you."

If only we could spend the next few days talking and fucking and laughing as well as figuring out how the hell we were going to make this work when he was headed back to Boston soon and I was headed to New York.

But we were too close to the finish line now.

"I'm good." I squeezed him in reassurance. "Just stay safe. There's plenty of time to figure out the future."

"As long as you're in it, I don't care."

I pulled back. "I should let you get packed up. I've got my marching orders from Sara, and I won't let you down, boss."

His eyes softened. "You could never let me down."

We regarded one another for a moment too long. I wanted to say it, but I couldn't get the words out. It would be so natural and easy right now, here in the building where we'd first met.

But the words got stuck in my throat.

He coughed and took a step back. "I should get organized."

I nodded, giving him some space and helping to arrange some of the papers spread out on his desk.

"You know, it's only noon, and I've already yelled at two Hebert brothers today."

Owen barked a laugh. "You want me to find Finn? You can tell him he's too tall."

"Ooh, I'll tell him his hair is too shiny. That'll wound him."

"Or that, as a dad, he's too perfect."

I giggled.

"You should go for the hat trick. I find your yelling very sexy." He gently smacked my ass.

I swatted him away. "Take care of yourself."

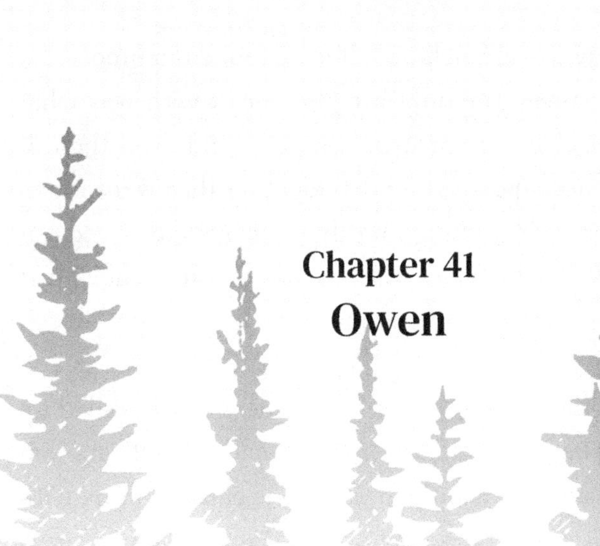

Chapter 41
Owen

Life at lumber camp was a lot harder than I expected. And busier. We were up loading trucks at four a.m., and Gus never stopped moving. If he wasn't jumping in and out of machinery, then he was taking phone calls and directing people like an air traffic controller on speed.

As a kid, I did everything I could to avoid coming out here. By the time I was old enough to be helpful, I'd resented my father so much that I didn't want anything to do with his business.

Now, I was getting the ass-kicking of a lifetime.

Gus and Jude had assembled a small crew, including Cole and me. Adele's due date was in three days, so Finn had stayed home.

The ragtag crew included our remaining Hebert employees, a few guys who worked for other companies but had offered to help, and Mike, who had retired a few years ago but had jumped at the chance to get back out there.

Day one was overwhelming, but we found our groove.

In my business, the only lumber I dealt with was what had been delivered to construction sites, and even then, it was mostly the paperwork and budgeting that went along with purchasing. Watching muddy trees being dragged out of the woods, knowing that they would go on to their next life as the frame of some family's home, was mind-blowing.

I slept in the bunk room with the other guys, huddled up in a sleeping bag Gus had lent me. He had a small cabin on the property since he was the boss, but he chose to bunk with us too.

The trip felt a little like a strange version of summer camp, and despite my reservations, I found myself having fun.

Everyone gave each other endless shit, and I marveled at the rapport Gus and Jude had with the other guys. Gus was mostly grumpy and Jude was always quiet, but seeing them here, in their comfort zone, was incredible.

Especially Jude. He seemed to know what everyone needed and had us rolling with laughter.

"You gonna tell us about that girl, Jude?" Gus called across the kitchen. "You're busting Chris's balls for proposing to Erica on their second date, but I saw you on stage. You never looked away from her."

Jude's face turned pink, and he focused on his paper plate of mac 'n' cheese. This was news. He was so secretive and reclusive, I'd assumed that he was celibate. Not that it was any of my business.

"And Finn said he followed her around the bar between sets," Cole added. He elbowed Corey out of the way and sat next to Jude. "Must be one special girl. This guy never takes anyone home."

Instead of responding, Jude got up from the table, threw his plate away, and grabbed his guitar case. Ignoring us, he started to tune, and soon the guys were making requests, and the topic had been forgotten.

While the rest of the guys played cards, I helped Mike with the dishes. I was already exhausted and knew we were in for a long day tomorrow, but spirits were high and, for the first time, I felt confident that we could really get things wrapped up and the company sold.

It was strange to realize that leaving didn't seem as attractive as it once did. I was growing attached to Lovewell, and to my brothers, who I felt like I was still getting to know. And then there was Lila. Another person I'd be leaving.

I was helping Mike dry dishes when Cole tapped on my shoulder. His hands were in his pockets and he was staring at his boots. He seemed so different out here. He was wearing beaten-up Carhartts, a hoodie, and his medium-brown hair was overgrown and in his eyes. I was used to seeing him in a suit after hockey games or dressed in head-to-toe Under Armour. Like my dad, he'd always been vain about his appearance. This was jarring.

"Can we talk when you're done?" he asked.

I nodded, drying the pot Mike had handed me, and then followed him out the back door.

He'd been strangely quiet since we'd arrived. Did everything that was asked of him, but barely spoke. Not that I was complaining. It was just out of character. But he'd shown up and was willing to pitch in, and that in itself was a surprise. So I'd hear him out.

We walked a few paces from the building, marveling at the sky above. This was darkness. True darkness. No artificial light for miles, and the stars looked almost close enough to touch.

"I wished I knew what they all were," he said, still marveling at the sky up above. "I never cared a lot about school. Always assumed I was smart. But these days, I'm realizing more and more that the universe of stuff I don't know is vast."

"There's still plenty of time," I offered. "You're young. As soon as we get the sale wrapped up, you'll have some money, then you can do anything."

He shook his head. "Probably not. I'm not like you. I've got nothing to offer. If I went to school, I'd just fuck it up."

We stood for a few moments in silence, contemplating the sky. It was chilly, cold enough to see my breath, but I felt strangely comfortable out here.

"I need to apologize," he said. "For so many things."

I crossed my arms, nodding for him to go on.

"I'm not going to make excuses or try to explain myself because there is no excuse for all the shit I've pulled."

"Good."

"And not that you care, but I'm going to therapy now. Debbie is kicking my ass, and I'm owning my shit and working to fix it."

"I do care. You're my brother."

"Half brother. I know you all hate me. It's because of me your parents got divorced."

"Stop," I said. "No one blames you. That was Dad. And my mom was way better off without him anyway." I could feel the guilt rising in my chest. I hadn't always been the most welcoming to Cole, mainly because of my own jealousy about my father's attention as well as our nine-year age difference. He'd grown up with the twins, and I always assumed that, after thirty years, we'd let all this shit go. Apparently not.

"Your birth was a wonderful thing to come out of our father's terrible behavior. And you're a huge pain in the ass, but you're one of us."

He nodded and kept staring at the stars. After a few minutes of silence, he spoke again.

"I know you think you had it hard because Dad ignored you. But it was no picnic being his favorite either. The constant pressure, the put-downs, the need to be the hockey star son who made him look good."

I hadn't really considered that. I'd always just assumed Cole was a privileged brat my dad threw money and attention at because he was a talented athlete.

He kicked at the gravel. "I had no one. I was alone with him. My mom didn't care, and all he did was scream at me, tell me what a loser I was, and push me to train harder.

"He used to wake me up at five and make me shoot a thousand pucks before going to school. And I did it. I did it to please him and make him proud. And it wasn't like I was good at anything else."

I put my hand on his shoulder, the guilt of being older and wiser and missing all of this weighing on me. "You're a lot more than hockey, Cole."

He shrugged my hand away. "Easy for you to say. You've got degrees and a whole life you've built for yourself. I had hockey, but I wasn't good enough. Couldn't handle the pressure, keep my mind focused, train instead of party. Nope, I fucked it up good." He sniffled.

Dammit, he was crying. God, now I felt even worse. I'd been so hard on him, and I'd said and thought such unkind things.

"I drove Lila away in the process. But that's the only good thing to come out of this. Because now she's gonna go to school and live in the city and have the life she always wanted."

I put my arm around his shoulders, which was difficult, as he was a lot taller than me. "We're all fucked up," I told him. "Dad did a number on us. But we're all we've got. I don't hate you, and I don't want you to hate me. You've fucked up, but things can be fixed, and I'm your brother. I'm here to help you."

We stood there, facing the forest, as he cried. And I let him. I couldn't fix the past, and neither could he, but standing there in the cold, I realized that I didn't have to keep living in the past. I didn't have to carry all this anger around with me anymore. I could make my peace and let it go.

"Anyway." He wiped his nose on the sleeve of his hoodie. "Lila came to me and told me about you two. I was really shitty to her."

Another spark of anger flared up inside me, but I smothered it.

"We were never right for each other. We were just kids trying to figure ourselves out. I was a terrible partner."

He ran his hands through his hair. "Seeing her face when she talked about you, though? I could tell that you're good for her."

That was incredibly generous of him. I was furious that he'd been such an ass to Lila, but whatever she said must have stuck with him, because I'd never seen him so contrite and accountable.

"But." He turned and glared at me, drawing up to his full height. "Just because we're over doesn't mean I won't step in if you hurt her."

"I would never hurt her," I snapped. But could I even make that promise? She'd been so upset with me when I offered to pay for school. And I'd brushed her concerns off instead of validating her. Cole wasn't the only one who needed to do better.

"She deserves good things, Owen. I'm trusting you to do right by her."

I gave him a solemn nod. "I will. I swear."

We stood for a few more minutes before the cold started to get to me. I elbowed him. "Let's go to bed. Gus will have us up at the ass crack of dawn tomorrow."

By five, I was already guzzling my second cup of coffee. Gus appeared and clapped me on the back, bright-eyed, like he lived for this shit.

And I supposed he did. This was Gus in his element, at his best.

Out here, he was a natural leader and strategist. He commanded a lot of respect. I'd had to leave Lovewell to figure out who I was. Gus only had to come out to the woods.

More and more, I hoped that, when this was over, we

could stay close. Despite how close in age we were, it felt as though I was just beginning to get to know him.

"We're doing this." His smile was so broad I could see his teeth through his thick beard. A rare occurrence. "If we stay on schedule, we'll get it done."

With a hum of agreement, I surveyed the guys. Cole was checking the numbers and fuel, while Mike, the driver, secured the load Jude had packed with the crane. It was like a symphony of lumberjacks, everyone doing their jobs in harmony.

"I'm proud of you," Gus said.

My chest tightened at the compliment. "Me? I'm just a bystander."

"No, you're not. We got so much done yesterday because of you. Someone needs to check the lists and yell out the directions. You're a natural."

I shook my head. My goal was to stay out of the way and make sure the work got done.

"I had my doubts about you, city boy. But you've surprised the shit out of me. Since you got here, you've worked damn hard. I know you hate this place, but you've done right by us. I'll always be grateful to you for coming back when we needed you."

I pressed my lips together to keep from teasing him. In all my life, I didn't think my older brother had ever spoken that many words to me at once.

"Thank you," I said with a small nod. "And for the record, you are fucking phenomenal at your job. I'm sorry Dad kept you out of leadership for so long."

He shrugged. "I've made my peace with it. I just want our guys taken care of." With a small cough, he clapped his hands and shifted back into work mode. "Good talk. Now get your ass to work so we can celebrate at the Moose tomorrow night. I'm buying."

The hours passed quickly, each of us taking our shifts and breaks. We were moving through the orders, and yesterday's trucks had returned, ready to be reloaded.

I was on the loading platform, level with the truck bed, counting the trees as they were loaded, making sure they were the right sizes, and radioing Jude, who was operating the boom log loader, when weight or balance needed to be adjusted.

Cole was on the ground, signaling to Jude with safety flags about how to place the trees in the truck bed. His height and long arms lent themselves perfectly to the job.

We'd found a good rhythm, and Cole seemed different after our heart-to-heart the night before. It was such a cliché, but being out here in the wilderness was good for all of us. I was connecting with my brothers in ways I'd never expected, and we were even having some fun.

Cole had a long way to go, but at least he was getting help.

Maybe it was Lila's influence, or maybe it was the camaraderie we were developing out here, but I felt some sympathy for him. He'd lost his entire identity almost overnight.

And he'd lost Lila. That alone was a devastation I couldn't fathom.

That kind of loss would break me.

So I was glad that we had started to mend fences. It would take time, but I hoped that he could figure himself out. And I'd be ready to help if he needed me.

He signaled that the next tree was incoming, and I stepped back, noting the size and approximate circumference of the pine.

Jude slowly lifted it and swung the boom around with precision.

Then I heard a deafening crack.

And the world went dark.

Chapter 42
Lila

I couldn't think, and I couldn't breathe. From the moment I'd answered the call, dread had enshrouded me.

Gus had called in the early afternoon. Said there had been an accident.

Owen had been hurt and taken by helicopter to the hospital.

Fuck. Fuck.

Adrenaline had taken over, causing my body to shake and my teeth to chatter.

Somehow, I made it to the hospital in Bangor.

I'd walked right through reception and straight into the ICU. An angry receptionist snapped at me when I ran to the desk.

"I'm here for Owen Hebert," I said, already breathless and panicked.

"You family?"

I hesitated. No, technically I was not. But I needed to see

him. I needed to make sure he was okay. My heart was ready to explode in my chest. So I just took off without responding, studying the names written on whiteboards outside of each door.

"Excuse me," she shouted as she followed me. "This is a closed ward. Come back here."

I broke into a jog. Fuck the rules. Fuck being polite. I was going to find him, dammit.

"Miss," she yelled again. "I'll have to call security."

Ignoring her, I turned down another hallway—*how big was this damn hospital?*—and ran smack dab into a set of double doors. I wrenched one open and ran inside, immediately skidding to a stop.

I was in a tranquil waiting room.

With the entire Hebert family. And every one of them was staring at me.

The nasty nurse followed. "Miss, you need to leave. You're disrupting the patients."

Gus stepped forward. "What's the problem?"

"This woman isn't family, and she's running around the ICU like a lunatic. Nancy at the front desk already called security," she hissed, out of breath.

I turned and narrowed my eyes at this person. She seemed to think she could keep me away from Owen, but the joke was on her. Security would have to tase me to get me out, and then I'd climb in a window if I had to.

I put my hands on my hips. "I'm his—"

"Assistant," Gus interrupted.

Slowly, I turned to face him. "You," I said, shoving his chest hard. "You were supposed to protect him. Keep him safe!"

"Who is this woman?" the nurse shouted. The door opened, and a kindly looking security guard walked in.

"I'm Lila," I said, looking around the room. Debbie was knitting, her hands trembling as she watched my display. Jude sat next to her, his head in his hands. Finn was standing, rubbing Adele's shoulders. She was reclined in a chair, her hands on her round belly. In a corner, Cole was slumped over his phone, looking up at me through his hair.

My stomach twisted. I hadn't thought this through.

"I'm Owen's Lila," I said, trying to sound authoritative. "I'm his. And he's mine. And I don't care what the hospital policy is. I'm not leaving until I see him." I crossed my arms and glared at the security guard, who didn't seem like he wanted anything to do with this display of crazy.

Hello, awkward. Everyone was staring at me in confusion. So I tilted my chin up and scanned the room. "Owen and I are together."

Adele's eyes widened, and Jude's head snapped up.

Debbie looked confused. "But...?"

"I'm in love with him," I blurted out, too exhausted to be more eloquent than that. "We've only been together for a few weeks, but I love him. Gus called me, and I panicked because, if anything happened to him—" My throat closed up, and I burst into tears.

What a way to make an impression on my boyfriend's family.

"Oh, sweetheart." Debbie hopped up and pulled me close. "That's wonderful. And he's going to be alright." She patted my back, soothing me as sobs racked me.

She looked at the security guard and Nurse Asshole. "Leave us. She's family," she barked.

With quick nods and contrite expressions, they made a beeline for the door.

For such a sweet lady, Debbie was not to be messed with.

She cupped my face in her hands. "I know it's scary. Loving someone is the most terrifying thing in the world."

I should be the one consoling her. This woman's son had been in an accident, yet here she was, whispering reassurances and comforting me. My mind spun and panic continued to course through my veins. My hands shook as I tried to make sense of everything.

Jude stood and took off his glasses. His eyes were red rimmed and his breathing was choppy. "It was my fault," he said. "I fucked up."

"You did not," Gus growled. "It was a machinery failure. Not operator error."

Finn padded over and put his arm around Jude in silent support.

"In fact," Gus continued, "you probably saved his life. If you hadn't gotten control, it would have hit him so much harder."

Debbie gasped and cupped a hand over her mouth, her eyes welling with tears.

Jude hung his head and shook it. "Still my fault."

"Accidents happen," Gus argued. "You and I know it. And we were going fast, which was my fault."

My chest heaved as I willed coherent words to form on my tongue. "What happened?"

Gus put a hand on my shoulder. "He's gonna be okay. He's just banged up pretty good."

I pushed his hand away, still shaking. "Start talking. Now."

"He was on the loading platform, and the hydraulics on the knuckleboom loader failed."

"None of those words make any sense to me." I rubbed at my head and closed my eyes.

Jude sighed. "The tree slipped, and the boom swung, knocking him off the platform."

Jesus. My stomach lurched. "You hit him with a tree?" I punched his shoulder so hard a sharp pain shot up my arm.

"It was an accident," Gus said, stepping between Jude and me. He bowed his head. "Trust me, no one feels worse about this than me. I am the captain of this ship, Lila, and my brother could have been killed."

Though it hurt to breathe, I forced in a shallow breath and let it back out. "How bad is it?"

"Broken collarbone and dislocated shoulder. Concussion and some cuts and bruises. Could have been so much worse. He was knocked out cold, and we were worried about a potential spinal injury, so we radioed for MediVac."

I nodded, mentally assuring myself that he would be okay. My brain comprehended, but my racing heart did not. I put my face in my hands, only beginning to see how scary this must have been for Gus.

"I'm sorry," I said. "It must have been terrifying for you. I just didn't have enough information, and I panicked. I care about him so much."

Gus put an arm around me, his warmth comforting. "It's okay. I get it. And I'm glad he has you."

Taking a small step to the side, I peered in the nearest door, desperate to lay eyes on Owen.

"We can't see him yet. He's sleeping. His body is in

shock, but he's stable. Here," he said, "have a seat and wait with us."

I nodded, feeling the adrenaline start to subside. Suddenly, my body felt exhausted. I took a seat next to Debbie and tried to keep myself from spiraling further. He'd be okay. Minor injuries. I kept repeating those phrases in my head like a mantra, praying we could see him soon.

We were silent, the hours having blurred together, when Adele heaved herself out of the chair with a grunt.

I assumed she was headed to the restroom for the tenth time, but halfway across the room, she froze and doubled over.

"*Fuck*," she ground out.

In an instant, Finn was at her side.

"What the fucking fuck?" she yelled, standing straight again but looking down at her legs.

Her gray leggings were wet.

"Holy fucking shit, Stretch. I think my water just broke."

Finn's face morphed from concern to exhilaration. "Fuck yeah!" He pumped his fist. "It's baby time."

Adele hit his chest and moaned again. "You and I both know we have hours. Don't get too excited."

His eyes were dancing as he kissed the top of her head, like he was totally delighted by the way she was yelling at him in the hospital waiting room.

She clutched her belly and leaned against him. "Can we please go to the maternity ward?"

Gus, who I hadn't noticed leave the room, appeared in the doorway with a wheelchair. "Got you a ride."

Finn helped Adele into the wheelchair, but rather than

rushing out of the room, he pulled his phone out, crouched behind her, and snapped a couple of selfies.

"Push me upstairs so I can get your massive baby out of me, please!"

"Got it, She-Ra." He spun her wheelchair, and as he pushed her out into the hall, he turned back to us and grinned. "You know where to find us. Just follow the sounds of Adele threatening my life."

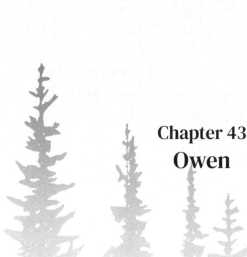

Chapter 43
Owen

Blurry. It was all blurry. My vision and my memories.

I'd fallen. Then there was a helicopter. And then doctors.

I opened my eyes a second time, only to immediately close them again. The harsh fluorescent lights felt like they were burning my corneas.

Everything hurt. Even my eye sockets.

Voices sounded close by. I cracked one eyelid just a sliver and caught sight of an older woman dressed in scrubs hovering over me. She pressed two fingers to my wrist and checked her watch, then ran a thermometer across my forehead.

"Can I get some water?" I rasped.

The nurse smiled down at me. "Sure can." She raised the head of my bed slightly, then picked up a pitcher and a small cup from a rolling table nearby. "Your family is in the waiting room. Would you like me to get them? Or would you prefer to rest?"

I took a sip from the straw she held to my lips and let the cool water soothe my throat. "You can get them," I said, leaning back against the pillow. I'm sure my mother was losing her mind.

It only took a moment for what sounded like a herd of elephants to stampede down the hall. Yup, that was probably my family.

"My baby," my mother cried as she hurried into the room, her hands clutched to her chest. She pressed herself against the edge of my bed and peppered kisses all over my head.

"Mom, that hurts." I winced. My entire left side was wrapped, and my arm had been splinted to my chest. No one had been in to tell me what was actually broken, but it felt like everything.

"Shh." She kissed my forehead. "I was so worried. We were all so worried."

When she stood up again, the rest of the crew came into view. Gus, Jude, and Cole were clustered in the doorway.

And then she walked in.

Lila.

Her face was blotchy and her eyes were red. The sight of her made my heart ache.

"Come here," I said, gingerly lifting my right arm.

With a hiccup, she darted for me, and when she was at my side, she cupped my cheek and pressed her lips together, as if holding back tears. "I don't want to hurt you."

"I don't care." I grasped her arm, snagging the IV in the process, and tugged, urging her closer.

"We were so worried," Mom said, pulling up a chair on my other side.

"Finn was here," Gus explained. "But then Adele's water broke."

"What?" I asked, immediately wincing at the pain in my head. "The baby's here?"

"Not yet. They're upstairs right now. Finn's sending nonstop texts and photos. I think Adele may kill him if he doesn't stop."

I laughed, but the sound was cut off by a stabbing sensation in my chest. Shit, that hurt.

"Take it easy." Mom patted my leg. "There's no rush. The baby won't be here for hours. She's only four centimeters."

"Mom. Gross." Jude hissed.

"It's the miracle of life," she quipped. "Get over it."

I closed my eyes and soaked in the chatter of my family. It was strange to be surrounded like this. I'd been on my own for so long that I'd forgotten what this felt like, having everyone together, talking over each other while my mom tried to keep order.

"He needs rest." A nurse had appeared in the doorway and was scanning each person in the room with narrowed eyes. She was probably right. I'd been hit with a wave of excitement when I saw my family, but I was already drained.

Mom bent down and kissed me again. "We'll be out waiting, and we'll update you about the baby."

"Lila," I croaked. "Can you stay?"

With a sweet smile, she nodded.

My mom was beaming as she herded my brothers out of the room.

"So I guess my mom knows," I said, patting the side of my bed.

"I don't want to hurt you." She wrung her hands and frowned.

"There's room. I just want you close."

With a soft sigh, she scooted next to me on my good side and squeezed my hand. "She knows because I told her."

My eyes widened in surprise, making my head pound.

"When I heard you'd been hurt, the hiding seemed so silly. So I burst into the hospital, demanding to see you. The nurse wouldn't let me in because I wasn't family, so I just ignored her and ran around the ICU looking for you."

My head was already so foggy. Rule-following good-girl Lila had a nurse chasing her through the ICU?

"Someone called security, but then I burst into the waiting room by accident and your whole family was there. So I freaked out and started shouting about how much I love you."

Those words had my lungs seizing. I couldn't get enough air, but it didn't matter. *She loved me?* The elation that came with that admission was short lived as I coughed and gasped, trying to fill my lungs, then was hit with a searing pain along my left side.

"Jesus, Owen. Do you need me to get the nurse?"

I shook my head and wiped at my eyes with my good hand. Despite the excruciating pain, this was the greatest moment of my life.

"I'm sorry I told your family I was in love with you first." She cupped my face. "I'm such a mess."

I kissed her palm. "It's okay. As long as you love me."

Her eyes filled with tears. "You scared the shit out of me. You promised me you'd be safe."

"I know." My heart ached at the fear in her tone. "I'm sorry."

"Don't apologize." She sniffled. "I'm just feeling a lot at the moment, and seeing you in a hospital bed isn't helping."

"Then I'll get out." I braced my elbow against the mattress and pushed up.

With a huff, she put her hand on my chest. "Don't you dare."

Obliging, I pulled her down toward me instead, guiding her head until it was resting on my chest. It hurt like hell, but I didn't care. I needed this moment with my girl.

As much as my ribs ached, I couldn't help but chuckle. "You know," I said, kissing the side of her head, "all I wanted was to casually tell our friends and families we were together. I certainly didn't expect you to break into a hospital ward and nearly get tackled by security trying to declare your love for me."

"I'm a mess," she murmured. "But I do love you. I've got a lot of stuff to work on. A mature, adult relationship is new for me."

"Me too. We can take it slow and figure it out together. Because that's all I need, to enjoy every day with my girl."

"I love you," she said into my chest.

"I love you too," I said back, closing my eyes and letting the euphoria of saying those words wash over us. Despite my aches and pains, this was a major achievement. One I'd never take for granted. Because whether she liked it or not, I was going to love this woman forever.

Our beautiful moment was interrupted when Jude burst through the door.

"Guys," he said, more excited than I'd seen him since he was a kid. "The baby is here. It's a boy!"

Lila sat up and smiled. "Look out world, the next generation of Hebert boys is upon us."

"We can go up to see him in thirty minutes. Do you want me to steal a wheelchair and smuggle you out of here?"

"Why don't we call the nurses and just ask them?" Lila, apparently back to being a rule-follower, suggested.

Knowing it wasn't worth arguing with her, I nodded once.

Then, after another vitals check, a visit from the doctor to review my injuries and treatment plan, and the arrival of two nurses who had to move all my lines and wires so I could be transported in a wheelchair even though I could walk just fine, we made our way to the maternity ward.

When Lila pushed me into the room, Adele was propped up in a bed, holding a tiny baby wrapped in a plaid blanket.

Finn was hovering nearby, snapping photo after photo.

My mom sat in a rocking chair, beaming at all of us.

"Ready to meet him?" Finn asked, almost bouncing as he took the baby from Adele's arms. "This," he said, bringing his son over, "is Theodore Francois Hebert."

The baby was tiny but had chubby cheeks and tufts of golden-blond hair.

"Ten and a half pounds," his father bragged. "He's a big boy." He rounded his shoulders, pulling the infant closer to his chest, and kissed his head. "You're such a big, strong boy.

Daddy's gonna get you such a cool plane. What's that? You like trucks too? It's fine, mommy's got you covered there."

Adele snorted. Her eyes were tired, but her smile was blinding. "The kid's only three hours old, and he's already promising him his own baby ATV."

Gus snorted. "In fairness, that's the Maine equivalent of promising your kid a pony."

"Touché," Adele admitted, shaking her head at our ridiculous family.

"You've only got a couple of minutes before my crazy family descends," she said. "And when Merry gets here, she gets her baby time, okay?"

The room was filled with grunts of affirmation. Finn stood in the middle of us all, chest puffed, looking so happy and confident, holding his son. A year ago, he'd been a mess, angry and unemployed and searching for his purpose. And he'd found it in the most unlikely of places. Lovewell.

He had the most impressive capacity to grow and evolve. And maybe I could follow his lead. Maybe I, too, could make peace with my past and my father and grow into the man I wanted to be.

Lila patted my shoulder, pulling me from my musings.

I smiled up at her as she wiped happy tears from her eyes. With her by my side, anything was possible.

Chapter 44
Lila

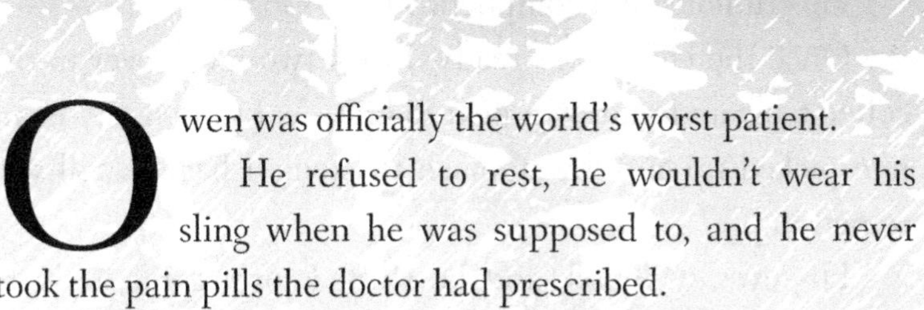

Owen was officially the world's worst patient.

He refused to rest, he wouldn't wear his sling when he was supposed to, and he never took the pain pills the doctor had prescribed.

"Sit down," I shouted. "And let me help you with the sling. If you don't wear it, you're never going to heal properly."

"I'm bored and have a lot to get done. It's a terrible combination. Just let me work woman, I need both hands."

Shooting a scowl his way, I snatched the laptop off the kitchen island and clutched it to my chest. "You will do no such thing. I'd have it all covered if I didn't have to spend all my time chasing you around and forcing you to take it easy."

He gave me a boyish smirk. "I love it when you chase me."

I rolled my eyes and fought a smile. We'd been holed up in the cabin since he was discharged a few days ago and were scrambling to get everything ready for the sale.

"I'm bored," he complained. "How about we go in the bedroom, and I'll make you come. It's been ages since you let me eat your pussy."

"You have a broken collarbone," I hissed. "You have to keep it stable so it heals."

He tilted his head and hummed. "Then sit on my face. I'll stay perfectly still. I promise."

I threw a dishtowel at him. "Sit down." I pointed to the couch. "And put on the damn sling. If you behave, I'll make a pot of coffee and sit beside you with my laptop so we can review documents together."

He grumbled but complied. Thank God.

Once the coffee was ready, I took two mugs over to the coffee table and sat down next to him. As I settled, my heart rate picked up and my stomach twisted. "I have to tell you something."

His eyes widened, and he shifted toward me, only to wince at the movement.

I snatched his sling off the back of the couch and gently eased his arm into it. "I, um..." Adjusting the strap, I peeked up at him. "I accepted admission at the University of Boston this morning. Sent the paperwork and everything."

"Lila," he sighed. "Don't derail your plans for me. Please. We can do long distance. New York is a quick helicopter ride from Boston. I'll come visit whenever you want."

This man was ridiculous. I gently patted his chest and cocked one brow. "Despite your rich and famous friends, you do not have helicopter money. Nor do I want to be that far away from you."

"New York is your dream."

I curled my legs up under me and turned to face him. "It

was my dream. But my dreams have changed. Willa is moving back to Lovewell to take over her dad's medical practice, and Magnolia may move too. I only wanted to move to New York to be with them. And then I found you."

He winked at me. Cocky bastard.

"Boston's program is excellent, and they offered me a decent scholarship. I love the city, and it just so happens that I'm madly in love with a guy who lives there."

He grasped my hand and brought it to his lips. "I'll do anything for you, Lila. I mean that."

I knew it. Together, we'd worked through so much. Our future was complex and unknown, but it was so, so bright. Every time I thought about moving to Boston with him, a peace settled over me. This was the right move for both of us.

"When you move in, we can turn the guest room into an office so you'll have a designated space to study. Just tell me what you need, and I'll have it arranged."

My heart lodged itself in my throat. "Move in?"

He leaned in and kissed me. "Of course. My condo is only a few stops from the school. It'll be a quick ride on the T, and on nice days, the walk isn't bad. It makes sense."

I frowned at him.

"I know you don't want to be a kept woman, but why pay for housing when my condo is so close to campus? Plus, do you really want to move into student housing?"

I most certainly did not want to move into student housing, but that was beside the point. He could not just tell me where I'd be living.

"Surely I can find something decent and cheap not too far from campus."

He dropped his head back and laughed. "In Boston?"

Yes, I was being hopelessly naïve, but the thought of compromising any of my hard-won independence still terrified me. But I wanted to spend every free moment with Owen, so I'd be at his condo a lot, right? And the place was amazing...

He leaned in and kissed my forehead. "You know what? I love you so much that I'll live in a rat-infested basement in Brighton if it makes you happy. I don't care where we live, as long as I get to wake up next to you every day."

God, could he be any more perfect?

His eyes were twinkling as he pulled back. "Screw my condo. The views are overrated. Who needs all those pretty places within walking distance? Or the gym? The doorman? Way too much. Don't even get me started on the rooftop pool."

"Rooftop pool?" I asked casually. "You've never mentioned that."

He winked. "Only the best for my Maple Sugar Queen."

I settled back into the couch and put my head on his good shoulder.

We were quiet for a long time before he cleared his throat. "I had another idea. Maybe someday we could find a cabin up here. Just for vacations. I think Maine is growing on me."

"Is that right?"

"I want to visit more, spend time with Merry and Theo, come up for holidays, that kind of thing."

I closed my eyes and exhaled. "I'd like that. We could come up during the summer and work on finishing our list of hikes, waterfalls, and strange roadside attractions."

"Our list is very long," he agreed.

"Hmm. Yes, it'll take many, many years to complete it." I snuggled up closer to him.

"Then I guess you're stuck with me for a long time."

"Guess so."

"Good." He dropped a kiss to the crown of my head. "Because I plan to love you like Lloyd loves Diane. I'll never hold you back. I'll always champion you. And I'll be the guy rooting for you every day."

Tears stung at the backs of my eyes as my heart tripped over itself. In the space of a month, this man had made me feel so seen and cherished.

"You taught me that we get to create our own futures," he mused. "That we can grow and heal from the past and chase our dreams. I want to do it with you, as a team, every single day."

Epilogue

Owen

2 Weeks Later...

Today was the day. We were finally closing.

Gus, as the acting CEO, had hundreds of pages to go through and dozens of places to sign.

Sara had come through for us. She and her team had fiercely negotiated and made sure every single detail was wrapped up.

The work Lila and I had done had sped the process along, and Strategic Timber was impressed. We hadn't shored up every detail, but they were happy enough to throw money at us without concern over the unanswered questions.

My injury and Finn's paternity leave had slowed things down, but the Gagnons had stepped up to help clear the decks, make sure our remaining customers were satisfied, and wrap up the financials. Lila had been invaluable, taking care of me while I was laid up while also double-checking every detail and motivating everyone.

The closing had been set in Boston, so Lila, Gus, Jude, and I had driven down together. We'd had a blast joking, listening to true crime podcasts, and consuming our weight in gluten-free snacks.

In many ways, Lila knew my brothers better than I did, so she fit in perfectly. I was still catching up, but despite my history of prickish behavior, Gus, Jude, and Finn had welcomed me back into the fold.

Things were still chilly with Cole. Gus had invited him to come to Boston with us, but after stepping up and helping out over the past few weeks, he'd gone dark again. My mom had mentioned that he was continuing with therapy. With any luck, he'd find some peace soon.

I'd miss them when I returned to Boston for good next week. Hell, I'd probably miss Lovewell too, and that was saying something.

But Lila had opened my eyes and forced me to move past so much of the anger I'd been carrying around over the years. I was already looking forward to visiting. I had a new nephew to see, after all, and I looked forward to checking in with my mom and brothers.

Today would be a day of celebration. Once we made it through all the boring legal shit, we had big plans. Gus, Jude, Lila, and I were headed out to my favorite restaurant to celebrate together. We'd Facetime Finn and baby Theodore when we toasted the sale.

I'd pulled some strings to get tickets to the Revs game tomorrow, where we'd meet up with Enzo, Delia, and

Amara. My Boston family was desperate to meet my Maine family.

We took the elevator up to the forty-ninth floor and followed the receptionist to a massive conference room that looked out at the Charles River. No wonder these bastards' hourly rates were insane. This was prime real estate.

Lila squeezed my hand as we walked in, sending a rush of gratitude through me. Not only had she made this happen with her hard work and brilliance, but she had successfully helped me get my head out of my own ass about the company, the town, and my family. With her by my side, I was truly at peace with the situation. And I was excited to start the next chapter with her. Not as boss and employee, but as partners in all things.

The conference table was large enough to seat thirty, and there were microphones and docking stations running along the middle.

We were directed to our assigned seats near several thick binders filled with the closing documents and piles of neatly tabbed papers.

The firm had supplied a notary, a small woman with gray hair and glasses, who sat at one end, doing a crossword puzzle while she waited for us to assemble.

The buyers were on their way, but apparently their flight from Toronto had been delayed.

While we waited, Gus groaned, fiddling with his tie. He looked like he was ready to jump out a window, rappel down the side of the building, and hike back to Maine, and the meeting hadn't even started yet.

On the other hand, Jude was taking everything in with bright eyes, excited to be here and loving the city. He'd made us stop for pizza last night, *after* we'd already eaten dinner, at some hole-in-the-wall place he'd found on Yelp. It was worth the indigestion, because the food was incredible. Despite the dullness of the sale process, he seemed content to eat his way through the city and come along for the ride.

Gus, the poor guy, was only here because he had to be. I felt for him. He was about to get a small windfall that could set him up for his next chapter. But instead of heading west for his fresh start, he'd be stuck in Lovewell for at least another year, working for the new owners.

I'd insisted that I'd negotiate to remove that requirement from the contract. Hell, I would have turned the whole offer down if he wanted. But he never even considered saying no. Gus was wired to take care of his people, and if staying meant we got a much better deal, then he'd stay. Even if it meant he would become just another employee of the company he'd always dreamed of running one day.

It had to sting. But he would never complain. He'd put in his year running operations, then get the hell out.

Sara clapped her hands. "While we're waiting, let's get started. The preliminary documents don't require a buyer's signature anyway. And Mr. Wilder," she gestured with an open palm to the other side of the table, where the buyer's legal team sat, "has the power of attorney if need be."

After what felt like the longest hour of my life, we broke for coffee and wandered the floor, enjoying the views.

"We almost done?" Gus asked, staring out over the skyline.

I shrugged. "No idea. But I hope so."

"Can we get hot pot after?" Jude asked, looking up from his phone. "There's a great place a few blocks from here."

"We have dinner reservations," I said.

He shot me a look. "It's early, dude."

Lila nudged him so she could see the screen. "Looks awesome. I'm starving."

"Fine," I said, scratching at my beard. "Let's finish up, and then you can get hot pot."

"I may want dim sum later too," he added.

I nodded. Whatever. I'd need a stiff drink after this, but if we could get it over with quickly, I'd be more than happy to stuff my face with dumplings too.

The buyer's counsel was droning on about the title insurance and various zoning stipulations in the contract when the large oak door opened and a couple of middle-aged men in suits stepped into the room. Behind them was a younger man with a trendy haircut who looked bored, and a woman.

She was physically small, but she commanded attention the instant she stepped over the threshold. She wore sky-high heels and a black pantsuit. Her deep red hair was thick and cascaded down her back.

There were more than a dozen people in that room, but everyone stopped and stared.

"Sorry we're late," she said, gesturing for her associates to take seats. "Fucking commercial flights."

Next to me, Gus gasped.

When I turned to him, his face was red and his breaths were coming rapidly. His hand jerked, sending his coffee cup careening across the table, drenching our paperwork.

"Fuck," he uttered, grasping at the stack of napkins in the middle of the table with a shaky hand.

"Don't worry about it," Sara said, gesturing for one of her

associates to deal with it. "We have triplicate copies of everything. Sam will clean it up, then we'll proceed."

Gus sat back and hung his head while the young associates buzzed around, cleaning up and depositing fresh copies in front of us. He gripped his armrests so violently his knuckles were white, and sweat beaded on his brow.

The redhead sat across from us, pulling my attention away from my brother, and casually flipped through the papers. "Looks like you're pretty far along. Just tell me what you need me to do."

Her fingernails were painted jet black and filed to dangerous points. As I observed her, I was hit with a sense of déjà vu, as if I'd met her before. But if I had, I was sure I'd remember a redheaded corporate assassin.

Gus was directed to sign a few more pages, and as he picked up his pen, his hand still trembled.

The lawyers droned on, passing documents and sending their paralegals out every few moments to make copies.

The woman was watching us closely. She hadn't introduced herself, but it was safe to say that she was one of the principals of Strategic Timber. I'd seen several names on the offer and the presale documents, but none had stuck out to me. Did we go to college together? She looked like she could be around my age.

"Okay, last one," Sara said, handing it to me.

When I slid it to Gus, he didn't even look down. His eyes were locked on that woman. I nudged him, and he dropped his pen, like I'd startled him. He picked it up quickly and hastily scribbled his signature, then handed it to the notary.

I exhaled. Okay. It was done.

The woman was still watching me. I could feel her scrutiny, even as the room went quiet while we waited for final copies. Rolling my good shoulder, I glanced up, ready to stare right back if it meant she'd look away. But no, she wasn't looking at me. She was staring straight at Gus.

"August," she said softly, her voice deep and raspy. "I was hoping I'd see you today."

He looked up and locked eyes with her, his jaw rigid. The room went dead quiet, and the hair on the back of my neck stood up. I was clearly missing something. What the hell was going on?

"Do you two know each other?" I asked my brother, trying to break the tension.

Gus said nothing, but all the color had drained from his face.

The woman stood and offered me her hand across the table.

"Gosh, I'm so rude. My apologies. I'm Chloe LeBlanc."

She paused for a moment, a feline grin spreading across her face.

"I'm Gus's ex-wife."

Bonus Epilogue

Want more Owen & Lila?

Download the Bonus Epilogue HERE

Also by Daphne Elliot

LOVEWELL

The Lovewell Lumberjacks Series

Wood You Be Mine?

Wood You Marry Me?

Wood You Rather?

Wood Riddance

The Maine Lumberjacks Series

Caught in the Axe

Pain in the Axe

Axe-identally Married

Axe Backwards

Axe-ing for Trouble

THE MOM COMS

Mother Hater

HAVENPORT

The Quinn Brothers Series

Trusting You

Finding You

Keeping You

The Rossi Family Series

Resisting You

Holding You

Embracing You

Acknowledgments

Thank you for taking this trip to Lovewell with me! My 15th published book, and one that is so near and dear to my heart.

This book would not have been possible without the help of so many talented and dedicated people. Every book starts off feeling impossible, and I'm only able to get it over the finish line with a lot of support.

This, or any of my other books, would not exist without Erica Connors Walsh. Thank you for being my friend, my cheerleader, and the best PA ever. From cover design to finding photos and editing blurbs, you are truly in my corner every single day. We have cried and laughed and yelled together over the past three years, and I am a better person and writer because of you.

To the incomparable Jenni Bara, you are so talented, humble, and kind. Your friendship is a true gift. I continue to be amazed by all the things you manage to do while never losing your sunny attitude. Every book I write is better because of your ideas and energy. Thank you for being a true friend and for teaching me to just roll with things.

Beth, thank you for your thorough editing. I am amazed by your patience, professionalism, and kindness. You've worked through this series with me, tolerating my late add-ons and last-minute changes. Your careful work has helped bring these characters to life, and I am truly in your debt.

Amarilys, you are the kindest, most positive person I know. I cherish your friendship and feel so lucky to have you on my team. Thank you for believing in me.

Morgan, thank you for being a trusted member of my team, a lovely friend, and my eagle-eyed final proofer.

Amy Jo, you are loving, hilarious, and incredibly talented. Thank you for sharing your creativity with me.

Becca, thank you for your professionalism and excitement about this series. You and the Author Agency have been such wonderful partners throughout this process.

Andi and Jenn, thank you for your friendship, encouragement, and willingness to Peloton with me.

Austin, thank you for the gorgeous cover. You took a simple idea and elevated it with your immense talent. I am so grateful to get to work with you.

Lindee, thank you for your beautiful photos. This is our fourth book together and I appreciate your dedication to hunting down beautiful people to grace my covers.

To my hype teams, thank you from the bottom of my heart for loving these books and this crazy world I've created. Most days, I pinch myself that I'm surrounded by such an amazing group of positive, kickass people.

Thank you to my mother, who always pushed me to do my best and believed in me even when I did not. I am the kind of person who decides to write books in my nonexistent free time because of you.

To Claire, my IRL friend and confidant. Your love and support mean so much to me. A greater power brought us together, and I am thankful every day for your humor, wit, and heart.

Thank you to my family for being hilarious and loving and silly. To my children, G & T, you push me and challenge me and surprise me every day. Thank you for never going easy on me.

And finally, thank you to my patient and devastatingly handsome husband. Thank you for the inspiration and endless support. You are my original Alpha Roll.

About the Author

In High School, Daphne Elliot was voted "most likely to become a romance novelist." After spending the last decade as a corporate lawyer, she has finally embraced her destiny. Her small town steamy novels are filled with flirty banter, sexy hijinks, and lots and lots of heart.

Where To Find Daphne:

daphneelliotauthor@gmail.com

Stay in touch with Daphne:

Subscribe to Daphne's Newsletter
Join Daphne's Reader Group
Follow Daphne on TikTok
Like Daphne on Facebook
Follow Daphne on Instagram
Hang with Daphne on GoodReads
Follow Daphne on Amazon